TEMPTATION

Cynthia Blair

BALLANTINE BOOKS • NEW YORK

Copyright © 1993 by Cynthia Blair

All rights reserved under International and Pan-American Copyright Conventions. Published in the United States by Ballantine Books, a division of Random House, Inc., New York, and simultaneously in Canada by Random House of Canada Limited, Toronto.

Library of Congress Catalog Card Number: 92–97322

ISBN 0–345–37129–1

Manufactured in the United States of America

First Hardcover Edition: May 1993
First Mass Market Edition: April 1994

10 9 8 7 6 5 4 3 2 1

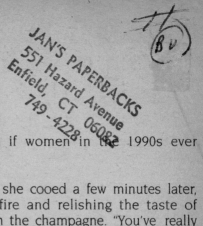

Rachel wondered if women in the 1990s ever swooned.

"This is so nice," she cooed a few minutes later, staring into the fire and relishing the taste of berries mixed with the champagne. "You've really thought of everything, haven't you?"

He shrugged modestly. "I figured if you're going to do something, you should do it right."

In a voice that was a bit more strained, he added, "It was important to me that we get things started on the right foot."

" 'Things'?" she repeated, knowing she was teasing but unable to resist. Maybe it was the blue eyes, maybe it was the intensity behind them, but something about Ryder made her feel more alive than she ever had before. It was like being in a play, a wonderful, perfectly constructed play, knowing what the outcome was going to be but still savoring every moment it took to get there. "What do you mean exactly by 'things'?"

"You and me," he said. His blue eyes were burning into hers. The glass of champagne on the floor beside him had been forgotten. "Don't you feel it? Isn't it just as clear to you as it is to me?"

Also by Cynthia Blair
Published by Ballantine Books

ALL OUR SECRETS
CLOSE TO HOME
SUMMER HOUSE
THE THREE OF US

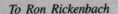

To Ron Rickenbach

Chapter One

"*If God had meant* for us to bake cakes from scratch, He wouldn't have given us Sara Lee," muttered Rachel Swann.

She tore off the limp apron she had tied over her Guess jeans and her brand-new Adrienne Vittadini T-shirt, a two-thirds-off find from Daffy's, and tossed it onto the kitchen counter. Then she stepped back to survey the two lumpy layers she had just turned out of their pans and onto recent copies of *The New Yorker.*

A low whimpering sound escaped the back of her throat.

When she had first cracked open *The Joy of Cooking* earlier that afternoon, Rachel had been envisioning two perfect golden circles. Instead, what she now had on her hands looked more like odd geological formations, foam-rubber models demonstrating the devastating effects of too much shifting beneath the earth's crust.

"It's the thought that counts . . . isn't it?" she said aloud. "Or did that sentiment go out with white gloves and pillbox hats?"

Rachel was about as much at home in a kitchen as she would have been at a mud-wrestling match. Sure, she could do okay with peanut butter and jelly on white bread, the main staple in her daughter Becky's diet. She was similarly skilled in the areas of Jell-O and Kraft Macaroni and Cheese. Even thumbprint cookies were not beyond her.

Today, however, it was not for Becky's benefit that she was tackling kitchen duty. It was her boyfriend Howard's daughter's sixteenth birthday. And Rachel was taking advantage of the occasion to try, one more time, to chalk up a few brownie points with Heather.

The moment Howard had left for his usual Saturday pickup of number-one daughter and her younger sister, Kimberly, from his ex-wife's house—an activity that pretty much paralleled that of Rachel and her ex, Boyd, the evening before—she'd dashed into the kitchen of his large suburban house in Scarsdale. It was a sprawling ranch with about as much charm as the *Leave It to Beaver* set. No wonder Howard's ex-wife had been willing to let it go, opting instead for their lakeside weekend retreat in Connecticut.

Rachel had been hoping that some secret Betty Crocker tendencies she had never before been aware of would magically surface. If anything could bring them out, she reasoned, it should be this Formicaed fulfillment of someone else's dream, a kitchen fitted with every modern appliance, gadget, and toy invented in the past five years. If a digital electric can opener couldn't inspire her, then there truly was no hope at all. So far, however, that was turning out to be precisely the case.

"It's amazing what a little cosmetic surgery can do," Rachel told herself bravely. "Isn't that why frosting was invented?" She studied the cookbook she had propped up against the counter-top convection oven. *The Joy of Cooking*: wasn't *that* a contradiction in terms.

" 'Cream one-half cup butter.' I can do that. I learned how back in junior-high home economics.

"Besides," she went on, "it's high time I conquered my fear of frosting. I mean, look at me. I'm a capable, independent, professional woman. I've weathered childbirth, divorce, grueling interviews at some of the top nursery schools in Manhattan. I'm a free-lance journalist who's paid my dues, making the rounds, pounding the pavement. . . .

"Okay, so maybe my in-depth interview with Monty Hall didn't set the world on fire. And my incisive coverage of the annual tiddlywinks championship up at MIT won't win me a Pulitzer. But what about my last assignment? Not every writer could toss off an article for *New York Life*, probably the slickest, most sophisticated magazine in town, rating the top ten baby clothes boutiques for their Layette Olympics. Surely somebody with credentials like those should be able to follow a simple recipe."

Still, a nagging voice at the back of her mind reminded her that *her* daughter, her own flesh and blood, had been perfectly satisfied with a store-bought cake on her last birthday, when she turned five. Not some chi-chi overpriced bakery, either. They were talking Baskin-Robbins here. True, ice cream had recently become Becky's number-one passion, so much so that she'd renamed her favorite teddy bear Rocky Road. And it was similarly true that Baskin-Robbins was one of the few establishments around that was willing and able to sculpt a cake in the shape of Barbie—currently Becky's second greatest passion—watching *Brady Bunch* reruns on cable.

"Now, now," Rachel muttered. "There's a world of difference between my Becky and Howard's two little darlings. Besides, chances are that Heather never had the crush on Bobby Brady that Becky has."

Dutifully Rachel beat the butter until it looked like whipped cream. When she dumped in half a box of confectioners' sugar, gave it a few more turns, and discovered that she had created a substance very much like frosting, she was heartened.

"See? This isn't so hard, after all. Apparently any fool who can read can cook."

She reached for a bottle of red food coloring and cavalierly dropped in five or six splotches. She had intended to dye the frosting the pale pink of roses, the official flower of turning sweet sixteen. Instead, it turned fire-engine red.

Rachel just stared, nervously twirling around her finger a scraggly strand of her shoulder-length black hair, a lock that was joining all the others in rebelling against a week's worth of remedial mousse. It took everything she had to resist the temptation to sob. Finally, in a last-ditch effort, she began to beat the mixture furiously, hoping the color would fade. But red food coloring, she was finding out, was like diamonds: It was forever.

She heard Howard and his daughters coming in through the front door just as she was sticking in the sixteenth pink candle. Everything was ready. The cake, lounging in the middle of the kitchen table, managed to fall just inside the acceptable range. Lying at each of four place settings was a colorful, campy Happy Birthday, Sweet Sixteen! paper napkin. A few limp balloons hung from the mock-Tiffany lamp. In the background, Mr. Coffee perked optimistically. All in all, Rachel was pleased.

"Hi, Heather! Hello, Kimberly!" she called gaily.

As the two girls appeared in the doorway of the kitchen, their father not far behind, she cried, "Surprise, surprise!"

The expression on the older teenager's face quickly changed from its usual one of boredom to something dangerously close to disgust. She pushed up the sleeves of her pink Esprit jacket—a delicate pink, Rachel noticed—and placed her hands on her hips.

"What is *that*?" she demanded.

Kimberly peeked out from behind her. "Oh, my *God*!" the thirteen-year-old squealed. "It's so *red*!"

"It's also crooked. It looks like . . . it looks like a hat that Roseanne Arnold sat on." Heather flipped her long blond hair—a little longer and a little blonder every time Rachel saw her—over her shoulder, looking triumphant over what she obviously thought was a very clever turn of phrase.

Rachel smiled wanly. "It's supposed to be a birthday cake. I thought I'd surprise you."

"Oh, yuck," pronounced Kimberly, today serving as the Greek chorus. "I bet that thing has enough red dye number two in it to kill all of Westchester County."

"I thought they banned that stuff," Rachel mumbled. "Or else decided it wasn't so bad for us after all."

"Honey, I think it's a lovely gesture." Howard had finally come to her aid. He ran a hand over his balding head, a gesture Rachel had come to associate with his conflict over Daughters vs. New Girlfriend. "You kids should be a little more appreciative. Especially you, Heather. Rachel put a lot of effort into trying to make your birthday special."

"Mom already got me a birthday cake." Pouting, Heather dropped into a kitchen chair. "We had it after dinner last night."

"I bet it wasn't homemade," Howard insisted. Half to himself, he added, "The only thing Sydney ever baked was herself—in the sun in St. Thomas."

"It was from Decadent Desserts of Scarsdale," Kimberly chimed in. "A chocolate hazelnut torte. Boy, was it good. The best cake I ever had in my life."

"I bet it cost me about as much as a week in St. Thomas, too," Howard grumbled.

"Well, I always think homemade birthday cakes are the best," Rachel said brightly. "Anybody can go out and buy one, but not everybody can, uh—why don't we light the candles and have some? We'll have a little party."

Heather, sitting hunched over, her hands still shoved deep inside the pockets of her jacket, looked up just long enough to glare at her. "You didn't have to do this, you know. I mean, it's not as if you're my mother or anything." Coldly, she added, "Isn't one daughter enough for you?"

Zap. "I know I'm not your mother, Heather," Rachel said in an even voice. It took everything she had not to sound as if she were pleading. "And I'm certainly not trying to be. But since the four of us spend so many of our weekends together, I just thought it would be nice if we all had a little celebration in your honor. In fact, I even got you a present."

"A present?" Heather's ears pricked up. She had just heard one of her favorite words in the English language. "What is it?"

"Why don't you open it and find out?"

Rachel was feeling pretty cocky as she reached into the cabinet underneath the microwave and pulled out a rectangular box. It was wrapped in yellow paper with pink roses and tied with a pink satin ribbon. Heather's favorite color combination, at least at last report. Rachel had gone to three different Hallmark's to find that wrapping paper.

Another valiant effort down the tubes.

"Pink and *yellow*?" Kimberly was smirking. "Oh, Heather. I thought you said just the other night that you *hate* those two colors now!"

"It's just wrapping paper, for heaven's sake." Howard pulled out a kitchen chair and sat down. "Say thank-you, Heather. It was very nice of Rachel to get you a present."

"Rachel *always* gets me presents," Heather returned. "She got me a Christmas present, a Valentine's Day present ... I mean, it's not as if it's a big surprise or anything."

Still, she wasted no time in pulling off the ribbon and tearing through the paper. As she opened the box, her face actually reflected something resembling enthusiasm.

"Oh, Rachel, you got them! The turquoise Reeboks I wanted!"

"You've only been hinting about them for three months," Howard observed dryly. "Now where's that thank-you?"

"These are so cool! I can't wait to see how they look with the new jeans Mom got me." Heather tossed them back into their box and put them on the counter behind her. "And she got me this really awesome shirt. She took me to Bloomingdale's and said I could pick out any outfit I wanted. Mom has such great taste, though, that I had her help me. She always finds the greatest clothes, you know?"

"That was very nice of your mother," Rachel offered.

"Do you want to see how I look in my new outfit? The pants are really rad. They have these great pockets. . . . Here, I'll go try them on for you."

"Heather, what about the cake?" Howard called after her.

"Oh, I don't want any. I just started a new diet today."

She left behind a dead silence, broken momentarily when the coffeepot burped. Rachel stared at the floor, vaguely aware that she had never really noticed Howard's linoleum before. As she gripped the edge of the kitchen counter, she wondered which would feel more satisfying: screaming in anger or crying in frustration.

Howard, meanwhile, remained glued to his chair, earnestly studying the salt shaker. Only Kimberly appeared un-affected by the scene that had just transpired. She reached toward the cake and ran her index finger across the top. She stuck the fingerful of red frosting into her mouth and made a loud sucking noise. And then her face twisted into a grimace.

"Oh, yuck!" she whined. "This tastes awful. Rachel, are you sure you followed the recipe right?"

"I guess I owe you an apology for the girls' boorish be-havior this afternoon," Howard said later that night. He lay down next to Rachel on his king-size bed, a piece of furni-ture so large that whenever Rachel curled up at one end, she invariably found herself thinking about football fields. "That mother of theirs never did teach them a thing about manners."

It had been after eleven by the time Heather and Kimberly finally fell asleep in front of the *Dirty Dancing* tape, sprawled across the chocolate-brown leather couch amid empty Diet Coke cans and boxes from Pizza Hut. There was the usual whining as the grown-ups roused them and shooed them off to bed. Alone at last, Rachel and Howard retreated immediately to the bedroom, a roomful of mirrors, sharply angled furniture, and thick carpeting that brought to mind model homes.

"Heather and Kim have had it tough," said Howard. "I think they're still in shock from the divorce. It has been only a little over three years. You can imagine what a hard time they're having."

Besides, Rachel couldn't help thinking, it must be ex-hausting, constantly playing one parent against the other, milking the guilt of both Mom and Dad for all it's worth . . . and thinking up new ways to torture their father's girlfriend.

"It's not easy being a kid these days," Howard went on. "All the emphasis on how they look, who their friends are, not to mention the way their hormones are taking over. I get a cramp in my stomach whenever I think of all the pain those girls have gone through. No wonder they're a little selfish sometimes."

"Don't give it a second thought, sweetie."

This was not the time to remind Howard not only that she herself had once been a little girl, but also that she now had a daughter of her own. In fact, she found herself bringing up Becky only on rare occasions. Howard Becker happened to be a victim of parental myopia, a syndrome characterized by blindness to the faults of one's own children with a concurrent hypersensitivity to the faults of everyone else's. And that included Becky.

"Rachel, I'm too old for this," he had groaned just the weekend before, when she'd suggested that an outing to the season's hot Walt Disney classic might be a good way for Howard, Rachel, and Becky to spend their rainy Saturday afternoon. He was also "too old" for renting the *Little Mermaid* video, playing Uncle Wiggly, giving piggyback rides, and covering aluminum cans with contact paper and yarn to make pencil cups.

But who could blame him? He had already been through all that once. There was no good reason why he should embrace another round of playing daddy to a kindergartener. At least, that was what Rachel was always telling herself.

As far as his offspring went, her original notion that Heather and Kimberly would welcome the opportunity to play big sister to a charming, precocious five-year-old lasted about as long as her fantasy of her and the two young Beckers giggling together and exchanging beauty tips over hot chocolate and Mallomars. It was just as well that Rachel and Howard usually ended up entertaining their children on different weekends.

"Listen, Rachel, I'm sure Kim and Heather appreciate you, even if they're not always very good at showing it."

He reached for her, his hand cool against her warm skin as he slid it over the exposed flesh between the bottom edge of her Vittadini find and the waistband of her jeans. Attempting to sound seductive, he murmured, "I certainly appreciate you. And the good news is that I do know how to show it."

He began tugging at her sweater. "Here, why don't you get this thing off?"

"Ummm . . . not yet." In response to Howard's puzzled expression, she said, "Let's make out."

"What?"

"You know. Kissing, hugging . . . copping a feel here and there. . . ."

Howard laughed, but there was a definite undertone. "What is this, junior high?"

"Oh, come on, Howard. Don't you remember how wonderful it used to feel when you were in high school, when you would make out for hours and hours until you thought you couldn't stand it for another second, until you thought you were going to burst or, or end up with hormones dripping out of your nose. . . ."

"That's gross."

"It was meant to be devilishly clever, so much so that you'd start kissing me with wild, passionate abandon."

"Wild, passionate abandon? Sure. I can handle that."

Howard's version of passion, Rachel observed, not for the first time, was what she would have classified as wooden, one-sided . . . controlled. The exasperated sigh she let out, however, was interpreted by him as ecstatic response to his finesse.

"*Now* can we take off our clothes?" he murmured between sloppy kisses.

Well, I tried, Rachel thought, wriggling out of her jeans. I just hope Masters and Johnson aren't watching.

Once she was naked, she couldn't help giving herself the once-over, doing a sort of bodily inventory. It was habit, every woman's compulsion to quiz herself constantly, eager to see whether she passed or failed. Everything checked out fine, she was glad to see. No flab, no cellulite, no ugly stretch marks or even unsightly moles. Just long, slender legs, toned up by jogging, aerobics, or whatever happened to be the latest panacea. No threat of middle-age spread around the middle, even though the countdown to the big four-oh had already begun.

No, the body was in fine shape. Not *Playboy* material, maybe, but good enough so that taking off her clothes in front of a man didn't require turning off the lights.

Tonight, Howard wasn't in the mood for aesthetics. He was ready to get down to business. Already he had taken off his own clothes, interrupting the action for a few seconds to fold up his beige Armani sweater as carefully as if he were a new salesman at Bloomingdale's. Rachel, meanwhile, pulled down the bedspread and slid in between the sheets, shivering a little.

"Cold?"

"Ummm. I need some body heat."

He stepped over to the bed. Rachel closed her eyes and reached for him eagerly. Instead of the warm flesh she was anticipating, however, she felt her arms close around air.

"Howard?" Her eyes flew open.

"Hold on a sec." He was hurrying over to the bedroom door, the semi-erect protrusion bobbing up and down against his hairy legs looking nothing short of ridiculous. "I thought I heard one of the girls."

"It's almost midnight. They're fast asleep."

"Well, I thought I heard something, that's all. See? I'm already back." He jumped onto the bed, wearing a big, leering grin. Abruptly his moment of joviality faded. "Wait a sec. Don't tell me you didn't hear that. Wasn't that Kimberly, calling for me?"

"I didn't hear anything. Maybe it was the wind, or the house settling."

"The wind doesn't say Daddy. Let me just go check."

"Fine. Go check." Rachel flopped against the pillow, her eyes fixed on the ceiling.

"What? What's wrong?" In a fraction of a second Howard's tone had switched from concerned to petulant.

"Nothing's wrong."

"Give me a break, Rachel. I can see something's bugging you."

Still talking to the ceiling, she replied, "I just wish that for once you and I could act like . . . like a couple. Instead, I constantly feel as if we're knocking ourselves out of joint trying to make our relationship fit around everybody else's schedule. It's as if it's okay for us to see each other only as long as it doesn't inconvenience anybody."

Howard sighed loudly. He sat up, his arms folded across his chest. "Come on, Rachel. Don't start on me. You've known all along that this was the way it was going to be. My arrangement with Sydney is that I have Heather and Kimberly every other weekend, the same as you and Boyd. You know full well it's the only chance I have to see them."

"It's the only chance you have to see me, too," Rachel reminded him.

"Well, what do you expect me to do? I'm only one person, you know."

There was that gesture again, running his hand over his shiny head, his version of wringing his hands. Internal conflict over the women in his life. This time, however, there was no doubt that in the struggle between her and his daughters, Rachel was coming out the loser. The two of them were being driven even further apart. This would probably be their only chance this entire weekend to be alone together, and it was being spoiled by a pointless argument—one that they had had practically every weekend since they first got together.

That had been a little over a year before. While Rachel's personal life hit a new low with her divorce, her vicissitudinous free-lance writing career had reached a new high: She was doing an article for *Business Week*. It was exactly what she'd needed, and she'd thrown herself into the human interest piece profiling ten graduates of the Wharton School of Business twenty years after their graduation.

Howard Becker was the centerfold. After graduating first in his class, he had gone on to get a law degree at Yale, signed on with one of the big oil companies that in the mid-seventies everyone loved to hate, and climbed the corporate ladder steadily. Howard Becker was what every little boy and girl with a toy briefcase dreamed of becoming. In fact, her article opened with a vignette describing his typical day: high-level meetings, lunch at '21,' an afternoon flight to Paris on the Concorde.

Howard obviously liked what he read. While during their interviews Rachel had felt *he* was interviewing *her*—for the position of file clerk, no less—he was positively bubbling over with personality when he telephoned her the day the story broke.

"Ms. Swann, you are a genius." He was nearly gurgling with delight. "Now, tell me. Have *you* ever had lunch at '21'?"

Over a lunch of steak tartare, Rachel found Howard talkative, charming, even flirtatious. After that he kept calling and she kept eating. They were both new to the dating scene, and they found in each other a sympathetic sounding board for the problems of readjusting to life after divorce. Before she knew it, she found herself smack in the middle of a relationship.

At first, the two availed themselves of all the cultural wonders that New York City had to offer. Rachel's black peau de soie heels, formerly virtual prisoners of their Maud Frison shoebox, actually began to wear out. She felt as if she had risen from the dead, thriving on being wined and dined and escorted to every worthwhile event in town.

It wasn't long, however, before those cosmopolitan evenings at the opera or at Broadway shows began to ease into weekends at Howard's house in Westchester, with or without Becky at her side. All of a sudden, instead of enjoying Pavarotti at Lincoln Center, Rachel found herself watching Kimberly play Buttercup in her elementary school's production of *H.M.S. Pinafore*. Instead of dining at La Grenouille, eating out was starting to mean Burger King. The long, romantic evenings gadding about New York City stepped aside, a type of family life that was already familiar to Rachel taking their place. But even that felt comfortable. It was almost a relief to relegate the Maud Frison slippers to the back of the closet, instead investing in a second pair of Nikes.

The idea of living together had come up on occasion. It was inconvenient for Rachel, having to buy two boxes of Tampax and stash them in two separate bathrooms almost thirty miles apart. But Rachel had serious doubts about leaving the city, especially once Becky had her heels dug in at a really fine school, right in the neighborhood. Howard, meanwhile, frequently voiced his fears that his daughters simply wouldn't be able to handle it. In the end, it would have been impossible to say which of them was more relieved.

When the telephone rang, Rachel muttered, "Oh, great. This is all we need," before she could stop herself. Howard responded with an icy glare.

"Well, it *is* almost midnight, on a Saturday night, no less," she pointed out. "Who else could it be?"

"Hello?" Howard greeted the caller politely, as if he didn't also know full well who it would be. "Oh, hello, Sydney. No, I'm not doing anything important."

Rachel snuggled beneath the blankets. This was bound to be a long one, and it was getting drafty.

"Sydney, I . . . Sydney, do you really . . . ?" Covering the receiver with his hand, Howard glanced over at Rachel and whispered, "Kimberly's supposed to go to Courtney Ringwald's birthday party tomorrow afternoon. Sydney didn't know anything about it until she stumbled across the invitation just now."

"*Now*? She's poking around Kimberly's stuff now? What is she, the Midnight Raider?"

But Howard had already turned his attention back to his ex-wife.

"Yes, Sydney, I *know* it's something you couldn't foresee, but that doesn't mean I should be expected to change my plans." He paused, nodding furiously as he listened. "Yes, yes, I know she'll be disappointed. But a deal is a deal. The girls and I are scheduled to spend all day tomorrow together, and I'm not about to give that up because of some stupid birthday party."

Oh, why not? Rachel was tempted to say. Would it be so terrible for *us* to have some time alone together? She blinked hard, telling herself that those weren't tears in her eyes; she was just tired.

"What are you talking about, it's important that Kimberly be seen at Courtney's party? We're not raising her to be some kind of goddamned debutante, for heaven's sake. That kid is destined for Harvard!"

With a sigh, Rachel reached for her sweater curled up on the floor beside the bed like a loyal pet. She pushed her arms through the sleeves. They were still warm. Pulling the blanket up to her chin, she rolled over so that her back was to Howard.

At this point, she mused, I don't know which is worse. Being alone in bed on a Saturday night . . . or being one of three people crowded into a bed meant for two.

As she closed the door of her apartment behind her on Sunday evening, Rachel felt the way she always did upon returning home: as if she were crawling back into her warm, welcoming cave, shutting out the rest of the big bad world.

The apartment that she and her daughter, Becky, shared was modest. But what would have been considered basic by the rest of the world's standards was luxurious for New York. A living room, a kitchen, two bedrooms—one the size of a shoebox, the other the size of a packing carton. At the front door was a foyer just big enough to pull on a coat without banging an arm against the wall. All in all, it took up no more than six hundred square feet of the island of Manhattan. But it was the one place in which Rachel could allow herself to let out a loud sigh of relief.

This place, after all, was hers. After her divorce, she had made a point of throwing out the old and deliberately replacing it with the new—"new," in this case, translating to things that were precisely the way she wanted them. True, her budget had been limited. All the more reason to select every piece of furniture, every square inch of fabric, every throw pillow and ceramic mug and bath towel, with the greatest care.

Those who knew Rachel Swann could see her signature everywhere. The wineglasses from Pottery Barn were sleek, the Conran's lamps elegant in their simplicity. The soft, inviting colors that dominated the room, peach and mint green and pale aqua, reflected her passion for the intoxicating pastels that were found in flower gardens.

Even the bright colors of Becky's possessions, superimposed over the more delicate shades, did not detract. In fact, they added a certain hominess that might have otherwise been lacking. And those touches were everywhere. The bold painting of an orange sun rising up over a rainbow, tacked to the refrigerator with a magnet modeled after a miniature Hershey bar. A pile of loops and the small square loom that promised to turn them into potholders, half-hidden underneath a pile of *Vogue*s and *Elle*s. The tiny artifacts of Barbie's life, scattered in the most unlikely places: a plastic high-heeled shoe balanced on top of the pink Wedgwood box, a small nylon stocking draped across a Venetian glass paperweight.

In one corner of the living room sat a long wooden table housing Rachel's computer, her files, and a chaotic assortment of papers. This was her work space, her place to write. Yet even this section of the apartment conscientiously combined prettiness with functionality. Office supplies had been dumped haphazardly into a large multicolored straw basket from Guatemala. The paper clips were bright green and blue and yellow. Even the Bic pens were the jazzy variety, neon colors decorated with slashes and zigzags in contrasting tones. Amid all the happy clutter was a large framed photograph of Howard, wearing a stiff smile.

Within this small space, Rachel had created a home for herself and her daughter. Personalized, fun, decidedly feminine. Yet she hadn't realized just how protective she felt about it until the first time she brought Howard there.

It was back when they had just started seeing each other, the painful moment when it was time for that dating rite of passage, bringing the man in to see how he looked framed by one's own home. Taking advantage of Becky being away at Boyd's that weekend, Rachel had spent Saturday cleaning: tucking away toys, scouring and polishing and re-arranging, hunting down dust bunnies with an ugly vindictiveness.

She had even considered running down to ABC Carpet to buy the pink and green dhurrie she had been drooling over for weeks. She had been conducting an ongoing debate, agonizing over the practicality of owning a light-colored rug in a grimy city and routinely subjecting it to the wanton ways of a four-year-old. In the end, catching herself in the act of going overboard in the name of dating, she was able to resist the urge to jump into a cab and snatch it up.

Howard bowed his head as he came in, unconsciously acting as if he were entering a dollhouse. "So!" he said with that forced cheerfulness people so often feel compelled to use in social situations when they'd prefer to be doing something else. "This is where you hang your hat."

"This is it, Howard." She watched him closely, eager for his reaction. "Do you like it?"

"Do I like it?" he repeated. Not a good sign.

He perched awkwardly on the edge of the flowered peach and green camelback couch. How out of place he looked, more because of his own discomfort than because he was a man superimposing himself over a room that shouted "feminine!" He couldn't even bring himself to sit back against the ruffled cushions. Tensely he clutched his wineglass, obviously afraid of putting it down in the wrong place.

"I guess it's not your style, huh?" she asked, politely offering him a way out. "No chrome, no leather, more flowers than a Monet—"

"Rachel," he pronounced, looking her straight in the eye, "this place is very *you*."

She could have taken that a lot of ways. What happened, however, was that his words struck home—in a very complimentary way. She understood then that she had fiddled with her budget and shopped the January sales and lugged her latest finds home on the subway rather than splurging on a cab not to create a place for socializing, but to make a nest that was just for her and her daughter.

She also realized that she didn't really want him there. He didn't belong. She could compromise enough to fit into his life, but he was unable to do the same for her. She decided there and then to go ahead and buy that pastel dhurrie.

Tonight, as she pulled off her shoes and kicked them into a corner, Rachel could feel the tension flowing out of her. The train ride from the suburbs back into the city; the long trek across Grand Central Station, dragging her weekend bag, calculatedly casting mean looks at everyone she passed; the subway ride uptown: it was already retreating to some remote corner of her memory. Instead, she fussed around her apartment, taking advantage of her few minutes of solitude before Boyd showed up with Becky.

She snapped on the radio and tuned to a classical station, picked two or three parched blossoms out of the otherwise fresh bouquet, took a quick inventory of the refrigerator, and turned on the kettle to make some herb tea. The red light beaming off her phone machine urged her to check in. First, however, she turned to the mail.

For the most part, it was a disappointment: the usual pleas for donations, announcements of bedding sales, offers of five or six useless sample-size cosmetics with the purchase of some grossly overpriced item of makeup. There were some highlights. Not one but two birthday party invitations for Becky. A nice fat check, payment for a recent free-lance assignment interviewing the queen of household hints for *Woman!* magazine. It cheered her up for a few seconds, then reminded her that in twelve hours she was going to have to switch gears, snapping on that dynamo personality she kept in reserve. She had a nine o'clock meeting with Grayson Winters, editor-in-chief of *New York Life* magazine. Aside from doing a bit of mental preparation, she would have to take action: hunt down a pair of panty hose, find her missing beige pump, check under eighteen sheets of unrecyclable plastic to see whether or not the dry cleaner had been telling the truth when he claimed to have gotten the spot out of her Anne Klein skirt.

There was one more piece of mail: the June issue of *Cosmopolitan.* Rachel had mixed feelings about subscribing to a magazine like that. It was a secret indulgence, one that most people would hardly consider terrible but that she wasn't particularly proud of. She preferred keeping this fascination to herself, rather like her habit of dishing ice cream into a cup whenever she was eating at home alone, then holding it up to her mouth and using her tongue as a spoon.

What would Howard think, she wondered, thumbing through the magazine, if he ever found out there's a side of me that savors such articles as "What Your Gynecologist Will Never Tell You About Orgasms" or "Fifteen (Never Before Revealed!) Bedroom Secrets That Hookers Have Known for Years"? And Molly, her politically correct sister. She cringed at the very thought of the sarcasm that would come spewing from her sister's lips if she ever saw Rachel poring over the advertisements, the enticing hair color ads that promised the moon or the two-page spreads with the tantalizing copy featuring lingerie-clad models whose accessories were the hands of square-jawed young men with excellent haircuts.

Tonight, *Cosmopolitan* was exactly what she needed. She dropped it into her lap and greedily skimmed the table of contents, meanwhile pushing the buttons on her answering machine.

"Hi, Rachel." The voice belonged to her sister Molly. "It's late Saturday morning, around eleven. I guess you're at Howard's again this weekend, making the scene in Westchester. Listen, I just got some great news. It's so great, in fact, that I just have to tell you in person. How about dinner at my place tomorrow night? Mike's cooking, but I have peanut butter and jelly on hand for Becky. Give me a call. *Ciao!*"

There were a few messages from friends, a couple of hangups, and an invitation to try home delivery of *The New York Times.* Aural junk mail, for the most part. She made a mental note to call Molly as soon as Becky was in bed, then returned to her perusal of *Cosmo*'s table of contents.

The screaming teakettle called her back to reality a few minutes later. She had barely had time to dunk her Wild Forest Blackberry tea bag into her mug when the buzzer sounded. Her daughter was back. It was time to switch roles.

"Becky!" she cried, crouching down in the hallway and extending her arms in response to the sound of the elevator doors sliding open.

"Good God, Rachel, can't you even buy her a decent pair of shoes?"

Boyd rounded the corner, his handsome face made ugly by his scowl. He carried the compact blond, tousled-haired beauty with a sense of triumph that Rachel found irritating.

"What's the matter with her sneakers?"

Becky, her head resting on Boyd's shoulder, murmured, "They started hurting, Mommy."

"But you've been wearing those same sneakers for weeks," Rachel insisted. "You've never complained about them before." Pulling out all the stops, she added, "They're Keds."

"You'd think you could manage to find a respectable shoestore." Boyd planted Becky in the doorway of the apartment. "Or are you too busy writing those . . . those articles on the ten best ways to fight mildew to find the time?"

"Are you planning to come in, Boyd, or would you prefer to continue berating me from out there in the hall?"

"Look, all I'm saying is that I'm concerned. I want to make sure you're able to take care of Becky, that's all."

Rachel bristled. " 'Able?' This from a man who couldn't

remember the date of his daughter's birthday if his annual bonus depended on it?"

"Let's not get into this now, all right?" He was suddenly all sweetness and concern, bundled up and packaged in Ralph Lauren sweats and a pair of two-hundred-dollar running shoes.

The crunch on Wall Street doesn't seem to be affecting him, Rachel noted. Who knows? Maybe he could even afford to spring for a new pair of Keds.

As she closed the door after he'd left—this time taking care to turn all three locks—Rachel observed that spending ninety seconds in the company of her ex-husband was as exhausting as the ninety-minute commute home from Howard's. For Becky's sake, she filed her cynicism away.

"So, Becky, how was your weekend?" She knelt down, wanting to collect a hug or two before her daughter scurried off. "What did you and Daddy do?"

"We went shopping," Becky announced happily. "Look, Mommy! Daddy bought me Cheerleader Barbie!"

Rachel's motherly smile faded. "Becky, I thought you and I had decided to hold off on any new Barbies for a while."

Becky grinned, undaunted. "When I told Daddy that, he said it makes him happy to buy me things. I also got new paints, another set of Legos, and two sundresses. Daddy says I look so grownup."

Rachel's eyebrows shot up. "Since when does Daddy know anything about shopping for dresses?"

"He doesn't." Becky shrugged. "Ariana does."

A chill ran down Rachel's spine. "Ariana?" she finally croaked after taking a few deep breaths. "Becky, honey, who is Ariana?"

"Daddy's new friend." Becky was already absorbed in attempting to squeeze a miniature pom-pom into Barbie's slender plastic hand.

"Is she . . . nice?"

"She's really nice. She let me try on practically every

dress in the store. She's pretty, too. She has yellow hair, just like my Barbie."

"I see. Is this . . . this Ariana Daddy's girlfriend?"

"Mommy," Becky said earnestly, focusing her attention back on her mother, "can I ask you something really, really important?"

"Of course, sweetie."

"It's something that I never even thought up until this weekend, but now it's really bothering me."

Rachel swallowed hard. "What is it?"

"Do angels help the tooth fairy build castles out of the teeth she collects, or does she have to do it all by herself?"

Chapter Two

"*Coffee, Rachel?*" chirped Mary Louise Finn, Grayson Winters's secretary. "I can never remember how you take it: with a little sugar and a lot of milk, or a lot of sugar and a little milk."

"Actually, this is one of those days when I need a lot of both." Rachel cast an appreciative smile at the soft-spoken redhead, no larger than a size six petite. "And if you don't mind, make it a double."

Last night's conversation with her ex-husband, combined with Becky's little tidbit about Daddy's new Barbie-blond girlfriend, had left her feeling defensive and on edge. Suddenly her assignment with *New York Life* had taken on great significance. An uncomfortable state of low-key anxiety was waiting for her when she woke up, greeting her like an overly enthusiastic lover. It stuck with her as she showered, blow-dried her limp hair into a style that looked as if it had been planned, and put on makeup, the cool tones that the Clarion computer had insisted were right for a woman with her coloring.

It followed her onto the subway train, into the midtown station as she communed with people with whom she was afraid to make eye contact. It was there as she entered the wood-paneled elevator of the Dominion Building, the publishing empire's headquarters, along with the chattering secretaries clutching paper cups of coffee, the dour corporate-ladder-climbing businessmen, and their meticulously groomed female counterparts, reeking of crisp, unrelenting efficiency.

Neither had it been banished by Mary Louise's good-natured banter when Rachel ran into her in the reception area, a little bit of Santa Fe right in the middle of midtown Manhattan. Between all the cactus, the geometric quasi-Aztec motifs in muted shades of rust and blue, and the grotesque oil paintings of animal skulls roasting in the summer heat, it was all that Rachel could do to keep from baying at the moon, coyote-style.

The mood still enshrouded her as she entered the office of the magazine's editor-in-chief, with its Chippendale library table-cum-desk, austere paintings in ornate frames, and thick burgundy carpeting. Part of her nervousness, of course, stemmed from the fact that the particular editor with whom she was meeting was Grayson Winters. While the Incident, as she labeled it in her own mind, was something that was never mentioned, it was still there, hovering between them like a balloon that had already lost half its helium but hadn't yet given up the fight.

But this was neither the time nor the place for dwelling on past nastiness. Rachel kept reminding herself that she was a professional, and that professionals didn't allow themselves to be distracted by bogeymen, things that went bump in the night, or the memories of close encounters of days gone by.

"Had a tough weekend, did you? Well, if this doesn't perk you up, I'll have to call in the medics," Mary Louise quipped. Grinning, she handed Rachel a Lenox cup of sweet, pale coffee, so full it threatened to spill over into the gold-edged saucer. Fine china instead of polystyrene or, for the ecology-minded, cardboard: This was a typical Grayson Winters touch, one of the little luxuries designed to make people feel important. Or perhaps to put them in their place.

It was while Rachel was working on perfecting her balancing act that Grayson strode into the office. His presence immediately filled the room, changing its atmosphere from informal to businesslike.

"Rachel. Sorry to get you over here so early—on a Monday morning, no less—but it's already promising to be one of those weeks."

He didn't notice her sympathetic nod, so intent was he on giving orders to the woman who was his second pair of eyes, ears, hands, and feet. "Mary Louise, get Thompson on the phone and tell him I'll have to cancel lunch today. Tell the printer to call me between ten and ten-thirty. Oh, and tell Jack Richter I need to see him sometime this morning."

He was an impressive man, well built, over six feet tall, with blond movie-star looks. Grayson Winters was a man who had undoubtedly been a surfer in a previous life. In this one, however, he had emerged as a wunderkind on the staff of *Los Angeles* magazine, then at the age of forty-two emigrated to the East to take his rightful place at the head of the floundering *New York Life* empire. In his four years as head honcho, he had let down no one, performing all the magic that had been expected of him.

His attention immediately focused back on Rachel as he dropped onto the straight-back chair that complemented the dignified desk. Confident, well-spoken, totally in control. Cool as the proverbial cucumber, as always—and about as difficult to read as the packing label on one.

"Now," he said, lapsing into the approachable-but-still-authoritative persona he invariably switched on for dealings with his underlings. "Where were we? Oh, right. Your next article."

"Is there anything else I can get you, Rachel?" Mary Louise offered. She was already halfway out the door. "We've got danish, bagels, doughnuts . . ."

"Thanks," Rachel said, "but just coffee is fine."

Actually, she was starving, having suspected that even attempting anything resembling breakfast that morning would have only aggravated the knot in her stomach. But being in the presence of Grayson Winters was increasing that knot to basketball proportions. As much as Rachel hated to admit it, she—a woman who prided herself on being fearless, who as a reporter thought nothing of barging in where she knew she was unwelcome, who had once spent three hours stuffed inside a locker so she could write a feature article on how the members of her alma mater's football team handled pregame tension—had yet to conquer the feelings of intimidation that just being in the same room with him invariably elicited.

"Okay." Grayson folded his hands across his desk and directed his gaze at Rachel. Mary Louise, meanwhile, had slipped away, silently closing the door behind her. "Rachel, I've got what I think is a really exciting assignment for you."

Rachel nodded, meanwhile arranging her face into an expression of what she hoped was pleasant anticipation. The truth was that she was skeptical. So far, every assignment she had been given on *New York Life* had been introduced as "exciting." That had been the word used to describe the article investigating the rumor that the toy chain Kiddie Town U.S.A. might be opening a branch in Manhattan, she could recall, as well as the interview with the mayor of the city of New York's dry cleaner.

"We've been keeping an eye on you," Grayson went on, turning up the volume on the twinkle he kept on reserve in his startlingly blue eyes, "and so far we like what we've been seeing. We loved the piece on the dry cleaner. It was so . . . witty."

As if there had been any other way to approach an exposé on caviar stains.

"Anyway, we think you're ready for something a little meatier."

Involuntarily, Rachel sat up a little straighter. She pulled herself up to the edge of her chair. A meatier assignment; that sounded promising. Perhaps she had been too quick to judge. Maybe this really was the end of those fluff pieces. New York was, after all, a city full of competition and crime, stories of enviable successes and devastating failures, eight million tales of blood, sweat, and tears. Was it possible that she was finally going to get to tackle the kind of news story she could really get excited about?

"There's a new exhibit opening at the Metropolitan Museum of Art, something that's somewhat of a departure from their usual stuff." As if responding to a cue, Grayson flashed a smile, exposing two perfect rows of gleaming teeth. "And, well, it's your baby."

Rachel cocked her head to one side. "Excuse me?"

"The art exhibition. We'd like you to take it and run with it."

"An art exhibition?" Rachel blinked, still not certain she was understanding this correctly. "That's the meaty assignment?"

"That's right." Grayson was nodding enthusiastically, looking like one of those Charlie Brown wobbleheads that had been so popular back when Rachel was in junior high school. He stopped bobbing and looked at her questioningly. "Quite an opportunity, Rachel, don't you think?"

She smiled at him wanly. "Uh, yes. Yes, it certainly sounds that way."

"I knew you'd be excited. In fact, the moment I first heard about it, I said to myself, 'We've got to get Rachel Swann on this. It's the kind of thing that's really her cup of tea.' "

Winking at her conspiratorially, he added, "And I bet you thought we wouldn't be able to come up with anything that would really challenge you. Something this . . . meaty."

That word again. *I think there would be more meat on a spare rib,* Rachel was thinking.

Aloud, she said, "Yes, it sounds quite interesting."

"Interesting! That's an understatement. Why, this is the exhibit that all of New York is going to be talking about this season. It's going to be as big as King Tut or Manet at Giverny. . . ."

"Oh, yes. The Monet exhibit," she interjected tactfully.

"Whatever." He waved his hand in the air. "It's going to be as popular as the Nijinsky costumes. We're talking coffee table books and a Bloomingdale's event . . . even shopping bags!"

"That big, huh?" Rachel's enthusiasm was burgeoning. "Are we talking cover story here?"

"Well, maybe not *quite* as big as King Tut and Nijinsky . . . but big, believe me."

Rachel's flush of enthusiasm was already slipping away. "I think I understand. Big enough for shopping bags but not big enough for the cover of *New York Life* magazine." The irony was wasted on Grayson. "Uh, what exactly *is* the exhibit?"

"The native art of Mocambu."

"Mocambu?" The file cards in Rachel's mind flipped to the geography section. "What are we talking here, Africa?"

"The Caribbean."

"Oh. Mocambu, huh? Is there a Club Med there?"

"Hardly. Mocambu happens to be the second poorest nation in the world. Not exactly the kind of place yuppies like to let down their hair for a week of scuba diving."

"Second poorest, huh? Which country has the distinction of being number one on that list?"

"Haiti."

"I see. Okay, then, if this place is so poor, what's the art like?"

"Actually, the word *art* may be something of an exaggeration." Grayson had begun tapping a pencil on the edge of his desk. "Artifacts is more like it."

"You mean folk art." To herself, Rachel added, "Folk art is really big these days."

"I think that's a safe label to pin on it." Grayson nodded his approval. "Anyway, from what I understand, the exhibition is going to consist of pottery, textiles, and all that everyday stuff that New Yorkers love to compare with their own version from Conran's and Laura Ashley. You know how it goes. 'Oh, look at that brown earthenware cup, sweetie. Isn't that just like those awful coffee mugs from Pottery Barn that the Feinsteins gave us for our wedding anniversary last year?' "

Rachel was nodding. Perhaps there would be some human interest stuff here after all. Us versus them—and are we really so different? Already a list of adjectives was coming to mind.

"There are supposed to be a lot of religious articles in the exhibition, too," Grayson went on.

"Religious?" Rachel's bubble hadn't quite burst, but it was definitely leaking air. "You mean like crosses and prayer shawls and things like that?" Hardly the stuff for a whimsical piece on Mocambu, the kind of cheerful writing, chock full of cute turns of phrase and hyperbole, that *New York Life* was noted for.

"Fortunately for you—and the wonderful piece we all know you're going to turn out—it's nothing that ordinary. The Mocambians practice a brand of religion that has African roots, one that's very much like voodoo."

"Voodoo?" This put everything in an entirely new light. "You mean magic potions, the evil eye, secret spells, zombies, voodoo dolls—all that?"

"Or some variation on it, anyway. Why, does that appeal to you?"

"Of course it does. It appeals to everybody, doesn't it? That stuff turns everybody into an eight-year-old kid again, about to venture into the haunted house at the amusement park or . . . or finding an empty beer bottle on the beach and looking inside, hoping to find a treasure map. . . . All that black magic mumbo-jumbo brings out a hidden side of everyone, the side that believes in Good with a capital G and Bad with a capital B.

"You know," she went on, a smile creeping across her face, "I think I may already have a hook for my article."

Grayson laughed heartily—too heartily. "Rachel, why don't you at least wait until you see the exhibition before you start writing the article? It would be nice if you found out the facts first."

"What? And violate the first law of journalism?" Rachel couldn't resist adding with feigned innocence. "So how many tickets to the opening am I getting?"

"Only one, I'm afraid. They're harder to get than tickets to a Stones concert."

"One ticket?" she repeated.

Grayson looked offended. "Do you know there are people in this town who would kill for that ticket?"

"In this town, there are people who would kill for a used copy of *New York Newsday*."

Despite her cynicism, Rachel found that she was actually looking forward to the opening. And even though she hated to admit it, the idea of writing it up for the magazine was not entirely without appeal.

So what if it's not the Wedtech scandal? she was thinking as Grayson fed her more of the details. So what if it's not even the latest on Donald Trump's sex life? At least it will be a night out. Another by-line. Another paycheck, too— part of which is slated for a new pair of Buster Browns for Becky.

Rachel only hoped that far away in the hinterlands of Rochester, New York, Tom Vogel, the man who had been the single most important influence in her life, wasn't at the moment supplementing his well-stocked literary larder with a subscription to *New York Life*.

The first time she saw Tom Vogel, Rachel had been singularly unimpressed. The graying old geezer in a plaid flannel shirt and a string tie promised to be just another employer, someone who saw her as little more than a robot who typed, filed, and tried to sneak out of work early.

It had been more than fifteen years earlier, when Rachel was still getting used to the idea of thinking of herself as a college student. Instead of being one of those freshman lucky enough to spend her time doing nothing besides memorizing the plots of Shakespeare's plays and practicing the correct method of lighting a Bunsen burner, Rachel had to work her way through college. Henry and Mildred Swann had made it clear from the start that while the family's hardware store may have been one of the more prosperous businesses in the suburban Long Island town they all called home, the sale of nuts and bolts and Red Devil paint hardly yielded enough to put three daughters through college. A scholarship helped; even so, during her freshman year at Marbury College in upstate New York, Rachel ended up spending fifteen hours a week in the school cafeteria, shoveling macaroni and cheese and fielding sarcastic questions about the true identity of the mystery meat coagulating inside the shepherd's pie.

It was hardly a stimulating complement to the liberal arts education she was seeking. But a job—any job—wasn't easy to come by in a small town like Marbury, New York. Even though it was a mere two-hour drive from Rochester, the small town had a character all its own. Having a population somewhere around four thousand was only part of it. It was also smack in the middle of farm country, complete with wide open fields and endless clear blue skies, a setting quite alien to a young woman who had grown up surrounded by tract houses, shopping malls, and six-lane expressways.

When she'd first come to Marbury, Rachel had assumed that no matter how small the town, the college nestled within its borders was bound to assert itself in virtually every facet of life. So she was surprised to discover that in this small rural town, even the local 4-H Club had a higher profile. At supermarket checkout counters there were magazines like *Farm and Ranch Living* and *Gun World*. The movie theater barely had enough business to survive, while the feed store had them waiting in line on Saturday mornings. The only books available for sale outside of the Marbury College Bookstore were the thick romances with lurid covers displayed in a revolving wire rack at Scooter's Drugs.

It had occurred to Rachel that the best way to make some good money would be working on a farm. But that, she quickly concluded, was taking her youthful urge for more life experience just a little too far. So freshman year found her learning the ins and outs of the food service business. It was tedious, but her weekly paychecks kept her in textbooks and ball-point pens.

During her second year she would have been welcomed

back with open arms. Her line, after all, had always moved the fastest. But come sophomore year, the mere thought of spending yet another two semesters with a stainless steel ladle in hand was enough to take away her appetite. In September Rachel headed toward the job placement office, determined to find a better way.

She found that better way on the bulletin board outside the placement office, a chaotic free-for-all on which would-be employers and would-be workers communicated via hand-lettered index cards and photocopies on goldenrod paper. There, amid the offers of yard workers and baby-sitters and foreign language tutors, among the pleas for warm bodies to deliver newspapers and make doughnuts, Rachel found Tom Vogel's ad.

"Wanted: Person with reasonable intelligence to do clerical work. Job requires decent typing and working knowledge of the alphabet. Two dollars an hour. Apply Mr. Vogel," and a phone number.

"At least the guy has a sense of humor," Rachel muttered, copying the number onto the cover of her spiral notebook. And not knowing if the man who had tacked up the index card was a librarian or the maven of a mail-order pornography business, she headed for the nearest phone.

"Can you type?" Mr. Vogel barked when he heard why she was calling.

"I'm a decent typist," Rachel replied evenly. "That is what your ad asked for."

"Filing?"

"A, B, C, D, E, F, G . . ."

"Can you use a telephone?"

"Isn't that what I'm doing right now?"

A breathing noise came across the wires. Rachel didn't know if he was sighing with impatience or laughing.

"You're hired."

She reported to work at the *Marbury Express* the next day, dressed in a denim skirt and an embroidered Indian blouse.

"Know anything about newspapers?" the crusty editor-in-chief greeted her, not bothering to get up out of his swivel chair.

"No."

"Know anything about writing?"

"Not much." Rachel wondered if her verbal interactions with him would always be based on the Socratic method.

"That's okay." At last, a statement. "You don't have to do much writing on this job. You don't have to do much thinking, either. In fact, the less thinking you do, the better off you'll be. Ever use an IBM Selectric before?"

Tom Vogel, she had learned as she sat in front of a type-writer in the cramped *Express* office, was the driving force behind one of Marbury's two newspapers. In a town that needed a second newspaper about as much as a five-story parking garage, the *Express* held a firm second place. Its competition, the *Daily Reporter*, consisted mainly of adver-tising, interspersed with photos of prize-winning cattle and the latest victor in the weekly sixth-grade spelling bee.

The *Marbury Express*, meanwhile, actually had news in it. It offered updates on local issues as well as interpreta-tions of national and international news. It even offered a place for students to air their views, reflecting Tom Vogel's belief that young people who spent nine months of the year in this town had as much right to express their views as anyone. It was no wonder that his newspaper's readership was about a quarter of its competitor's.

At first, as Rachel logged in her hours at the typewriter amid the framed photographs of Pulitzer Prize winners, it was just a job. Working at the *Marbury Express*, typing other people's articles and filing away bits of paper that might one day be of use, was better than working the caf-eteria line. Rachel tried to turn off her brain the moment she walked in. After all, that was how she'd survived sup-plying the college's student body with its minimum daily requirement of starch. But it wasn't long before she began finding it impossible to resist adding the occasional comma or checking a date or the spelling of some local news-maker's last name.

"What the hell is this?" Tom demanded one day after she'd been working at the *Express* about a month.

Rachel blinked. "As I was typing the bank robbery story, I noticed that Pete had put in what I thought was the wrong address for this bank. So I checked it. Sure enough, I found that he'd put 108 instead of 118. I also found out that it happens to have had the highest incidence of robberies in the county." She shrugged. "That little fact seemed to add to the story, so I stuck it in."

"What are you doing, bucking for my job?" Tom growled.

"I'll take it out, then."

Tom looked at Rachel over the page he'd been reading. She had expected to see anger in his face. Instead, she saw something that looked very much like admiration. "I like it," he said. "Leave it in."

After that, fiddling around with other people's writing became part of the job. She corrected grammar and fixed misspelled words but also took every opportunity to check facts and add whatever extras she could find. Always her slant was toward the human interest side rather than simply the regurgitation of facts. She strove to answer questions like, What does all this mean? How will this affect *you*, our reader? After a while, Tom stopped commenting on her changes. He simply accepted them as a matter of course.

"What now?" he growled one afternoon as she walked into the office. It was a few weeks before Christmas, and Rachel was already as much a part of the newspaper office as the thirties-style metal furniture.

"Uh, I guess I kind of rewrote Pete's story." Her tone was apologetic.

"What, Pete's writing isn't good enough for you anymore?"

"Not this time. He was in a hurry, I guess. He had all the facts, but somehow it wasn't clear what the point of it was."

"Great." Tom tossed the article onto his desk and folded

his arms across his chest. "Now I suppose you want your own column."

"I never—"

"Okay, okay, you got it. But that doesn't mean you can shirk any of your other duties."

Rachel was still dazed when she saw her first column in the paper the following Monday morning. Even more surprising than seeing her name in print was seeing her own words. "From Where I Sit" her column was called. In it, she dissected one of the week's hot stories, a possible change in national legislation that looked favorable for the state's dairy farmers but which, she predicted, would in the long run mean nothing but trouble. Her point of view was controversial, she knew. But she knew just as well that Tom Vogel was not one to let a little controversy within the pages of his newspaper get him all bent out of shape. And when at about the same time her column started appearing regularly the newspaper happened to pick up more than a few new subscribers, so much the better.

She stayed at the *Express* for the rest of her college days, making money, of course, but also making a career choice. When she picked journalism as her major, she had no doubts as to who was responsible.

"Now what?" Tom demanded a few months before graduation. "I suppose you're going off to Rochester or Buffalo or some big city to become a reporter, right?"

"Actually," Rachel replied after clearing her throat nervously, "I was kind of hoping you'd offer me a job."

"Oh, really?"

"Sure. I know I still have a lot to learn—and, well, I can't think of a better teacher. Besides, after three years here, I know this paper pretty well." She took a deep breath. "I think . . . I think you need me as much as I need you."

Tom Vogel sighed tiredly. "Terrific. I suppose you'll be expecting more money, too. How does three twenty-five an hour sound?"

* * *

Even though her stomach was begging for a croissant as Rachel left Grayson's office, she couldn't resist stopping off at Jack Richter's to say hello. While she and Jack had never actually worked together on a project, he was an institution around this place. She couldn't even remember how they had first met, just that they had gotten to know each other in the same way she'd gotten to know her way around the company cafeteria.

She peered inside his open door, finding him in his usual condition. His shirt-sleeves were rolled up to expose lean, muscular arms so white that they looked as if they hadn't seen the sun since the day his parents packed away his inflatable kiddie pool. As always, a cigarette was dangling from his lips. Jack's face was scrunched up in concentration as he communed with his computer, the tension in his forehead and the eerie reflection of the screen's green light making him look older than his forty-odd years. All that was missing for his portrayal of the role of editor was a green visor.

His office complemented his appearance like an artfully chosen accessory. The top of his desk was a blizzard of white paper, and from out of his trash can spilled whatever didn't make it to the Out box. Sandwiched between three empty cardboard cups of coffee was a plastic statue of a hula girl with pointed bare breasts and a yellow grass skirt capable of undulating.

"Hey, Jack, got a second?"

At the sound of her voice, he glanced up from the screen of his word processor. It took only a second for the identity of the intruder to register.

"For you, doll? Any time." He leaned back in his swivel chair, looking relieved to have an interruption, especially by a slender, pretty woman in a spotless white linen skirt and a silk blouse the exact shade of blue-green as her eyes.

While Jack Richter couldn't be considered good-looking by traditional standards, he was one of those men who grew on people over time. His dark brown hair, hazel eyes, and plain features were rarely deemed worthy of a second look.

It was his broad smile that roped people in, that and his easygoing personality. Even when he was going out of his way to be offensive, Rachel had reflected more than once, you couldn't help but like the guy.

"What are you doing here?" he demanded. He was already on his feet, clearing a stack of computer printouts off the torn leatherette chair that was pushed into one corner of the small office. He looked around helplessly, then dropped them onto the floor. "Business or pleasure?"

"Pleasure?" Rachel repeated with raised eyebrows. She sat down gingerly on the chair, hoping she wasn't subjecting herself to a social disease. "Is such a thing possible within the walls of the Dominion Building?"

"Hey, babe, I've been offering to answer that one for you for years."

"Yes, I know."

Rachel's tone was dry. Even so, despite the lightly antagonistic quality of their banter, there were absolutely no hard feelings between her and Jack. Coming on to women was a habit for him in the same way as chain smoking or being a slob or putting up pictures like the one currently tacked up on the wall, right above his head so that it was impossible to miss. A bleached blonde in hot pants so short you could see almost as much as her gynecologist was bent over the gas tank of a sleek, imported sports car, about to insert a shining silver nozzle.

"I'm here within the hallowed halls because I had a meeting with Grayson."

"Ah. The man after whom the gloomiest season of the year is named."

"Hey, look, he's from California. Their idea of winter is kicking up the temperature of the heated pool four or five degrees. So how the hell are you, Jack?"

He shrugged. "Only the good die young."

"I'm asking for a general life report and you're giving me Billy Joel."

"Oh. In that case, I guess you could say I'm fair to middling."

"Not bad for an editor who works fourteen hours a day. And that's just on the weekends. How's Gillian?"

Jack's expression darkened. "Is that supposed to be funny?"

"No, I, uh . . ." Rachel was aware of the unmistakable feeling of her foot creeping into her mouth, but she had no idea why. "Uh, the last I heard, you and Gillian were seeing a marriage counselor."

"Yeah, a therapist."

"That didn't work out?"

"It did for Gillian. I finally figured out that practically the whole time we were seeing the guy, she was also . . . seeing him."

"I don't—" All of a sudden, like a chill spreading quickly over her body, the meaning of his words came clear. "Wait a minute. Are you joking?"

"Do I look like I'm joking?"

She had to admit that he looked more like someone about to liberate an embassy taken over by terrorists than someone who was joking.

"I'm really sorry, Jack. I honestly hadn't heard. So where does that leave the two of you?"

"Well, it leaves Gillian with a new fur coat, a baby-blue Jaguar, and a half interest in a very successful marriage counseling business."

"Poor Jack."

"As for poor Jack, it leaves me drinking too much beer, smoking too many cigarettes, and religiously reading the personal ads in *New York* magazine while humming 'Looking for Love in All the Wrong Places.' "

He took a long drag on his cigarette and sighed. "I keep telling myself it's just as well. That I'm not really the marrying kind and that it simply was never meant to be. You know, the whole 'Jack and Gillian' thing did get to be pretty tiresome after a while."

"I can see where it would."

"How about you, Rachel? How's that guy you brought to

the company picnic last year? The one who totally embarrassed himself during the Frisbee competition?"

"You mean Howard. You weren't impressed?"

"Sure I was impressed. I've never seen anyone eat so many chili dogs at one sitting before. He still your number-one heartthrob?"

"I guess you could say that."

"Honeymoon's over, huh?"

"It's just a little crowded, that's all."

"Don't tell me good old Howard is into kinky stuff. Ménage à trois, ménage à quatre, ménage à cinq . . ."

"Believe me, even that would be an improvement."

"Oh, yeah?" Jack's eyes lit up. He leaned across his desk, leering at her. "You know, Rachel, maybe you and I should—"

"Relax, Jack." She dismissed him with a wave of her hand. "I'm talking about Howard's two teenage daughters."

Jack pretended to ponder her words. "Two teenage daughters? I could live with that."

"I give up! There's no use trying to talk to a sex maniac."

"Why, Rachel. *Thank* you."

She rolled her eyes upward in mock exasperation. "So, Jack, how's the editing business?"

"That, at least, is going well." Jack was lighting up another Marlboro. "The guys upstairs seemed pleased, anyway."

"I suppose that's the best any of us can hope for. Still doing the same guy stuff, I see."

"Sure. Sports, stereo components, cars . . . the things that really matter. How about you?" He gestured toward Grayson Winters's office with his match, filling the room with that distinctive odor of sulfur that invariably brought birthday parties to mind. "What did Uncle Grayson have to say?"

"I just got a new assignment."

"What is it this time? Another round-up article highlighting a thousand and one things to do with the kiddies over the Fourth of July weekend? The place to go on Fire Island this summer? Or perhaps, if we're lucky, a roundup of the hottest lingerie boutiques in this great city of ours?"

Rachel grimaced. "Not quite that bad. But not much better, either. There's an exhibition opening at the Metropolitan Museum of Art next week. I'm supposed to write it up."

"What, you mean the exhibit from that Caribbean island that nobody's ever heard of?"

"Yes, that's the one. It's called Mocambu."

"Oh, yeah. I heard about that. Isn't it supposed to be full of creepy masks and icons and all that stuff that's used in voodoo-type rituals?"

"You got it. And yours truly is supposed to come up with a human interest slant."

"That should be easy. How about 'Dos and Don'ts for Holding a Human Sacrifice in Your Studio Apartment'?"

"I was thinking more along the lines of 'How to Put a Hex on Your Co-op Board'." With a sigh, Rachel said, "There are other things in that exhibit. You know, artwork and weavings and housewares. . . ."

"Hut-wares."

"Whatever."

"It sounds like fun."

"I don't know, Jack. The bottom line is that I'm still not getting the kind of assignment I want. At first, I was hoping this one might pan out. Grayson was acting like this was such a big deal, you know?"

"I'm telling you, it's the kind of thing that's bound to have all of New York a-buzz."

"A certain sector of New York, anyway." Rachel puffed out her cheeks and blew a stream of air out of her mouth. "It's still not the kind of article I want to be doing. It's not even close. But I suppose that until that chance comes along, I'll keep plugging away at this fluff stuff." With a shrug she added, "I just hope I can find something sexy to say about this exhibit."

"Hey, Rachel?"

"Hmmm?"

"Speaking of sexy, if you ever do get assigned to research that round-up article—you know, garter belts and edible underwear and all that—promise you'll let me tag along, okay?"

Chapter
Three

"Why are you walking so fast, Mommy?"

Rachel, absorbed in brooding about her new assignment on the Mocambian art exhibit, tuned back in to the present. She had lapsed into her own world as she hurried up Broadway, an ice-cold bottle of champagne tucked under her arm. Becky, meanwhile, skipped along beside her, eyes wide as she greedily sucked in the circus that was the city's streets.

"I'm sorry, honey. Am I going too fast for you?"

"I *like* skipping. I just wanted to know why you were going so fast."

"I always walk fast in this neighborhood," said Rachel, remembering to adopt the mean expression she wore whenever she was on her way to her sister's apartment, uptown in an iffy neighborhood near Columbia University. "It's not as friendly as our neighborhood."

"Those boys look friendly," Becky said a little too loudly. "See them over there? Standing in front of that store on the corner?"

"You're right, they do look friendly." Rachel grasped her daughter's hand even more tightly and dragged her across the street. "But I'm not sure those are the kind of boys you and I want to be friends with."

"Maybe we shouldn't live in the city anymore," Becky said in a matter-of-fact tone. "Maybe we should live in a big house with a big backyard. And swings. And a Volvo."

Rachel chuckled. "You mean like the house where Howard lives?"

41

"I mean like the house Daddy and Ariana took me to see last weekend."

Rachel stopped in her tracks. Even the potential danger of drug dealers had suddenly paled. "A house? Where was this house, Becky?"

The little girl frowned. "I think maybe in France. Is that what it's called out where Aunt Sis lives?"

"That's Long Island, honey. Did the house look like the kind Aunt Sis lives in?"

"Oh, no. This was much bigger. It had so many rooms that my Barbie and me could hardly even count them. There was a big, big room, right at the top of the stairs. Ariana said that could be my room. Just pretend, of course."

"Of course." Rachel was walking much more slowly. "Sweetie, does Ariana live in that house?"

"She *wants* to live there. That's what she told Daddy. That's why she took him to see it. She wants him to buy it for her. It's her dream house, she told me. You know, just like Barbie's Dream House."

Rachel scrunched her eyes together, wanting to hold back the tears that were threatening to turn her meticulous makeup job into a cruel joke. She no longer felt like going to her sister's house for dinner, celebration or not.

But she and Becky were practically on Molly's doorstep. Besides, she knew that a little moral support—or at least a little distraction—was precisely what she needed. And even if chances were slim that she would find the former, the latter was practically a given. She stepped inside the entryway of the dignified prewar building and pressed the button labeled Swann/Hollinger.

"So?" Dr. Molly Swann cried excitedly, flinging open the door of her apartment. "Do I look any different?"

The emotions that only moments earlier had surged up in Rachel were already leveling off. The buxom woman with wild shoulder-length black hair was holding out her arms in an imitation of Lynn Redgrave in a Weight Watchers commercial. Her blue eyes were shining with the same triumph that Lynn apparently felt over having lost unwanted pounds while gorging on chicken divan and Dutch apple pie.

"You've lost weight," Rachel tried, not seeing any obvious reduction in her sister's ample girth but figuring that was probably her best bet. As usual, Molly's roundness was left undisguised by her unflattering choice of clothing: a bulky pink popcorn-stitch sweater with short, puffy sleeves, a shapeless brown dirndl, shiny panty hose, and a pair of flat black shoes that were pitifully scuffed and stretched out.

"No, I haven't lost weight." Molly's face crumpled, but only for a moment. "It's something even better than that. Becky, can you guess?"

"Can we come in while we guess? Lately I find myself holding too many important conversations in the hall."

Rachel and Becky came inside the apartment, a compact one-bedroom. Its thick white plaster walls were dotted with African artifacts, advertisements for Molly's year-long research project some ten years earlier, an escapade that earned her both a Ph.D. and a stubborn rash that to this day persisted. Some of her souvenirs, like the oversize masks scowling from the wall above the well-worn beige corduroy couch, were grotesque. Some, like the display of blowguns and other weapons hung between the intercom and the teak wall unit, were simply bizarre. Still others, like the graceful hand-woven reed baskets and the primitive weavings made from coarse, colorful yarns, were actually kind of pretty.

Becky headed straight for her favorite souvenir: a crude doll with burlap skin and hair that resembled seaweed. Rachel had always suspected that it had been designed to serve as a warning to little African girls who resisted the notion of moisturizing and conditioning.

She watched Becky sit down cross-legged on the floor and attempt to give her a make-over. Then, turning to her sister, she said, "I got champagne for the occasion." She handed it to her sister. "So what *is* the occasion?"

Molly clasped her hands in front of her, posing like a little girl about to give the welcoming speech to the parents in the audience at the annual kindergarten pageant. "I've been promoted. Yours truly is now an associate professor of sociology."

Rachel let out a shriek. "Molly, that's great! Congratulations! I'm so happy for you." She threw her arms around her sister. "Wow. My sister, an associate professor. At Columbia University, no less."

"It's great news, isn't it?" Mike Hollinger called in from the kitchen. He was standing at the stove, wooden spoon in hand, stirring the contents of a saucepan with dogged determination. A linen dishtowel was tucked into the waistband of his jeans. "Sorry I can't come in, Rachel. I just made my roux, and you know how temperamental *they* are. The soufflé will never forgive me if I abandon it for even a moment."

"Yes, I know how vengeful those soufflés can be."

Rachel headed into the kitchen, a tiny strip of a room that looked like something that belonged in a motor boat rather than in a home. But that was New York apartments for you.

Despite the modest accommodations, however, Mike was in the midst of creating a celebratory feast worthy of a four-star rating. The white ceramic soufflé dish was buttered, the asparagus was waiting to be steamed—just five and a half minutes, not a second longer—and a perfect tart topped with a pinwheel made of raspberries, blueberries, and kiwis was on the counter, warming to room temperature.

Rachel was appropriately impressed. "Wow, Mike. It looks fantastic."

She leaned over to place the requisite kiss three quarters of an inch away from his lips. There was an unsettling incongruity between the luscious food in production and its stick-thin orchestrator. Mike's gaunt face was more reminiscent of a poster child than a gourmet chef. His dark hair had finally reached ponytail length, she noted, wondering if he had chosen the yellow elastic band because it so tastefully matched his lemon-colored Fifth Annual FolkFest T-shirt.

"Here, why don't I stir while you open the champagne?"

"Rachel Swann," he said accusingly. "You mean a strong, competent, independent woman of the nineties like you is still afraid to open a bottle of champagne?"

"Guilty as charged. I'm afraid that opening champagne is a skill that, in my day, was exclusively the domain of the menfolk. Don't forget, I grew up in a decade when we were told it was dangerous for girls to do deep-knee bends in gym class because they might damage their childbearing organs." She shrugged. "You can't expect me to overcome everything."

"That's a good point, Rachel." Molly came into the kitchen and retrieved three tulip glasses from a high shelf while her sister stirred and her live-in lover wrestled with gold foil, wire, and a plastic cork. "It explains why I have a phobia about exercise."

"You're perfect just the way you are," Mike insisted. He poured the champagne and handed her a glass. "And isn't it nice that the whole world recognizes it?"

"Well, the world of Columbia University, anyway," Molly said with a proud grin.

"How could they not?" said Mike. "You're a famous author. *Tribal Rituals in Contemporary America* just missed being on the *New York Times* best seller list by this much. You were the toast of the American Sociologists Association's last convention. You were on *Donahue*, for God's sake."

"Yes, but you never know how the academic community is going to react to success in the real world. It's so easy for them to feel threatened."

"Hah!" said Rachel. "They're probably all dying for a chance to meet Marlo."

"Wait, don't drink that. Not yet. Not until we make a toast." With one hand, Rachel reached for the glass Mike held out to her. The other hand, still clutching the wooden spoon, never missed a beat.

"To the new associate professor of sociology," said Mike.

Rachel raised her glass high in the air. "And a helluva gal to boot."

After they'd had the obligatory sip of champagne, Mike reclaimed his wooden spoon—and his sovereignty over the kitchen.

"Now, scoot, you two," he insisted. "Go sit down in the living room, make yourselves comfortable, and plot how you're going to take over the world. And send Becky in here. I want to hear her recipe for chocolate milk."

"You know, this wasn't as much of a surprise as you might think," Molly said once the two women had settled in, Molly on the threadbare couch, Rachel on the blue canvas swivel chair from Jensen-Lewis. "Mike's psychic predicted this a few weeks ago."

"Mike's psychic?"

Molly looked surprised. "You mean I never mentioned her? She's great. Madame Chrissie can really see into the future."

"Madame *Chrissie?*"

With a shrug Molly said, "I think she's originally from California. Anyway, Mike was in for a consultation—back in May I think it was—and she told him that she could sense that someone very close to him was about to take a step upward on a ladder."

"Maybe Madame Chrissie thought there were home repairs in your future."

"Give Rachel her business card," Mike called out from the kitchen.

"Good idea. She's really great, I'm telling you. In fact, I'm thinking of going in for a consultation myself one of these days. Of course, the way things are going lately I'm already pretty sure what my future holds."

As she spoke she went over to the wall unit and reached into a crude earthenware pot shaped like a skull with feathers in its ears and oval-shaped seeds for teeth, and pulled out a business card the color of Bazooka bubble gum. "Here's her card. She's downtown in the Village, and—"

"Oh, *shit!*" came the agonized cry from the kitchen. "Pardon my French, Becky."

"That's okay," said Becky. "Daddy says that all the time."

"Mike, are you okay? Did you get burned?" Molly was already on her feet.

"No, no. Nothing like that." He appeared in the doorway, an anguished look on his face. "Molly, you're not going to *believe* this. The only butter we have in the house is salted."

In response to the two blank stares he encountered, he explained patiently, "The hollandaise recipe calls for unsalted."

"Can't you just make do?" Rachel gave a bewildered shrug.

Mike reacted with indignation. "Not unless I were willing to compromise the integrity of the sauce. No, I'll just have to run out to the Korean grocery across the street. Come with me, Becky. It'll take only a minute. Besides, I can use this as an opportunity to teach you how to choose the freshest arugula."

"Goodness, these new men," Rachel commented.

"New and improved." Molly was beaming with pride.

As Mike hustled out of the apartment on his holy mission with Becky in tow, Rachel placed her champagne glass on the pile of thick, dusty books sitting on the floor beside her, creating a makeshift table. "Gosh, associate professor. This is such wonderful news, Molly. Did you tell Mom and Dad?"

"I called them as soon as I found out."

"Were they excited?"

"You know how they are. When I told Dad I'd been promoted to associate professor, he said, 'Isn't that what you were before?' " She laughed, but not without bitterness. "I think the Florida sun is drying out his brain. I knew it was a mistake for them to move down there after he sold the store."

"Don't feel too bad, Mol. I remember the very first time

I had a piece accepted for a national magazine. I think it was *Bon Appétit*. When I told him he said, 'Why don't you do something for a real magazine . . . like *TV Guide*?' And that was when they still lived up here. How about Mom? What did she have to say?"

"No surprises there, either. She just kind of sighed and said, 'You and your sister Rachel. I don't know why the two of you work so hard.' For a minute there, I almost ended up feeling like I'd done something wrong."

"I know. Believe me, I know. And what about Sis? Was she happy for you?"

"Oh, sure. Although I can't help feeling the baby of our family inherited some of Mom's confusion over why a woman would want to do anything besides make babies and wrestle with grass stains. But Sis is a good egg. She knew she was supposed to act excited. She even said she'd try to come up with something special to celebrate at her annual Fourth of July barbecue next week. By the way, she asked me to remind you about it."

"Not only have I not forgotten; I can hardly wait," Rachel said wryly. "Maybe you'll be honored by getting your name written in red gel on the Carvel ice cream log. The barbecue is Monday, right?"

Molly nodded. "That's right. She said to come around noon."

"Okay. I just have to check with Howard. . . . But tell me—what about Mike? Is he excited about your promotion? He certainly seems to be."

"Oh, Mike," she said vaguely, waving her hand in the air. "You know Mike. He's . . . he's great."

Rachel picked up her champagne once again, this time seeking fortification. "Wasn't he—how can I put this— even a little bit threatened?"

Molly pulled herself up indignantly. "Of course not. You know Mike isn't like that. He's sincerely happy about my successes. That's one of the things that makes us so right for each other."

"Right. It's all part of his being a new man." Rachel was

trying hard to keep the skepticism out of her voice. "So how is his free-lance work going?"

"Pretty well. You know, he's very much in demand. He's such a whiz with computers." She paused to twist a knot of hair at the back of her head into a makeshift chignon, then stuck it up haphazardly with three bobby pins she retrieved from the pocket of her dirndl. The result definitely said Charwoman. "Mike could work seven days a week. He has companies calling him all the time, begging him to come in and revamp their computer systems. He could make gobs of money if he wanted to."

"If he wanted to?"

Molly shrugged. "You know Mike. He's never wanted to be part of the rat race. He prefers to work however many hours he needs to to make enough money to live, and no more. The rest of his time he devotes to reading or studying or thinking."

Brightly she added, "Did I tell you he was teaching himself ancient Greek? He wants to be able to read the classics in the original."

"Seems to me he'd be better off learning something useful, like Japanese."

"Oh, Rachel. Give the guy a break, will you?"

Molly was scowling, looking exactly the way she had when Rachel was eight and she was five and her big sister had just indulged in one of her favorite sibling displays of power—pulling off her Barbie doll's head.

"Just because Mike isn't pulling down a six-figure income, wheeling and dealing and screwing the little guy so he can afford custom-made suits and those, those ridiculous toys for grown-up little boys they sell at Hammacher Schlemmer . . ."

"Come on, Molly. You know as well as I do that Mike is—"

"Mike is Mike."

This was the no-nonsense Molly speaking, the one it was never worth arguing with, the one who had boosted Phil Donahue's ratings by accusing the ultraconservative sociol-

ogist who had appeared with her on his show of being the
1990s version of a male chauvinist pig: a male chauvinist
warthog.

"So," Molly went on cheerfully, not even attempting a
graceful transition as she steered the conversation over to
Rachel and the dirt in her life, "how about you? How's the
writing going?"

"Couldn't be better." Rachel forced a wide smile. "In
fact, I just got one of the most intriguing assignments of
my life. It's for *New York Life* magazine."

"Great magazine to be writing for. High visibility, excellent circulation, nice reputation ... I bet they pay well,
too." Molly was nodding in approval. "And how about
Howard? How are things between you and the man in the
pinstripe boxer shorts?"

"Oh, Howard. What can I say?" Loftily Rachel waved
her hand in the air. "The man is crazy about me."

"And you?" Molly asked doubtfully. "Are you crazy
about him?"

"Well ... sure."

"I don't get it, Rachel. I know you probably don't want
to hear this from anybody, especially a younger sister, but
you really do deserve someone better."

Rachel looked her sister in the eye. "Howard is Howard."

But her moment of triumph rapidly faded. Suddenly her
entire body slumped.

"Oh, Mol, who am I trying to kid? Why am I pretending—in front of you, of all people? Things with Howard
are lousy. He never has any time for me because his obnoxious kids are always around. It's the same old story. Except
that I'm beginning to think he likes it that way. He must;
otherwise he'd be as frustrated as I am and he'd try to
change it."

She shook her head and grimaced. "Take this past weekend, for example. We spent all day Saturday and Sunday
catering to the little darlings. It was even worse than usual,
in fact, since it was Heather's birthday. She was acting as

though she'd been elected queen or something. I try; I really do. I got her a present, I put a little family party together with balloons and candles and birthday napkins. . . . I even made her a cake."

"You? You baked?" Molly's hand flew to her heart. "Mother of God, this must be love."

"Believe me, it's not out of the goodness of my heart. It's out of desperation to be accepted into the Becker enclave."

"Can't you slip the kids a twenty and send them off to a movie?"

Rachel grimaced. "I know that sounds good in theory. But the sad truth is that even when Howard and I do manage to get some time alone together, all we end up doing is arguing about them."

Tiredly she rested her head in her hands. "I don't know, Molly. It's as if, all along, I've been fooling myself into thinking that maybe this relationship was really going somewhere. But now I'm starting to wonder if the only place it's going is closer and closer to that brick wall I keep banging my head against."

"Maybe you need a vacation," Molly suggested helpfully. "A little time away from Howard. How about a week at a spa? One of those really rustic ones, where you pay them big bucks to torture you. You know, hiking twenty miles at dawn, being fed one piece of lettuce for lunch, having cold mud glopped all over you in the name of beautiful pores . . . I'd say you're ripe for a make-over."

"Hah! Forget mud and hiking. I need a make-over for my *life*, not my body."

Molly shrugged. "Well then, maybe it's simply time to say bye-bye to good old Howard."

Warily Rachel eyed her sister, meanwhile thinking that Molly was one of the lucky ones who had both success and love. She and Mike had moved in together almost two years earlier, and while Rachel had always had her doubts about the relationship, from the way Molly acted, she and Mike complemented each other as well as Ozzie and

Harriet. And it didn't seem to bother Molly one bit that she was Ozzie . . . and Mike was Harriet.

"It has occurred to me that it might be best to break up with Howard," Rachel said in answer to her sister's question. "The problem is, I have a hard time believing that I'd be able to find anyone who's any better. I mean, single men in this town are about as easy to find as taxis during rush hour."

Involuntarily she shuddered. "Besides, there's been some funny stuff going on with Boyd that's threatening to turn me off men completely."

"And he always looked so good on paper." Molly sighed. "What now?"

"Apparently he's got himself a new woman."

"Is that supposed to be news?"

"Becky says she looks like a Barbie doll. She's already taken her clothes shopping. She's also taken her shopping for houses."

"Houses? You mean dollhouses?"

"I mean real houses. Houses with pink bedrooms that she's using to entice *my* daughter."

Molly patted Rachel's arm. "Don't worry about it. Even if this woman has got plans for Boyd, that doesn't mean he's going to go along with them. I predict that by the end of the summer, she'll be old news."

"It's funny; even though this whole thing is making me sick, it's not her I blame. It's Boyd. And myself, too, for misjudging him so badly. When I first met him I thought he was Prince Charming—with a steady job."

"Give yourself a break. You were young, just a few years out of college."

"Still, my track record makes me seriously doubt that I'll ever find somebody I could really be crazy about."

"Oh, come on. Good men are out there, if you're just willing to look for them."

"Really?" Rachel was skeptical. "Do you know any you can introduce me to?"

Molly gave her question serious thought for a few seconds. Her forehead tightened in concentration. "Well, there are lots of available men in my classes. Especially in the graduate seminars. Of course, the oldest ones are only about twenty-five years old. . . ."

"Oh, that'll do me a lot of good. If Cher couldn't pull it off, how on earth am I supposed to? I don't have her legs *or* her clothes."

"All right, all right, so I can't come up with the names of any Prince Charmings at the moment," Molly said impatiently. "But that doesn't mean they don't exist. *And*," she added pointedly, "whether there's somebody out there for you or not, that still doesn't mean you have to put up with somebody like Howard. You know, somebody you're not satisfied with."

"Maybe you're right." Rachel took a sip of her champagne. "Actually, my sagging love life is the least of my concerns right now. I mean, that's pretty much an ongoing thing. What I'm really depressed about right now is my career. Maybe I've managed to ward off middle-age spread, but my career sure hasn't."

"What's so terrible? You're working, aren't you? Don't forget, you're in a super-competitive field. Half the kids who get out of college with an English major dream of doing what you're doing."

"Yeah, I'm working. But the point is that I'm not getting the kind of work I want—the kind I always just assumed I'd get."

"What kind is that?"

"Molly, I want to delve deep into the ugly underbelly of this city. I want crime, I want corruption, I want scandal. And do you know what I get? Fluff. Human interest. Round-up articles on the best places in Manhattan to find . . . I don't know, wool socks."

She shook her head in frustration. "I met with Grayson Winters this morning to talk about my next assignment. He's the editor of *New York Life*. And, well, the bottom line is that I'm really disappointed in what I've been given."

Molly's expression was sympathetic. "No ugly under-belly?"

Rachel shook her head. "Not at all. It's just more of the same mindless filler. Another human interest piece that does little more besides take up space in the magazine. Oh, sure, people read it, and they do enjoy that kind of thing. But it's not the kind of thing I thought I'd be doing by this point in my career."

"Poor Rachel. You've got the career blues. But it's probably just a temporary slump." Curiously she asked, "Are you really researching wool socks?"

"Not quite, but almost. I get to cover some precious exhibit at the Metropolitan Museum of Art whose main purpose is to provide the mink-coat set with new shopping bags to show off to their friends."

Molly's face lit up. "Rachel, you're not by any chance talking about the Mocambian exhibit, are you?"

"You've heard of it?"

"Of course I have! It's the hottest thing to hit this town since . . . since King Tut! At least, it is in my circle."

Rachel remained sour. "I'm sure that a bunch of crummy wooden artifacts are a big thrill for people who've spent their whole lives studying that kind of thing, but for the rest of us—"

"Hey, don't forget who you're talking to here!" Molly cried with mock indignation. "Besides, those are not just *any* crummy wooden artifacts, you know. They're part of a fascinating Caribbean culture that we're just starting to learn about."

"I know, I know. A charming little culture that was founded on firm principles of devil-worship."

Molly frowned. "Well, that is a bit of an oversimplification. Devil-worship is a label we've pinned on it, but from what I understand, the Mocambian interpretation of good and evil was quite different from ours. I seem to recall reading that rather than seeing those two forces as directly oppositional, the Mocambian culture is based on the idea that both elements exist in everyone and everything. It's kind of like the Oriental concepts of yin and yang."

"Should I be taking notes?" Rachel interrupted. "I mean, is this going to be on the quiz?" Instantly she regretted her surliness. "Look, I'm sorry, Mol. I don't mean to be taking this out on you. Especially since you're riding high on such great news. I'm a cretin for bringing up all my problems when we're supposed to be celebrating your promotion. Here, let me get you some more champagne. Where is that bottle, anyway?"

"It's in the kitchen."

Now that Rachel had changed the subject, Molly was back to glowing, although whether her cheeks were pink from experiencing pride in her accomplishments or from downing a full glass of champagne on an empty stomach was impossible to determine.

"Thanks," she said, holding out her glass for another round. "You know, I really do feel that this is the beginning of an exciting new chapter of my life." She sighed. "I only wish you were feeling that way about your life, too."

"Oh, don't worry about me."

"Look, I'm certain this is just a lull. You know, things with Howard could get better. If he ever starts to appreciate you, that is. Even if he doesn't, I have every confidence that you'll find someone better. And don't let Boyd have the satisfaction of getting you down. As for your writing . . ."

"Oh, let's be optimistic." Rachel spoke with forced gaiety, trying to make up for having poured out her heart to her sister during what was supposed to have been Molly's moment of triumph. "Besides, who knows? With a little elbow grease and a bit of creativity, I may be able to take this piece on the Mocambians and make it the turning point of my career."

"That's the Swann spirit. Don't forget, Rachel, you're a pretty tough cookie."

Rachel eyed her warily. "I guess I am. But you know what they say."

"What do they say?"

" 'Tough cookies get stale.' "

I wonder what someone has to do in order to become a "guest curator"? Rachel mused as she sat on a crosstown bus edging toward the Metropolitan Museum of Art. Is it something you take a course in? Maybe it's one of those New School specials, a ten-part lecture allegedly for self-edification and personal fulfillment but in reality just an egghead version of a singles bar.

At any rate, the title certainly sounded formidable, Rachel reflected. She glanced at her watch for the fifteenth time, desperate to be prompt for her eleven o'clock appointment to interview the guest curator of the museum's latest extravaganza, "Darkness Untamed, Beauty Unspoiled: Five Hundred Years of the Arts and Crafts of Mocambu."

The past few days since her meeting with Grayson Winters had been hectic. With the help of Molly and the Columbia University library, she'd thrown herself into Mocambian history and culture. She'd plowed through so many erudite journals and wordy, dust-covered tomes that she ended up grateful Molly had turned out to be the only academic in the family.

But at least she felt prepared. She was even wearing her most dignified outfit: a somber suit in go-everywhere gray. She had accessorized with a belt, shoes, scarf, and a lapel pin so unmemorable, they were bound to be perceived as tasteful. She had pulled her hair back into a severe ponytail, not wanting to be mistaken for a mere dilettante by Dr. Cornelia Pellings Ashcrofton.

Following the instructions that the secretary in the special exhibitions department had given her over the telephone, Rachel bypassed the grand staircase that led up to the museum's front entrance. She barely glanced at the two huge banners hung overhead, announcing the exhibitions that the museum was currently featuring. True, they were well publicized, but they weren't quite shopping-bag caliber. Rachel couldn't resist a smug smile.

The entrance that led to Dr. Ashcrofton's office—her *guest* office—was much less dramatic. Still, passing through the simple, unmarked black door that led to the enormous edifice's bottom floor—the very pulse of the place, since this was where the majority of the offices were—gave her a little thrill. Only a privileged few were allowed through there. This wasn't an entrance for the casual museumgoer, or even the dedicated Derain devotee or the true Flemish freak. Only those who had serious business with the mavens of the art world were permitted in this part of the museum.

The secretary who greeted her—Patty Rogers, according to the plaque on her desk—looked as out of place in this milieu as a suit of armor accidentally placed among the mummies. Somehow, streaked hair and eyeliner and the concentrated perusal of a fashion magazine just didn't cut it when it was injected into an atmosphere that said "*This* is where the world's great treasures are given sanctuary."

"Can I help you?" the young woman asked, reluctantly tearing herself away from the printed word. She punctuated the question by snapping her gum loudly.

"Dr. Ashcrofton, please."

"She expecting you?"

"Yes. I'm Rachel Swann? Eleven o'clock?"

The woman glanced at the appointment book left open on her desk. Meanwhile Rachel read, upside down, the title of the magazine article the young woman had been studying: "What Really Runs the Show, Your Mind or Your Heart?" Pretty metaphysical stuff. "Oh, yeah. Here y'are. Go on in. Her office is right down the hall."

The young woman went back to the latest issue of *Mademoiselle*, not at all aware that she'd just played catalyst in uniting two great and ambitious minds.

Any questions Rachel had about the qualifications necessary for being invited to guest-curate were answered as soon as she peeked inside the doorway of Dr. Cornelia

Ashcrofton's office. Copies of the no-nonsense books she had written were placed in strategic spots all over the tiny space, as were academic journals on whose covers her name was prominent. There were photographs, black and white mostly, of the good doctor with Margaret Mead, Jane Goodall, Louis Leakey, and various dour old men whose wrinkled knees were boldly displayed by their meticulously pressed khaki shorts.

Rather than feeling intimidated by this less-than-subtle exhibit of Dr. Ashcrofton's accomplishments, Rachel found herself relaxing. After all, she had one of *these* in her own family.

"Dr. Ashcrofton? I'm Rachel Swann, from *New York Life* magazine." As she held out her hand—friendly, yet authoritative; she'd read about that in *Self* magazine—she saw that Dr. A. was giving her a thorough once-over. She, meanwhile, responded in kind.

Dr. Ashcrofton's persona could be summed up in one word: crusty. She stood less than five feet two inches tall, with graying hair shaped into a prim pageboy. Her stocky form was clad in a white blouse, a navy-blue cardigan, and a plaid skirt with an uneven hem. Her glasses, a pair of bifocals, were on a chain, at the moment resting on her amorphous chest. Yet despite her appearance, the woman exuded intelligence, insightfulness, and a brusque no-nonsense quality that Rachel had occasionally gotten glimpses of in her sister.

"Rachel Swann," Dr. Ashcrofton repeated, finally extending her hand toward Rachel's. Peering at her uncertainly, she asked, "Any relation to Molly Swann?"

"Why, yes. Molly is my sister." Rachel smiled brightly.

"Really?" Dr. Ashcrofton perked right up. "You know, I caught her on *Donahue*!"

Immediately she reeled in her enthusiasm. "Not that I have time for that sort of thing very often, of course . . . She's done some fine work. Very fine. Clever idea, taking the tribal customs of what most people consider primitive cultures and superimposing them over the traditions that we claim make us civilized to show just how similar we really are. I particularly enjoyed her comparison of the emcees so commonly used at our weddings with the buffoonish performance of the head warrior at the Mozambican marriage ceremony."

It would be clear sailing from here on in, Rachel knew. Her credentials had gotten her in: She was one of the fold. In addition, she recognized that given Dr. Ashcrofton's apparent appreciation of the mass media, she was bound to be cooperative. She was undoubtedly thrilled over the opportunity to splash her own life's work across the pages of a magazine that featured articles on which deli offered the leanest corned beef in town.

Dr. Ashcrofton moved some papers and journals to clear a chair for Rachel, meanwhile muttering incoherently. It was already clear who was going to lead the interview. This woman was used to being the star of every occasion. She certainly hadn't gotten here, to the bowels of one of the finest museums in the world, by being coy.

"Now." She sat down at her desk, thereby putting a formidable barrier between her and Rachel. "How can I help you?"

Rachel opened her notebook and placed it in her lap. Her pen was posed in midair. "As you know, I'm doing an article on the Mocambian exhibition for *New York Life* magazine. Basically, I'm looking for background. Some insights into Mocambu's history, something on the people perhaps, their culture . . . plus whatever you can tell me about the exhibition itself."

Rachel waved her hands in the air in a gesture designed to say, "It's your baby. Roll with it."

"Well, if there's one thing I'd like your article to convey," Dr. Ashcrofton began slowly, "it's that the Mocambians are not all that different from us. They have their social codes, they have their ways of dealing with the natural cycles, they have their religion. . . ."

"Yes, what about their religion?" Rachel interjected. "I understand it's very much like voodoo."

She watched Dr. Ashcrofton's face carefully, searching for some reaction, since *voodoo* was one of those words that elicit strong reactions in almost everybody, a word like *war* or *cholesterol* or *Jesse Helms*.

But the woman just smiled. "Yes, the religion of Mocambu is very much like Haitian voodoo. That's mainly because Mocambu, like Haiti, has its roots in West Africa.

"That, in fact, explains why Americans are bound to find the religious customs and beliefs of Mocambu so strange. Using herbs and potions, subscribing to such primitive beliefs as hexes and curses, worshipping both good forces and evil forces . . . those are all very much a part of African religions. They're quite commonplace. It's seeing them transplanted here, so close to the Judeo-Christian culture, that makes them seem like such a novelty."

"What about the worship of both good and evil?" Rachel asked, drawing upon the wealth of knowledge she'd gained over the past few days. "Does that, in your mind, translate to devil-worship?"

Dr. Ashcrofton's expression was stern. It was clear she wasn't pleased by the use of such pop phrases. She had no interest in equating a fascinating, complex culture, one rooted in a colorful if primitive society, with heavy-metal rock bands.

"Actually, the Mocambians have a rather sophisticated view of good and evil, especially when compared with those put forth by our own so-called civilized religions," she said coldly. "The Mocambians believe that good and evil coexist side by side, that both elements exist in everything—nature, people, even their gods. Rather than being mutually exclusive—an either-or situation—they are two forces that are in constant struggle. Rather than simply being written off as something that nice people should strive to avoid, evil is respected because of its inevitable presence."

Rachel paused, scribbling away on her pad. Two forces . . . constant struggle . . . this was good stuff. She didn't want to miss a word of it.

"Dr. Ashcrofton, is there actually a figure in the Mocambian religion that's comparable to what we would consider the devil?"

Dr. Ashcrofton nodded. "Yes, there is. And he is treated with due respect. The Mocambians attempt to appease him in special ceremonies, and there are potions conjured up to deal with his spells. They even build small temples in which they pay their respects to him. But there is also an appreciation of the fact that the devil's real power comes from human weakness."

"I'm afraid I don't follow."

"The point is that evil—the devil, if you will—is no more powerful than people's own tendency toward greed and lust and all the other vices will allow him to be."

"Ah. I see." Rachel was getting the distinct feeling that there was little room for vice of any kind in Dr. Ashcrofton's life. Perhaps that was what accounted for her fascination with the Mocambians.

She glanced at her notes, suddenly realizing that too much of this devil stuff would make for a very heavy article, not at all the kind of thing Grayson Winters was looking for. Slyly glancing at her watch, Rachel said, "Goodness, the time is flying right by. . . . We'd better move on. Tell me, how would you characterize the social structure of the Mocambians?"

Dr. Ashcrofton was off, just as well informed about this topic, just as eager to spout off about it. Her enthusiasm was rubbing off on Rachel. As she nodded and took notes and said "uh-huh" to show she was still tuned in, the article was already beginning to take shape in her head.

Maybe it won't change the world, she was thinking as she scribbled away. Maybe it won't even shake up the city of New York. But I can certainly do my best with it, make it something good, something I can be proud of.

Besides, at the moment the idea that one particular article could change her life sounded utterly ridiculous.

Chapter
Four

"How *come* they call these flea markets?" asked Kimberly. Trustingly she slid her hand into her father's as they hurried out of the way of a beat-up old Chevy whose driver was taking the fact that he was in the parking lot of Yonkers Raceway just a bit too much to heart. Much to Rachel's astonishment, Howard's younger daughter's voice actually registered something resembling enthusiasm.

"Because, flea-brain," her sister cut in nastily before Rachel was able to construct some colorful, if not altogether accurate, response, "you've got to have a mind the size of a flea's to want to come to something like this in the first place."

"Come on, you two," Howard said heartily. "Trust me, this is going to be fun. Who knows what great things we're going to find? At some pretty unbelievable prices, too."

"Yeah, right." Heather indulged in an arrogant toss of her head, number one on her list entitled Obnoxious Body Movements. "If I'm really lucky, maybe I'll find myself a tomato-red polyester blouse for nine ninety-nine. Just what I always wanted."

Despite her resolve that today she was going to have a good time—even in the presence of Heather and Kimberly Becker, Westchester County's double-duty answer to the Antichrist—Rachel cringed with every word. After all, coming to Yonkers Raceway for the Sunday flea market had been her idea. With Becky at Boyd's and Rachel needing a way to play The Good Mother to Howard's daughters, she had frantically speed-read the Sunday *Times*, zeroing in on this option with more than a little relief.

"It's such a gorgeous spring day. Let's do something different," she'd suggested that morning over breakfast.

She spoke in the chirpy tone of voice that always made her feel like a character on *Mister Rogers' Neighborhood*. The four of them—Rachel, Howard, and the little Beckers—were crammed around the kitchen table, heads bent with religious fervor as croissants and scones from the closest yuppie bakery were consumed. Another long day loomed ahead, and, as usual, Rachel was the only one interested in how they were going to fill it.

Heather had perked up immediately. "I know. Let's go to the mall."

"We always go to the mall," whined Kimberly.

"Do you know how people shopped a long, long time ago, before there were any malls?" Rachel asked. There was that voice again.

Heather blinked, her eyelashes so heavily mascaraed that she created a draft. "Mail order?"

"No. Back in the old days, people used to shop in open air markets."

"Oh." Heather's interest was already waning. "You mean like in the Middle Ages. The only stuff there was to buy in those days was, like, pigs and cheese."

"Well, whatever they had to buy and sell, going to market was pretty exciting," Rachel insisted. "Imagine what it must have been like, living back in the Middle Ages. Once a week—or, uh, however often they did it—you'd leave your isolated farm in the middle of nowhere and go to market. There'd be stalls set up, and people would be selling all kinds of terrific things. And there'd be wonders you'd never seen before. Jugglers and strolling minstrels and mimes . . ."

"And cock fights, right?" Kimberly looked pleased over her ability to contribute to the conversation. "I saw that on TV once."

"What exactly are you suggesting, Rachel?" Heather asked in exasperation. "A field trip to the South Bronx?"

"I feel like I'm torturing them," Rachel said an hour later as the four of them joined the throngs who were making their way into Yonkers Raceway.

Today the teeming masses were not there for the sport of horse racing, but the equally exhilarating sport of bargain hunting. Stands were set up in more or less straight lines, selling everything from clothing to toys to junk—at one particular stand, annoyingly labeled "anteeks." It was food that appeared to be the hot seller, however. Pizza, sausage heroes with peppers and onions, shish kabob, souvlaki— Rachel wondered how much she could make moonlighting here on weekends with a Maalox stand.

"You're not torturing them. It's good for them," Howard insisted, distractedly patting her on the back. "I like them to be exposed to other life-styles. It builds character.

"Boy, it's hot." He glanced up at the sky, as if annoyed that the sun was hanging out there, ruining his day. "Maybe I should have worn a hat. I don't want to get a sunburn on my head." Protectively he touched the expanse of skin he wore like a cherry on top.

"You came to the right place. You could probably pick up a hat for a few bucks."

"I don't wear hats."

"I just want everybody to have a good time, that's all." Rachel sounded meek—defeated, even—as she added, "It would probably help if I could get a little more support."

But Howard didn't hear her. He had rushed over to a stall selling flashlights for two ninety-nine.

"How long do we have to stay here?" Kimberly demanded. "This stuff is all so cheesy."

"You call this cheesy?" Howard was holding up a one-hundred-percent cotton flannel shirt priced at eight ninety-nine. "This is a steal. You know, I could really get into this."

"Kimberly, there's a stand selling tapes and CDs over

there," Rachel said, pointing. "Why don't you go see if you can find any good ones?"

Whereas once upon a time words like *abracadabra* and *open, sesame* could cast magic spells, the words *tapes* and *CDs* now had the same powers. Presto, chango: In a flash, Heather and Kimberly were off, groaning and squealing in ecstasy as they flipped through the red and blue plastic bins.

"At last, vee are alone." Rachel's vampire imitation may not have been Comedy Store quality, but it got her through the embarrassment of the point she was trying to make. "Howard, there's something I've been wanting to talk to you about."

"Can't it wait?" He was fingering some argyle socks, three pairs for ten dollars.

"Howard, those are Orlon. Look, I want to ask you something."

She caught herself in the slip. Five seconds earlier, she had been talking to him about something. Now, here she was, suddenly *asking* him.

"Ask away, Rachel. I'm listening."

"Next weekend is the Fourth of July weekend, and, uh, I—"

"Already? God, summer's practically over. Where does the time go?" Howard had picked up a pair of baggy shorts in a Hawaiian print, lush salmon-colored flowers against a background of turquoise and jade-green leaves. "Are these me or what?"

"Anyway, that weekend my sister always has kind of a barbecue thing, and—"

"Molly?" Howard's low-level contempt for Molly Swann, usually kept fairly contained, was leaking out around the edges.

"No, not Molly. Sis."

"Oh. The black sheep of the Swann clan."

"She's hardly what you'd call a black sheep."

"She's a housewife, right? She's the baby sister of a successful free-lance journalist and a talk show feminist, but she never even got it together enough to finish college."

"Thank you, Howard, for reducing all three of us to laughable caricatures of our true selves."

Rachel took a deep breath, reminding herself that she was asking Howard for a favor, not doing field work for Ten Ways to Start an Argument.

"Anyway, Sis is planning this family thing, and of course Becky and I are going, and . . . well, it would be nice if you came, too." A lame finish for a sentence that, at least in her mind, had had a pretty strong start.

"Rachel, you know I have the girls that weekend."

"Yes, I know, but—"

"And they'd feel out of place at something like that. Hanging around with *your* family, I mean."

"Yes, I can imagine how they'd feel." Better than you know. "So I thought that maybe they could spend the weekend—or at least part of it—with their mother."

"What?"

"That way, we could have some time alone together."

Please, *please*, don't make me hear "But it's the only chance I have to see my daughters" again for the quadzillionth time.

Howard was silent. Rachel didn't know if he was considering her request or debating whether or not to buy himself one of the enameled "I *#$! New York" keychains, two for a dollar, he was examining.

"Yeah," he finally said. "I guess I could do that."

"You could?"

"Sure. You're right, Rachel. We hardly get any time alone together."

"Do you think Sydney would agree to keep the girls?"

"I don't see why not."

Instead of saying "Goody, goody, gumdrops," as was her first inclination, Rachel simply nodded in a dignified fashion. "Great. Then it's settled. The barbecue is Monday. We should plan to leave midmorning, around ten."

"Ten sounds fine." Howard held up a keychain. "Want me to buy you one of these?"

"Maybe this would be a good time for us all to discuss our plans for next weekend," Rachel suggested gently a few minutes later. Kimberly and Heather had returned to the fold, having between them spent more on CDs than Rachel routinely spent on a winter coat.

"What's happening next weekend?" Kimberly asked brightly. Her mood was substantially improved by having made a sizable investment in a mode of musical entertainment that the Japanese were no doubt working at that very moment to make obsolete.

"Hey, look. Car stuff."

Howard had stopped in front of another stall, Arnie's Auto World. The really flashy items, the fuzzy dice and the Garfields with suction cup legs, were up front. In the back were cables and clamps and oddly shaped metal things, automobile innards that invariably aroused feelings of great anxiety in Rachel. In between were the impulse items: sheepskin seat covers, leather steering wheel covers, and plastic clip-on contraptions that held coffee cups, designed for people so addicted to caffeine that they had to have it available to them even at speeds upward of sixty m.p.h.

"Why don't you tell the kids about the Fourth of July weekend?" Rachel prompted.

"Hmmm? Oh, sure. God, I always wanted sheepskin seat covers. But I don't want people to think I'm a pimp. Hey, look at these seat-cover jobbies, with the wooden balls. What, are these supposed to be good for your back? They look like something left over from the Spanish Inquisition."

"What's happening on the Fourth of July?" Kimberly asked. Heather, meanwhile, was making it clear by her body language that she was bored both by the conversation and by being surrounded by automotive accessories.

"It's not a big deal," said Howard. "Rachel's got this family thing she wants me and her to go to on Monday, so I figured you girls could spend that day with your mother.

Look at these. BABY ON BOARD. Who the hell cares, anyway? Kidnappers, maybe."

"Daddeee." Heather had decided to join in. Something in what he'd said had sparked her interest. Rachel felt her heart drop into her stomach with a thud.

"Hey, check this out." Gleefully Howard picked up a detachable red flashing light, the kind that police officers and firefighters stuck on top of their cars whenever they experienced the uncontrollable desire to weave through traffic at eighty miles an hour. "Think I should get one of these? It'd be a great way to deal with tie-ups on the Triborough."

"It looks like a hat," Kimberly quipped.

"Oh, yeah?" Grinning, Howard stuck it on his mostly bald head. The no-nonsense suction cup at the bottom of the light clung to the smooth skin of his head like a barnacle on the underside of a fiberglass hull.

"Turn it on!" Kimberly insisted, laughing.

Howard complied. The rotating red light radiated out from the top of his head, spinning round and round, turning him into a human beacon.

His appreciative audience of one applauded. "You look great, Dad."

Heather was not at all amused. "Daddeee! You said you'd take me to the beach party on Monday. Remember? Me and Hillary and all my friends?"

"I did?"

"Yes, you did. You don't remember?" Heather's face was twisted up, a warning to all that she was dangerously close to tears. "Oh, Daddy. How could you have forgotten?"

"Sweetie, can't you just—"

"It's so important to me. Besides, Daddy, you *promised*."

"Howard," Rachel said, rather close to tears herself, "can't the three of us talk about this in a calm, unemotional way?"

"Well, Rachel, it seems to me that if I *promised* . . ."

"Take that thing off, will you? I'm trying to have an adult conversation here." Rachel glanced around, suddenly self-conscious. "Besides, you're beginning to attract attention."

Howard reached up. "Okay, I—wait a second. I can't get it . . . this damned thing is stuck."

"Come on, Howard. Stop trying to be funny."

"Take it off, Daddy. You look weird." The novelty was wearing off even for Kimberly.

"It's stuck, I'm telling you." Howard's expression was quickly growing panicked. "This suction thing is so strong, I can't—"

"Daddy, you're embarrassing us!" Heather began pulling on his arm. "Take it off right now!"

"I'm telling you, Heather, it's really stuck on there." The color of Howard's face perfectly matched the light emanating from his head, rhythmically illuminating his surroundings, making him the center of a bizarre, newly formed universe. "I'm *trying*, but I can't. . . ."

Rachel, watching this scene in disbelief, suddenly could stand no more.

"Oh, Howard, forget it. Just forget the whole thing."

She turned away, disappearing into the crowd of flea-market shoppers that had gathered to gawk, their embarrassed titters quickly elevating to guffaws.

"Rachel? Rachel Swann? Is that you?"

Rachel had just settled into a seat on the commuter train that ran between Yonkers and New York, curling up with her face pressed close to the soot-covered window. The air-conditioning was a relief, and she was just beginning to relax, looking forward to a nice, long sulk, when her reverie was shattered.

She glanced up, curious about who the culprit was. It took her a few seconds to connect with the pretty, carefully madeup face beaming down at her. It was the accent, more southern than a bucket of grits, that tipped her off.

"Gayle?" she breathed. "Gayle Shipley?"

"It is you! Rachel, how y'all doin'? Goodness, how long has it been?"

As the woman settled in beside her, a walking tribute to Seventh Avenue with her designer clothes, designer accessories, and designer attitude, both of them began muttering calculations.

"I guess it's been nine years since we worked together," Rachel finally concluded.

"That sounds about right. I was workin' in the art department of *World Today* when you came in to do that series of articles on youth clubs. Golly, it's hard to believe it was really that long ago."

Time had been a friend to Gayle Shipley, Rachel noted, discreetly taking inventory. Aside from the slender woman's enviable look, one that could be achieved only with a good eye for fashion and a generous credit line at Bloomingdale's, she was positively radiant. Rachel glanced down at her own jeans, her idea of the appropriate fashion statement for slumming it at a flea market. Instead of feeling zany and madcap, she found herself feeling like the hired help.

"We had some great times back then, didn't we?" Gayle was saying, her selective memory glossing over what had, in fact, been a rather hellish period of deadlines, uncertainty, and personality conflicts. "Things were just so crazy at *World Today*."

"Crazy," Rachel repeated, still trying to get her bearings.

"My Lord, it feels like it was yesterday, not nine years ago."

"That's right. I had just moved to New York." Rachel's voice grew wistful as she found herself drifting back in time, remembering places and people and feelings that these days were rarely dragged out of the dusty cartons in which they had been packed away in the back of her brain.

That stint with *World Today* had been her first real writing job in the city. The Big Time, as she used to think of it. Upon arriving in New York with two solid years' experience with the *Marbury Express*, Rachel quickly discovered that her credentials qualified her for little more than proofreading, copyediting, and making trips to the deli for other people's coffee and bagels. She was living in the West

Village, in an apartment on Perry Street so tiny that it was just as well she couldn't afford any furniture besides a single bed, two director's chairs, and a wicker trunk that served as both dresser and dining room table.

Then the friend of a friend got her into the *World Today* offices. Suddenly it all seemed worth it: coming to a city so congested that it took forty-five minutes to travel on public transportation the two miles to work; living on Campbell's tomato soup and saltines; spending long evenings trying to get comfortable in a director's chair, relying on *Star Trek* reruns to take her out of her claustrophobic quarters.

She was a writer—a real writer. With her improvement in status came a resulting leap in the self-esteem department. And it showed. Men started flocking around. Rachel kissed Mr. Spock good-bye. Her evenings were now spent taking in arty movies at the Film Forum or drinking cappuccino at Bleecker Street cafés or downing beers at the historic and very literary White Horse Tavern. Her companions were a long and ever-changing list of young men, most of them just starting out, most of them intense, all of them as taken with their newfound urban lives as she was.

Dashing about the city, playing femme fatale, was new to Rachel. In college she'd had little time for serious dating, between her heavy courseload and her job at the newspaper. Then, once she was living in Marbury for real, still plugging away as Tom Vogel's top reporter, she found few suitable males to play Romeo to her Juliet. So it was almost a relief that, finally, she found herself smack in the middle of the life she had dreamed about as a child, watching Sandra Dee and Doris Day dash about New York in a basic black dress and a string of pearls, juggling romance and career.

Of course, all that had changed when one of those faces with whom she exchanged gay banter over mesquite chicken and kir belonged to Boyd Tanner. She found herself at the end of those Doris Day movies, at the part where her career suddenly seemed less important than choosing an engagement ring and having real estate agents show her larger, sunnier two-bedroom apartments with better addresses, addresses suitable for an up-and-coming Wall Street bond broker and his wife.

"Imagine," Gayle was musing, "nearly a whole decade has gone by. I hate to say it, but it seems like just yesterday. I remember you were goin' out with some young man who I thought was most inappropriate. A poet, or somethin'. I remember him havin' shoulder-length hair." The way she pronounced the word "hair" gave it at least three syllables.

"Actually, he wrote for the *Village Voice*," Rachel said defensively. "He was brilliant, if a tad too close to the edge."

"But what about you? Remember that character who was always following you around like a puppy, begging you to go for sushi with him? You know, that guy from accounting . . . Gil, Gilman . . ."

"Gilbert Lefkowitz."

"Right. That was his name. Gilbert Lefkowitz." Rachel shook her head as if in disbelief. "I wonder whatever happened to him?"

"He's now an executive vice president of finance with the Hearst Corporation."

"No kidding. You mean you kept in touch?"

"I guess you could say that. Gil and I have been married for seven years now." Already the leather wallet was being lifted out of her Judith Lieber pocketbook. "Here's my sugar," she said proudly, flipping through the photos. "This was taken just a few months ago." She peered at the photograph, smiling coyly. "Hiya, honey," she greeted it.

There he was. Gilbert Lefkowitz, coated in plastic. Looking a hell of a lot more appealing than Rachel remembered him, too.

"And look at these little cuties," Rachel said dutifully, noting the two grinning towheads, a boy and a girl, a complete set. They were dressed up for Halloween in pumpkin costumes, looking Hallmark cute. "Your kids?"

"Darlin', aren't they? Megan Rae Louise is five, and Jesse just turned three."

"Jesse? Just Jesse?"

"His middle name is James." Gayle wrinkled her nose. "I kind of liked the sound of it. You know, the two Js?"

"Very catchy. So you've been married seven years?"

"Oh, I know what y'all are thinkin'. The seven-year itch, right?"

"No, actually, I—"

"To tell you the truth . . ." There was a gleam in Gayle's eye as she said, more to herself than to Rachel, "We're still like newlyweds, even after all this time."

"That's terrific. Really terrific." Rachel swallowed hard, wondering how she could change the subject to something more pleasant. The possibility of nuclear war in their lifetime, for example.

Too late.

"What about you, Rachel? Surely y'all must be married by now."

"Actually, I'm, uh, divorced."

"Oh, *Rachel*. I'm so *sorry!*" Gayle reached over and grabbed Rachel's hand. Kneading it, she cooed, "Oh, honey. You must be just destroyed. What a terrible, *terrible* thing."

"Uh, to tell you the truth, I really believe it was for the best. Boyd and I—"

"There aren't any children, are there?" The kneading continued.

"I have a bright, beautiful, wonderful daughter. Her name is Becky. . . ."

Gayle let out a loud gasp. "Oh, you poor, poor dear. And that poor child!"

Rachel simply offered a wan smile.

"Now, the best thing for you to do is get right back in that saddle. You know what they say. Just because you failed once . . ."

"I am involved with someone new." Rachel gave in to the urge to add just a hint of loftiness to her tone. "His name is Howard." She found herself wishing his name were something more along the lines of Dirk or Rutherford or even Armand.

"Howard?" Gayle perked up. "What a charmin' name. Anyone I know?"

"He is if you read *Business Week* and *The Wall Street Journal*."

Gayle was frowning. "No, I'm afraid I'm not really in touch with that kind of thing."

"In fact, that's how I first met him. Interviewing him for *Business Week*."

"I'm sure Gilbert has heard of him," Gayle insisted. "What did you say his last name was?"

"Howard Becker."

"I'll check with Gil."

Rachel was certain she would.

"And how is that writing career of yours goin'? Still writin' those perky little articles?"

Rachel cleared her throat. "I'm, uh, working free-lance now. Doing a lot of different things."

"Would I have read anything you've written?"

"It's possible." Especially if you spend a lot of time in supermarket checkout lines. "At the moment I'm doing kind of a fun piece for *New York Life*."

"*New York Life*!" Gayle was clearly impressed. "Why, Gil and I subscribe!"

"Then you'll be reading it. I'm covering the opening of a new art exhibition at the Met."

Gayle gasped. "Not the Mocambian exhibit?"

"Yes. You mean you've heard about it?"

"Of course! My, what a coincidence. I'm catering it!"

Rachel was bewildered. "You're catering an art exhibit?"

"The opening. It's a fund-raising thing for the museum. Just champagne and canapes, but it's one of the Met's big social events this month. You mean you didn't know that?"

"Oh, I just . . . you're catering it?"

"That's right. Uptown Catering is a little business I started with two of my friends, Mandy Carp and B. J. Morton. Mandy's husband is a psychopharmacologist and B.J. is married to the president of a firm that imports Italian designer furniture. Anyway, the three of us put our little ol' heads together and came up with the idea of starting a catering company. Just somethin' to keep us out of trouble. And, well," she concluded with a shrug, "it kind of took off."

"It must have if you're doing parties at the Met." Rachel was having a hard time hiding how impressed she was.

"It turns out we have a flair for it. Mandy's a great cook—you should see some of the things she does with truffles—and B.J. has great connections. Me, I'm the organizer." Gayle chuckled. "We're making so much money that even our husbands are amazed. Gil has been teasin' me, sayin' that for our tenth wedding anniversary he expects me to take him on a first-class cruise around the world—and pick up the tab myself!"

Gayle leaned forward as if she were about to share a secret. "But you know, Rachel, the best part is that I really love it. My own little business that I created by myself, with two of my dear, dear friends . . . It's important to me, bein' involved in somethin' I care about. I know it sounds corny, but for the first time in my life, I feel fulfilled." She sighed peacefully. "I'm really, really happy."

"Gee, Gayle," Rachel said lamely, "it sounds like you've got everything."

"You, too, Rachel. Look at you. You have a terrific new man, a daughter, a successful career you love. . . . What else is there?"

Rachel forced a smile. "Not much, I guess."

"Oh, my, is this Grand Central already?" Gayle looked up, blinking as if she'd been in a trance. "Well, back to the city."

"So you still live in Manhattan?"

"We actually live in Bedford Hills, but we have a small place in Murray Hill. Nothing fancy, but it's convenient since a lot of Uptown Catering's work is here—including a breakfast I've got tomorrow for the mayor." She rolled her eyes upward in exasperation. "It's going to be another one of those crazy periods, when all we do is work. We've got the mayor's thing tomorrow, a little shindig for the Sony

Corporation over the Fourth of July weekend, the party at the Met the following Wednesday . . ."

Gayle had begun gathering up her things. "Well, Rachel, it was great seeing you again. I'm so glad we ran into each other."

"Me, too." Rachel smiled, all the while thinking, The perfect way to spend the afternoon before going home to slit my wrists.

"We should really get together for lunch sometime."

"Definitely. I'll call you. Uptown Catering, right?"

"We're in the book. I'll look for your name in print. And who knows? Maybe we'll run into each other at the Met next week."

"Just don't make any native Mocambian specialties for the reception," Rachel couldn't resist saying. "I don't think New York is ready for mesquite iguana yet."

"Oh, Rachel, you always did have such an incredible imagination," Gayle called across the train before disappearing.

Chapter
Five

"Are we there yet?" demanded Becky for the eighth time, her voice getting two points higher on the whine scale with each repetition.

"Soon, honey. Soon," Rachel replied through gritted teeth.

"I can't believe we're not at Aunt Sis's yet." Becky's tone had moved on to pouty.

"And *I* can't believe we're actually renting a car," Molly muttered from over on the passenger side of the front seat, her posture reminiscent of a hunchback on his way to a GI series. "I especially can't believe you're making us pay half."

"Relax, Mol. I'm telling you, it still works out cheaper than if all four of us had taken the Long Island Rail Road. When you add on the cab fare we'd have had to pay, it's an absolute steal."

Rachel gripped the wheel of the Budget Rent-a-Car dark blue Fury, her level of tension a barometer of the outrageousness of the other drivers on the Long Island Expressway. Sure, it was cheaper to drive out to the family barbecue at the home of Sis and Company, at least in dollars. When the cost in terms of wear and tear on the driver was factored in, however, that left the whole issue open for debate.

And Rachel's mood hadn't been that terrific in the first place, even before she and Becky waited in line with the thirty other impatient New Yorkers who'd come up with the brainstorm of renting a car and leaving the city over the Fourth of July weekend. Last Sunday's fiasco, courtesy of Howard and his two omnipresent sidekicks, still weighed heavily on her mind. She didn't know which was worse, having gotten so disgusted with Howard that she'd walked out on him, or the fact that he had yet to call her to apologize. Or at least to beg for the chance to tell his side of the story.

"You know, this is actually kind of interesting," Mike piped up from the backseat, where he and Becky had been playing Go Fish since the Triborough Bridge. "From a psychosociological perspective, I mean."

"Translate, Mike." Rachel's tone was patient. No use taking out on Mike her frustration over the passive-aggressiveness of the other drivers. After all, he couldn't even drive. While in his work life he had conquered the computer with its mind-boggling confusion of bits, bytes, and megahertz, he had in his personal life never mastered any machine more complicated than the Cuisinart.

"What's interesting," he said, "is that here on the country's expressways, highways, and byways—"

"Go fish!" Becky squealed joyously.

"What are byways, anyway?" Molly mused, not speaking to anyone in particular. "I don't think I've ever actually been on a byway."

"Here on the roads is where people play out the battle between the superego, the ego, the id. . . ."

"You mean the id-i-ot." Molly was watching in disbelief. "God, Rachel, that guy cut you off with about an inch to spare. Hey, I just thought of a new theory. Maybe the amount of space a guy allows between bumpers when he cuts you off is equal to the length of his you-know-what." Over her shoulder she cast a sweet smile at Becky.

"Fascinating," Rachel said dryly. "Just fascinating."

There was a long silence. In a perverse way, Rachel was actually beginning to enjoy herself—aside from the guerrilla warfare she was engaged in with the other drivers on the expressway. It was a beautiful July day, balmy and dry with only a minimum of pollution. This was the ideal kind of weather for getting out of the city, out to where the trees were. How lovely it was to have the whole day off, how nice it would be to see Sis. Then there was all the traditional Fourth of July junk food, the kind of thing she rarely let herself indulge in—potato salad and tortilla chips and rich creamy dips that had started out as dried flakes in a soup box.

Her reverie was interrupted by Molly's loud sigh.

"We didn't even rent a car last January when Fortunoff's had its white sale. I mean, I like the fact that it's called a Fury—that has a nice ring to it—but still. All this fuss just because Sis and her macho mate Vito decided to spend the U.S. of A.'s birthday charring greasy chopped meat over an open flame."

"Go fish!" Becky cried again.

"His name is Jerry, not Vito," Rachel shot back. "You know, Molly, our baby sister has been married to the man for close to two decades. I don't think it's too much to ask that her big sister be polite enough to call the woman's husband by his correct name."

"Vito, Jerry, it's all the same to me," Molly muttered.

"So where's good old Howard today?" Mike asked brightly, not actively trying to change the subject but instead totally oblivious of what the subject was.

"Why is it that everybody always insists on referring to him as 'good old Howard'?" Rachel said crossly.

"There's just something about him," Molly replied with mock sweetness.

"I like Howard," Mike piped up from the backseat. "I think he's a great guy."

"Yeah, such a great guy that his woman is spending one of the three major cholesterol-consuming weekends of the summer without him."

"He's busy."

"Busy? On the Fourth of July? The only people who are allowed to be busy on the Fourth of July are Good Humor Men and those guys at Jones Beach who rent out the umbrellas. It's positively un-American to work on the Fourth of July."

"I didn't say he was working."

Molly's only response was a raised eyebrow.

"Look, his daughter Heather wanted to go to some beach party up in Westchester, and Howard got roped into carpooling."

"What a guy." Molly let a stream of air escape through her tight lips. "Good old Howard."

"I don't think that's so bad," Mike commented from the backseat. "It's important for a man to spend time with his daughters. Especially a suit like Howard. Any clone who spends his weekdays logging in the hours for the power-hungry corporate machine . . ."

"Here we go again." It was Rachel's turn to mutter.

"What's that, Rachel?"

She glanced at him through the rearview mirror. "Just another bottleneck, Mike."

Sis lived in the middle-class suburb of West Islip, a town whose major claim to fame was that it was home to Jessica Hahn. Sis's house was one of a dozen nearly identical ones, all built in the early 1950s, all in the then-popular ranch style, all with two-car garages that announced anyone who bought in automatically qualified for the American dream.

Carol Street, named after the builder's daughter, was like a child's puzzle: All the houses looked the same at first glance, but there were really many differences that it would have been fun to circle with a red crayon. This one had aluminum siding, this one had a statue of the Virgin Mary in front, this one had an addition stuck onto one side, comically distorting the building's proportions.

Sis's house was easy to spot: It was the one that looked as if it were being renovated. In fact, it had looked that way for fifteen years, ever since she and her brand-new family had moved in, thrilled to be out of the Brooklyn rental they were quickly outgrowing. Bricks were piled up in the front yard, a promise of better things to come. Bags of cement and piles of lumber filled the garage. Most of the shingles were painted white, but the area underneath the bay window in front was still a pale green.

Then there was the truck, parked in the driveway next to the 1982 Nova with a fender that looked as if it had wrestled with a Mack truck. The pickup was green with the weathered look of someone who had spent too much time in the sun. In back were tools and more construction materials. On its side was printed GERALD CASAMANO. CONTRACTING.

"Hey-ey-ey!"

At the sound of the Fury's tires crunching over the gravel driveway, Jerry Casamano of truck-door fame emerged from the backyard. He came around the side of the house, wearing a blue and white checked apron over his jeans and brandishing a pair of barbecue tongs. "Here dey are. I'm always glad to see three a my favorite ladies. Get over here, Becky. Give yer uncle Jer a big hug. Here's Rachel, the famous writer. And here comes my sister-in-law, the doctor."

Turning to give Mike a big wink, the type that was definitely a part of the secret language of guys, he added, "The way I see it, it always helps to have a doctor in the family, y'know?"

He descended upon Molly with outstretched arms. "Too bad you're not the kind who could take out my appendix. Hey-ey-ey, check this out. Are these two somethin' or what? You city girls really know how to dress."

"You don't look too bad yourself," Molly returned, smoothing her size-sixteen Bermuda shorts. "Love the T-shirt, Jerry. What, today you're not rolling up the sleeves and storing your cigarettes there? You didn't have to dress up for us."

"Hey-ey-ey, you gotta love her, am I wrong?"

"I do," Mike said simply.

"How ya doin', Mike?" As he shook his hand, Jerry's biceps and triceps swelled like Popeye's, stretching the fabric of his white T-shirt to the limit.

"Mommy, I need something to drink," Becky insisted. "I want a Coke."

"Hey, come on around back, Becky. All youse guys. Sis is waiting for you. *Marone*, she's been gettin' ready for this thing for days. It was like she was up for the potato salad prize or somethin'. Sis! They're here!"

Margaret Swann Casamano, a.k.a. Sis, was draped across a lounge chair, a king-size plastic Bart Simpson tumbler in her hand. She jumped up the moment she spotted Rachel and Molly, splashing the tiniest drop of Hawaiian Punch on her fuchsia knit halter.

"Rachel! Molly! Hey, Beck, how's it going? You made it. Traffic okay?"

"Sure, if you happen to possess a strong death wish." Rachel threw her arms around her sister. "You're looking good. Like an advertisement for suburban living."

"Me? Nah." Demonstratively, Sis took hold of the insignificant band of flesh peeking out from between the bottom of her halter and the elastic waistband of her shorts. "Look at this. Gross, huh? But that's what beer and nacho chips'll do to you."

"French wine and soufflés do the same thing," said Molly. "How are you, Sis? Rachel's right. You look terrific."

"Doesn't she?" Jerry had deposited his tongs next to the grill and come over to the women. His dark brown eyes were shining as he slid his arm around Sis's waist. "She's really something, this one. You'd never guess she had two teenage kids, wouldja?" Winking at Rachel, he added, "A teenage husband, too."

"Oh, you!" Sis punched him in the shoulder. Rachel noticed that her eyes had the same glow as Jerry's.

"Where are the kids, anyway?" Rachel asked, suddenly feeling inexplicably defeated.

"They'll be out in a minute," said Jerry. "Hey, what kinda host am I, anyway? Listen, what can I get you to drink? We got beer, iced tea, Coke, diet Coke, anything you want."

"I'll have a beer," said Mike. "What about you, Molly? What would you like?"

As Rachel glanced over at Mike and Molly, she couldn't help noticing that there was nothing in their eyes that came even close to what she had seen in Sis's and Jerry's.

"So come on, come on, sit down," Jerry insisted once everyone had a plastic glass or beer can in hand. "Pull up a lounge chair. It's gonna be a couple minutes till those burgers are cooked, but we got chips, pretzels, all kindsa stuff. Lookit all this. Help yourselves, please. So tell me. What you guys been up to?" He perched on the edge of a redwood bench and leaned forward, beer in hand, his elbows resting on his knees.

"Come on, sweetie. Give 'em a break. They just got here."

Sis had returned to settle comfortably on her lounge chair, looking very much like the queen of the manor in her regal costume of a daringly bare halter top and shorts that were similarly revealing. Her hair, tinted reddish-brown, was piled up into a sort of impromptu topknot, an afterthought held in place with many bobby pins. It tended to frizz up in summer, and today was no exception. Still, there was something charmingly innocent about the way the tendrils framed her round, cherub face, with its blue eyes, thick lashes, and pouty pink lips.

"Yeah, but I wanna hear all about how it feels to be an *associate* professor at Columbia University." Jerry was beaming proudly. "Imagine me related to somebody like that. Me, who never even went to college . . .

"Hey-ey-ey, here he is. Here's my man. Get over here, Vincent. Say hello to your family."

Twelve-year-old Vincent awkwardly held up his hand in a sort of wave as he wandered into the backyard. As always, his thick eyeglasses with their similarly thick black frames gave him a confused look. He was dressed in full Eagle Scout regalia, having just come home from the gala celebration that always followed his pack's participation in the Fourth of July parade.

"Hi, everybody. Aunt Rachel, Aunt Molly, Mike."

Both his skin and his voice, Rachel observed, were un-

fortunate casualties in Vincent's painful transition from boy-
hood to manhood. They added, no doubt, to the almost
pathological shyness that had characterized him since he
was old enough to crawl away from the threat of an imminent social encounter.

Today was no exception. The boy was acting as if he
hoped there was a way he could merge with the group
without actually being noticed.

"Hi, Vincent," Mike said brightly. "Boy, you're getting
big, aren't you?"

"He sure is," Rachel agreed solemnly. "How was the parade?"

His father answered for him. "Ah, they were great, every
one of 'em. I was so proud, standin' out there, watchin' my
kid leadin' the parade, holdin' the American flag. . . . Hey,
you know, don'tcha, that Vincent here is the youngest Eagle
Scout in all of Long Island's history? The kid's got more
badges than . . . than I don't know what."

"Daaaad," Vincent pleaded.

"Hey," Rachel observed, "that's not a mustache I see
growing over your lip, is it?"

The shade of red the boy turned made her regret the
comment. The moment was salvaged, however, as Shelley
Casamano suddenly made her dramatic entrance from the
house, announcing her arrival by slamming the screen door
behind her.

"Oh, hi," she said, blinking as if she were astonished at
finding a party in her backyard. She paused just long
enough to give the impression that she was posing for a
fashion shoot, a habit not at all uncommon in fourteen-year-
old girls. Her long straight brown hair, highlighted with
blond strands just a shade too light, was lightly disheveled,
creating that distinctive just-climbed-out-of-the-backseat-at-
a-drive-in look. Shelley was wearing skintight jeans and a
baggy white T-shirt that magically clung in just the right
spots, showing off an alluring amount of perky, youthful
breast.

"Hey-ey-ey, Shell, come on out." Her father beckoned. "Can I getcha a beer?"

"Jerry, she's too young," Sis scolded, laughing. "You're gonna start her on the road to ruin."

"Hey, listen. I never heard of a fourteen-year-old kid who needed any help at all gettin' on that road. If they're gonna travel it, there's not a hell of a lot you can do to stop them."

"I'll just have a diet Coke." Shelley drifted over to the picnic table covered with a flowered paper tablecloth, looking as if being among such cretins was causing her great pain. "I don't want to get fat," she added more to herself than anyone else.

"Hey, fat chance of that, if you'll excuse the pun," Jerry returned. "I'm tellin' ya, this kid eats like food was already outa style." He guffawed loudly over his own joke.

Shelley just cast him one of those "oh-Daddy" looks.

"So listen. Who's ready for some chow? I think those burgers should be just about ready by now. I see Becky found the chips. Way to go, Beck! The way I figure it, ya gotta start eatin' early in the day. Then ya can just keep goin'!"

"I've got all kinds of stuff in the fridge," said Sis. "Rolls, macaroni salad, potato salad . . ."

"We know. We already heard all about the potato salad Olympics," said Molly.

"What?"

"Listen, let me help." Already Mike was bounding toward the kitchen, showing more enthusiasm than he had since arriving.

"I'll come with you," Jerry offered. "I want to toast some of those buns on the grill." He leaned over and nuzzled his wife's neck. "Sis over here knows how much I love hot buns."

"Oh, you!" Giggling, Sis waved him away. "Get in the kitchen, where you belong!"

"God, I'm getting horny just watching you two," Molly commented to her sister as soon as the men were out of earshot. "I had no idea I was coming to an X-rated barbecue."

"You know how Jerry is."

"I can see. It doesn't look like you mind too much, either."

Sis just shrugged. But that glow was back in her eyes. "How about you, Molly? How are things with you and Mike?" She fixed her wide blue eyes on Molly, making it obvious that she was seeking the truth.

"Great. Great. Couldn't be better." Molly glanced toward the kitchen. "I bet right about now he's garnishing the cole slaw with carrot curls."

"Howard sends his regards," Rachel offered meekly, not wanting to be left out. "He got tied up with his daughters today."

"That's too bad." Sis cast her oldest sister a knowing look but said nothing more.

"Hey, Sis, where's the Tabasco sauce?" Jerry called through the window.

"Tabasco sauce? What on earth do we need that for?"

"I dunno. Mike here insists he's got to have some."

Sis sighed. "Guess I'm gonna have to get off this lounge chair, something I swore I would not do today. Listen, why don't you two come inside and see what Jerry's doing with the playroom?"

"Don't tell me: red flocked wallpaper," Molly muttered. She let out a little yelp when Rachel jabbed her elbow into her arm.

"You were wrong," Rachel said a minute or two later, not without triumph in her voice. "It looks like Jerry's building in a whole wall unit. Look at that. A place for the TV, a special shelf for videotapes and one for CDs. Over there he put in bookshelves. . . ."

"For their leatherbound copies of the *Reader's Digest*, no doubt." Molly had walked over to the Casamanos' video collection and was perusing it. "You think those two watch porn movies together?"

"I don't think they need them, Mol."

"I only want to find out what their secret is. How they keep that, you know, that spark in their lives. Sis and Jerry have been married for eighteen years, don't forget."

Rachel shrugged. "Maybe they're just in love."

Molly cast her a scornful look. "Really, Rachel. Sometimes I think the only things you know about life are what you learned in *Seventeen* magazine."

"Everything's about ready," Jerry said cheerfully when they came into the kitchen. "Come on outside. We got everything set up. Hey, grab some mustard from the fridge, will ya?"

"I got it." Molly went over to the refrigerator. Rachel was about to leave the empty kitchen to go outside with the others, when she heard her say, "Hey, Rach. Wait a sec. Check this out."

Grinning, she handed a small piece of paper to Rachel.

"Where did you find this?"

"In the meat keeper."

Rachel began to read aloud. " 'I walk into the house, tired from a long day's work.' Honestly, didn't the guy ever study grammar and punctuation in school?"

"Shhh, not so loud. Rach, you're not going to believe this, I'm telling you."

" 'I walk into the house' . . . wait, where was I? Okay. 'All the lights are out, and I think nobody's home. I walk into the living room, and it's so dark I can hardly see. I'm just about to turn on the lights when I hear you say, "Don't turn on the light, Jerry." I'm standing there in the dark, and all of a sudden I feel you come over and put your hands on my belt.' . . . Molly, what the hell is this?"

"Kinky stuff, Rach. Don't you see? I bet Jerry and Sis leave these little sexy notes about their fantasies all over the house."

"What about the kids?"

"Shelley and Vincent obviously aren't into meat."

"Here, put this back." Suddenly Rachel couldn't wait to get rid of the thing. "God, Mol, how are we ever going to look either of them in the eye again?"

"Are you kidding? I have new respect for those two." Slamming the refrigerator door shut, she mused, "Gee, I wonder if Jerry has a friend for me. I mean, Mike would never do anything like that. Howard would?"

Rachel snorted. "My Howard? A man whose idea of foreplay is reading the Dow Jones report aloud?"

"God, I'm jealous. It's just not fair."

"Molly, bring out the pepper mill, will you?" Mike called in from the backyard. "We need just a dash more fresh pepper in the slaw."

Molly gave her sister a rueful look. "Duty calls."

It wasn't until two hours and three beers later that Rachel was able to play true confessions with Sis. Shelley was off to Jones Beach with a carful of friends. Becky had drifted off to sleep on a chaise longue. The boys, meanwhile, including those over the age of thirty-five, had retreated to the back portion of the yard, where they were engaged in a competitive game of Frisbee. So far, it looked as if youth was easily outdoing experience, since Vincent was the only one of the three able to bend over without wincing.

"You know," Rachel said, leaning back on her lounge chair and hiking up her shorts a little bit more in order to provide easier access for the sun's tanning rays, "I wasn't telling the whole truth when I told you that Howard wasn't here because of his daughters. I mean, he is carting his darling Heather all over Westchester County today, but it's more complicated than that."

Molly, stretched across her own chaise, glanced over lazily, lifting her sunglasses as if it were a great effort. "Don't tell me you're finally starting to see the light, Rachel. Phasing Mr. Good Times out of your life once and for all."

"That's not fair. Actually, I always kind of liked Howard," Sis offered. "He seems so . . . so stable."

"Stuffy is more like it," said Molly.

"It's not even that," Rachel said. "A little stuffiness I could live with. What bothers me is that he doesn't seem to have made any real commitment to the relationship."

"Uh-oh," said Molly. "The C word."

"You've got it. Every time he has to make a choice between me and his daughters, I lose."

"You can hardly blame the guy for that," Sis insisted. "I mean, imagine how poor Howard must feel, trying to be there for everybody. And nobody's ever satisfied."

Rachel was about to ask exactly whose side her sister was on when Molly blurted out, "For God's sake, Sis. Why are you always so quick to defend the creep? Can't you see he's treating Rachel like a doormat? He doesn't appreciate her, he hardly ever puts her first. . . ."

"I guess it's just hard for me to understand, that's all." Sis shrugged. "Me and Jerry never had any problems like that."

"Oh, so it's all been perfect, huh? Right from day one?"

"Well, no, but . . . I guess what I mean is, sooner or later Jer and I have always found a way to work our differences out."

Rachel could sense that Molly was about to let loose with her interpretation of what it was about Jerry Casamano that made such simple solutions possible. Eager to cut it off at the pass, she said, "You know, I don't feel as if I want too much. All I want in a man are three basic things. It doesn't sound like that big a deal, at least in theory. Not that I managed to find them in the man I chose to marry. Maybe what I want really is impossible to find."

"What are those three things, hon?" Sis asked encouragingly. For the moment, it was hard to tell which of them was the big sister.

"Okay. First of all, a sense of humor."

"Mike has that." Molly was nodding.

"Jerry has that," Sis added.

"Howard is not exactly what you'd call the life of the party. Okay, that's the first. Next comes strong moral fiber."

Sis frowned. "What does that mean, exactly?"

"It means he's . . . solid. You know, that he's committed to things—social issues, things that matter in terms of the world—but also to being a good person. And that means working on his relationships instead of expecting them just to fall into place all around him."

"Commitment," Molly muttered. Both of Rachel's sisters were nodding away as they silently evaluated their own relationships, once again looking smug. "The C word again."

"Right. And the third one . . . fun in bed."

Molly lapsed into pensive silence. Sis, however, giggled.

"You're right, Rachel. That is important. I guess Howard strikes out once again, huh?"

Rachel sighed, then reached for the potato chips that so far she had managed to resist. She plopped the bowl into her lap and mindlessly began shoving them into her mouth, her blue eyes meanwhile becoming glazed.

"I have this image, this fantasy of being involved with a man who doesn't want just sex, but who wants sex with *me*. Somebody who catches my eye from across the room while we're at a crowded party and gives me such a burning look that I get turned on just standing there. Somebody who brings a jar of honey to bed and—"

"Great. Here comes the X-rated part," Molly quipped.

"You know, Rachel, it doesn't sound to me like you're asking too much." Sis's eyes were wide. In fact, she looked as if she couldn't quite believe that all these elements were missing from her sister's life. "Especially that part about the honey."

"Oh, my God," Molly breathed. "But wait a minute, Sis. Maybe you and Jerry are hot in bed. But what about the rest of your life together? You know, *real* life?"

"What about it?"

"Well, look. You've got a house that's been under construction for a million years, and it's never going to be done. . . ."

Sis shrugged. "We never seem to have enough money. Besides, he's working on it a little at a time. Haven't you seen the home entertainment center?"

"Yeah, right. I bet you're in debt right now."

Sis frowned. "Isn't everybody?"

"Look at how you live. You're on the edge here. You're

just scraping by financially, you never go anywhere or do anything. . . . I just don't think this is much of a life, that's all. Don't you ever want *more*, Sis?"

Her reply was a look of confusion. "You mean more than two great kids and a husband who adores me?"

All of a sudden Sis sat upright. "Hey, wait a minute. You know, your relationship with Mike isn't exactly ideal, either."

"What do you mean?" Molly's defense system was instantly in place.

"Come on, Molly." The tone of voice Sis used was considerably softer than the one the middle Swann favored. "He's not even working. You support him, don't you? Doesn't that bother you?"

"Just because we've been able to rise above the traditional male-female roles, the confining sexist stereotypes that people have just blindly accepted for hundreds of years . . ."

"Forget the sociological jargon. The fact is, Mike doesn't work. He stays home and cooks. He's . . . he's more of a housewife than I am."

Molly stuck her chin in the air. "He's liberated."

"He's unemployed."

"He supports me in my career."

"He allows you to support him in his lack of career."

"Hey, hey, come on, you two," Rachel interjected, unable to stand it any longer. "So none of us has a perfect relationship, right? So what? Who does?" She indulged in a loud, slow sigh. "What does it really matter that the cards you get dealt in life don't add up to exactly what you want? Did any of us ever really think that was the way things would turn out?"

"I did," said Molly. "I always thought you could have whatever you wanted. All you had to do was figure out what it was and then go after it."

"Haven't you ever heard that expression?" Sis teased. " 'Be careful what you wish for . . . because you just might get it'?"

"It would be nice to find out just how true that saying really is," Rachel grumbled. "I'm with Molly. You know, I can remember one time when I was a teenager, hanging around with you guys. It was a Saturday, and it was raining. . . . The three of us were having a really good time, playing the piano and laughing our heads off."

"Must have been 'Heart and Soul,' " said Molly. "That was the only thing I could ever play."

"Maybe. Anyway, there I was, feeling really good, and I just kind of stepped out of the moment for a few seconds and thought, Wow. Life can really feel good. It can be *fun*." She shook her head. "Now when I look back on that moment, I feel like those days are gone. It's as if, somehow, I'm missing out on all the fun."

"Maybe you just need a little more heart," Sis offered.

"And a little more soul," Molly added. She broke into an old song from the sixties, "A Little Bit o' Soul."

"Spare me!" Rachel cried, laughing. "Your singing certainly hasn't improved since the old days!"

Just then the Frisbee came *whoosh*ing by, landing right in the potato chip bowl that was planted in her lap.

"Oops, sorry." Mike came jogging over, huffing and puffing as if he'd just run the New York Marathon. "Guess I'm a little rusty."

He looked at the three of them, grimacing. "Sorry if I interrupted something."

"No, Mike, you didn't interrupt a thing. We three Swanns were just reminiscing about the good old days." Sis was climbing out of the chaise longue. There was a checkerboard design imprinted on the back of her legs. "As a matter of fact, I was just about to get up. Talking about fun and getting what you want out of life reminded me that I've got something I want to show you two. Be right back."

"Maybe it's one of her marital aids," Molly whispered.

"Ta-dah!" Sis cried a few minutes later. "Well, everybody? How do I look?"

Rachel glanced over at the back door, expecting to see her sister modeling a new jump suit or perhaps a daring new bathing suit, a K mart special. Instead her eyes grew wide and her mouth dropped open as she found herself witnessing the arrival of Tammy Wynette, suburban-style.

Sis was decked out in complete cowgirl regalia—fringe, rhinestones, and all. The crimson vest and flared miniskirt she wore were trimmed with white cactuses made from sequins. Her white blouse with full sleeves had a kind of shine to it, a satiny look that one did not ordinarily associate with daywear. The stiff, deep burgundy boots were obviously plastic, their silver trim looking as if it would at some point require Crazy Glue, and the fuchsia cowboy hat was a tad too small. All in all, the effect was nothing short of unforgettable.

"Isn't she something?" Jerry cried, dropping the Frisbee and running toward her. He was speaking for them all. "Sis, you're gorgeous. I tell ya, if the kids weren't around right now . . . come on out here, babe. Let's get a better look at you."

Mike cast Molly a questioning look. She, in turn, simply shrugged.

"Sis?" Rachel asked timidly. "Uh, what's up, exactly?"

Becky, now awake, was beside herself. "Is that your Halloween costume, Aunt Sis? Oooh, I want to be a cowgirl, too!"

"Not quite, honey. Us grown-ups were talking before about having fun, getting what you want out of life. So that's what I'm doing. I decided it's time to get the lead out and make one of my dreams come true."

"I told you they were into kinky stuff," Molly whispered, leaning across the condiments.

"Yup," Jerry agreed, reaching for his wife and sitting her down on his lap. "Sis here's always had a secret fantasy of becoming a country-western singer. And, well, I've been encouraging her to go for it."

Sis nodded. "This outfit was his birthday present to me." Turning to Molly, she said, "See? There is more to my life than shopping at Pathmark."

"It's . . . it's really something." Rachel swallowed hard.

"There's only one thing. I don't want you to take this the wrong way, but, uh, do you think there's really much call for country-western singers on Long Island? I mean, the metropolitan New York area isn't exactly filled with cow-pokes."

"Well, of course it's not. And you're right; country music would be kind of out of place around here. At least, the usual kind." Sis was explaining with the patience of a kindergarten teacher. "But Jerry and I have been writing our own songs. You know, kind of customizing the country-western sound, adapting the lyrics so they're more in tune with the greater New York metropolitan area."

"Sounds good to me," Mike interjected agreeably.

"That's right. And as soon as she feels she's ready, the little lady here is gonna be making her singin' debut at the Beach Club Inn." Jerry had thrown a protective arm around his wife. He was holding her in a sort of permanent squeeze, meanwhile smiling down at her.

"The Beach Club Inn? What's that?" Mike asked.

In response Molly muttered, "I don't think I want to know."

"You've heard of it, haven't you? It's a club down by Tobay Beach." Sis was growing more and more animated. "Usually, it's just a bar. A hangout for locals, with a live band on weekends. But on Thursday nights they have an amateur show. Anybody can be in it. You just have to show up. Anyway, I thought it'd be a good place for me to get my feet wet."

"That explains the plastic boots," Molly said under her breath.

Despite her halfhearted attempt at being discreet, Jerry overheard her.

"Okay, okay, so this pair is plastic," he said. "Right now we can't afford leather. But I promise one day I'll be able to buy this lady here any damn thing she wants."

"Oh, come on, Jer." Sis giggled. "You know I don't care about that."

"Well, Sis, I think this is great." Rachel was almost beginning to believe it. "I mean, if this is something you've always wanted to do, then you might as well go for it."

"That's what I been telling her." Jerry planted a noisy wet kiss on Sis's cheek. "Believe me, she's got talent. There's no telling how far she could go with this gift of hers."

"Talent?" said Molly in a soft voice. "Somehow, during those piano-playing sessions of our idyllic childhood, I don't remember Sis being much more than the page turner."

"Make sure you tell us when you're going onstage," Mike insisted. "I'd never forgive you if we missed this."

"Oh, I'll tell you. And I hope you'll all come. Sure, I'll be nervous, but it's really important to me that you all be there."

"I know I wouldn't miss it," Molly said, deadpan. "Not for a million dollars."

Rachel glared at her, but Sis didn't notice. She was too busy gazing up at Jerry.

"Don't worry, baby doll," he assured her, fondling her puffy shoulder. "We'll all be there for you. I know I will. You can bet on that."

"I know," said Sis. She reached up and placed the palm of her hand against his cheek. "I know I can always count on you."

"Somebody get me an airsick bag," Molly muttered.

But Rachel was watching them with a dull ache in her heart.

Chapter Six

Maybe I've been overreacting, thought Rachel, bending her knee Rockette-style and sticking her thigh underneath the shower's spray. Ponderously she rubbed her palm over the cake of avocado soap, vaguely aware that she was washing with something that smelled like guacamole. *I mean, it's not as if Howard does these things to hurt me. His life is just . . . complicated.*

The Fourth of July weekend was by that point just a fond memory, a bit of indigestion that still lingered, and a pair of sunburned shoulders. Now that summer had settled in and Rachel had no real distractions, she had begun to miss Howard.

Or maybe it's just the sex I miss, she thought, soaping up one shoulder with languorous movements. Mediocre sex, admittedly. But frequent sex, dependable sex, *comfortable* sex, all the same.

At any rate, she decided to call him. It was just past seven o'clock, and there was a slim chance that if she hurried, she would still find him holed up in his midtown office. She was suddenly desperate to reestablish contact. To apologize, even, if that was what it would take to smooth things over. She was more than willing to blame the entire flea market fiasco on temporary insanity induced by the hot, feverish Yonkers sun.

She hurried through what she had originally intended to be a long, slow, self-indulgent shower. Then she slipped into something to get her in the mood: her shortest shorts and a clingy tank top. Finally, a quick check in Becky's room, where the little girl was already sleeping off the rigors of her first day of day camp, softly snoring as the tensions of learning how to make lanyards and singing endless choruses of "One Hundred Bottles of Beer on the Wall" drained away.

"I know what I'm doing," she muttered as she dialed. Then, in her perkiest voice: "Howard? Oh, good. I'm glad I caught you."

"Rachel." At the other end of the line Howard cleared his throat. "Listen, I'm glad you called. There's something I—"

"I know what you're thinking." Rachel lowered her voice to what she hoped was a sexier, more intimate tone. Meanwhile she draped herself across the couch, figuring it wouldn't hurt to play the part to the hilt. "You're still upset about that day at the flea market, aren't you? I don't blame you. But I've been thinking about it, and I realize now that we were both wrong. I got a little carried away, you were . . . you were . . ."

She was hoping he would fill in the blanks. Instead, he cleared his throat once again.

"You know, Rachel, this little bit of time we've had away from each other has given me a chance to think, and, uh, I . . ."

Suddenly things were starting to move in slow motion.

". . . I think it would be best if we took a bit of a break from each other."

A *break*? Rachel was thinking, panic rising in her chest. A break is what you take when you're getting eyestrain from reading too much or when you've been doing your aerobics tape more energetically than you should.

Somehow the idea of someone requesting a break from her gave new life to her mild indigestion.

"I think we both know that things between us have been getting a bit stale lately."

Stale? She wasn't about to subject herself to a mental list of the images *that* one conjured up.

And then the very last thing that Rachel would have expected happened. She experienced a great wave of relief. It was as if invisible strings that had been binding her were being snipped one by one. She was being set free. And that was cause for celebration, not sorrow.

"Maybe you're right, Howard," she said, and her words were sincere. "We *are* stale. And I do think a break would be good for us."

"You really think so?"

"Yes, I really do."

Howard sounded surprised, caught off guard by her readiness to agree with him. It was clear he had been expecting an argument—maybe a few tears, perhaps even desperate pleadings. Rachel was glad that she hadn't come through for him.

"Uh, okay, then. I guess it's settled."

"Good. I'm glad we got this cleared up," she said energetically. "Oh, and Howard? Be sure you give my love to Kim and Heather!

"Freeee again," she sang after hanging up, breaking into a dance that was a cross between an Irish jig and the bugaloo. She couldn't remember the last time she had felt this good. At last a decision had been made. Not that she and Howard were necessarily splitting for good. Who knew where this "break" from each other would lead? For now she wasn't interested in peering into any crystal balls. She was young, single, and footloose.

When the telephone rang again, mere seconds after she had heard the satisfying click that cut off communication with one Howard Becker, she immediately concluded it was he again. If Becky hadn't been asleep, she might not have answered. But since the last thing she wanted was for her daughter to reemerge, still cranky and exhausted but insisting on staying up anyway, she grabbed it before the second ring had begun.

"Hello, Rachel? It's Boyd."

"Boyd!" she cried. She sank onto the couch, modestly covering herself up with a throw pillow. "This is a surprise."

"How was your weekend?" he asked congenially. "Did Sis have her usual shindig out on the island?"

"Yes, as a matter of fact. It was fun, too. . . . Boyd, why are you calling?"

He laughed, brushing off her caution as if it were the silliest thing in the world. "Actually, I'm calling to invite you out to lunch."

"Lunch?" Okay, what's the catch? she was thinking, her guard snapping firmly into place.

But his tone remained casual. Chummy, even. "Oh, I just want to talk about Becky. Maybe the two of us can put our heads together and come up with some solutions to her growing pains."

"Growing pains? I haven't noticed Becky having any growing pains."

"How about tomorrow?"

The next day she was free. The art opening at the Met wasn't until six, and all she had planned was some reading about Mocambian culture, to help her better understand the exhibition.

"Sounds fine."

"Great. Café de Paris at noon."

As Rachel hurried through the congested streets of midtown Manhattan at five minutes to twelve the next day, a lump of fear sat in her stomach, weighing her down like the proverbial ball and chain. She had no idea why Boyd had suddenly invited her out to lunch, sounding so congenial over the telephone that she couldn't help being suspicious.

His phone call had dragged up memories she hadn't let herself think about for a long time. All of a sudden the smallest details were parading before her, details like what she had been wearing the first time they'd talked about marriage, the songs that had been popular during those early golden days, the exact way she had felt the first time they met.

Rachel Swann and Boyd Tanner had both been waiting in line at one of the movie theaters directly opposite

Bloomingdale's, she with her friend, Lynn, he with a buddy whose name she had by now forgotten. It was early on a crisp Saturday evening in late October, and since they were hardly the only people in New York who had come up with the idea of celebrating the invigorating night by tucking themselves away in a dark, stuffy movie theater, the line was endless. So was the wait. It was inevitable that she and Lynn began chatting with the two men in line in front of them.

Right from the start, sparks had flown. By the time they shuffled inside the theater, the foursome had decided to sit together. Boyd and Rachel were at the center. When the movie was over, they each said good-bye to their friends, then went off together to pour out their life stories over half-pound burgers and beer at Jackson Hole.

That was just the beginning. Next followed an intense period of dashing around the city, eating at the trendiest restaurants, and attempting to look cool enough to be let into the club of the month. But it wasn't long before that was replaced with a preference for staying in for the evening. They played house, preparing elaborate dinners in the tiny kitchen in her West Village apartment, experimenting with unusual vegetables and spices chosen painstakingly at Balducci's. They rented videos so they could watch movies while lying together in bed, playing footsie. Saturday nights, they read the Sunday *Times*.

Even the sex was terrific. That, Rachel finally admitted to Boyd, had been a great surprise.

"What do you mean?" Boyd challenged her. They were celebrating their one-month anniversary, lying in her bed, accompanied by a half-empty bottle of Beaujolais and a totally empty bakery box from the Patisserie Lanciani. He pulled the sheet around him protectively, making it clear that he was only pretending to be kidding. "Why did you assume that I'd be a lousy lover?"

"I didn't say *lousy*," she defended herself. "I just said I didn't think you'd be so—you know, free. You being a Wall Street-type and all."

"Oh, I get it." The tension in his face faded, and he laughed. "You mean the pinstripe suit and the wing-tip shoes scared you."

"Let's just say I expected you to be more of a challenge." With one hand she took a cursory inventory of his body. "Hmmm. But I can see now that basically you're easy."

"Piece of cake," he murmured, reaching for her.

Finally the two of them decided it was time to make a commitment. It was the mid-1980s, and elaborate, old-fashioned weddings were more in vogue than ever. Rachel was firm about keeping things simple, even in the face of strong resistance from his parents, a matched set of Boston Brahmins who thought that any gathering with fewer than two hundred fifty guests wasn't even worth getting dressed up for.

Her parents, meanwhile, were willing to accept whatever vision she came up with for her own wedding. Molly, then an intense graduate student at Columbia University, told her that getting married in this day and age was a form of social pollution. However, she did come across with a soup tureen from Tiffany's so gaudy that it looked like a Marie Antoinette hand-me-down. Sis, already married herself, was thrilled that her big sister was joining the club. Eagerly she offered up her daughter and son to play the role of flower girl and ring bearer.

In the end, the wedding was simple enough for Rachel's taste, traditional enough for Boyd's parents, and romantic enough to keep everybody else happy. They were married by a judge at the Dairy, a huge, funky building in the middle of Central Park. After the ceremony, their hundred or so guests stayed on for champagne and wonderful hors d'oeuvres that looked more like tiny sculptures than food.

Rachel waited for the reception to announce publicly that she was keeping her own name. Molly let out a triumphant whoop. Boyd's mother muttered that it was only because Rachel was a professional woman, a writer whose reputation was so closely linked with her name, that she was flying in the face of tradition. Mrs. Robert J. Tanner proceeded to drown her shock in champagne.

On the surface, Rachel and Boyd looked like thousands of other Manhattan couples tying the knot in the prosperous eighties. They bought a two-bedroom co-op, continued forging ahead on their same career paths, then, predictably, had a baby. But it was while Rachel was pregnant with Becky that she first tuned in to the signs that the walls of her marriage were crumbling.

Afterward she'd felt foolish for not having been able—or willing—to see it all much earlier. She had chalked up their constant arguing to being "a phase," blaming pressure at work for their inability to agree even over something as simple as what movie to see. When Boyd started staying late at the office more and more, Rachel was eager to believe his explanations and excuses. Finally, when he cut himself off from her entirely, barely speaking and making a point of sleeping way over on the other side of the bed, she blamed her pregnancy.

The less available to her he became, the more available she tried to be to him. Holding together the pieces of her shattering marriage became her number-one priority. After Becky was born, she was self-conscious about showering too much attention on the baby whenever her husband was around. With great reluctance she turned down a plum assignment that would have taken her out of town for two nights. She was on edge constantly.

"Give it time," her more experienced friends told her. "It's a big adjustment, having a new baby in the family. Boyd's just jealous, but he'll come around."

She knew for certain she would never be able to forgive him for the way he had ended their marriage. It was just three months after they'd celebrated their four-year wedding anniversary with a tense dinner at an elegant restaurant, saying no more than ten words to each other through the entire meal. That same tense mood was hovering on the Saturday night before Halloween, when they were invited to a costume party at the home of some friends, Jeff and Peggy Morrow, who lived in New Jersey.

The Morrows took their holidays seriously, and to show what good sports they were, both Rachel and Boyd were dressed to the hilt. Rachel was Little Bo Peep, complete with a wooden staff, a pair of lacy pantalets peeking out from underneath her flouncy skirt, and a headful of blond ringlets, courtesy of a very uncomfortable wig. Boyd was Dracula. His black satin cape was lined in blood-red, a perfect match for the drops oozing out of the corners of his black-lipped mouth.

"This should be really fun." Rachel's voice was hopeful as they veered off the New Jersey Turnpike in their rented car.

Boyd, gripping the wheel, grimaced. "I'm sorry, but getting dressed up like a dead person is not my idea of a good time."

"You look great, though," she offered feebly.

At the party she kept getting the feeling that her own husband was avoiding her. She saw him engaged in animated conversation with Cleopatra, a very shapely mummy, and two glamorous witches who looked as if they had quite a flair for casting spells. But every time she sidled up to him with some tidbit of small talk on the tip of her tongue, he found some excuse to move away.

Finally, on the way home, she confronted him, unable to tolerate the tension any longer. Sitting in the front seat, staring at the white ruffle bordering her full pink skirt, she murmured, "What is it, Boyd? We never talk about it, but it's always there."

He let out a long, tired sigh. "It's over, Rachel."

She glanced at him. In the pale light of other people's headlights, the ghoulish white makeup on his face almost glowed.

"What's over?"

He looked at her. "You know it as well as I do. I just don't see any point in pretending anymore."

"Is there someone else?" she asked in a thin voice.

He shrugged. "No one that's been particularly important."

After that, it was just the two of them—Rachel and Becky, wandering around in an apartment that had once seemed too small but suddenly seemed much too big.

"You're my family now," Rachel had whispered to her baby daughter the day Boyd came back to the apartment to pack up his things. She held her tightly as she sat in the most remote corner of the living room, trying not to listen to the sounds of closet doors and dresser drawers being slammed shut.

Now, almost four years later, Rachel didn't know which hurt more, remembering the good times or the bad. As she pushed against the heavy glass and wood door of the Café de Paris, she told herself this was hardly the time to decide.

"It's funny," Boyd mused, fingering his wineglass. "You and I used to live together. Now if we say three sentences to each other at a time, that's a lot. Do you ever step back and think about how strange that is?"

Rachel, her hands wrapped tightly around a glass of Perrier, was not in the mood for philosophizing. "Somehow I don't think wanting to share that observation with me was why you invited me to lunch," she said dryly.

He chuckled, a rather humorless laugh. "No, it's not. Actually, there's something very specific I want to talk to you about."

"Another lecture on footwear?"

"No." Boyd took a deep breath. "Look, there's no point in trying to sugar-coat this. You and I are both adults. Rachel, I'm getting married."

"It's Ariana, isn't it," Rachel said dully, making a pronouncement rather than asking a question.

Boyd looked pleased. "Why, yes! You mean Becky told you about her?"

"She said she has hair like Barbie."

"It's true that Ariana is a natural blond, yes."

Right. And I'm the empress Josephine, Rachel was thinking.

But pettiness about hair color was the least of her concerns. Even though being divorced from Boyd had been a fact of life for some time, even though she had more or less seen this coming, she still felt as if the rug had been pulled out from under her. All her insecurities, fears, anger, and jealousies were bubbling to the surface. But her determination not to let him have the satisfaction of seeing any of it forced her to remain on an even keel.

"Congratulations," she managed to say.

"There's more." This time he was having trouble looking her in the eye. Rachel braced herself. "Ariana has always wanted . . . I'm going to talk to my lawyers about getting our child custody ruling changed."

"What? Boyd, are you crazy? How . . . why . . . ?"

He was holding up his hands, looking as calm and as in control as if he were running an annual stockholders' meeting. His mouth was stretched to form just the hint of a smirk. "The way I see it, you'd be better off without the financial burden you're carrying around."

"Becky and I have been managing just fine. Of course, if your child support payments were on time . . ."

"I don't think it's me that's the problem here. It's you. Or, to be more accurate, that frivolous career of yours."

"Frivolous? What's frivolous about being a journalist?"

"Oh, come on, Rachel. Get off it, will you? Labeling the crap you write 'journalism' is like . . . like saying any jerk who sings in the shower is an opera star."

"I do not write crap! Besides, no matter what you may think of my writing, it provides me with a perfectly respectable income."

Boyd's smirk was by now in full bloom. "Rachel, exactly how much 'income' did this career of yours generate last month?"

"I don't think that's any of your business."

"Oh, it's very much my business. At least, my lawyers would say it is. Then there's the IRS, of course. . . ."

"So it wasn't my best month. I wrote three or four articles, and I made a few thousand dollars."

"A few thousand dollars?"

Rachel was finding the restaurant very warm. She tugged at the neckline of her dress, suddenly feeling strangled by it. "Just under two thousand."

"Barely enough to pay the rent and the electric bill, eh?"

"Boyd, if you hadn't been so . . . so sleazy about hiding your assets during the divorce proceedings . . ."

"Besides," he went on, annoyingly calm, "it's not as if you've ever made a real name for yourself, is it? I think it's high time you abandoned your fantasies about becoming a Nicholas Pileggi or a Jimmy Breslin—or whoever the female version might be," he added with a condescending smile.

"I have a very good name . . . with a certain audience."

Dismissively he waved his hand in the air. "The question at this point is, where do we go from here?"

"And where *do* we go from here? In your estimation, that is."

Boyd leaned a little closer, folding his hands deliberately in front of him. "I want Becky to come live with me and Ariana after we're married."

"Never!" Rachel yelled.

"A little girl needs a stable home, one with a mother and a father. She needs financial security, too. Any judge in the nation is bound to see—"

"Never!" This time Rachel's voice was a croaking sound. She stood up from the table, her eyes blazing. "I'll—I'll move to Mexico before I let you take Becky away from me!"

Boyd chuckled. "Thank you for that, Rachel. Your threatening to kidnap my daughter and take her out of the country will only make me look better in court."

Rachel turned and fled, not even aware that every eye in the restaurant was turned on her. She raced outside, wanting to get some air. She could hardly breathe; her heart was pounding too fast, too wildly. She ran and ran, bumping into scowling pedestrians on Second Avenue. Finally she was stopped by a red neon sign warning DON'T WALK.

She grabbed onto a pole, then leaned against it as if the cold metal structure were the only thing holding her up.

"Oh, God!" she sobbed, burying her face in her hands. "Somebody help me, please!"

Any excitement Rachel had ever felt about covering the Metropolitan Museum of Art's opening was completely gone as she trudged up the endless pyramid of steps that led to the front entrance of the museum. Her meeting with Boyd had left her unable to work for the rest of the afternoon. Instead of poring over the mildewed tomes on Mocambian culture extricated from the basement of the New York Public Library, she had paced around her apartment, unable to concentrate. Her lawyer never did find the time to call back, and both her sisters were apparently just as busy.

When Becky arrived home from day camp, climbing off the bus in a state of ecstasy over the six new songs she had learned, Rachel had grabbed her and hugged her for so long that the little girl began to squirm.

"Mommeeee," she had protested, "the other kids are looking!"

From what Rachel could see, the urchins still on the bus were too busy hurling damp towels at each other to notice a poignant curbside moment between mother and child. But she released her, instead settling for a small, sticky hand clutched tightly in her own.

"Becky, you know that I love you very, very much, don't you?" she said as the two of them headed back into their apartment building.

"I know," Becky said impatiently. "Hey, did you know Tommy Barrett can turn his eyelid inside out? It's so disgusting."

"And you know that I always try to do whatever is best for you, right? Do you know that, Becky?"

"Can you turn your eyelid inside out, Mommy?"

Rachel just grasped her hand more tightly, vowing to spend every moment of what was left of the afternoon with her daughter, not letting go until the baby-sitter was at the door.

Now she was having trouble caring about something as far away and seemingly insignificant as a distant culture that had all of a sudden been thrust into the public eye. Yet she could already see that she was probably the only person in the crowd streaming toward the museum who felt that way. Tonight even the stately building itself, usually so austere and imposing, looked ready to party.

Still, she tried to arrange her features into a reasonably pleasant expression as she followed the carefully coiffed and perfumed women and the well-tailored men with correct-width lapels to the section of the museum in which the Mocambian exhibition was on display. She was almost there when she heard a familiar voice calling after her.

"Rachel! Rachel, over he-uh!"

Automatically she turned. There was Gayle Shipley Lefkowitz, beaming and waving from across the room.

Aside from the white rosebud pinned on her chest, no one would ever have guessed that Gayle was anything but a wealthy patron of the arts here tonight for her share of champagne and culture. She was sleek in an understated sheath, nubby raw silk in a pale lemon yellow, a dress so sophisticated that it could have come straight out of Audrey Hepburn's closet. Her hair was swept up, although whether that look was designed to show off her mile-long neck or her diamond earrings the size of ice cubes, it was difficult to tell.

Exchanging polite banter, especially with someone as irritatingly cheerful as Gayle, was the last thing Rachel was in the mood for. But it was too late to hide, to blend in with the mass of bodies moving slowly toward the exhibition. Rachel forced a smile.

"And where's that Howard of yours tonight?" was the first thing out of Gayle's mouth.

"Only one ticket." Rachel shrugged, doing her best to look chagrined.

"Oh, Rachel, you should have told me. Why, I could have gotten you as many tickets as you needed!"

"It's just as well. After all, I am working tonight."

"That's right. We both are." Gayle glanced around, wearing a satisfied smile. "Although everything seems to be running smoothly, all by its little ol' self." She wrinkled her nose. "I bet I can even sneak away for a few minutes. Have you seen the exhibit yet?"

"Uh, no, but I'm sure I can—"

"Oh, come on. I'll walk y'all over. It's just fascinatin', really. Here, grab yourself some champagne and come with me."

Having little choice, Rachel did as she was told. As she followed her self-appointed tour guide, she took tiny sips from the tulip glass she had taken off a tray. At first she did it to reduce the risk of spilling. But on meeting up with an empty stomach, the champagne quickly began melting away her tensions. Her sips became gulps as she and Gayle pushed through the throngs that looked like extras in a film about prerevolutionary French aristocracy.

And then they turned a corner. Rachel gasped, caught completely off guard by what clever Dr. Ashcrofton and her sidekicks had put together. Poised at the entrance of the exhibition was a wooden statue, standing over twelve feet high, a demonic figure with glowing yellow eyes and an open mouth that was twisted into a horrific frown. Its body and face were distorted, mocking the human image in an unsettling way. In each hand it held a long spear, their tips pointed downward.

"Now, this piece really gives me the creeps." Gayle made a face back at the evil-looking icon glowering down at her. "I'd much rather look at the weavings. Come see them, Rachel. They're very colorful—and much more pleasant than this bozo."

"Just a second." Rachel's voice was barely audible.

She was mesmerized by the statue, captivated by its ugliness. Even though it was crudely made—all rough edges and incorrect proportions, a primitive culture's clumsy attempt at illustrating its worst nightmare—it positively emanated evil. Its stance was menacing, the expression on its face designed to terrorize. And the eyes, made of a glittering yellow stone that caught the light in a most peculiar way, seemed to be looking right at her—and only at her.

Rachel wasn't aware of how long she stood there. In retrospect, she couldn't remember what she was thinking as she stood eye to eye with the demonic icon. She did know that when Gayle touched her shoulder gently, she felt as if she were being jerked out of a trance.

"Rachel, I'm sorry about just abandon' y'all, but I'm afraid I'm going to have to run back," Gayle was explaining. "One of my people just gave me the high sign."

"Wait, Gayle." Rachel grabbed her arm. "Before you go, there's something I want to tell you."

"Rachel, I'm afraid I really should—"

"You know the man I told you about? Howard?"

"Sure. The wonderful guy you're so crazy about."

"That's what I wanted to tell you. He's not that wonderful, and I'm not even close to crazy about him. In fact, right now we're, uh . . ."

Rachel took a deep breath. This phrase still wasn't easy for her to say. "We're taking a break from each other."

"Mah goodness, Rachel." Gayle looked baffled. "Uh, thank you for being so honest."

"And another thing. My career is . . . well, I wasn't exactly telling the truth about that, either."

"Listen, Rachel. I really have to get back. Maybe we could have lunch sometime."

What on earth came over me just now? Rachel wondered, suddenly embarrassed as she waved meekly at Gayle, who was moving quickly across the room. She glanced back at the icon. The expression on his face seemed to have changed. Instead of looking scary, he now appeared to be laughing at her.

Wow. Better lay off the champagne, Rachel thought. She

made a point of depositing her glass on top of the next display case.

Work, she reminded herself. You're supposed to be working. Purposefully Rachel took out her small spiral notebook and began walking around the exhibition, jotting down clever phrases as they came to mind. She found it a relief to have something other than her own private agonies to think about.

"Hand-crafted weavings reminiscent of the Guatemalan place mats from Pottery Barn," she scribbled. "Graceful pottery in earth tones. Santa Fe inspired?"

As she continued through the exhibit, she became more and more absorbed by it. Still, she sighed in disappointment. Just as she'd feared, there wasn't much of substance here. Pretty, yes, at least some of it. Interesting, certainly. Still, as she wandered from room to room, taking notes, one single word was positioned firmly in the center of her brain: fluff. She kept wondering what Boyd would have thought of all this.

And then she wandered into the last room of the exhibition—the grand finale, as it were. This was the one that was meant to shock, to stimulate discussion, to make this exhibit one that would maintain public interest throughout its three-month stay in town.

THE RELIGION OF MOCAMBU, the sign over the doorway read.

"Okay, Swann," Rachel muttered, finally starting to get excited. She turned to a blank page in her notebook as she entered the room. "Let's sell some shopping bags."

Unlike the others, this room was dimly lit. Piped-in music filled the space with the spooky sounds of distant, unrelenting drums. Occasionally the sound of human voices broke in, an eerie monotonic chant in some undecipherable language.

Rachel felt uneasy as she shuffled through the maze of glass cases and wall displays. She turned away in revulsion from the hollow, unseeing eyes in the line of grotesque masks—life masks mixed in with death masks, the accompanying sign explained, the mixing of opposites in the true Mocambian tradition.

She was similarly repulsed by the display of pungent herbs and powders, the odd-smelling ingredients that were used in potions specially prepared for rituals that dated back as far as the Mocambians themselves. She tried to fight it, telling herself that what really bothered her was the Disneyland-style way in which the religion of these people was presented.

"It just smells funny in here, that's all," she muttered. She copied down the names of some of the herbs. Ground Lizard Claw, Dried Satan's Breath . . . these she would no doubt be able to use in her article. "And those relentless drums are enough to give anybody a headache."

In the center of the room was a small, squat building made of wood and mud. Despite its iffy construction, it looked fairly substantial.

"Obviously there are no building codes in Mocambu," she quipped to herself, aware that the champagne had made her giddy. Even so, the journalist in her recognized that describing this odd, primitive structure could provide a good beginning for her article.

"It looks like the devil's dollhouse," she muttered.

She peered at the sign off to one side, next to the maroon velvet ropes draped across the front of the platform on which it was standing, meant to prevent the curious from going inside.

"Hmmm. Interesting. A temple of black magic. A chapel for worshipping the devil. Well, at least the Mocambians are equal-opportunity worshippers."

Studying the temple, she noticed that there were some odd symbols carved into the wooden doorjamb, across the top.

"Wonder what that means?" she mused. "Abandon hope, all ye who enter?" She glanced back at the sign. "Ah, I see. 'Be careful what you wish for because you just might get it.' "

Whether it was the fact that she was talking to herself or

simply the natural ebb and flow of museumgoers, Rachel suddenly found herself more or less alone. Even the guard had moved away, politely explaining to an intoxicated invitee that he wasn't allowed to accept her kind offer of a glass of champagne.

This is my big chance, Rachel thought. This is my chance to go where no other journalist has dared to tread.

After another few quick glances around, she stepped over the velvet rope, paused to see if an alarm would sound, and then sneaked inside.

As she sat down on one of the crudely made wooden benches on the straw-covered wooden floor, Rachel the Fearless Journalist was worrying about getting a splinter in her butt. But she quickly forgot all about the risks: She was too busy taking in her bizarre surroundings.

The focus of the tiny room was what appeared to be a sort of altar, placed at the end of the two benches. It was a wooden table, over which were draped dark-colored weavings. On it were a few of the herbs she had seen on display, powders and gnarled twigs and dried leaves. There was also a haphazard collection of jars and boxes and beads.

Off to one side was a small skull, one that looked human but could well have belonged to some simian species. A line of thirteen waxy white candles was unlit, but past usage had burned them down almost completely. Along the edge of the altar were the same symbols that had been outside, above the doorway.

She kept her eyes fixed on them as, aloud, she said, "Be careful what you wish for . . ."

Then, in a voice that was almost a whisper: "I want to make some wishes. I wish that all of a sudden my career would take off like a rocket to the moon. If I could only get one really fantastic assignment to get me started, just one . . . That would show Boyd. And if I were a successful journalist, no lawyer in the world could find a way of giving that bastard even the slightest bit more control over Becky.

"And . . . and I wish I could meet a man who's gorgeous, smart, successful . . . and madly in love with me."

She laughed. "What I wouldn't give for those two things. And while I'm at it, I wish Molly would find herself a man who's as strong as she is, not somebody like Mike who rides on her coattails. And I wish she would start taking better care of herself. Losing weight, getting in touch with her body . . . For Sis, I wish for money. Lots and lots of money. More money that she would ever know what to do with.

"Oh, if only you could really make deals, if only you could really get what you want in life . . . I'd give anything. *Anything*."

All of a sudden Rachel became aware of a distinctive smell inside the temple. It was probably some herb, but oddly enough she found it both horrible and intoxicating at the same time. She also felt cold, as if some quirk in the building's construction caused drafts to cut through it. She shivered, part of her recognizing how nasty it was in there, part of her wanting to stay.

And then the cool draft in the hut became an excruciating iciness, almost too much for her to bear. The smell of the herbs became sickening, a burning sensation that filled her nose and throat, made her eyes tear. A roaring sound rose up inside her ears, a deafening noise that seemed to come rumbling from deep beneath the earth.

Rachel clasped her hands over her ears and clamped her eyes closed. She curled up, almost in the fetal position, recoiling from some sensation that she could not name.

And then: "What are you doin' in here?"

She opened her eyes, blinking and shaking her head. She felt strange. Yet the terrible noise she thought she had heard was gone. The cold was gone, too, as was the smell. All she saw was the guard, standing in the doorway of the temple, scowling.

"You're not supposed to be in here," he snapped. "I'm not sure this thing is even safe." He reached his hand inside, begrudgingly offering to help her out.

Rachel felt as if she had just lived through an earthquake. Yet as she let the guard lead her out of the temple, then glanced around nervously, she saw that all around her everything was proceeding exactly as always.

"I—I think maybe I passed out or something," Rachel mumbled. "I felt so dizzy."

"The air in there probably isn't so good," the guard said sullenly. "Didn't you see the ropes? Ya think we put those up for our health?"

"I, uh, I'm sorry, I . . . listen, I'm feeling kind of queasy. Is there a bench around here? I really need to sit down."

It took a few minutes for Rachel to regain her composure. She sat on a bench in the room full of weavings, their lively colors seeming to mock her. She was actually glad when she saw Gayle marching toward her on a pair of stiletto heels, frowning with concern. She was carrying a glass of champagne and a plateful of oddly shaped goodies.

"Rachel, I heard the guards talkin' about somebody faintin'. I had no idea it was you. Are you okay? Here, drink some of this. You need liquids."

Doubting that French champagne was what the American Medical Association had in mind, Rachel dutifully gulped it down.

"And eat some of these. Y'all shouldn't be drinkin' on an empty stomach. Honey, are you okay? You look terrible—like you just saw a ghost." Gayle wagged an accusing finger at her. "I know what happened. You didn't eat anything before you came here tonight, did you?"

Rachel hung her head in shame.

"You should always have at least a little yogurt before you come to something like this. It coats the stomach. Now, have yourself a shrimp roll with curried mustard. Would you like me to walk you out and help you find a cab?"

When Rachel got home, she still wasn't feeling quite right. Her head ached and her eyes felt like marshmallows as she paid the baby-sitter and forced herself to respond to the girl's in-depth report on every word Becky had said that evening before falling asleep. The relentless pounding of the Mocambian drums, that awful tape Dr. Ashcrofton had insisted upon having pumped into the exhibition's religion room, continued to echo through her head.

"Stop, please stop!" she moaned once she was alone in the living room. She kicked off her shoes and fell across the couch, pledging to get up in a few minutes to seek out the Advil. But as soon as her head hit the cushions, she was sucked into a thick, all-consuming sleep.

Chapter
Seven

"Mommy, are you in there?"

Through the horrifying nightmare, one in which grotesque faces leered, drums pounded, and her feet seemed to be encased in concrete, Rachel heard a familiar high-pitched voice that simply did not belong.

"Mom-meee, wake up. I'm hungry."

Abruptly, the murky dreams filling Rachel's head began to swirl away like dirty bathwater being sucked down the drain. In their place was the unpleasant sensation of small fingers prodding persistently at her eyelids. Squinting, she saw Becky leaning over her, wearing an impatient scowl.

"What time is it?" Rachel's mouth was coated in cobwebs.

"Three oh eight. That's what it says on the digital clock."

"Three oh eight? In the afternoon?" Still struggling to shed her cloud of confusion, she glanced at her watch.

"That's eight oh three, Becky."

Things were finally clicking into place. The art opening the night before, the champagne, the bizarre way in which she had suddenly passed out in that god-awful temple of doom, her inability to get any farther than the living room couch . . .

And the headache. That was still there, she discovered as she struggled to sit up. Rachel contemplated asking Becky to hunt down the Advil, then immediately rejected the idea of forcing her five-year-old to play drug runner.

"The bus comes at eight-thirty, Mommy. I have to get ready for camp. Did you buy me more Kix?"

Kix. Camp. Buses. It all seemed so overwhelming. "Let Mommy get a glass of water first."

Rachel stumbled to the bathroom, where she gulped down three Advil tablets with a huge glass of water.

"I'll never drink champagne again," she told the bathroom mirror. "Not unless I've just won the Pulitzer."

"Today is Orange Day," Becky informed her gleefully, trotting along behind Rachel as she headed toward her daughter's room. "We have to wear orange. Mommy, do I *have* any orange clothes?"

By the time Rachel put together an outfit that in dim light could pass as orange, discovered that there was still enough cereal in the old Kix box to fill the small plastic Fern Gully bowl, enforced some halfhearted toothbrushing and hair-combing, and escorted her eternally chirpy sidekick to the bus, the Advil had kicked in. Two cups of coffee and three pieces of dry toast completed the cure. When the telephone rang at one minute past nine, she was feeling close enough to human to fool just about anyone.

"Hello?"

"Rachel, honey, are you all right?"

Gayle Shipley Lefkowitz. Coping with all that southern charm at this hour of the morning would be no easy feat.

"I think so. But one thing's for sure. From now on, Gayle, I'm going to follow your advice. Yogurt, right?"

"Absolutely. Even a couple of spoonfuls of the stuff will do the trick." Earnestly Gayle added, "Don't leave home without it."

"Words to live by."

"Actually, there's another reason I called."

Gayle's voice had changed from concerned friendliness to the casual tone that always betrayed an underlying hint of nervousness. Rachel braced herself.

"I don't usually do this, Rachel. . . . In fact, I *never* do this. . . ."

Where exactly was this leading? Rachel wondered. Was Gayle about to invite her to embark with her upon a life of crime? A chocolate binge, perhaps? Something kinky, something madcap, something fattening, something fun?

"Rachel, how do you feel about blind dates?"

None of the above.

"In my book, they're about two notches below internal examinations." Rachel hesitated before adding, "Why do you ask?"

"Well, it was the strangest thing. Just this morning I was plannin' a wedding brunch for five hundred—at least, that's what I was supposed to be doin'. Instead, I found myself thinkin' about what you said about Howard last night."

"Howard? What did I say about Howard?"

"That the two of you had decided—very congenially, of course—to take a little break from each other. And I started thinking, 'Poor Rachel, stuck in this mean, cold-hearted town without a special man on her arm. . . .' "

Spare me, thought Rachel.

"Anyway, almost like I was having a psychic experience or somethin', the telephone suddenly rang. It was a client of mine, the wife of a very high roller. He's somebody whose business demands that he entertain quite a bit. In fact, she had called to schedule a little end-of-summer thing, an itty-bitty garden party for a hundred people out at their summer place in the Hamptons. But we got to talkin', and the next thing I knew she mentioned that she had this wonderful guy she'd been tryin' to set up for ages."

"Ah, yes," Rachel interjected dryly. "The famous paradox of blind dates. If he's so wonderful, why does he need to have his friends set him up?"

"Rachel, let's try to be fair here. The man sounds terrific." Gayle had lapsed into her no-nonsense tone, one Rachel remembered from their days of working together. "The point is, as she was talkin', your name just sprang to mind. It was like some kind of karma, you know? I mean, think about it, Rachel. The way you and I ran into each other on the train last week, totally out of the blue and after such a long time, and then meetin' up at the museum . . . Look at how the two of us have started following parallel paths."

One evening of sharing champagne, shrimp rolls, and death masks did not a pair of parallel paths make.

Rachel glanced down at the slinky black dress she was still wearing. Somehow, after doubling as a nightgown, it had lost a lot of its slink. She felt grimy, raw, in need of a long, hot shower. She did not feel the slightest bit like a femme fatale.

"Thank you for thinking of me, Gayle," she said politely. "But at this point in my life, I'm just not interested in putting myself through the horrors of a blind date."

"I understand, Rachel. Really I do. Believe me, it's not as if I spent the mornin' ransackin' my address book, lookin' for somebody to match you up with. But the way this woman just called me, makin' this man sound too good to be true ... I couldn't help myself. The next thing I knew, it all just kind of ... happened."

Rachel froze. "*What* just kind of happened?"

After a long silence Gayle said, "I gave her your name and number and told her to have the man call you."

"You *what*?"

"Rachel, it's not that big a deal. Look, the whole thing was just a natural progression."

"A natural progression."

"Sure. Last night you made a point of telling me that you had suddenly found yourself on your own, am I correct?"

"Yes, but I wasn't exactly handing out résumés."

"There's no need to get huffy. If you don't want to go, don't go. When this guy calls—*if* he calls—just say no."

"Oh, I'm fully aware that I can do that." Rachel paused. "Uh, what's he like, anyway?"

Gayle giggled. "From what I understand, he's funny, very bright, and quite tall."

"Terrific. So far we have a nerdy basketball player who knows a lot of knock-knock jokes."

"Now, Rachel. You're not being very open-minded about this. You could at least give him a chance. He came with a very high recommendation."

Rachel could feel resignation setting in. "Okay, Gayle. So what's his name, this dreamboat who fell from the sky?"

"Lance Firestone."

"Lance, huh? I've never dated a Lance. And you can honestly tell me that you trust this woman's assessment of him?"

"My goodness, Rachel. Why on earth would she lie?"

Rachel snorted. It was clear that Gayle did not know much about blind-dating.

But maybe it's not such a bad thing, Rachel thought a few minutes later, sitting in front of her word processor. She had intended to start typing up the notes she had made the night before. Instead, she was letting her mind try on the different possibilities that all of a sudden seemed to lie ahead. I mean, how terrible could this Lance be?

What were the words Gayle used? Funny? Bright? I could get used to that, she decided. Especially since it's been quite some time since I've been wined and dined by a new man.

Besides, she thought with a devilish little smile, flicking on her computer, who knows what we'll end up having for dessert?

It was a good thing Rachel's initial reservations about partaking of the blind-dating scene had faded so quickly. Rather than receiving an invitation to go out with Lance Firestone, what she got was more of a summons.

"Lance Firestone will be meeting you at eight o'clock on Friday night." The nonnegotiable message she found on her answering machine later that same day had been left by a woman, presumably an assistant or a secretary. The restaurant the faceless voice named was one of Manhattan's most elegant, a place that made even calf's brains and cow's stomachs sound palatable by translating them into French.

Rachel was glowing with anticipation as she stepped out of the taxi and into the restaurant the following evening. And knowing that she looked terrific was part of it. After reluctantly turning Becky over to Boyd a few hours earlier, she had focused all her attention on creating a knock-'em-dead look. She had revived her skimpy black dress, considerably spiffier after a visit to the dry cleaner. She swept up her hair and indulged in unusually intense eye makeup. Thanks to her sheer smoky stockings, there were little black diamonds running up her shins.

Standing in the foyer, Rachel took in the soft lighting, the rich colors, the arrogant waiters. Within these walls, well-dressed people made clever conversation in low voices, laughing appreciatively at all the right moments. Huge bouquets of fresh flowers dotted every corner of the room, and the deep red carpets were thick enough to muffle every sound. The candles on each table completed the transformation into otherworldliness.

There's something to be said for an evening of being treated like a princess rather than a scullery maid, Rachel observed with a small, satisfied smile.

"This way, *madame*." The headwaiter beckoned. His nose was so high in the air that Rachel involuntarily glanced up at the ceiling. Head held high, shoulders back, stomach sucked in, she paraded through the restaurant, ready for anything.

And then she caught her first glimpse of her mystery man. Her initial impression of him was that he was tall, dark, and handsome. Tall, certainly; Lance Firestone was well over six feet tall. More like six four, in fact. Solidly built, too, so that his mere presence made a statement. In the handsome department, he offered a square jaw, decent cheekbones, and an unoffensive nose. As for the dark part, his eyes were easily the darkest she had ever seen. They were so black, in fact, so very intense, that they practically glowed.

He was dressed in what was obviously an expensive suit. It looked custom-made by someone who knew his way around a needle and thread. Italian shoes, silk tie, Pima cotton shirt: everything he wore was of the finest possible quality.

That was the good news. The bad news was that the reason Rachel was able to get such a good look at him was that he was standing up, gesticulating wildly as he argued with the waiter.

"Whaddya mean, this is one of your best tables?" Lance was demanding in a voice so loud that at least a third of the restaurant's patrons were able to tune in. "I'm practically sitting in the kitchen over here."

"Monsieur," said the waiter, "when you requested a quiet table, we made a point of choosing this one because it is our most private."

"Yeah, right. What, I'm not a good enough tipper?"

Rachel, meanwhile, was attempting to sink through the floor, or at least to will herself into an invisible state. She obviously wasn't managing to do either. Already Lance had noticed her, his face lighting up as he realized that the red-faced woman standing beside the headwaiter, watching this scene, was his date.

He held up both hands in surrender. "Awright, awright. Forget about it. *This* time, anyway."

"Very good, *monsieur*." The waiter stalked off.

"These guys, I'm telling you," he said to Rachel by way of greeting. "They'll get you coming and going."

Rachel stretched her shiny red lips into a smile. "You must be Lance."

"You got it. And you're Rachel, right? Come on, come on, sit down. Let's see if we can get these clowns to bring us some wine." He muttered to himself as he folded up his endless legs so he could fit on the narrow red leather banquette, then added, "I wonder who you have to screw around here to get a wine list."

Never again, Rachel was thinking. You would think a woman my age would have learned that blind dates are about as much of a sure thing as the slot machines at the Las Vegas airport. You would think that.

Having never been one to make a scene, she gingerly took a seat opposite her date for the evening.

"Hey, can I get a wine list, please?" he was yelling, snapping his fingers.

Surprisingly—or perhaps not—a waiter miraculously appeared with one in hand.

"See that? All you gotta do in a place like this is make yourself heard. The first thing you have to do is make these guys understand that they're not dealing with some— Whoa, will you check out these prices? Three hundred bucks for a lousy bottle of Beaujolais!"

Rachel cleared her throat. "Uh, perhaps you'd feel more comfortable if we went someplace else for dinner." Preferably in two separate countries.

"No, no, this is fine. The food here is supposed to be worth the obnoxious way they treat you. Hey, it's not like I can't afford to pay three hundred dollars or anything."

He looked over at Rachel, focusing on her for the first time since she had arrived. He was wearing a big grin as he commented, "Besides, the number three has always been kind of lucky for me."

His eyes were still fixed on her. He looked her up and down, soaking up every detail. "So you're Rachel. Wow. I guess I got lucky this time."

Not that lucky, Rachel was thinking. But she simply smiled.

When Lance ordered the wine—the three-hundred-dollar wine—she was amazed that he did so in flawless French. She couldn't help being impressed. Even the wine steward treated him with respect, going so far as to mutter, "Excellent." Whether it was a comment on the choice of wine or the precision of his accent, Rachel couldn't say.

"Where did you learn to speak French like that?" she asked once they had been left on their own again. "Have you lived abroad?"

"Oh, I've lived all over the world," Lance replied with a wave of his hand. "As a matter of fact, I think you'd be hard pressed to name a place I haven't been."

"Were you an army brat?"

"Not quite." He hesitated before saying, "You might say I have a rather extensive background in the area of diplomacy."

"Diplomacy, hmmm? Is that what you do?"

"Right now I'm on Wall Street." The light from the candles on their table was reflected in his dark eyes. "What I actually do is rather complicated, so I usually just tell people that I dabble in futures."

When a basket of rolls arrived, Lance pounced upon them as if he hadn't eaten in days. By the time Rachel had maneuvered a sliver of butter onto her plate, he had wolfed down two and was starting on his third.

"Don't tell me you're one of those lucky people who can eat as much as he wants and still not put on weight," she remarked, determined to give this evening her best shot. "Do you work out at a gym?"

"Nah. Who has the time?" Lance shrugged. "I'm just lucky, I guess."

Rachel, nibbling on her roll, shook her head. "Boy, I'd give my eyeteeth to be able to eat whatever I want and still stay fit."

Lance let out a loud guffaw. "Your eyeteeth? Is that all?"

Rachel glanced at him quizzically, but he was too busy attacking another roll to notice. Fortunately the wine steward was back, doing his little song and dance: uncorking the bottle; pouring a few drops into *Monsieur*'s glass; waiting, expressionless, during the initial tasting.

"Fine, fine," Lance said, waving his hand with impatience. "Great stuff, Rachel. You gotta try it."

The wine was, indeed, excellent. In fact, Rachel concluded as the first taste led quickly to the second and third and fourth, it was very possibly the finest she had ever had. She drank some more. It was certainly potent. Already she could feel herself getting a buzz on. Her champagne experience of the other night set off warning signals in her head, but this stuff was very hard to resist.

She was in such a fog, in fact, that she paid little attention as Lance ordered dinner for them both. *Mousse de foie de volaille, côtes de veau belle des bois, crevettes jardinière* . . . it all sounded like the lyrics to a beautiful French aria, playing somewhere in the distance. Rachel glanced at her wineglass and was startled to discover that she had barely drunk a third of it.

It's my own fault for forgetting Gayle's advice, she scolded herself. That damn yogurt.

She made a point of going easy from then on, even though she knew full well she would probably not be seeing another three-hundred-dollar bottle of wine in this lifetime.

Afterward, she would remember little of the meal itself, or the conversation that took place while she was eating it. All she did remember was the feeling of being in a wonderful dream, one in which everything was pleasant and vague, like an Impressionist painting viewed without wearing one's eyeglasses.

She was uncharacteristically mellow as empty plates vanished and delinquent crumbs were brushed away. She sat nursing the remains of her single glass of wine, feeling very distant from her companion but at the same time strangely tied to him.

This isn't so bad, after all, she thought, feeling more comfortable than she ever would have imagined.

It was over the coffee and the *poires au gingembre* that the mood changed. Rachel was pulled out of her reverie, back into reality. Her head cleared, so much so that she noticed for the first time that there was a *mousse de foie de volaille* stain near the hem of her dress. Instead of being enveloped by her own little world, she was suddenly very aware of her dinner companion—his size, his proximity, the sound of his voice, the piercing gaze of his black eyes, seemingly pinning her against the back of her chair.

"Ah, dessert," he said casually. "Time to get down to business."

"Business?"

"You know, I wasn't exactly telling the truth before. About working on Wall Street, I mean." Lance spooned a third teaspoon of sugar into his coffee.

Rachel, a spiced pear slithering around in her mouth, simply stared at him.

"Here, why don't you have some more wine? I think it might ease the shock of what I'm about to tell you."

"Thanks, but I think I've already had enough wine."

"Just a little. I insist."

He emptied the last of the wine into her glass. The bottle had looked almost empty, yet the remaining drops filled her glass up to the top. Rachel took a sip. The wine traveled down her throat like the flames on a fire-eater's torch.

"All right," she said, blinking hard a few times to keep her eyes from watering. She looked over at him expectantly. "If you were lying about the Wall Street bit, then what do you do for a living?"

"For a living?" Lance chuckled. "Interesting choice of words. Actually, you already know all about what I do. Most people do. Of course, they know of me—and my work—under other names."

"Other names?" Rachel was not in the mood for playing guessing games. "It sounds like you're a writer."

"No, not quite. Although I do consider myself creative, my mind works in a slightly different way. I like to leave the word business to other people. Daniel Webster, for example. Now, there's a guy who knows his stuff."

Rachel was beginning to feel uneasy. Lance's eyes, she saw, were glowing again. As she looked into them, she felt repulsed. Yet at the same time she was unable to look away.

"Who are you?" she whispered.

"You can choose from a hundred different names. Zamiel, Ahrimanes, Belial, Abaddon." He was wearing a cold smile. "Or, more commonly, the Prince of Darkness, Beelzebub, Lucifer, Satan."

Rachel stared at him, her eyes wide. Lance settled back in his chair, a smug smile on his face.

"Impressed?" he asked, folding his arms across his chest.

"What kind of turkey are you, anyway?" she gasped once she finally managed to speak. "Did Gayle put you up to this, or is this entirely your own warped sense of humor?"

"Gee, thanks." Lance was beaming. "I'm hardly ever credited with having a sense of humor."

"Ugh," Rachel grunted. "Lord help me, this is so junior-high. If you can't even be straight with me ..."

"Oh, but I am being straight with you. I'm being perfectly straight. What do you expect, a little miracle or something? Something flashy? Would you like me to turn this glass of Perrier into wine in order to make my point? No, thanks. It's always been my policy to leave the theatrics to the other side."

"The other side, huh?" Rachel jeered. "What, is that supposed to be terribly clever or something?"

"You know, that's something I'll never understand about you mortals," Lance said, shaking his head in disgust. "If I show up in the form of a cloven-hoofed fire-breathing demon, everybody accepts it. They really get into it, in fact. But every time I put in an appearance looking like some regular guy ..."

"You don't look like a regular guy," Rachel countered. "You look like a regular *nerd*."

"Go ahead. Sticks and stones can break my bones. . . . Come to think of it, they can't. Even so, there's no reason to get nasty."

Rachel sighed. Holding up her hands in surrender, she said, "Okay, you're right. Look, Lance, you're probably a very nice guy and all—"

"Why, thank you." Lance bowed his head modestly. "Jeez, I'm not used to this. I think I'm getting more compliments tonight than I've received in the last two thousand years."

"But no one can expect every blind date to work out. You and I are just ... not each other's type, that's all."

"Oh, but you *are* my type." Lance was leering at her across the table. Just for a second Rachel was almost certain she saw tiny flames glimmering in the pupils of his eyes. The wine again, no doubt, playing tricks the way wine sometimes did.

"Look, I'm flattered," she said, having decided to try a slightly different tack. "But—"

"And do you know *why* you're my type?"

"Don't tell me." Rachel's voice was oozing with sarcasm. "You're attracted to brainy women."

"Nope."

"You adore independent types."

"No, not really."

"Oh, *I* know. You can't resist ambitious women."

"Now you're getting warm. The fact is that you, Rachel Swann, possess the single most important quality that draws me to someone."

"And that's ambition?"

"Not quite. Not ambition as much as . . . shall we say, desperation?"

"Desperation?" Rachel blinked. Her stomach gave an unpleasant lurch.

"Wait, wait, let me see if I can do this." Lance paused, rearranging the expression on his face and shifting around on his chair. And then, in a voice that sounded identical to her ex-husband's: "I want Becky to come live with me and Ariana after we're married. A little girl needs a stable home, one with a mother and a father. She needs financial security, too."

Rachel's mouth had dropped open. "What? How did you . . . ?"

Lance looked pleased with himself. "Wait. There's more." He took a moment to change his posture and his expression once again before speaking. "I want to make some wishes. I wish that all of a sudden my career would take off like a rocket to the moon. And . . . and I wish I could meet a man who's gorgeous, smart, successful . . . and madly in love with me." This time she heard her own voice, speaking in a near whisper, coming out of his mouth.

"Who are you?" Rachel croaked.

"Not that you're entirely selfish, of course. How kind of you to think of your sisters. A better man and a better body

for Molly, lots and lots of money for sweet little Sis . . .
Sounds rather like Santa's list, doesn't it?"

At the sound of his self-satisfied laugh, Rachel snapped
back into reality. "Wait a minute. Wait just a minute. Put
away the tarot cards, hotshot. Somebody—I don't know
who—has obviously been clueing you in on the details of
my life. Gayle, probably, although I don't know how she
knew all that. As for the voices, a lot of people can do that.
I mean, just look at all the impressionists you see on cable
TV late at night."

Lance shrugged. "Suit yourself. You can rationalize anything, I suppose, if you want to badly enough. First, why
don't you finish off your wine? It would be such a shame
to let it go to waste. In the meantime, let me ask you just
one simple question."

Dutifully Rachel took a small sip from her wineglass.
"Okay, Lance," she said. Uh-oh. There was the buzz again.
Both her speech and her mind were becoming blurred. "Hit
me."

He leaned against the table in such a way that the flick-
ering candle cast odd shadows across his face. Rachel saw
the flames in his pupils again. Only this time she realized
that all they were were two tiny reflections of the candle's
flame.

"Would you be willing to give your soul in exchange for
having those three wishes come true? One for you, one for
Molly, one for Sis?" He was speaking in a husky voice.
Was she imagining it, or was she really detecting an under-
current of eagerness in it?

"Ah, yes. The age-old question." Rachel strove to maintain an intellectual tone, the one that had served her so well
back in college and which, in adult life, had gotten her
through many an uncomfortable situation. "The mere mor-
tal's chance to make a deal with the devil. Signing away
one's soul in order to make one's wishes come true."

"Yes? Yes? And would you do it, Rachel? *Will* you do it,
Rachel?"

She took another sip of wine. She was thinking, thinking

hard. But instead of hearing her own thoughts, there was a voice superimposed over them, like an announcement made on a loudspeaker in an auditorium.

"I want Becky to come live with me and Ariana after we're married. I'm going to talk to my lawyers about getting our child custody ruling changed. You'd be better off without the financial burden . . . that frivolous career of yours . . . any judge in the nation is bound to see . . ."

This time it wasn't Lance who was speaking. It was Boyd, his words echoing through her brain. She could see his face, more evil than any demon's, more threatening than any supernatural force.

She put down the wine. She felt totally clear-headed, in complete control, as she turned to Lance. "Yes," she said calmly. "I would jump at the chance to make a deal like that."

Lance sat back in his chair, wearing a smug smile. "I was hoping you'd say that." His face had taken on a hard, ugly expression. The handsomeness was gone; she wondered how she could ever have thought that he was the least bit good-looking. "Of course, there's the usual *quadraginta quattuor dies* thing. . . ."

But she was hardly listening. All of a sudden the wine—or perhaps it was the rich food, an overabundance of cream and butter—had begun to rebel. The lurch her stomach had given earlier was proving to be just a warning.

"Uh, will you excuse me for a minute?" she said, standing up and looking around wildly for the rest room. "I think maybe I got a little carried away. . . ."

A few minutes later Rachel was standing in front of the mirror in the women's room, studying her red face as she mopped off with a wad of cold, wet paper towels whatever was left of her makeup. Her head was pounding. Never before had she so well understood the expression about feeling as if one's head were about to explode.

Some party girl, she was thinking, staring at the hollow look in the eyes that were staring right back at her. So you had a lousy blind date with a creep who has an odd sense of humor. So you ate too many *crevettes*, even though you have absolutely no idea what they are. So what? What's the big deal about tossing your cookies like a fifteen-year-old at her first beer bash?

But the worst was over. She had to admit that, headache and all, she was beginning to feel better. In fact, she was even feeling a little bit euphoric. She celebrated the unexpected upswing in her mood by brushing on a little blush and wielding a few strokes with her lipstick.

What next? Rachel wondered as she made her way back to the table. She quickly got her answer: Lance was gone.

A moment later the headwaiter was at her side, making an irritating clucking sound.

"I am so sorry, *madame*. The gentleman said you would understand."

"But . . . what . . ."

"He said you had accomplished your business for the evening," he added, sounding sympathetic.

A feeling of panic rushed over Rachel.

"What about the check?"

"Everything is taken care of, *madame*."

"That's a relief. I'd hate to have to take on a second job to pay for a bottle of wine. Especially since I just left most of it in your ladies' room."

"Pardon, madame?"

Rachel cast him a wary look. "I really need a taxi."

Chapter
Eight

"They're not headaches, exactly," said Rachel, staring down at her freshly shaven shins peeking out from underneath the crisp green paper robe that crackled whenever she moved. "I mean, they *are* headaches, but there's this whole other feeling that goes along with them. Sort of like . . . spells."

"Spells?" Dr. Ashwandi's jet-black eyes peered at her above his thick color-coordinated mustache. "Exactly what do you mean, Ms. Swann, by 'spells'?"

"Well, uh, it's like all of a sudden I get dizzy, and it feels as if the room is spinning around. Sure, my head aches—it pounds, in fact—but mainly I start feeling kind of disconnected from myself." Her tone was almost apologetic. "I know, I know. The whole thing sounds very weird."

"Umm-hmm. Umm-hmm."

Rachel could only wonder what a man like Ashok Ashwandi must think, a man who came from a land of caste marks and saris. He had his roots, after all, in a society where it was probably rare indeed that a woman complained of feeling disconnected from herself or pronounced her condition "weird."

What made the whole situation even more uncomfortable was that Dr. Ashwandi wasn't her regular doctor. Her usual internist was Dr. Amy Pitkin, an almost frighteningly intense woman of about Rachel's age whom she had in the past consulted about a bronchial infection, a shoulder with all its muscles in spasm, and a colony of undesirables growing in a place where they really didn't belong. Dr.

Pitkin was one of those doctors who, mercifully, was never more than a few inches away from her prescription pad. Her philosophy seemed to be: If you can describe it, we can medicate it.

However, when Rachel had telephoned the office a few days earlier, not long after her disastrous blind date and the second episode of suddenly feeling "weird," she had been told that Dr. Pitkin was on vacation in Mexico and would be away for another two weeks. Rachel was a tad envious, picturing her floating on a raft in the middle of a pool, smothered in sun block 15, her Sportsac packed with free samples of Lomotil, Maalox, antibiotics, and everything else required to ward off the almost inevitable side effects of a vacation south of the border.

But what was good news for Amy Pitkin was bad news for Rachel. She was, for the moment, without medical guidance. At least this Dr. Ashwandi was filling in during his colleague's absence. Rachel only hoped he was as quick on the draw when it came to scribbling notes to pharmacists. So far the only thing she'd been able to ascertain about the chubby Dr. Ashwandi was that America was being very, very good to him, at least if his pinky ring sporting a diamond the size of the Taj Mahal's gift shop was any indication.

"There's something else," Rachel said hesitantly.

"What's that?"

"I think I've been . . . imagining things."

Dr. Ashwandi eyed her curiously. "You mean hallucinating?"

"Yes. No. Not exactly." Rachel grimaced. "Things happen to me, things that at the time seem totally plausible and very real . . . but when I look back on them afterward, I realize that they couldn't possibly have happened. Not the way I remember them, anyway."

"You are hearing voices?"

"No. Yes. Not quite. What I mean is, I hear the voices only of people I know." Rachel frowned. Somehow, none of this was coming out right.

"These feelings you describe. Do they come upon you in the morning?"

"No—at least, not so far." Rachel crossed her legs at the ankle, trying to maintain the highest level of dignity possible while sitting with her feet dangling. She felt like a kindergartener sitting in the principal's chair. "It's happened to me only twice, and both times were in the evening. I guess I should mention that both times I had been drinking. The first time it was champagne, the second time wine. But not a lot, by any means. . . ."

"Any vomiting?"

"Just once."

"Fainting?"

"No. See, it's less of a physical thing than a sensation of being . . . I don't know, as I tried to explain before, sort of separated from myself."

"Yes. That's the part that puzzles me. If you could describe it a little more clearly . . ."

"Hypnotized, maybe? No, that's not it. It's like losing the ability to differentiate reality from unreality." She could tell he wasn't following. "I'm not explaining this very well, am I?"

"Ms. Swann, from what you are saying," Dr. Ashwandi said with great patience, speaking in a lilting voice, "it sounds to me like you may be pregnant."

"Oh, no. I'm not pregnant. I'm sure."

Dr. Ashwandi's bushy black eyebrows blended into his hairline. No doubt he had heard that one before.

"No, really. I know that's not it."

The good doctor eyed her warily. "Let's have a look at you."

A few minutes later Rachel was sitting on a regular chair, opposite his desk, this time dressed in her own clothes. She was afraid Dr. Ashwandi wouldn't recognize her.

"Well, Ms. Swann, you were right about one thing. You are not pregnant." He folded his hands across the desk, his pinky ring flashing. His voice was stern as he added, "In fact, I couldn't find anything out of order."

As if I were a Maytag washing machine, Rachel was thinking. And I'm getting about as much sympathy as one. She imagined she was supposed to feel guilty for taking up his precious time without any interesting pathologies to justify doing so.

He crossed his hands on his desk, weaving one hairy finger over another. "You are a successful career woman, I take it?"

Rachel brightened. "I guess you could say that. In fact, I have an article in the *New York Life* magazine that just came out today. I don't suppose you happened to see it? . . ."

"And you are a single mother?"

She simply nodded. She was catching on to the fact that Dr. Ashwandi was not interested in wordy explanations.

"Do you have a boyfriend?"

"Well," Rachel said with a frown, "that's not as easy to answer as you might think because—no, I guess not."

"Ah. As I expected. I think I have discovered the cause of your problem."

"What, not having a boyfriend?"

"Stress," Dr. Ashwandi announced triumphantly. "Your symptoms are rooted in stress. Ms. Swann, I suggest that you learn how to relax."

"Relax?"

"Take a hot bath, take a walk, do whatever you need to do to cut down on your level of tension. I predict that doing so will result in the elimination of your symptoms."

"That's it? That's your diagnosis?"

"You are not alone, Ms. Swann," Dr. Ashwandi told her in a serious voice. "I see many women who display these symptoms. And ninety-nine times out of a hundred, I can trace them directly to stress."

As she left his office, a hundred twenty-five dollars poorer and considerably disheartened, Rachel found herself muttering, "And what about the hundredth?"

* * *

"Sorry I'm late, guys," Rachel said breathlessly, breezing into the small bistro tucked away in the East Sixties. "I was busy paying someone a hundred bucks to advise me to take more showers."

"That's all right." Sis, beaming with pride, held up a copy of the latest issue of *New York Life*. "Today, Rachel dear, you can do no wrong."

She and Molly were already sitting at a round table in the noisy restaurant, packed to the gills with the weekday lunch crowd. The meeting place of choice for the Swann sisters' rendezvous was the New York version of a French café. A red and white striped awning outside, red and white checked tablecloths inside, a menu written in such elaborate French that ordering became a game of Twenty Questions. The best part, however, was that it was just a stone's throw from Bloomingdale's.

"Congratulations, Rachel," Sis gushed. "Your article is brilliant. I read it coming in on the train this morning. It made the Mocambian exhibition sound like so much fun that I just might pack up my whole family and bring them into the Met. What a colorful people the Mocambians are! And so primitive. They're completely untouched by modern civilization."

"I'm sure Jerry will feel right at home," Molly commented. "Here, let me see that."

"I haven't seen it, either." Rachel peered over Sis's shoulder, attempting to view the magazine as if through someone else's eyes—someone objective. The first thing she noted was that Grayson Winters had unfortunately been true to his word. Rather than using the face of the exhibition's welcoming demon as this week's cover girl, as Rachel had suggested, *New York Life* instead featured a blonde in a peach-colored bikini, licking an ice cream cone and pulling an "I Love New York" baseball cap down over her eyes. "The Enticements of Summer," the headline read. And right under it, "One Hundred Reasons to Stay in Town This Summer."

As Molly flipped open the magazine, Rachel saw that her article covered three pages. In addition there was a full-page color photograph of one of the exhibit's more eye-catching pieces of pottery, a cup molded into an animal that was part cow, part chicken, and part something that looked like a bull terrier. There were three smaller photographs as well. The first was of some Mocambian natives doing some sort of dance—or perhaps it was simply a West African form of aerobics. Alongside it was a snapshot of Dr. Ashcrofton sitting at her desk in the museum's underbelly, looking serious and knowledgeable and veddy, veddy prim.

The third picture was of the temple. Glancing at it, Rachel got an odd feeling. For a moment she felt as if her headache might be coming back. Fortunately it failed to materialize. She decided, in the stark light of day, that it was simply a case of associating that grimy little Caribbean outhouse with her newly developed allergy to wine, champagne, and geeks.

"I'm pleased with it," she admitted to her sisters. "Of course, it's not the sort of thing I'll be thrilled to show my grandchildren."

"Oh, Rachel, you're such a good writer, I'm sure you'll eventually start doing the kind of journalism you want to be doing." Good old Sis, the eternal cheerleader. "I just *know* you're heading toward great things."

"Well, there is one way you could find out, you know," Molly said matter-of-factly, squinting at the menu.

Sis looked over at her, surprised. "Don't tell me you've starting going to a psychic, Molly."

"I won't tell you, then. But can I tell you that Mike has?"

Rachel groaned. "Not Madame Chrissie again."

"I'm telling you, Rachel, she's fantastic." To Sis, Molly explained, "Madame Chrissie told Mike that someone he knew very well was going to be climbing up a step on a ladder. That was right before I was promoted to associate professor."

Sis did not look convinced. "Sounds kind of abstract to me."

"Look, Rachel, what have you got to lose? Maybe she'll even have something to say about your future with Howard."

"How is Howard?" This topic of conversation was much more up Sis's alley. She was, after all, someone who watched *Love Connection* nearly every day.

"I don't really know how Howard is," Rachel replied in a lofty tone. She was suddenly absorbed in scanning her menu. "We've, uh, decided to take a little break from each other."

"Good old Howard finally dumped you, huh?" Molly jeered.

"Molly! That's not nice!" Sis protested. "Maybe it was Rachel's idea."

"That'll be the day." Molly turned to confront Rachel. "Well?"

"Actually, it was Howard's idea," Rachel admitted. "But once I thought about it, I realized that it really was for the best."

"Poor Rachel," Sis cooed. "But it's not too late. Maybe you two will get back together again."

"Oh, I don't know." Rachel couldn't resist adding, "As a matter of fact, I've already had a date with someone else."

"Oooh! Tell us!" Sis cried.

She was tempted to spill her guts, to tell her sisters the entire outrageous tale. But something stopped her—mainly, the fact that it *was* such an outrageous tale. She could just hear Molly and Sis, speaking in soothing tones, trying to convince her that a short stay at the Little Flower Rest Home could only be good for her.

"Actually," she said lamely, "there's not much to tell. It was a blind date and, uh, it didn't work out."

"Do they ever?" Molly said dryly.

"Don't worry, Rachel," Sis assured her. "You'll find your Mr. Right. You deserve to be happy."

"I do, don't I?" Rachel shot back. She was trying to

sound flippant. Instead, she sounded a tad morose. "You and Molly and I, we *all* deserve to be happy."

More to herself than to her sisters, she added, "That's what I want for all of us."

"It'll take me only a minute to pick up those extra copies of the magazine," Rachel said apologetically as she and Molly padded down the thick carpeted hallway. "And if you don't mind giving me an extra five minutes, I'd like to stop off to say hi to a friend of mine."

"And have her tell you how wonderful your article is, right?" Molly teased.

She had accompanied Rachel on her after-lunch stop-off at the Dominion Building. Sis had declined, saying that she, too, was eager to see the place, but that she was even more eager to hurry downtown to Odd Lot Trading to do a bit of serious shopping.

"In the first place, the person I'm seeing is a him, not a her," Rachel corrected her. "And in the second place, what's wrong with a bit of basking in one's glory?"

"Nothing. Hey, bask all you want. I'll join you in a sec. I just want to stop off in the women's room." Even when it came to bodily functions, Molly strove to be politically correct.

"Bathroom's that way, Jack's office is that way," said Rachel.

As she had hoped, Jack was in his usual place: holed up in his office with his shirt-sleeves rolled up, surrounded by a cloud of smoke and enough empty polystyrene cups to pollute an entire river.

"Hey! Here she is! Star of the day!" he greeted her. "Can I be the first to congratulate you?"

"Well, the third, anyway," Rachel quipped.

"In that case, can I be just one more in a long line of fans telling you you did such a great job that you deserve to be the next president of Mocambu? Maybe even to be sacrificed to their rain god?"

"That you can. The first one, anyway." Rachel was glowing, loving every second of this.

"Seriously, Rachel, you did a very nice piece. You should be pleased."

"Oh, I am, I am."

"And . . ."

Suddenly Jack's voice trailed off. The look that had come into his hazel eyes was the type that in Rachel's experience was most commonly motivated in men by reports of a two-for-one Black & Decker sale at Sears.

"And who is this?" he asked in an odd voice.

Rachel, expecting Fergie or at least Princess Di, turned, only to be disappointed.

"Oh. It's just Molly."

"*Just* Molly?" he repeated.

"Sorry. I didn't mean it the way it sounded."

Jack's eyes remained glued to "just Molly." And, Rachel was at least as surprised to observe, that same brand of glue appeared to have been applied to Molly's eyes as well.

"Rachel," Molly said, speaking in a voice Rachel had never heard before, "why don't you introduce us? You're being awfully rude, you naughty thing."

Rachel wondered if her younger sister's body had just been taken over by aliens, aliens who lived on a planet where the inhabitants spoke like southern belles stepping out onto the veranda to announce that it was time for the Virginia reel.

"Uh, sure. Molly Swann, this is Jack Richter. Jack, my younger sister, Molly. Jack and I have known each other for years—although not as many years as I've known Molly, hah-hah. . . ."

But Rachel had become irrelevant. She suddenly understood how cleaning people must feel as they bustled around occupied offices or homes, not particularly welcome but considered so unimportant that their presence was barely even noticed.

"Gee, I wonder if it's going to snow tonight?" she commented, curious to see if either of them would remember that today was one of those scorching ninety-five-degree July days.

She passed the test with flying colors—or failed it, depending on one's perspective. Neither Molly nor Jack took the least bit notice of the fact that she had lapsed into senseless blather.

"Rachel's sister, huh? Oh, I'm sorry. How thoughtless of me. Here, let me move those for you." Jack was tripping over his own feet as he raced through the obstacle course created by his own compulsion to live the life of Oscar Madison. In a dramatic gesture he lifted a two-foot pile of books, papers, and computer output from the chair in the corner of his compact office, placing them on the floor. Shoulder muscles bulged from beneath his shirt, muscles that Rachel had never before even suspected were in existence. "Here, Molly. Please, sit down."

"Oh, that's okay, Jack," Rachel said pointedly. "I'll just stand, thanks."

"So, Molly, are you a writer, too?" Back at his desk, Jack wore a moon-pie expression that would have been more appropriate to a Looney Tunes character than an award-winning journalist.

"Actually, I teach sociology up at Columbia."

"Really? That's *fascinating.*"

"But I do some writing, too."

"Molly wrote a book comparing rituals that are performed in contemporary American society with the rituals performed by people that we like to label primitive." Rachel couldn't resist tacking on the punch line that was guaranteed to get 'em every time. "She was on *Donahue* a couple of months ago."

"Wow! That's really wonderful, Molly."

Jack's tone was dripping with sincerity. Molly, meanwhile, was actually blushing.

"I have to admit that I'm pleased with my book's success."

"Molly was also promoted to associate professor of

sociology just a few weeks ago," Molly's big sister reported proudly.

Molly was nodding shyly. "At the beginning of the summer." A noise then escaped her lips that sounded suspiciously close to a giggle. "How about you, Jack? You're an editor here, right?"

"Yup. I've been with *New York Life* since the day it started." All of a sudden Jack's eyes lit up a few more watts. "Hey, have you two had lunch yet?"

Molly looked crestfallen, almost as if she had just found out she'd graduated into a higher tax bracket. "Yes, we did."

"It *is* almost two-thirty, Jack," Rachel reminded him. "Not everybody lives on eastern editors' time."

Her tone of voice clued her in to the fact that she was very irritated. That realization took her by surprise.

What's the matter with me? she wondered. What am I being so crabby about?

Then she realized. It was the look that was in both Jack's and Molly's eyes. The glint. The exact same glint she noticed in the eyes of Sis and Jerry every time they looked at each other.

Jealous—again, she thought morosely. This is becoming a *trend*, for God's sake.

Just this once, instead of being her usual good sport, she decided to indulge this rare foray into the den of the seven deadly sins.

"Look, you guys, we really should get going. Molly, weren't you just saying you have to teach a graduate seminar at four?"

"W-what?" Molly glanced over at her, looking so zoned out that Rachel considered having a word with her about the dangers of drinking wine with lunch.

"Graduate seminar, Molly? Remember? Intense twenty-four-year-olds eager to pick your brain dry so that in five years they can steal your job?"

"Oh, of course. I almost forgot." Molly blinked hard, as

if trying to force herself back into the real world. "You're absolutely right, Rachel. We really should get going."

She turned her attention back to Jack. "Well, Jack, it was really nice meeting you."

"It was nice meeting *you*, Molly."

Oh, *pul-leez*. Any more of this and I'm going to need a shot of insulin. Rachel watched in amazement as Jack actually rose from his seat, hurrying around his desk and knocking over an almost empty polystyrene cup of coffee in his effort to walk his female guests to the door. It was a distance of a good five feet.

"Maybe I'll, uh, run into you again sometime," Jack was saying.

Molly cast him a bashful smile. "I certainly hope so, Jack."

As the two sisters rode down the elevator, Rachel expected a barrage of questions from Molly.

Is he married? Is he seeing anybody? What's he really like? Is he really as sweet as he seems?

Instead, Molly didn't say a word about Jack Richter. And that, Rachel knew, was even worse.

There was bound to be fallout. And it was bound to come soon. Sure enough, not even twenty-four hours had passed before Rachel received the telephone call she had been expecting.

"Rachel, he *called* me," Molly squealed into the phone. It was a quiet squeal, one that revealed a need for secrecy, a fear of being discovered, and more than a little glee over the whole damned exciting thing.

"Who?" Sometimes it was fun to play dumb.

"Jack Richter, that's who."

"Oh. Am I supposed to be surprised or something?"

"I couldn't believe it." Molly was acting as if Rachel were nothing more than a sounding board. "I was sitting in my office at school, and the phone rang, and it was him. He tracked me down at work."

"Clever fellow, that Jack."

"Rachel, I wish you'd be a little more serious about this. He called to ask me out!"

"I'm sorry, Molly, but I just don't understand what the big deal is. It was obvious from the minute you two met that there was real chemistry between you. I mean, I felt like I was an extra in a Swedish porn flick or something."

"But Rachel!"

"But what?"

At the other end of the line Molly was sighing in exasperation. "What about Mike?"

"What *about* Mike?"

"For heaven's sake, Rachel. Surely you haven't forgotten that I'm living with the guy."

"So what are you saying? That only floosies make lunch dates with guys they're attracted to?"

"It's not a lunch date. It's a dinner date." Molly was silent for a few seconds. "Oh, Rachel, what am I doing? What's going on here? Mike and I are a couple!"

"Do you love Mike?"

"I'm . . . I'm very fond of him. You know, he and I have been together for a long time. Two years, Rachel. That's a very long time."

"I don't hear you saying the L word, Mol."

"Oooh, I wish I'd never met Jack Richter!"

"Do you really?" Rachel asked dryly.

"Well . . ." Molly giggled. "Did you notice how . . . how *hazel* his eyes are? And did you notice that cute way he clears his throat?"

"Cute? The last time I heard him do that, I urged him to go in for a chest X ray."

"And he's witty, too. Don't you think he's witty? I mean, when we talked on the phone just now—we must have talked for half an hour—he kept saying these really charming, funny things. . . ."

Molly groaned loudly. "Oh, God, Rachel. What am I doing?"

"Look, Molly. You're not running away to Tahiti with the guy. You're having lunch. . . ."

"Dinner."

"Dinner with him. That's a perfectly reasonable thing to do. You just want to get to know him a little better, right?"

"Actually, what I want to do is check into a motel that has a hot tub and . . . oooh, I shouldn't be saying these things, should I?"

"Not to me, anyway."

"Okay, okay. I'll get a grip on myself. See? I'm acting like a nice, normal human being, a professional woman with a Ph.D. and a respectable position shaping young minds and a hard-cover book with my photograph on the back. . . . Rachel, who has a better lingerie department, Lord & Taylor or Saks?"

"Molly," Rachel said with a sigh, "given the direction in which you're obviously headed, I don't think that the kind of underwear you wear is going to make a hell of a lot of difference."

Chapter
Nine

Rachel *couldn't help feeling* a little foolish as she trekked down University Place in pursuit of a psychic reading. Yet ever since Mike and Molly had first mentioned their experience with Madame Chrissie, she hadn't been able to stop thinking about it.

The opportunity to consult with someone who had a hot line into the future was enticing—and in the end irresistible. So what if this extra unbudgeted cost meant canceling her haircut at Barney's and taking buses instead of taxis for a week or two?

East Eleventh Street, Rachel discovered as she turned off University in search of the address printed on Madame Chrissie's bubble-gum-pink business card, was one of the main drags in the city's antiques district. The sidewalks were swarming with elegant women in designer panty hose supervising husky men in nondesigner T-shirts lifting and carting and unpacking treasures that had traveled great distances, through both miles and years. A bigger-than-life-size marble statue of a headless woman was parked on the curb next to a fire hydrant. Lined up in front of a coffee shop were six ornate dining room chairs with needlepoint seat covers.

"Aw, shit, Harry," muttered one of the huskies, holding up the tail end of a library table that he and his three cohorts were unloading off the back of a truck. "We chipped the Chippendale."

Madame Chrissie was located at the end of the block, in an office building. Most of the other tenants were designers and interior decorators, dealing very heavily in the here and now. Not surprisingly, the psychic had been relegated to the top floor, upstairs with a handful of others who didn't quite fit the building's profile: a food co-op's headquarters, the editorial offices of a Polish language newspaper, a few psychotherapists.

At the end of a corridor lined with closed, locked doors, Madame Chrissie's door had been left ajar.

"Come in," a gentle voice beckoned at the sound of Rachel's heels clicking against the hard linoleum floor as she traveled down the long hallway. "I felt that your presence was imminent, so I left the door open."

"Uh, I did have an eleven o'clock appointment."

Rachel walked in slowly, not sure of what she would find. Surely beads hanging in the doorway, thick dusty carpeting and pillows with red silk fringe, incense. Instead, Madame Chrissie's office could have belonged to an accountant. It was all clean lines and high-tech accoutrements, leftovers from the eighties. Track lighting, wire shelving, a red metal In-basket. She only hoped that none of those designers ever wandered in there by mistake.

Madame herself was young, probably in her mid to late twenties. She had pale blond hair and a vague, ephemeral way about her. Probably, had she been born twenty years earlier, she would have made cover girl of *Life* magazine's special issue on the emergence of the flower child. Instead, she was wearing a smart gray business suit, high heels, and pearls. Quite a far cry from a shawl and a pair of large hoop earrings.

"Come in, Rachel. Oh, wow. Did you hear that? I just called you Rachel without even asking you if it was okay. I guess I just *knew* I could call you by your first name. You know, like I'm getting vibrations that tell me you're the kind of person who feels comfortable with that."

"That's true." Rachel sat down on the couch, feeling positively dowdy.

"I'm getting good vibes from you," Madame Chrissie went on, going over and sitting next to her on the couch.

"I can tell that you're a good person. You're kind, thoughtful, considerate of others. . . ."

Is this woman psychic, or did she simply get hold of my Girl Scout records? Rachel wondered. But she quickly reminded herself that if she was going to get anything out of this at all, she would have to suspend all cynicism, at least for a while.

"Thank you," she mumbled, embarrassed. "Actually, I was, uh, looking for some information about my future."

"I knew that!" Madame Chrissie said brightly.

"Didn't I mention that on the phone?"

"Oh, right. I thought it sounded familiar." Madame Chrissie smiled apologetically. "You see, when you're in constant contact with other planes of existence the way I am, sometimes you forget who told you something. Clients, dead people, spirits . . . they all get mixed up together."

"I can imagine. Madame Chrissie, what I was hoping was that you could give me some idea of where my life is headed. You see, I'm at a point where I'm struggling with a few different things, and I—"

"Wait. I see a man." Madame Chrissie squinted as if she were slightly nearsighted when it came to seeing into other people's lives. "He's very important to you. His name is Jim . . . Bob . . . Dan . . ."

"Howard?"

"Howard! That's it!"

Rachel was beginning to regret the sacrifices she was making in her attempt to tamper with fate, or at least do a little spying on it. "Howard is—"

"Wait, don't tell me!" Madame Chrissie held up her hands. For a moment Rachel thought they were playing charades. "This man is a . . . a doctor?"

"No. . . ."

"An accountant?"

Rachel sighed. "Not quite."

"Oh, I know. He's a lawyer. He has two teenage daughters. He lives in Westchester County, he's getting bald, and he's lousy in bed."

"That's exactly right!" Rachel cried. "How did you know?"

Madame Chrissie shrugged. "When you're born with the gift, you don't ask questions. I've always been able to do this, ever since I was a little girl back in California. That, and wiggling my ears."

She pulled back her hair from either side of her head and demonstrated. It was, indeed, impressive. "I'm also very good at imitating a French accent."

"What about Howard? Do you see a future for him and me?"

Madame Chrissie frowned. "He's kind of fading fast. That's not a good sign."

"I suppose that all depends on how you look at it." Rachel shrugged. "Is there . . . somebody to replace him?"

There was a long pause. Rachel could practically hear the gears turning. "Um, I'm afraid that's kind of fuzzy, too. I see this shadowy kind of thing, and I *think* it's a man, but I'm not sure. It could be something else."

"Something else? Like what?"

"Like, oh, I don't know, a deadly disease or an increase in your rent. It's kinda hard to tell."

Rachel sighed. "I was hoping for something a little more specific."

Madame Chrissie didn't seem to be listening. "Wait, now there's something else. I see a boy. No, a man." She frowned. "Wow, this is really freaky. I'm getting both man signals and *boy* signals. . . ."

"Could it be a man whose name is Boyd?"

"Yes! That's it! Whoa, don't tell me you're psychic, too?"

"Not quite. Boyd is my ex-husband."

"Oh. That explains why I'm also getting a lot of bad karma signals. But who's that?" Madame Chrissie screwed up her face. "I know this sounds really crazy, but I could swear he's holding cotton candy . . . *yellow* cotton candy."

"I think her name is Ariana," Rachel offered dryly.

"Well, cotton candy or not, the two of them together

look pretty menacing." The pale blond woman shivered. "I'd watch out for them if I were you."

Rachel simply nodded. She didn't need a psychic to tell her that.

"There's a little girl. . . ."

"That's Becky."

"I would have said Betsy, but you know better than I."

"Is she with me?" Rachel asked eagerly. "Or is she with . . . with . . ." Somehow she couldn't quite manage to say the words.

Madame Chrissie's face was all scrunched up. "It's not clear. Right now she's kind of floating between you and them." She glanced at Rachel, wearing a sympathetic smile. "She's definitely closer to you, though."

So far, not so good. "Anything else?"

"Wait, wait, there *is* something else. . . . It has to do with your job. You're—don't tell me—a dental technician, right? No, no, that's not it. Something more creative."

"You're getting warm."

"You work for a plastic surgeon?"

Rachel scowled. "Wrong field."

"Gee, this is hard. Some days are better than others, and . . . oh, I know. You're a free-lance journalist who's disgusted with the way your career is going. You're writing too many fluff pieces when you want to be involved with more serious stuff."

Rachel stared at her. "You're amazing!"

Madame Chrissie beamed. "You should hear me do Leslie Caron in *Gigi*."

"So what's going to happen with my career? Is it going to improve? Am I going to start getting assignments doing the kind of articles I want to do?"

"I don't know, Rachel. There's that cloud again. . . ." She shook her head in frustration. "I'm sorry. It's just that the vibrations I keep getting from you are so . . . so mixed.

"Maybe if we made bodily contact. Yeah, that's a good idea. It usually helps."

Rachel nodded eagerly. "Okay, what do I have to do?"

"Give me your hands. If I'm holding both of them, that should strengthen the vibrations. It's kind of like adjusting the antenna on your television set."

Dutifully Rachel held out her hands, and Madame Chrissie took hold of them. As she closed her eyes, there was a placid smile on her face.

Then the smile faded. She began to tremble, and her expression became one of horror.

"Oh, my God!" she cried, dropping Rachel's hands as if they were hot potatoes.

"What is it?" Rachel demanded.

"I—I don't know. I've never seen anything like it." Madame Chrissie stood up. "I need a cup of herb tea really bad."

"But what does this mean? Am I going to die? Is something really terrible going to happen? Am I sick? Am I going to have an accident?"

Madame Chrissie looked at her. "All I know is, your future is being controlled by some force that doesn't want me or anybody else butting our noses in."

Molly, Sis, and Jack Richter were obviously not the only ones impressed with Rachel's article on the good citizens of Mocambu. It wasn't long before Mary Louise was summoning her to Grayson Winters's side once again.

"He has another assignment he wants to talk to you about," Mary Louise told her over the telephone as both women simultaneously checked engagement calendars.

"Oh, goody. What is it this time?" Rachel asked herself after she'd hung up. "The dynamic new History of the Crayon exhibit at the Children's Museum?"

On her way to the head honcho's office, Rachel couldn't resist poking her head into Jack Richter's office. Nothing like a good tease to start the day off right.

"So you and my sister are an item, huh?" she greeted him, lounging in the doorway of his chaotic office.

Jack looked up from his computer screen. "Oh, hi, Rachel."

She swung in and dropped into his Leatherette chair, miraculously free of pulp products at the moment. "I guess if I were a really good friend, I'd warn you."

"Huh?" Jack blinked in confusion as he pulverized a cigarette butt into an already full ashtray.

"Come on, Jack. Don't play dumb with me. Especially since Molly called me right after she hung up from her conversation with you and spilled the beans."

"She did, did she?"

Rachel's mouth dropped open. "Why, Jack Richter! I do believe you're blushing!"

"Nah. It's just a little hot in here, that's all."

"Hot? *Hot?* The way they've got the air conditioner turned up, I thought I'd accidentally stumbled into the *Refrigeration World* offices."

"You know, Rachel, now that we've got our cards on the table, there are a couple of things I'd like to ask you." Jack looked around nervously. Then he stood up, strode over to the door of his office, and closed it.

"Goodness. What exactly is the nature of these 'things'?" Rachel asked, feigning horror.

"I just don't like to mix business and pl . . . uh, my personal life. You know how it is."

"Oh, sure. I know. Mr. Macho here doesn't want anyone to know he's got a crush on my little sister."

"I wouldn't call it a crush, exactly."

"You're right. Mr. Macho has got the hots for my sister."

Instead of coming up with a snappy comeback, Jack hesitated, his face softening into a smile. "She's really special, isn't she?"

"Molly? *My* Molly?"

Jack groaned. "Come on, Rachel. Give me a break, will ya?"

"You're right. I shouldn't be giving you such a hard time. Actually, I should, but for entirely different reasons."

"Oh. I get it. You mean Mike, right?"

Rachel's surprise was genuine. "No. To tell you the truth, I wasn't thinking about Mike at all."

"What about him, anyway? That's what I wanted to ask you about. I mean, the two of them are living together, aren't they?"

"I guess you could say that. Or you could say that Mike is Molly's housekeeper. Or maybe her indentured servant."

Jack frowned. "I'm afraid I don't follow."

"Look." Rachel let out a loud sigh. "The truth is, I've never really approved of Mike. Not as a match for Molly, anyway."

"You think he's bad for her?" There was an expression of glee bubbling underneath the concern on Jack's face. "Why?"

"He's not *bad*, really. Just . . . not good. Mike is so passive. Not exactly what you'd call a go-getter. The way Molly is, I mean."

"Yeah, that gal is a real go-getter," Jack mused, not without pride.

"Hold it right there, buddy. Let me give you lesson one on my sister. You don't call her a gal, okay?"

"Woman. Right?"

"Ten points. Tell me, have you two actually gone out yet? Or are you still at the stage of whispering sweet nothings over the telephone?"

"We had dinner. That's all . . . so far."

Rachel rolled her eyes. "Look, Jack. I feel like I'm caught in the middle here. You know I like you. We've been friends forever. You're almost a brother to me. But Molly is my sister. My real sister. We're connected by blood, by experience, by years of sharing boxes of Tampax. . . ."

"So what's your point?"

"Jack, there's no way I can put this delicately, so I'll just come right out and say it. You and Molly are . . . you're totally wrong for each other."

He considered her point. "You're right. That's not delicate at all."

"I thought you could take it," she muttered.

"Look, Rachel. I hear you. And I believe that you're saying this in the spirit of wanting to do what's best for both of us. . . ."

"To be perfectly honest, I can't imagine what either of you see in each other."

"Pardon?"

"Well, to put it bluntly, my sister is a smart-ass who prides herself on being a cynic. She's a die-hard feminist, she's ambitious as hell, and, well, she doesn't exactly have the body of the usual nymphet one would assume you consider your dream date. To sum it up, Molly Swann is not your type."

"And what about me?" Jack said coldly. "How would you categorize me? For some reason, I have this weird feeling that that's what's coming next."

"Well, you . . . well, let's just say that your view of women is not exactly, shall we say, progressive. You're undoubtedly more interested in—oh, I don't know—how long a woman's tongue is than how many of Shakespeare's sonnets she can recite."

"I can change, Rachel," Jack insisted in a voice so soft and sincere that it startled her. "I have changed. Already."

"Uh-huh." Slowly Rachel stood up. "Well, just excuse me if I don't start shopping for a maid of honor dress, okay?"

Jack was nodding knowingly. "Molly warned me about this."

"Huh?"

"She told me there was a good chance you'd react this way."

"*What* way?" Her tone was tart.

"I hate to say this, but, well, Molly told me you might be jealous."

"What?" She dropped back onto her chair. "May I ask what it is I'm supposed to be jealous of? What, are you secretly supposed to be the man of my dreams, Jack? Or am I supposed to be protective of my little sister?"

Jack was gazing at her coolly, meanwhile lighting a cigarette. He paused to puff. "Molly said she was afraid you'd

be jealous that she was getting involved in a new relationship while your thing with Howard has been getting a
bit . . . stale. So much so that the two of you actually decided to cool it."

"Stale? Is that the word she used?" Rachel snorted.
"Knowing Molly, she probably said something like 'moldy'
or 'contaminated' or . . . or 'rotten.' "

Jack was thoughtful for a few seconds. "I wouldn't say
that *rotten* was a Molly-type word."

"Then you don't know Molly." Rachel stood up, taking
care to maintain perfect posture. "Look, Jack, I know that
this is really none of my business. None of it is my concern, not even the way you two are gossiping about me and
my relationships and the childish way in which you expect
me to react to the fact that you two are flirting and sneaking around and maybe even playing spin the bottle."

She waggled a finger at Jack. "But when this turns into
disaster city, don't say I didn't tell you so. Don't say I
didn't warn you."

"Fine." Jack gave a firm nod of his head. "I hereby consider myself warned."

"Good. The subject is closed."

She was about to leave his office with as much dignity
as she could manage when he called after her, "By the way,
do you have any idea what size bustier Molly would
wear?"

As Mary Louise ushered Rachel into Grayson's grand office, he was standing at his desk, talking on the telephone.
Politely Rachel hesitated in the doorway, performing the
mime routine that translates to "Oh, no! I'd never want to
listen in on a telephone call!" But he beckoned to her, then
without ceremony turned his back on her.

Rachel, suspecting she was *supposed* to feel uncomfortable, sat down on a chair and did her best not to squirm. As
usual, being surrounded by the many fine and intimidating
things gathered together in Grayson's office made her feel
as if she were browsing at Cartier's, meanwhile being

watched by a high-tech security system that had pegged her as a potential shoplifter.

"I know, I *know* I said that," he was muttering into the phone. "But I had no idea that this ... this charity thing was going to come up."

It wasn't what he was saying; it was the way in which he was saying it. That low voice tinged with desperation and annoyance, that posture that hovered somewhere between defensive and defeated. He was talking to—negotiating with, squirming out from under—a woman. A woman who was not his wife, that faceless, nameless creature who lurked somewhere at the back of Grayson Winters's life.

This realization caused a big lump to lodge itself deep in the pit of Rachel's stomach. Overhearing him in this way was bringing it all back. Once upon a time she had been his target, his pick of the litter for part-time party girl. And while the whole sordid incident was something that neither of them ever alluded to, it was still there between them.

It had been a meeting not unlike this one. Rachel had come in to talk to him about an assignment. One of her very first for *New York Life*, in fact. She had been so excited to be part of this slick magazine, the definitive word on what was in and what was out in all of New York's different scenes, from politics to fashion to theater, she could hardly believe she wasn't simply indulging in a richly detailed daydream.

So she had been very flattered that the powerful force behind it all had seemed so interested in her. He had come around from behind the big desk, taking a seat next to her on the leather couch—a place that, back then, she didn't know better than to avoid. She had started out chirpily telling him the story of how she had first become interested in journalism. She had ended by forcefully pushing his hand away from a place where it did not belong.

He had acted hurt, then angry, then cool. Mainly he'd made it clear that he was not a man who handled rejection well. Throughout it all, Rachel did her best to remain calm and professional.

These things happen, she kept telling herself.

Part of her wanted to call the police. The other part was thinking, Please, *please*, don't let him take this assignment away.

In the end, neither event occurred. She wrote the article and said nothing; he gave her another assignment and said nothing. The End. Except, of course, that since neither of them had contracted amnesia in the interim, the Incident continued to haunt their relationship, acknowledged or not.

"Look, Nicole, I'll have to call you later. There's someone in my office."

Rachel shook her head to clear out the cobwebs—or, more accurately, to send the bad memories back to the attic of her mind so that, once again, cobwebs could cover it. She flashed him a broad, friendly smile, telling herself, Think perky.

"Rachel," he said heartily, sitting on the edge of his desk. He was towering above her—in fact, looking way, way down at her. "Nice job on that Mocambian piece. I knew it would turn out to be your type of thing."

"Thank you," she said simply.

"So, are you ready to talk about what we've got next on the agenda?"

"Shoot."

"Good." He left the desk in favor of his chair. As he leaned back, the force of his muscular shoulders, submitted to torture three times a week on the Vertical Club's Nautilus machines, made it creak. He crossed his long legs, legs that you could just tell had a deep, even tan underneath those gabardine pants from Barney's.

His piercing blue eyes were fixed on hers. "This next assignment is really going to turn you on."

"Great." Rachel tried to sound enthusiastic. But she'd been down this road before, and had learned the hard way that one person's caviar was another person's salty fish eggs.

In the meantime she began scrounging around in her purse, looking for a pen. She suddenly felt clumsy and incompetent. Having Grayson Winters reach across his desk, as cool as cucumber dip, and hand her a gold Cross pen didn't help a bit.

"Thanks," she sputtered. But he was already in high gear.

"Have you ever heard of an organization called Grass Roots?"

Rachel blinked. Grass Roots, Grass Roots ... she was shuffling through the file cards of her memory bank once again, trying to come up with something from under the G's. Somewhere, deep in the fog, she had a dim recollection of the name. Annoyingly, she couldn't quite match it up with a memory.

"Grass Roots," Grayson was saying patiently, now treating the polished edge of his desk as a footstool for his equally polished Bally shoes, "is an organization dedicated to preserving the earth's ecology."

"Oh, right." Ecology—that was the key word. "They're kind of like Greenpeace, right?"

"Except that they're much less mainstream. Greenpeace might have started out as a radical organization—in terms of the public's perception—but by now it's become positively middle-class. Grass Roots is still a relatively unknown quantity. Still, it's gaining acceptance. Better media attention and all that. And the perception by the percentage of the public that does know of them is that they're basically a bunch of good guys, genuinely concerned with environmental issues."

Rachel was nodding. "I think I remember now. It was started by a bunch of latter-day hippies, right?"

"An interesting categorization." Grayson let out a hearty, if insincere, chuckle. "It's true that Grass Roots was started by a couple of guys with beards and flannel shirts somewhere out in the wilds of Oregon. And it became just what the name says: a grass-roots organization. It caught on. People started jumping on the bandwagon. It truly became a 'grass-roots' movement."

He sighed, meanwhile gazing out the window at the towering user-unfriendly steel structure outside, a fifty-five-story monolith that almost exactly matched the one he and Rachel were in. It was hard to tell what his sigh meant. She was tempted to ask him whether he was for or against clean water and air.

When Grayson returned his gaze to her, there was a distinctive glint in his eye, a look that told her excitement was bubbling underneath the surface. It was a look she hadn't seen yet today.

"It seems there's a bit of dirty linen within the Grass Roots organization," he said slowly. It was clear that he was relishing every word. "It turns out that this organization that's supposedly dedicated to making our planet squeaky clean isn't quite so squeaky clean itself."

Suddenly Rachel understood that it wasn't that Grayson was for or against pollution, it wasn't his personal feelings about Grass Roots that was responsible for that glint. It was the fact that there was a story here. A juicy one, one that was just a fraction of an inch away from being tabloid material. One that promised all kinds of delicious gossip. Scandal, but scandal against a backdrop of what happened to be a very hot topic. It was precisely the kind of thing that *New York Life* readers loved.

Grayson Winters had never looked happier.

"I've got a source—an insider, some guy who's pretty far down on the organization's totem pole but who apparently has a bone to pick with them. This guy says that part of Grass Roots' funding comes from private companies, the kind of companies that it purports to be investigating." He was looking at her meaningfully. "Are you getting my drift?"

"Sure. Payoffs. We'll pay you to keep quiet about the fact that we're using the local swimming hole as our toxic waste dump."

"Exactly." Grayson folded his arms across his chest. He looked as satisfied as if he had just finished a six-course meal. Or as if he had just had the best sex of his life.

"And the best thing about this," he went on, "is that the guy who's ready to spill the soy beans on these alleged do-gooders is giving us an exclusive story. He called the office last week, saying he wanted to speak only to me. When I realized there really was something there, I told him I'd have to hand the story over to one of my people. He agreed."

And I'm that people, Rachel was thinking, nodding.

"Here's the deal, Rachel." Grayson was looking at her seriously. "This guy, the insider from Grass Roots, will be calling you at home. He wanted your number there so he wouldn't be traced to the *New York Life* offices."

Great, Rachel was thinking. I just hope his idea of a hot Saturday night isn't breathing heavily into his latest find from the AT&T Phone Store.

"His name is Johnny."

"Johnny?" she repeated, doubtful.

"That's his code name."

"Code name!" She didn't mean to sound naive, but that one just slipped out. She felt like Bob Woodward or Carl Bernstein, even though *Deep Throat* was a lot more colorful than *Johnny*.

"Hey, Rachel," Grayson said, "this is a *very* big story. A lot of people are going to get hurt when it breaks. Careers are going to be ruined, fortunes are going to be lost, respectable businesses—seemingly respectable businesses—are going to collapse like outhouses in an earthquake.

"And *you're* going to be behind it all. This time around, Rachel, you're going to make a real impact."

It wasn't until then that, slowly, dramatically, a rush of understanding washed over her.

This is it. The story I've been waiting for. The chance to rake muck, to delve into scandal, to get my hands dirty in a story worth a little extra scrubbing with turpentine.

Her heart felt as if it had just merged with her stomach. Surprisingly, that was actually a pleasant feeling.

This is it. This is really, really it.

* * *

"Are you okay, Rachel?" Mary Louise Finn asked as one pale journalist with a stricken look on her face came out the door of Grayson Winters's office, walking like a zombie. "Can I get you anything?"

"No, that's okay." Rachel's voice was hoarse, an inevitable manifestation of the fact that she felt, at the same time, deliriously happy, petrified, and, above all, overwhelmed. She wouldn't have recognized it, in fact, if it hadn't just come out of her own mouth. "I'm fine, really."

"You don't look fine." Mary Louise wasn't about to let the wool be pulled over her eyes. "How about a cup of coffee?"

"That's funny; I was just about to suggest the same thing," a booming voice broke in.

Rachel was grateful to look up and find Jack standing there, his hearty tone and big grin thinly masking his concern. Seeing the look in his eyes jolted her out of her semihypnotic state.

"Do I look that bad?"

"You look good enough to eat," he returned. "So let's go eat. I gotta go to the bank anyway." Casting a rueful look at Mary Louise, he added, "I gotta get myself out of this building every once in a while, just to remind myself I don't live in Toledo, Ohio, anymore."

"You never lived in Toledo, did you?" Rachel asked once she and Jack were sitting in a booth in the coffee shop downstairs, the toe of the gigantic body of the Dominion Building.

"No, but it sounds good, doesn't it?" Jack rested his elbows on the table and looked at her intently. "Now, enough about me. What the hell just went on in there? You look like you've seen a ghost. I know that Uncle Grayson has his bad moments, but I've never known him to affect anybody quite that way."

"I—I guess I'm just in shock." Rachel shook her head brusquely, as if trying to snap all the parts back into place.

"Good shock or bad shock? I can't tell."

"Jack, I just had the most incredible thing in the world happen to me. Grayson just—"

"Can I get yez some coffee?" offered the chirpy waitress, having just sashayed over to the table, coffeepot in hand.

Jack glanced up at her. "Sure, Madge."

"Doris," she corrected him, efficiently filling two of the four cups that were placed on the table, upside down.

"I was sure it was Madge," Jack muttered as she took off as quickly as she'd come, leaving two red plastic menus with more listings in them than the Toledo phone book.

"Jack, I just got the most exciting assignment of my life. It's supposed to be top secret and all that, but I guess I can tell you."

Jack shrugged. "It's forgotten already—and you haven't even said a word."

"I'm going to investigate a scandal inside an environmental organization called Grass Roots."

Before she had a chance to expand, Jack let out a low whistle. "Wow!" he said. "Go for it, babe!"

"So you know Grass Roots?"

"Sure I do! And I know all about their holier-than-thou attitude, too. Oh, not that they're not doing great work. Necessary work. But they piss off an awful lot of people in the process, and that makes them really newsworthy. I mean, bringing close to a thousand schoolchildren to watch the demolition of a playground for a high-rise parking lot— and stopping it, I might add—is terrific showmanship."

"It's a good opportunity, isn't it?"

Jack looked at her quizzically. "Yeah, I guess you could say that. Why? Is there some question . . . ?"

Rachel let out a loud, deep sigh, not unlike the one that Grayson had treated her to less than half an hour earlier. "It's just that it's such a double-barreled situation, you know?"

"No." He reached into the pocket of his jacket. "But maybe having a cigarette will help my comprehension."

"Grayson himself said that doing this story is going to destroy a lot of people's careers."

"Hey, don't tell me you're going all soft on us all of a sudden." Jack paused to light his Marlboro, his brow furrowing in what appeared an almost spiritual experience. "Don't forget that the careers you're going to be destroying belong to the slimeballs that are selling your planet down the river."

"Well, sure. That's true of some of the people." Thoughtfully Rachel stirred a packet of sugar into her coffee. "But if this turns out to be as big and as important as Grayson was making it sound, there are going to be repercussions for other people, too. I mean, what if some company closes down and all kinds of innocent people are suddenly out of a job?"

"That could well happen, my dear." Jack's tone was less than sympathetic. "But that would happen even if the government closed them down, or . . . or they got caught in some of the other shady dealings they're involved in, or—" He paused to take another drag of his cigarette. "Or if some other reporter broke the story, which is exactly what would happen if you backed down."

"Oh, I'm not going to back down," Rachel said. She sounded weak and uncertain, not at all like Lois Lane.

"That's my girl!" Jack sat back in the red-plastic-covered booth. "Now, let's talk about the up side of being at the top of the heap—which is where you have suddenly found yourself. How'd you manage it, anyway? What did you do, sell your soul to the devil?"

Rachel turned white. It was as if the force of gravity had suddenly exerted itself on her features. She seemed to age about thirty years.

"Oh, my God," she breathed.

"No, actually I don't think he makes deals," Jack said lightly. "I mean, I've been offering to negotiate for a bigger apartment for years, and I'm still in the same rent-controlled rat trap. . . . Rachel, what's wrong?"

She opened her mouth to speak, but no words came out. She reached for her coffee, took a few big gulps, and then set her cup down in its saucer with too much force.

"Nah, it's ridiculous," she said more to herself than to Jack.

"What's ridiculous?"

She started to laugh. "It's so ridiculous I can't even bring myself to tell you about it. You'd lose all respect for me."

Jack's response was predictable. "My goodness, Rachel, what makes you think I have any respect for you now?"

"It's . . . it's just craziness, that's all. I had this totally weird blind date a week or so ago, and this guy said . . . oh, never mind. Really. Look, let's order something."

"Oh, sure," Jack jeered. "Exclude me from lurid tales of your sex life. Keep me in the dark about those blind dates of yours with bizarre men capable of making you turn the color of Casper the Friendly Ghost."

Rachel chuckled. "I don't know what's the matter with me. I should be celebrating, not complaining. Honestly, how do you put up with me?"

Jack's eyebrows jumped up and down. "I'm just using you to get to your sister," he replied. In a much warmer tone of voice he added, "That, plus I'm hoping some of your good luck will rub off on me."

Chapter
Ten

"Really, *I'm not interested,*" insisted Rachel's neighbor, the fiftyish man down the hall whom she nodded to almost every day but with whom she had never exchanged a single word. "How did you get into the building, anyway?"

Rachel peeked her head out of the tiny room that had once been home to her apartment building's incinerator, but in these more environmentally conscious days had become a recycling dump for used magazines. She had just dropped off a thirty-pound stack of *Kid City*'s and *Sesame Street* magazines, taking advantage of Becky's absence to do a Saturday morning cleanup.

She had not expected to encounter any drama as she stepped out of her apartment in a pair of gray sweat pants and a baggy purple T-shirt. Yet here was an intriguing little scene unfolding right before her eyes.

"Look, I'm busy right now," her neighbor barked. "Bug off or I'll call the super."

The woman standing on his doorstep—on a mat printed with GO AWAY—was large in height, width, and breadth. She towered above Mr. Crabby, in fact, and he, Rachel estimated, stood at least six feet tall. She weighed in somewhere in the low two hundreds. Her hair had been dyed a color that did not exist in nature, a bold red-orange that could light up a dark alley. It was carefully set and sprayed. Her makeup was in similarly garish tones—tomato-red lipstick, two thick smears of robin's-egg-blue eyeshadow, lots and lots of rouge.

She obviously had money, if not much taste or moral fiber. Even though it was July, folded across the crook of her arm was a jacket that looked like real leopard skin. Her skin-tight black stretch pants would have been better suited to someone a third her age—not to mention a third her size. She was wearing spike heels, made of what looked like dyed alligator skin. Her jewelry was similarly flashy: large diamond earrings that looked too big to be real, an armful of bangle bracelets, a clunky necklace resting on her ample bosom. She was carrying a tote bag, olive-green plastic printed on the side with the logotype of Harrods.

The man down the hall was slamming the door in her face as Rachel attempted to slink back to her apartment, unnoticed. No such luck.

"Excuse me. Excuuuuse me," the woman bellowed, her voice not surprisingly matching the rest of her. "I have to speak with you, miss."

"I, uh, the . . ."

Rachel hesitated in her doorway, unable to follow her neighbor's lead and simply slam the door and triple-lock it. Being rude was not something that came to her easily.

In seconds the woman was on top of her. She stopped, gave Rachel the once-over, and frowned. In a hoarse voice thick with the accent of one of New York City's outer boroughs, she croaked, "So what's this? You're not wearing makeup?"

Rachel, caught completely off guard, immediately retreated to a defensive position. "It's nine-thirty on a Saturday morning. I'm supposed to be worried about whether I look like a Do or a Don't?"

The woman was shaking her head, obviously disapproving. "Such a pretty face, and you let it just sit there like a *latke*."

Rachel blinked. "Excuse me?"

"A *latke*. You know, a potato pancake. What, you're not from New York?" The woman sighed. "It's a good thing I'm here. It looks like I made it just in time."

"Just in time for what?"

"Look. I'll show you." Shaking her head—in disbelief or

perhaps in disgust—the woman walked right into Rachel's apartment. She dropped her tote bag onto the couch and began rummaging through it.

Rachel hurried in after her. As she glanced over her visitor's shoulder—no easy matter, since she was forced to stand on her toes—she saw that the bag was filled with a haphazard collection of junk, bottles and tubes and jars. The woman rifled through it until she found what she'd been looking for: a small *TV Guide*—size booklet. She held it out triumphantly.

"I'm your Avon lady," she announced, "and as I said, I got here just in the nick of time."

"Oh, dear." Suddenly it all made sense. "Look, before I take up any of your time, I have to tell you that I'm not in the market for cosmetics. I already have everything I need. In fact, I've got closets full of the stuff."

But the woman had already turned around and was scrutinizing Rachel's face close-up. So close-up that Rachel could hear her wheezing. It was as if carrying around all that heavy jewelry were too much of a strain for her.

"Those are some earrings," Rachel couldn't help commenting, confronted with them up close. "Are they Avon?"

"Are you kidding? These are real diamonds, honey." With an odd little smile she added, "I like supporting the South African government however best I can." She appeared to be studying Rachel's pores.

"And is that necklace, uh, ivory? I thought people were, you know, cutting back on ivory. The massacre of elephants and all that."

The woman shrugged. "Call me quirky. But enough about me. Let's take a look at you. What I see is, you got bags under your eyes, you got a few wrinkles here, you got a patch of dry skin over there. . . . You're too young for this. What are you, bucking forty?"

Rachel cringed. "I'm thirty-six."

The woman clucked disapprovingly. "And I see gray hairs. Look at this one here. It looks like it belongs on a fox terrier, not on a thirty-six-year-old woman. What, you don't own a mirror?"

"I just don't seem to have the time to fuss with things like that, that's all." Rachel had wanted to sound indignant, to imply by her icy tone that she had much more important things to worry about. Instead, her words came out sounding apologetic.

"Not enough time. Hah! That's everybody's excuse these days." The woman seemed exasperated. "Listen, I'm an expert on time. And believe me when I tell you that you've simply got to make the time. After all, if you don't look after yourself, who will?"

Rachel sank onto the couch, next to the leopard skin jacket. "I guess you're right," she admitted. "It's just that with my job and all, I'm always busy."

"Hey, don't think I don't know. Not enough time, not enough money, not enough energy ... But listen, I can help." She sat on the chair next to the couch, pulled the Harrods bag onto what there was of her lap, and once again began rummaging through all the clutter.

"I can put together a daily skin care regimen that you can do every morning lickety-split while you're listening to—you know, that woman, the one they got to replace the one who replaced Jane Pauley."

"Thank you, but ... how did you know I listen to the *Today* show while I'm getting dressed every morning?"

The woman waved her hand in the air. "You and everybody else in this town. Look, somewhere in this mess I got shampoo-in hair color that doesn't take any longer to use than that honey-lemon shit—pardon my French—you use. It costs a lot less, too."

Rachel's eyes popped open. "You mean you can smell my shampoo?"

"And listen. You just gotta try our new perfume. We're really pushing this stuff this month. It's called A Night in Heaven."

With a cackle she took out a small bottle and, pumping away at the atomizer with a thick finger, sprayed the room

again and again. The smell was horrible. Rachel, not wanting to be rude, took a little sniff and then began breathing
through her mouth. Even so, it was as if the perfume had
invaded every molecule of her body. She could still smell
it. In fact, she felt engulfed by it. It was making her head
throb, and she was beginning to get woozy.

"I got something else for you. It's this overnight
moisturizer that you're not gonna believe. Here, let me give
you a free sample."

As she handed the small white tube to Rachel, she cast
her a meaningful look. "This stuff can work miracles. And
believe me, I'm somebody who knows from miracles."

"Miracles, huh?" The perfume was making her feel light-
headed. Much to her amazement, she found she was actually warming up to the woman. "In that case, have you got
anything in that bag of yours that can find me a new man?"

She was trying to make a joke, a well-meaning attempt
at sharing a personal revelation. But the woman wasn't
laughing. In fact, when she looked up, her eyes were burning with a strange intensity. Rachel began to feel uncomfortable; there was something about her. . . . She began to
rub her temples in a futile attempt to lessen the throb in her
head.

"That's what you think would make you happy?" the
woman was saying. "A new man?"

"Not just any man," Rachel corrected her. She was having trouble focusing. It was that damned perfume. She
blinked hard a few times, wondering if the awful-smelling
stuff had gotten in her eyes. "The man who's—you know—
right for me."

"I know exactly what you mean." The woman was
nodding. "We're talking Mr. Right here. We're talking
somebody who's gorgeous, smart, successful, childless,
and madly in love with you."

All of a sudden Rachel's heartbeat shifted into fourth
gear. And the pain in her head reached a nearly excruciating level.

"Who are you?" she whispered.

The woman looked annoyed. "What, you have to ask?"

In the same breathy voice Rachel demanded, "Why are you here? What do you want?"

"Just doing a spot check, that's all." The woman shrugged. "I was wondering how you like the way things were going so far."

Even in her foggy state, Rachel understood. "The assignment," she said dully.

"What, you were thinking you got that because that Grayson guy likes you so much? After what happened with you and Mr. Feelgood?" The woman let out a loud guffaw. "Hah! Dream on."

"Oh, no," Rachel moaned. "I was afraid that was what was going on."

The woman stood up, her impressive bulk looming ahead of Rachel like a monolith. "Listen, you got some coffee? I'm telling you, this door-to-door stuff is hard work."

Rachel nodded. In a little-girl voice that barely sounded like her own, at least to her ears, she said, "I could make some coffee."

"Terrific. I take three spoons of sugar and plenty of half-and-half. And ya got anything to go with it? Some Entenmann's, maybe?"

"I don't have anything like that. I don't keep half-and-half in the house, either."

The woman gestured toward the kitchen with her chin. "I think you do, Rachel. Just take a look around."

With zombielike movements Rachel went into the kitchen and made a pot of coffee. Sure enough, when she looked in the refrigerator, there was an unopened container of half-and-half. And right next to it sat a white box containing an apricot danish.

Rachel hated apricot danish.

"So how does it feel, getting what you want?" the woman called from the next room. Rachel dutifully took the cream and the cake out of the refrigerator, set them both on the counter, and walked over and stood in the doorway, looking a little sheepish.

"It feels pretty good," she admitted.

"Pretty good?" the woman prompted, her head cocked to one side. She was wearing a wide, crooked grin. The odd shape of her mouth was emphasized by the gash of smeared red lipstick.

"It feels very good. As a matter of fact, I—I never knew I could feel so ... so fulfilled. So good about myself. So ... so ..."

"Go ahead," the woman urged Rachel. "You can say it in front of me. The H word."

"Happy," Rachel responded right on cue. "I never knew I could feel so happy."

"Hah! It does feel good, getting what you want, doesn't it? Despite what all those religious fanatics claim, there's definitely something to be said for the here and now. What is it that Janis Joplin used to sing? 'Get it while you can'? Words to live by, I always say."

She leaned over and patted the seat of the couch. "Come, sit down, my little Rachel. Tell Auntie Agnes all about how good it feels to get what you want."

"Agnes?" Rachel repeated, following her directions.

The woman shrugged. "It works for me. Now tell me everything."

Rachel began slowly. "All my life I've been striving for things. To do things, to accomplish things, to get the things I want. And it's fun to do that, in a way. But at the same time, there's always this frustration. Frustration that comes from the fact that the whole time you're out there, doing your best, knocking yourself out, you're never really certain whether or not you're actually going to get the payoff you so badly want."

She raised her hands to her temples again but discovered that as she talked, her headache was fading. "There's always so much involved that you can't control. It's like ... it's like you're on a merry-go-round, reaching for that brass ring. You know that, yes, you might get it. But there's an even better chance that you'll just fall off the horse. The merry-go-round will keep on going round and round, and you'll be sitting there with your butt sore and your skirt ripped, knowing that you went for it . . . and failed."

Agnes nodded. "Good girl," she said, her voice as soothing to Rachel as a caress. "All we're talking about here, after all, is you buying yourself a little insurance."

"Insurance?" Rachel repeated, her forehead wrinkling in confusion.

"Sure. You know, the way people buy car insurance to keep their car the way they want it, or health insurance to keep their health the way they want it. This is sort of like a new kind of *life* insurance." Agnes shrugged. "It's a way of being sure you can keep your life the way you want it."

Rachel looked over at her and nodded, acutely aware of how the perfume Agnes had sprayed had found its way into her entire apartment. But the odd thing was, it didn't smell bad anymore. In fact, it smelled wonderful.

The fragrance seemed to punctuate their conversation. That, too, was wonderful. Everything they were talking about seemed to make so much sense. Such beautifully perfect sense.

"Now, don't forget that skin cream I gave you," Agnes was saying in that same soothing voice. "It's important that you keep it. Use it every night, and don't forget to follow the directions. They're right on the back. Right under where it says all that stuff about *quadraginta quattuor dies*. But use it sparingly. It's only a *trial* size."

Her emphasis on the word *trial* made Rachel wonder if she was expected to offer to buy some. But then she remembered that this was one Avon lady who didn't particularly need to hawk the tubes of lipstick and gold-toned hoop earrings bought by women with a little extra cash after they'd paid off the electric company and the grocer and the baby-sitter. *Her* wealth came from much more lucrative sources.

"I'll be sure to try it," Rachel heard herself saying.

"Do that." The Avon lady looked at her with piercing eyes. "It's a great deal, I'm telling ya."

Rachel just nodded. "The coffee should be ready by now. You said you take three sugars, right?"

"That's a good girl," said Agnes.

When Rachel passed from the kitchen back into the living room, coffee in one hand and the Entenmann's apricot danish in the other, she felt a rush of coolness. And the smell of the perfume was completely gone. It was as if someone had opened both the windows and the door and allowed fresh, clean air to replace the stale air that had been trapped inside. She took a deep breath, aware that as she did so, the last lingering traces of the pounding headache she'd had only minutes before were completely gone.

Rachel wasn't at all surprised to find that all the windows and the door of her apartment were tightly shut. She was even less surprised by the fact that the Avon lady was gone.

Chapter
Eleven

It's not as if I can *tell* anybody about what's going on, Rachel thought as she sat cross-legged on the floor of her apartment, surrounded by books and pamphlets on just about every ecology-oriented movement that had ever existed—including Thoreau's *Walden*. If I had been any more honest with Dr. Ashwandi, he'd have me weaving baskets somewhere. And now, after what happened yesterday . . . Well, suffice it to say that reports of conversations about eyeshadow with the Avon lady from hell are not the kind of thing that sit well with the medical profession—or anyone else, for that matter.

It was first thing in the morning. The moment Becky headed out for day camp, Rachel hit the books. She was excited over the prospect of learning everything you ever wanted to know about save-the-earth organizations, background for her breakthrough article. Despite her noble intentions, however, she was having difficulty concentrating on the adventures of Greenpeace's boat, the *Rainbow Warrior*, instead agonizing over what on earth—or perhaps not—was going to happen to her next.

"Nothing, probably," she finally told herself, opening a back issue of *Mother Jones*. "Dr. Ashwandi was probably right. It probably *is* nothing more than stress. I really should try to schedule in a few more hot baths."

The telephone bleated. Rachel sighed, wondering if this was going to turn out to be one of those days when the most productive thing she would end up doing would be refilling the napkin holder.

"Hello?"

At the other end of the line she could hear a shushing sound.

"Hey, am I speakin' to Rachel? Rachel Swann?"

The voice was male, deep, and gave no indication of educational achievement beyond earning a solid C average in shop. Rachel's first thought was that this had to be a wrong number. Her second thought was that it couldn't be, not if the caller was asking for her by name.

"Speaking."

"Johnny here."

All confusion vanished. Rachel grabbed a pen, which, for a change, happened to be in the right place at the right time.

"You know who I am?" he went on.

"Yes, I do, Johnny. I've already spoken to ... yes, I know."

More shushing sounds. She realized that Johnny was calling from a pay phone, somewhere at the side of a road.

"I wanna meet with ya."

"Sure, sure. Just name the time and place."

"Okay, listen. There's a coffee shop at Twenty-third Street and Sixth Avenue. Y'know where that is?"

The heart of the fur district. A neighborhood in which men pushed racks of sable capes and lynx jackets down the sidewalk with the same casual air with which other men carried briefcases. "Yes, I can find it."

"Be there at one."

"Today?" Rachel croaked.

"Why, you too busy or something?"

No, smart-ass, I just didn't expect instantaneous results.

"Look, I'll be there. Uh, Johnny?"

"Yuh?"

"How will I know you?"

"Don't worry. You'll know me."

Sure I will, Rachel was thinking as she hung up the phone in response to the click and the dial tone she heard at the other end of the line. You'll be the guy in the black leather jacket, the one who looks like he's waiting for the casting call for *The New Dead End Kids*.

Johnny was a disappointment, totally lacking the colorful demeanor Rachel had been expecting. He was neither dark nor swarthy nor the owner of a black leather jacket. Instead, he was a lanky blond kid, probably in his early twenties, who actually had a gleam of intelligence in his eyes.

Just as he had promised, Rachel was able to pick him out of the late-lunch crowd at the Spartan Coffee Shop without any trouble. He was the only one in the joint wearing a Grass Roots T-shirt.

"D'wanna order?" he asked as she sat down at the corner booth, as far away from potential eavesdroppers as possible in a compact Manhattan coffee shop. "I'm havin' the vegetable plate myself. It's not bad in this place, though the sprouts could be fresher."

"Thanks, but I'm not very hungry."

"You meet somebody in a coffee shop, you gotta order something. Otherwise the owners get upset."

"Good point. I'll have iced tea. And a grilled cheese sandwich."

After ordering and then making the requisite amount of small talk, she folded her arms on the table in front of her. Some unidentifiable sticky substance immediately adhered to her skin, near the elbow. She chose to ignore it.

"So tell me, Johnny, how did you come to be involved with Grass Roots?"

"Well, let's see. I dropped outa college after two years—I was in school in Jersey, where I'm from—and I was kinda looking for somethin' to do. I hitched out to the West Coast with a friend of mine. Next thing you know, I'm in Portland, Oregon, of all places."

He grinned, for the moment becoming more boy than man. "Gosh, I mean whoever would've thought I'd end up in *Oregon*?"

"Life is funny that way. You never know where it's going to take you," she said, sounding like an ancient Chinese wise man. She nodded, encouraging him to go on.

"Anyways, I met this girl out there. She was active in this ecology group. Back then it was just starting to grow from a local thing to an organization with real presence. That was Grass Roots.

"Next thing I know," Johnny went on, sounding almost apologetic, "I kinda got into it. It was like the stuff they were saying made sense, y'know?"

"And what kind of stuff were they saying?"

"Actually, it's the kind of thing that everybody's saying these days. Only back then it was just startin' to heat up. They basically were saying that we all had to start makin' cleaning up the planet our highest priority. They said that if we didn't start doing that right away, treating it as an emergency situation, nothing else was gonna matter, anyway. Y'follow?"

"I follow." Graciously Rachel accepted her sandwich from the waiter. It turned out that she was hungry after all. Funny how the smell of grease could work up a person's appetite.

"So this group, Grass Roots, was basically made up of people—volunteers, I mean nobody was getting paid or nothing, not at first—who wanted to investigate companies that looked as if they might be bad polluters. You know, like maybe they were just keeping within the minimum government guidelines for pollution control, or maybe they were doin' stuff on the sly, like not disposing of toxic waste and garbage properly ... that kind of thing.

"What we'd do was target one particular company and then investigate just about everything it was doing. Whenever we found out they were doing something that wasn't kosher, we'd make a big stink in the media."

"It all sounds quite admirable." Rachel was sincere.

"Yeah, it was. Anyway, we started all this on a local scale, checking out businesses in the Portland area. Then we started to expand. Once we hit the cover of *Newsweek*, the contributions came rolling in. Things changed. All of a sudden we had the power to do our thing on a national scale. For the first time, there was money. Some of us even started collecting a salary. It was a really good time for everybody, you know? We were starting to make a difference. To be a real presence. To *matter.*

"Hey," he added proudly, "we even started getting hate mail."

"Yes, I can imagine." Rachel was nodding away nonstop, eager to show she was one of the good guys. "The whole thing sounds very exciting—and very worthwhile. Uh, let me ask you, Johnny. How did the organization choose the companies it was going to investigate?"

Johnny frowned, staring at his vegetable plate as if it were guilty of a lot more than simply containing sprouts that were over the hill. "To be honest, I wasn't involved in that at the beginning. We were told where we were supposed to go, and we went. I mean, I was only one of the little guys, and we weren't big on askin' a lot of questions."

"What exactly were you doing?" Rachel asked, wanting to clarify the term *little guys.*

"I was part of a team that would go into dumps and landfills and places like that to check out what was going on." He shrugged. "Not too glamorous, I guess ya could say, but somebody had to do it." This time, Rachel noted, he didn't look the least bit apologetic.

"But at some point you got involved?"

Johnny took a deep breath. When he began to speak, he had lowered his voice. Rachel's heartbeat quickened. They were about to get to the juicy part.

"After I'd been with Grass Roots for a couple of years, I started getting into the inside workings. Spending more time in the office instead of being out in the field all the time. I began finding out a little bit about how things worked, getting to know some of the people who made the organization run.

"I, uh, also had access to files, computer output, stuff like that." His voice was so low by this point that Rachel had to stop chewing in order to hear what he was saying. "That was when I got the shock of a lifetime."

She swallowed a wad of cheese. "Go on."

"I found out that some companies were paying off Grass Roots so as not to be investigated."

The unchewed mass of cheese stuck in her throat. "What?"

"Yeah, you heard me right. Turns out there can be corruption even in a group like Grass Roots. What was going on was that some companies who were getting a little nervous about the possibility that they might be next on our hit list were writing us checks with lots of zeros."

He shook his head, as if he still couldn't quite believe it. "That helps explain why we were gettin' so much money, now that we were big time, now that people were starting to listen when we spoke."

Rachel was struck by his unexpected loyalty to Grass Roots' ideals, this New Jersey boy who'd dropped out of college to hitch across the country to meet girls. He seemed as if he truly cared, as if he were not out for revenge or personal gain, but had a real interest in the purification of an organization whose goals had touched him—perhaps even given him a sense of purpose for the first time in his life. While the reporter in Rachel warned her to maintain a certain skepticism, Rachel's gut reaction was that he was sincere.

"There's more," Johnny went on. Once again his voice dropped a few hundred decibels. "Those corporate contributions—sometimes made in the companies' names, but more often not—were not all finding their way into Grass Roots' till. Some of that money was going to some of the people at the middle levels."

"Johnny, you're making some pretty heavy-duty accusations here. Before I knock myself out trying to verify them, I have to ask you: Are you completely convinced your information is correct?"

He nodded soberly. "I even got Xeroxes of checks and files to prove it. I can name names."

Glancing around the coffee shop and finding no one who looked particularly dangerous, he pulled out a manila folder. From what Rachel could tell, he'd been sitting on it.

"Look, here's one of the companies whose number was comin' up. I guess they got wind of it—maybe somebody inside Grass Roots made a point of telling them, I don't know. Anyway, they write us this letter, saying they applaud what we're doing and the U.S.A. needs more people like us, blah, blah, blah, and they're sending us ten thousand dollars to help further our cause."

Rachel scanned the letter, not even realizing she was still nodding. "I see. Uh-huh. The Bonnard Corporation of Yakima. What exactly do they do?"

His eyes were burning like a pair of sparklers on the Fourth of July. "Hospitals hire them to dispose of medical waste."

"Ah-ha." The cheese had by now made its way down into her stomach. It felt as if it had quadrupled in size.

Even so, she was experiencing a kind of euphoria she had rarely felt before. The adrenaline was pumping, her mind was functioning with supernatural clarity. Grayson was right; this *was* big. Bigger than even she had dared hope. So what if her source didn't have a cutesy name?

"I can feed you the names of the other companies involved in this kind of thing," Johnny went on. "If you're interested, I mean."

"Oh, yes. I'm interested, Johnny. I'm very interested. And so is *New York Life* magazine."

Johnny looked pleased. "So you think there's a story here, Ms. Swann?"

It was the first time he had called her by name. She was startled, as if she'd been caught off guard by hearing her name linked, for the first time, to what Johnny was telling her. It was her story. Her baby. The ball had just been passed to her, and she was responsible for running with it.

"Yes, I do, Johnny," she said evenly. "I definitely do."

And she knew, as she looked at him, that her eyes, too, were burning like a pair of sparklers.

* * *

Rachel was so exhilarated after her first clandestine meeting with Jersey Johnny—a nickname she found much racier than simply Johnny—that she decided to celebrate. And the place she celebrated best was Bloomingdale's.

She entered the department store on the Third Avenue side, a calculated choice on her part. Entering at Lex and Fifty-ninth would have meant being barraged by the pushy purveyors of pulchritude, as she liked to think of them—in other words, the cosmetics salespeople.

"Opium?" one would ask sweetly, brandishing a spray bottle.

"Obsession?" would come an offer from a shiny, red-lipsticked mouth.

No, no, *no*, Rachel would invariable cry, ducking from the intended assault. She often wondered why the candy department never resorted to the hard-sell approach.

The Third Avenue entrance put her right smack in the middle of the men's department. Silk neckties, leather wallets, shirts and socks and sweaters, all of them displayed calmly and rationally. Here there were no pushy purveyors to fight off, only businessmen and dapper dandies and staid female shoppers fingering the merchandise and frowning as they weighed the pros and cons, more often than not finding in favor of the pros.

Rachel immediately headed for the escalator, planning to head up to the second and third floors to engage in the act of browsing with the intent to buy. Passing through the men's department was simply a way of getting from here to there. But that didn't mean she couldn't enjoy the scenery. Lazily her eyes drifted over the delicious abundance of merchandise, the brilliant colors, the fine materials, the meticulous styling that just shouted *GQ*.

And then, suddenly, she froze. Lurking in the aisle between the hand-rolled linen handkerchiefs and the ninety-dollar leather wallets was Gayle Lefkowitz.

For almost two weeks Rachel had been avoiding her. Both of the chirpy messages Gayle had left on her telephone answering machine—actually, the first one chirpy, the second one closer to irritated—had gone unanswered. She had no desire to give a full report on her blind date. No doubt Gayle, matchmaker extraordinaire, expected a rave review—and normally Rachel could have risen to the occasion, calling upon that secret little-understood place deep inside her that would allow her to muster up enough enthusiasm for a discourse on her evening with Lance Firestone. In other words, she could have lied.

But that was under normal circumstances . . . and of course her evening with Lance Firestone had been anything *but* normal. So Rachel had done what any mature, intelligent, capable person would do: lie low and hope the problem would just go away.

Only it hadn't gone away. There it was, elbow deep in leather wallets and as big as any other Bloomingdale's shopper, trying to decide between the burgundy kidskin and the mahogany cowhide. Rachel panicked. All ability to reason vanished as she regressed to an animal state, dropping several substantial notches on the evolutionary scale. She took off, her mind filled only with the knowledge that to get away was to survive.

She turned a corner and found herself surrounded by an excess of soft fabrics, earth tones, and plaids. Her flight had led her straight to Ralph Lauren's Polo shop. She looked around, still alert, adrenaline pumping, her breathing so violent, it was only a step away from panting.

She spotted an exit just up ahead and made a beeline for it.

And then, "Oomph!"

Rachel had encountered an obstacle she hadn't anticipated, run smack into something with all her force. For a second she felt disoriented, a trifle confused. Then she looked up and found herself staring into the bluest, brightest, warmest eyes she had ever seen outside of a pet shop.

"You're a woman in a hurry," said a deep voice. And the eyes suddenly seemed to be laughing—not at her, but at the utter charmingness of the moment, the Fred Astaire–Ginger Rogers-ness of what had just happened.

Rachel just stared, blinking hard.

Fact or fantasy? she was thinking. But no answer was immediately forthcoming.

"I—I'm sorry," she stuttered. Slowly, through the fog, she was beginning to comprehend that the "obstacle" was a real person. A man, better looking than any one individual had a right to be. Slightly over six feet tall, she estimated, trim and muscular underneath a nubby cotton sweater the color of oatmeal, with thick brown hair, a delicious smile, and, of course, those eyes.

"Are you sorry? That's funny? I'm not."

His look was a challenge. Could Rachel rise to meet it? Under most circumstances, the answer would probably be yes. This time, however, she seemed to be more bowl of Jell-O than lightweight contender.

"I, uh, nearly knocked you over." She could feel her face turning redder than the Polo shirts folded on the wooden table right behind her victim.

"Not really. Actually, I'm a lot tougher than I look."

"Well, uh, next time I'll try to be more careful."

She eased away from him, embarrassed by the way she was reacting simply because she had just made bodily contact with a man who could have put Robert Redford to shame.

You should have been able to handle yourself a little more smoothly, she was thinking as she glided up to the second floor, sneaking a peek over her shoulder to see if he was still down there, in the crowd. But he was gone.

Still, a sweet feeling stayed with her as she "did" the second floor, attempting to root out some delicious tidbit that would serve as a tangible reward for her meeting with Johnny. She felt desirable, sexual, powerful . . . all because she had exchanged a few quips with a tall, fair, handsome stranger.

Actually, *he's* the one who did all the quipping, she reminded herself. I was simply . . . the quipee.

It took her the better part of an hour to bag her prey: a T-shirt dress, that perfect shade of blue that always made her eyes look luminescent. It was one of those purchases that was simply meant to be. Besides, any last doubts that may have lingered as she gazed lovingly at her own reflection in the mirror were shot down by the "40% off" scrawled in red across the price tag.

The dress was wonderful, one of those rare garments capable of making the wearer feel magically transported to a higher plane of existence. Sleek fit, cap sleeves that made it a strong contender for the "go-anywhere" category, and, of course, that color. *Her* color.

"I am woman," she could hear her reflection saying.

She responded in the obvious way. "I'll take it."

It was time for a coffee break, she decided. Clutching her Big Brown Bag in her hand, she rode up a few more escalators, luxuriating in her sense of triumph.

The Showtime Cafe was Bloomingdale's version of a coffee shop, one that appeared to have been decorated by a renegade designer from Disney World. The cute, heavily themed decor called upon a black and white color scheme against a backdrop of pink, colors that at some point had apparently been deemed Hollywoodesque. The whole thing was undoubtedly an attempt at taking the customer's mind off the prices of the upscale food, served cafeteria style.

After deciding she couldn't quite bring herself to indulge in the eight-dollar fruit salad, Rachel opted for a cinnamon danish and that much-coveted cup of joe. She headed toward a free table, fan-shaped plastic tray in hand, and sat down, planning to relish her few minutes of break time.

So she was surprised when someone pulled out the chair opposite her. And even more surprised when she saw who it was.

"This time you can't knock me over. There's a table between us," said Mr. Blue Eyes.

There it was again, the quipping. Rachel was beginning to understand where the concept of Prince Charming had come from.

"You don't mind if I join you, do you?" he went on.

The question was moot, since he had already done so. From his tray he took a cup of coffee and the fruit salad. A man with a strong sense of entitlement. She kind of liked that.

"The store's not as crowded as usual" was all she could come up with. She smiled, a smile that asked for his forgiveness.

But he acted as if she had just introduced a really fascinating topic.

"No, it's not. And I'm surprised. I had to exchange something, and I was dreading it. I figured I'd have to wait on line forever. Instead, I was in and out of there in ten minutes."

Almost apologetically, he added, "My parents got me a sweater for my birthday, and it was much too small. I guess they still think I'm twelve years old."

Rachel laughed. "Parents are like that."

"I don't usually go for those designer things, and I was thinking of exchanging it for something more practical. But . . . well, they're my parents."

What was this? A man who actually respected his parents? Rachel also made the observation that said parents were definitely in the well-to-do category. Ralph Lauren sweaters did not come cheap. Even in the twelve-year-old size.

"How about you?" he went on, looking sincerely interested. "Did you have any luck?"

"Actually, I did. I wanted to buy myself a little reward. And sure enough, I found it."

"A reward?"

Rachel hesitated. They had just met. In fact, she wasn't sure that they had actually met at all.

"I'm a journalist, and a few days ago I got the kind of assignment I've been dreaming about practically my whole career. I started doing some work on it this morning, and it seems to be going well, so . . ."

"Good for you!" He looked truly pleased for her.

Rachel was astounded. A man who asked questions, who reacted with warmth, who knew how to carry on a conversation . . . she found herself wondering how many teenage children he had.

Which brought her to the obvious question: Was this Mr. Blue Eyes married? Her heart sank. She took a big bite of her danish to counteract it.

"How about you?" she asked, not quite sure yet how to broach the subject. True, he wasn't wearing a wedding ring. But then, they rarely did. "What do you do?"

"I run my own company."

"Really?" That explained why he was exchanging sweaters at Bloomingdale's between nine and five on a weekday.

"What does your company make?"

"Toys."

Certainly better than nuclear warheads or girlie magazines, Rachel was thinking as she nodded and said the requisite "Oh!" But does that mean he lacks maturity? Is he one of those guys who spends his Saturdays playing Nintendo, giggling like a boy whose voice hasn't changed yet?

And then she could hold out no longer.

"Is this a family business?" she asked with a pretty smile. "You know, something you and your *wife* run together?"

She braced herself for what was to come: *Oh, no, my wife is a model and a heart surgeon* or *Why, yes. In fact, she's the heart and soul behind our multimillion-dollar firm.*

Instead, he said simply, "I'm single."

And then he added the words that every unmarried woman in an advanced state of Totally Charmed longs to hear: "I guess I just haven't met the right woman yet."

By the time the coffee was gone and Rachel had eaten her danish and a good third of the man's fruit salad, they were moving along at a nice pace. They had a lot in common, they found, things ranging from the mundane— hazelnut gelato, Mickey Rourke, crossword puzzles—to the global, particularly the great concern for the cleanliness of the planet. On this last issue it was all Rachel could do to keep from spilling the beans about her current investigative writing project. But keeping it secret until publication was the name of the game, so she managed to keep hold of her beans.

"By the way," he finally said, "you haven't told me your name."

"Rachel Swann."

"Pleased to meet you, Rachel. My name is Ryder. Ryder Thorn."

A name to match the rest of him, she was thinking as the two of them reached earnestly across the empty cups and the remains of the fruit salad to shake hands. But she realized that with the disappearance of the food, they were running out of excuses to be together. Rachel started to grow anxious.

"I guess we'd better get a move on," he said, glancing around and noticing that a group of four tray-bearing Japanese businessmen was eyeing their table covetously.

"I guess we'd better."

"Listen, I, uh, don't usually do this, but, uh—" A flush rose to Ryder's cheeks. "Do you think maybe you and I could get together sometime?"

"Wait a second. You mean outside of Bloomingdale's, right?"

Rachel was rewarded with a chuckle. She was glad that once again she had found the presence of mind to do some quipping of her own.

"How about if I give you my phone number? Here, I'll tear off the edge of this shopping bag and write it down. . . ."

"You could just tell me," he suggested. "I'll remember." In response to her quizzical look, he added, "I have a very good memory."

He'll never call, she was thinking as she walked away, feigning an interest in checking out the sheet department when in reality she simply wanted to avoid the embarrassment of riding down six escalators with him, only to have to go through the good-bye process all over again. But she fully realized that the only reason she was thinking such thoughts was to protect herself.

This time around, she sensed, she wouldn't need to.

Chapter
Twelve

"*Rachel? Are you still up?*"

The only thing worse than picking up the telephone at nine-thirty P.M. and finding my ex-husband at the other end, thought Rachel, is hearing Boyd talk to me in that annoyingly patronizing tone that he's perfected.

His question was particularly irritating given the fact that Rachel had of late begun running on a strange new kind of energy, even though she was doing none of those things that were supposedly guaranteed to put zip in one's step: no oat bran, no B_{12}, no brewer's yeast in her morning coffee. In fact, she rarely took the time to eat at all. She wasn't even logging in the recommended eight hours of shuteye, since all of a sudden she was too keyed up to sleep more than a few hours a night. Even Becky had noticed.

"Mommy," she accused Rachel one evening, hands on nonexistent hips, "have you been stealing my Flintstones vitamins?"

This new level of energy came from Rachel's excitement over her new project, the investigation of the Grass Roots scandal. She found that loving what she was doing, being totally wrapped up in it, quickly made irrelevant such mundane concerns as sleeping past sunrise and ingesting representatives of the four basic food groups.

These days she buried herself in her work. She holed up in the New York Public Library for hours at a time, continuing her mission of soaking up every word that had ever been written about the ecology movement, especially Grass Roots. She made countless telephone calls, chasing after every name she could get her hands on. It was fun, trying to find out more without giving away her little secret. At night, after reading a couple of Curious George books to Becky, she should have been too tired to do anything besides watch *Gilligan's Island* reruns; instead, she headed straight for her word processor, sitting there until the wee hours.

That was precisely what she was doing when Boyd interrupted her concentration.

"Yes, Boyd, I'm up," she replied tartly. "What is it?"

"I was calling to make you an offer you can't refuse."

She could feel her defenses locking into place like a suit of armor. "Let's hear it."

"How would you like the weekend off from mothering?"

"Boyd, you know that our agreement is that Becky—"

"Relax, Rachel. It's just one weekend. I'm not stealing her away . . . yet. Something special has come up. A friend just invited me out to his summer house in the Hamptons. The guy's got a pool, a tennis court, a Jacuzzi. . . . Becky would love it."

"Right. Becky's been saying she wants to work on her serve."

"Come on, Rachel. Don't stand in her way."

And will Ariana be there, brushing up on her mothering skills? Rachel wondered. But she didn't dare ask.

"All right, Boyd."

"Great. I'll be by on Friday around five."

"I'll make sure I pack her tennis whites."

She was about to return to her work when the telephone rang again.

"What now?" she muttered. Into the phone she barked, "What is it, Boyd?"

"Actually," said a voice she didn't readily recognize, "it's Ryder Thorn. Bloomingdale's, remember?"

Instantly Rachel was reduced to the proverbial schoolgirl, twirling the phone wire around her fingers, blushing to her hairline. "Of course I remember. Hello, Ryder."

"Good. I was calling to ask how you'd feel about having

dinner with me tomorrow night." He sounded completely self-confident. There was none of the usual embarrassing hemming and hawing, the endless chatter about the weather and health and all kinds of other pointless topics that would-be dates so often indulged in.

"Dinner sounds wonderful."

"I was hoping you'd say that. How does seven o'clock sound?"

"Great."

Rachel suspected that he'd already gone ahead and made the reservations. Instead of feeling manipulated, however, she was pleased. It wasn't that she was being taken for granted. Instead, it was simply a given that the two of them belonged together on a Friday night, laughing over red wine and fresh linguine.

The next evening Rachel dragged herself away from her computer at six. She carried out the usual predate routine— the showering, the disgusted wrestling with hair, the application of makeup accompanied by the heartfelt conclusion that every single shade she owned was wrong—but meanwhile experienced none of the usual nervousness or ambivalence about the evening ahead. She was looking forward to it, she realized, in a way that she had never looked forward to her time with Howard. Not even back at the beginning, when his bald spot still seemed cute.

As she stood in front of her closet, she wondered what type of restaurant Ryder would be likely to choose for their first date. On the one hand, he could go for a sophisticated place, one with appropriately rude waiters, inflated prices, and memorable sauces. She shuddered at the image, remembering the last time she'd endured an evening out with a man she didn't know very well. On the other hand, he could well go for a funkier-type place. One with loud music, perhaps, or the ethnic cuisine of some country that, most of the time, had its population living on bags of rice and Spam that the U.S.A. had sent over.

In the end, Rachel decided upon her new T-shirt dress, the one she'd bought the day she met Ryder. That seemed like a good omen. She dressed it up with some silver Native American jewelry, large pieces decorated with geometric designs that she suspected meant Give us back our land. A spritz of perfume, her beige Capezios, and she was ready for an evening of wining and dining—as opposed to *whining* and dining, as was the pattern with her last beau.

So she was caught totally off guard when she opened the door of her apartment and found that Ryder—standing there, grinning, looking so much at ease that it was as if he were the one who lived there, not her—was wearing more corduroy, suede, and nubby cotton than a university professor on his day off.

"Oh, I, uh . . ." she greeted him.

But he smoothed right over her confusion. "How does this sound? A late dinner on the terrace, overlooking a gorgeous lake about twenty feet away, sipping cold champagne and watching the moonlight flirt with the water. . . . Then an early morning swim, followed by a picnic brunch . . . an afternoon poking around quaint shops, chatting with colorful antiques dealers who are like something out of a novel. . . ."

Rachel was beginning to get the picture. "How does it sound? It sounds like heaven. What is this, some wonderful bed and breakfast you've found?"

"Not quite. It's a weekend place that belongs to my family."

"They stock the fridge with champagne?"

Ryder smiled. "You should see what else I've got packed in the trunk."

"Well, then." Rachel took a deep breath. "I guess I should change my clothes and throw a few things into a suitcase."

"I'll wait downstairs with the car. I'm double-parked."

A car. A family with a house on a lake. Better manners than David Niven. Is this really happening? Rachel wondered.

Moving faster than a speeding bullet, she pulled off the dress and pulled on a pair of jeans, the first pair of pants

she came across. A week ago they'd been a little snug.
Now, thanks to her lack of interest in food, they not only
zipped and snapped with ease, they also made her look
lanky. A few sweaters, shorts and T-shirts, a bathing suit—
two bathing suits—tossed into a tote bag. Next came a
quick sweep inside the bathroom. Not wanting to get stuck,
Rachel grabbed everything she could get her hands on.

Am I nuts? she was asking herself all the while. Going
off to a strange place with a man I barely know? Even if
he doesn't turn out to be Charles Manson's long-lost
brother, it's still rather extraordinary. Whatever happened to
the debate over whether or not you should kiss the guy on
the first date?

As she dumped her cosmetics into her bag, not even
bothering to pick out the Band-Aids and the dandruff shampoo, she reminded herself that she was a grown woman
who didn't have to do anything she didn't want to do.

"Ah," she said aloud, glancing into the mirror, "but I
want to. I *want* to."

His car was a Honda, she was relieved to see. No Jaguar,
no BMW, no flashy yuppie car to alert her to the fact that
there was a strong possibility of an overly strong attachment to acquiring and impressing. Ryder looked very much
at home in it as he sat at the wheel, grinning at her conspiratorially.

"All set?" he asked before putting the car into gear.

A quick glance over her shoulder, a triumphant wave to
her doorman, and they were off.

"I figured this would give us a chance to get to know
each other," he said matter-of-factly as he sailed confidently
through northbound traffic on FDR Drive. The six-lane
road was packed with other urban escapees panicked over
the prospect of spending a long, hot weekend in the city.
"Without any distractions, I mean."

"We should certainly know each other after spending an
entire weekend together," Rachel replied.

"Hey, you're not put off by this, are you?" Ryder
glanced over at her. There was concern in his blue eyes.

Rachel could feel herself melting into the seat. "I mean, I hope it's not too much."

"No, it's not too much. I wouldn't have agreed to come if I thought it was too much."

"Well, I'll tell you what. We can make a deal."

With the confidence that appeared to accompany just about everything he did, Ryder eased the car into fourth gear and smoothly crossed over into the fast lane. Rachel wondered if he made love with that same confidence. When she realized that she would probably have the opportunity to do some firsthand research if she so chose, she blushed.

"Let's make a pact. If you want a break, if you need time out," he said, "just say the word. I guess I should have mentioned that the house we're going to isn't exactly a one-room log cabin."

Rachel attempted to clarify his point. "You mean I can have a room to myself."

Ryder looked over at her again, but this time his expression was sheepish. "You can have an entire floor to yourself."

"I see. And where exactly is this lakeside mansion?"

"Upstate. About two hours' drive. So sit back, relax, and start deciding whether you want cold roast duck or grilled salmon for dinner."

When she cast him a puzzled look, not certain if he was joking or not, he explained, "There's a little barbecue grill up there."

And then he snapped his fingers, the ones that weren't busy negotiating the car onto the ramp headed toward the George Washington Bridge. "I almost forgot. I packed a little snack for the ride. I figured you'd be hungry. I know I am. Here, reach over the seat . . . see, back there? That bag?"

The paper bag from E.A.T. on Madison Avenue contained pâté, an assortment of French cheeses, and English water crackers.

"What, no caviar?" Rachel joked.

Ryder looked surprised. "I didn't know if you liked it. Not everyone does."

"Tell me, Ryder," Rachel said, arranging the delicacies on her lap and across the open glove compartment door, "how did someone like you get into the toy business?"

"I guess part of me is still a kid," he replied with a chuckle. "I get a kick out of the littlest things. My company specializes in wooden toys—you know, the old-fashioned kind like wagons and trains and those ducks on a string that little kids can pull around the house."

"I know the type." Rachel was nodding. "The ones grown-up people are always reminiscing about, saying, 'Hey, remember those little wooden ducks on a string? Those were great. How come they don't make those anymore?' "

"Well, we're still making them. But we've also expanded into educational toys. I'm not talking about those high-tech computerized jobbies where it's the computer that has all the fun. Not that we don't use all the technology that's available. But I'm talking about toys that make kids think, that force them to interact. The kind that teaches them things—basic things—without the kids even realizing they're learning.

"Anyway, the point is that nothing comes into our product line unless I personally get a kick out of it. It has to make me laugh or at least engage me for more than half an hour. I have to long to play with it again after I've left it behind. I have to lie awake in bed nights, thinking of new things to do with it.

"You should see this new thing we've just developed. We're about to show it at the big Toy Fair that's coming up. That's when all the Christmas orders come in, so it's a real make-or-break time. But I just know this is going to fly. It's called a Rubber Rainbow, and it's the coolest thing. . . ."

Ryder suddenly stopped, his cheeks pink. "Sorry. I didn't mean to get so carried away. I'll have to show it to you sometime." Laughing self-consciously, he added, "I guess you could say I'm my own market research department."

"It certainly sounds as if you love what you do," Rachel observed with admiration.

"Yeah, I figure you have to. If you're not having fun at what you're doing five or six days out of every week, then something is definitely wrong."

"I guess I'm flattered that you've taken some time off to . . . you know."

"To spend the weekend with you, you mean?" He looked at her for a long time, smiling. "I'm the one who should be flattered, Rachel."

Just as Ryder had promised, his family's little hideaway was, indeed, more than a one-room log cabin. It was more like a Victorian house that just happened to have been plunked down next to a lake. With its playful pink and lavender and baby-blue gingerbread trim, the wooden swing on the front porch, and the manicured flower beds all around, it looked like something out of a storybook. In fact, as she caught her first glimpse of it, Rachel found herself wondering if Pollyanna herself was secretly a member of the Thorn clan.

"So what do you think?" asked Ryder, lifting boxes and suitcases out of the back of the car.

"It's . . . it's . . . I'm overwhelmed."

She surmised that this house had at one time been part of a small summer community, the warm-weather retreat of wealthy city people. More than a dozen houses of the same period dotted the land that curved around the lake. Rachel could imagine this place at the turn of the century, when wives and children summered up here and Dad stayed in town, earning the money necessary for maintaining a multiple-dwelling life-style, sowing whatever wild oats he could while the rest of the family was stashed away.

She could see it all: girls in starched white dresses and big hair ribbons; impish little boys with slingshots and pockets full of frogs; church picnics and hoop-rolling con-

tests and awards for the best homemade peach pie—no
doubt made by a servant and then credited to the lady of
the house. The setting spoke of innocence, of an easier
time, of a sense of leisure that would probably never again
be recaptured.

"Come on inside," Ryder offered, looking very much at
home as he strode toward the front door, suitcases in hand.
"I'll show you around."

All three levels of the house, including the large single
room that comprised the attic, were furnished in antiques,
heavy wooden pieces that were consistent with the feeling
of the architecture. Instead of being oppressive, however,
the boldly patterned chintz fabrics in bright colors and the
ornate side tables and secretaries and armoires helped to
complete Rachel's notion that she was being permitted a
wonderful, if temporary, step back in time.

The bedrooms each had four-posters covered with hand-
worked quilts. The front room had a big fireplace, at one
time the only source of heat in the house, now used when
the season was extended into the fall or an unexpected cold
spell threatened to put a damper on summer frolic. Even the
bathrooms were perfect, with claw-footed tubs and marble-
topped washstands.

"It's magnificent," Rachel breathed, following her enthusiastic tour guide through the house. She glanced around,
wondering if there could possibly be any more, then noticed
the stairs leading up to the attic. "What's up there?"

"An attic. We can go up, if you're not afraid of a few
spiders."

She didn't see any spiders, but she did see a fascinating
collection of antiques. Odd pieces of furniture, trunks, dusty
photograph albums so packed with black and white snap-
shots that they would not quite stay closed. There was a
bentwood coat rack, slightly damaged, and two raccoon
coats covered in plastic. There was even a lumpy old bed
pushed next to the window, as if uncles or grandfathers occasionally snuck up there to take a catnap in relative peace.

"Ryder, this attic is incredible. It's like something out of a Walt Disney movie!"

"Yeah, this is kind of a fun place. Nowadays it's become kind of a general storage area for my parents and anybody else who needs a place to keep things. But in the old days . . ."

Lovingly he ran a finger along the dusty cover of one of the photograph albums. "I remember coming here every summer as a kid. Boy, it was great. On rainy days we would spend hours up here in the attic, playing. We would make up games—like Sherlock Holmes or haunted house—and use all this stuff as props. We had so much fun."

A glazed looked had come into his eyes.

"What about on sunny days?" Rachel prompted him, touched by his sentimentality. "There must have been many more of those."

"Oh, sure. Then we'd all be outside all day. Me and my brother and my sister, not to mention all the cousins who used to end up here for weeks at a time. We'd leave the house right after breakfast, and no one would see us again until dinnertime. At least, that's how I remember it.

"Now that I'm looking back on it, though," he said with a chuckle, "we were probably dropping into the kitchen every ten minutes for cookies or Kool-Aid or peanut butter and jelly sandwiches."

The glazed look was still in his eyes. "But we'd have incredible summers up here. There would always be a lot of kids around to play with. We'd go swimming or canoeing or play Indian scout in the woods around here. Or sometimes we'd get on our bikes and just take off, without any idea of where we were going. At night we'd build bonfires on the shore and tell ghost stories and toast marshmallows—you know, all that stuff you're supposed to do when you're a kid."

"It sounds great," Rachel observed, a little envious. "You know, I don't remember doing too much of that stuff when I was a kid."

He looked at her intently, his focus suddenly entirely on

her. "There's no reason we can't start doing it now," he said matter-of-factly.

Ryder volunteered to single-handedly take on the task of getting dinner ready. In the meantime, he suggested, why didn't she go upstairs and get settled in in what had been designated as "her room"?

There had been no discussion of who would sleep where, aside from her original intimation that the question concerned her. Instead, at one point during their tour of the magnificent house, Ryder simply said, "Here. This can be your room." They were standing in the doorway of a room with pink and white striped wallpaper and more ruffles than a Laura Ashley blowout sale.

She indulged in a bit of fantasy as she dumped her cosmetics into an empty basket she found in the bathroom. She decided to pretend she was the heroine in a romance novel.

"I've just come to stay at the house of Lord . . . Lord Periwinkle," she muttered, correcting her posture as she caught her reflection in the full-length mirror. Suddenly she was a swan, or at least a ballerina pretending to be a swan. "My name is Lady . . . Lady . . . Lady—"

"Dinner is served!" she heard Ryder call from below.

Arranging her mouth into a serene smile, Rachel floated down the stairs, her jeans and T-shirt magically converted to a formal gown made of the finest silk, her multicolored Swatch watch a pearl and diamond bracelet, her ponytail a sleek chignon. Then she realized that, Lord Periwinkle aside, there really was no one else in the world, either real or made up, whom she would rather be having dinner with than Ryder Thorn.

He had lit a fire in the fireplace—not really necessary, although it was cooler here than it had been in the city. Even so, it was a fine touch. Spread out on a blanket right in front of the fireplace was the food he had promised: cold duck, a basket of berries, and a bottle of champagne with two crystal glasses. Simple, but to the point. Rachel wondered if women in the 1990s ever swooned.

"This is so nice," she cooed a few minutes later, staring

into the fire and relishing the taste of the berries mixed with the champagne. "You've really thought of everything, haven't you?"

He shrugged modestly. "I figured if you're going to do something, you should do it right."

In a voice that was a bit more strained, he added, "It was important to me that we get things started on the right foot."

" 'Things'?" she repeated, knowing she was teasing but unable to resist. Maybe it was the blue eyes, maybe it was the intensity behind them, but something about Ryder made her feel more alive than she ever had before. It was like being in a play, a wonderful, perfectly constructed play, knowing what the outcome was going to be but still savoring every moment it took to get there. "What do you mean, exactly, by 'things'?"

"You and me," he said. His blue eyes were burning into hers. The glass of champagne on the floor beside him had been forgotten. "Don't you feel it? Isn't it just as clear to you as it is to me?"

She nodded, hoping he meant what she thought he meant. "That we belong together?" Her voice was husky, as if she were barely able to get the words out.

"Yes," he replied. "It's like this . . . this feeling of inevitability. Of certainty."

"But is it real?" Rachel's body language gave away what she was thinking. She was curled up into a little ball, all her defenses firmly in place. "I—I don't think it would do either of us any good to get swept away, to rush into something when we really don't know—"

"We have time," he interjected. "And I have no intention of rushing you." He paused, then added, "Rachel, I want you to be as certain about this as I am."

She waited, holding her breath. She was waiting for him to reach for her, to take her hand or put his arm around her shoulders. Instead, he stayed exactly where he was, the question still in his eyes. She understood then that he was going to wait for her to come to him.

The mood shifted then, with Ryder entertaining her with more tales of his idyllic childhood. Timeless summers up here at the lake, a fairly stable family life, all the advantages without any real pressure. It wasn't until later, he mentioned casually, that the tension between him and the rest of his family arose. He moved on quickly, making it clear that was one topic he wasn't in the mood for.

As he spoke, Rachel continued to be struck by how much at ease Ryder was with himself. Then, when it was her turn to fill him in on her own past and present, she found him an eager listener, someone who sincerely wanted to know more about her.

"Well, I guess it's getting late," he said finally, glancing at his watch. "Gee, did you realize it's past midnight?"

"I'm tired," Rachel admitted. "I put in a full day. And that was before I found out I was going to be taking a trip back in time, camping out in the Twilight Zone."

Ryder laughed. "Let me know if there's anything you need." He stood and began gathering up some of the plates and silverware from their fireside picnic. "There are towels in the bathroom and you'll find just about anything else you could possibly think of in the closet. You should be comfortable."

He gave her one more long look before turning and heading toward the kitchen with his hands full. "Good night, Rachel," he said in a soft voice. "Sleep tight. Don't let the bedbugs bite."

She lay in bed for a long time, surprised by her sleeplessness. Lying there, surrounded by Victorian splendor, was an odd experience. She should have felt misplaced, disconcerted by having ended up in a situation like this. After all, it was a far cry from what she'd been expecting six hours earlier. Instead, she felt at peace, as if, all the trappings aside, she were where she belonged.

And she knew perfectly well it wasn't the house. It wasn't even the idea of a delicious little lost weekend.

It was Ryder.

And then she knew why she was having trouble sleeping. She got out of bed and crept down the stairs to the room Ryder had staked out as his own. It was a den filled with lots of hearty male plaids and cool dark tones, fitted with a fold-out bed. Without reservation, without ambivalence, she went over to the partially open door and knocked.

"Rachel, are you all right?"

"I'm fine, Ryder." She walked shyly into his room, able to make him out easily in the moonlight shining in through the curtainless window. "I just . . . I just wanted to be with you."

She sat down on the edge of his bed, dressed in the cotton nightshirt she had so hurriedly thrown into her tote bag.

"Are you sure?" he asked, still not touching her.

"Yes." She reached for his hand then, finding it warm and strong. She held it in both of hers. "It's so strange. You know, we hardly know each other."

"That's funny," he replied. "I feel as if we've known each other all our lives."

She leaned down then to kiss him. He kissed her back gently, still not completely certain, still not wanting to rush her.

"I have a good idea," she said, pulling back. "Let's go upstairs, into the attic."

"The attic?"

She nodded, giggling a little.

"What, have you got a thing for spiders?"

"I like that room. I like the bed up there, next to the window. And I like the idea that probably no one else has ever made love up there before."

"I wouldn't bet on that." He was grinning, already climbing out of bed. He was trim and muscular, Rachel observed, and not at all self-conscious as he pulled on a robe. "But I'm game."

They made love like two people who did, indeed, know each other well. There was no nervousness, no tentativeness. There was only a sincere desire to connect. Rachel let herself go, wondering for a fleeting moment how what she and Ryder were doing could possibly be the same thing that she and Howard had labored over together so many times.

Afterward, after Ryder had fallen asleep with a tattered quilt partially pulled over him, she stayed awake for a while, just watching him. She was trying to absorb him, to know him even better than she already did. It was still so difficult to believe what had happened, the way it had happened, the certainty with which she was proceeding.

And if Gayle hadn't happened to be in Bloomingdale's the same time I was, lurking in the men's department, where I happened to be, I never would have met Ryder, she mused. Funny how things work. There's so much coincidence in life, so many important things that are nothing more than the result of random occurrences. . . .

As she reached out to place her hand on his shoulder, a chill suddenly ran over her.

It *was* coincidence, wasn't it? It really was nothing more than a random occurrence . . . right?

She drew in a deep breath.

In a soft, hoarse voice, one that was barely audible, she said, "Who are you, Ryder Thorn? Who are you . . . and where did you come from?"

Chapter Thirteen

"What a weekend," breathed Rachel, flopping across the couch.

It was late Sunday morning, and she had just floated into her apartment building. Her head and her heart were filled with Ryder. Her hands, meanwhile, were filled with the doggy bag he had foisted upon her with the determination of a mother.

Part of her feared that it hadn't really happened at all, that her overactive writer's imagination had conjured it up out of loneliness, desperation, and a need to fixate on something besides the Grass Roots scandal. Yet there was enough solid evidence to convince Miss Marple. Exhibit A was her blue T-shirt dress, Friday evening's discard, still draped across the chair. Exhibit B was the doggy bag. The leftover duck and the French cheese were emitting sufficient fragrance to stand up in any court of law.

Exhibit C was her favorite. From her purse Rachel pulled out the strip of four black and white photographs that she and Ryder had had taken by one of those machines that ate quarters and, in return, spat out a comic strip featuring you and yours. She snipped it in half, forming a square with two pictures on the left and two on the right.

With determination she picked up the picture frame that held Howard's photograph. In one fell swoop she banished the familiar bald head, tossing it into the trash basket. As she did, a fanfare sounded deep inside her brain. The new photos fit perfectly.

Now that she was home, reality beckoned. Yet she postponed responding to the red light on her telephone answering machine. There was plenty of time to catch up. For now she slipped off her shoes, settled back against the couch cushions, and closed her eyes.

She wanted to relive, just one more time, some of the highlights of her weekend with Ryder. Sex easily topped the list. That was a surprise—a welcome surprise. And not just the physical part; even more mind-boggling was the fact that afterward, she and Ryder actually had something to say to each other.

I'd forgotten how good it can be, she thought, hugging herself. Letting go like that, living in my body instead of exclusively in my mind . . .

But the list went on. What was even more amazing to her was that she and Ryder had actually had *fun* together. Fun. Now, that was a word that didn't apply much to adult life. Oh, sure, there was fun, but it was more along the lines of a party at which the guests were unusually animated. Or a movie that had earned that label from a reviewer. Running into a long-lost friend was characterized as "fun."

But the kind of fun she and Ryder had had . . . that was in a different category altogether. They'd had the belly laughs, experienced the letting go, reveled in the exhilaration that children feel sledding down a steep, icy hill or playing duck-duck-goose or sticking their hands into jars of finger paint and running them over sheets of white paper.

In short, they'd enjoyed the kind of fun that most people let go of once they leave childhood behind, not because they intend to, but because they simply *forget*. It wasn't supposed to be part of adult life. Behaving oneself and being responsible and fitting in supposedly earned an individual the rewards of adulthood, not laughing so hard that your stomach hurt, or doing something you'd never done before even though you were bound to be terrible at it, or forgetting all about everything except what you were doing at that very moment.

With Ryder, she had remembered. They had had so many

moments like that. They had gone skinny-dipping at the old swimming hole he had frequented as a child, whooping and screeching as they swung on a rope, Tarzan-style, then dropping thirty feet into the ice-cold water. They had lain in the cool grass after stuffing themselves with almost an entire pound of chocolate chip cookies. They had puttered around in the local shops, buying each other little surprises, toys and postcards and silly trinkets that would no doubt be saved for a long, long time.

And it's not over, Rachel reminded herself. In fact, she was certain that what she and Ryder had found in each other had barely begun.

"Enough!" she shouted suddenly, jumping off the couch. "No more mooning around. Like it or not, Rachel Swann, it's time to get back to real life."

She switched on the telephone answering machine, packing away her leftovers in the refrigerator as she listened.

"Rachel, where *are* you?" demanded Sis in an excited voice. "Call me, will you? The minute you get in!"

Vincent was probably crowned king of the Eagle Scouts, Rachel thought wryly, deciding that one could wait.

Next there was a call from Molly, pleading with her to call back and tell her whether or not Jack liked Thai food. In response, Rachel simply shook her head in amazement. Then came a couple of hangups—possibly calls from Johnny.

It was the last phone message that really caught her off guard. At the sound of the familiar voice, one she hadn't heard in a long time, she tensed up.

"Rachel? This is Howard." There was a pause. "Hey, long time, no see." Hearty laughter—*forced* hearty laughter. "I was, uh, just wondering how you were doing. I wanted to say hello, to see what was up. . . . Hey, call me back when you get a chance, okay?"

Rachel burst out laughing.

"Not in this lifetime," she said, talking to the machine as if its smooth plastic top were really Howard Becker's smooth bald head. "Sorry, Howard, but I don't think I'll get a chance to call you back for a long, long time."

She went over to the trash can and picked out his photograph. Matter-of-factly she tore it into tiny pieces, letting them drift back into the garbage like confetti.

"Good-bye, Howard."

She was still laughing as she turned to the pile of mail she had brought up in the elevator. Checking the top three envelopes reminded her that it was bill-paying time again. Now, there was a good solid piece of reality, in its most difficult-to-digest form.

But the next letter, the one just underneath, got her attention. It was a business-size envelope with her name and address written on the front in longhand. It wasn't a handwriting she recognized, and there was no return address.

As she held it in her hand, Rachel felt a chill. Suddenly she had the feeling someone was watching her. She turned but knew it was only her imagination. Even so, she couldn't help noticing that the room felt different. Nothing she could explain, not in terms of the usual things like temperature or smell . . . just *different*.

Her hands were shaking as she tore open the envelope. At first she thought it was empty. But there was a small white piece of paper inside.

Written on it, in the same handwriting in which the envelope had been addressed, were the words, "How am I doing?"

As she stared at the words, the paper suddenly felt hot—so hot that she feared her fingers would get burned.

"This is crazy!" she cried, dropping the letter. Instantly the feeling was gone. Yet she was only a little relieved. "Either I'm starting to see things, or . . . or somebody's playing a trick on me. Maybe it's Molly. Yes, that must be it. Or it could be Sis, or one of her kids. Maybe even Gayle."

Another thought occurred to her. Perhaps some crazy person had it in for her. Some man who was watching her, intentionally trying to frighten her, possibly even developing some weird sort of obsession with her.

It happened all the time. But to *other* people. She wondered if she should call the police.

But something stopped her. And that was the knowledge that maybe, just maybe . . .

"This is so ridiculous," she muttered, suddenly angry. She reached for the envelope and the letter with its bizarre message, then crumpled them both up in her hand. Deciding that the wastepaper basket near her word processor was much too good for this kind of trash, she tossed them into the kitchen garbage along with the remains of last Thursday's half-eaten bagel and a crumpled Lean Cuisine box. This time neither piece of paper felt hot. And she felt no chill.

Still, she wanted some noise in the apartment. She snapped on the television, rationalizing that it would be helpful to find out what tomorrow's weather would be. It also wouldn't hurt to catch up on what had happened over a weekend that, at the moment, was feeling far in the distant past.

But the face on the television screen was not that of a news anchor or a weather forecaster. Rachel was startled to see a face whose familiarity went far beyond that.

"Sis?" she squealed. *"Sis?* Is that you? What are you doing on TV?"

"I never in a million years expected that I'd really win," Sis was saying, looking as if she were about to burst. "The whole thing is so . . . so unbelievable."

It really was Sis. She was standing on the front lawn of her West Islip home, wearing jeans and a blouse with a small rip in the side, slapping her cheeks with her hands over and over again. The microphone was pushed up into her face. She looked dazed.

Rachel still couldn't make any sense of it. Was this a hallucination? All she could think of were the disasters that television journalists so loved to cover. But what could this mean? Had a tornado hit Long Island? A hurricane?

And then Jerry's face filled the screen. He was smiling; in fact, he looked like the cat that had swallowed half a dozen canaries.

"Jerry?" Rachel called out to him as if she expected him to hear her. "Jerry, is that really you?"

"This whole thing is too good to be true," he said, leaning into the mike. "I mean, winnin' the New York State Lottery, suddenly finding yourself a millionaire ... or, I should say, the husband of a millionairess." He chuckled, looking straight into the camera. "Anyways, it's just too much to take in, y'know what I'm tryin' to say?"

"And what do you plan to do with all that money?" the newscaster was asking, grinning stupidly. "Two million dollars is quite a sum. Do you expect it to change your life?"

Right there, on camera, Sis turned to Jerry and said, "I guess now we can afford to get the refrigerator fixed."

The anchor was chuckling as she turned to face the camera. "This is Norma Beacon, broadcasting live from West Islip. Back to you, Joe."

Joe McGregor, the co-anchor, was also indulging in a good, hearty chortle. And he kept it up even as he announced that the weather report, complete with the five-day forecast, was up next, right after a station break.

Rachel already had the receiver in her hand and was dialing Long Island's 516 area code.

"Damn!" she muttered in response to the busy signal. "I don't believe this."

But she did believe it. And she didn't need Sis's verification to convince her that it was true. She had heard it on the news.

"She just got lucky," Rachel mumbled as she dialed her other sister's number. "Molly will agree with me. I know she will—Molly? Is that you?"

"Oh, hi, Rachel. It is Rachel, isn't it?"

"Oh, I'm sorry, Molly. Were you asleep?"

"No, I wasn't asleep. I was just—"

Suddenly she was giggling, sounding far away from the phone receiver.

"*Stop* it! Can't you see I'm on the phone?" she cried.

"Molly, I only wanted to ask you—"

"Come on, honey. Please let me talk for just a minute, okay?"

"Molly, can you hear me? Molly, I—"

"Hey, give that back! I'm getting cold! Take your hand away from there, you beast. I'm trying to talk to my sister!"

"Molly Swann!" Rachel barked. "Get back on the telephone. You can play footsie later!"

"I'm not playing footsie."

"Is that Mike?"

"Oh, Rachel, you're not going to believe what happened."

"Try me."

Molly sighed. "Where should I begin?"

"Anywhere. What's going on over there?"

"Uh, hold on a second. Jack, sweetie, would you please go into the kitchen and get that second bottle of wine? It's in the refrigerator, right in the door."

"Jack?" Rachel breathed. "Jack Richter?"

"Oh, Rachel, you're not going to believe what happened."

"I have a feeling you're right."

"Mike went away this weekend. He's in Boston at a convention for amateur gourmet cooks. Saturday morning Jack called to ask if we could have dinner together. . . ."

Suddenly the dreaminess in her tone vanished. "You know, Rachel, it's not as if I were looking for this. I've been very loyal to Mike the whole time we've been together. I never had any intention of betraying him. I just—"

"I didn't say a word, Molly, did I?"

"It just *happened*, you know? It was one of those things that just appeared from out of the blue. It hit me like a lightning bolt, pulled the rug out from under me. . . . What are you thinking, Rachel?"

"I'm thinking that this sounds serious. I've never heard you speak in clichés before."

Instead of being offended, Molly giggled. "Oh, Rachel. I know this sounds crazy, but I think I'm in love."

Now it was Rachel who sighed. "I suppose I saw it coming. But can we drop it for now? You may find this hard to believe, but I didn't call to get the latest update on your sex life."

"Love life, Rachel. At least do me the favor of acknowledging that there's a lot more between me and Jack than just sex. Although that's certainly a large part of it."

"Spare me," Rachel interrupted. "I have to work with the guy, remember? Listen, this is important. Have you talked to Sis recently?"

"Not since the beginning of last week. Actually, she may have been trying to call me, but Jack and I had the phone off the hook. I'm expecting Mike to call tonight—you know, to tell me how the convention's going and all—and that's why I have it back on. Why? Is everything okay with her?"

"Oh, everything's great. Terrific, in fact. Our baby sister just won the New York State Lottery. Apparently she's now a millionaire."

Molly let out a squeal. "That's great! Wow! Hey, now she can afford to get that refrigerator fixed!"

"No one can ever accuse this family of thinking small," Rachel mumbled.

"What's that?"

"Nothing. I just . . . sure, it's great that Sis won the lottery. But don't you think it's strange?"

"Strange? What's strange about it?"

"Well, she was never interested in money before. I don't remember her making a big deal about playing the lottery."

"No, not until recently."

"What do you mean?"

"Oh, the last time I talked to her, she mentioned that—oh, thanks, honey. Just put it down over there. Listen, I'd . . . no, Jack! Not there!"

More giggles, accompanied by nearly hysterical shrieks.

"I should have called Dial-A-Porn," Rachel muttered.

"Get out of here, you wild maniac, you!" Molly was exclaiming through her laughter. "You . . . you X-rated thing!"

"Oh, *pul-leez*," Rachel pleaded. "Give me a break, Mol, will you?"

"He's gone now." Her voice dropped. "Rachel, why didn't you ever tell me about him before?"

"Maybe because I thought the two of you had about as much in common as—never mind. I want to talk about Sis right now, not your overactive hormones. Anyway, what were you saying about Sis and the lottery?"

"Only that she mentioned it a few days ago. Over the phone."

"What did she say, exactly?"

"Well, she didn't make a big deal about it or anything. She just mentioned that she'd been at the supermarket, and she noticed they were selling lottery tickets, and—just on impulse, really—she decided to buy one. Just for the heck of it."

"Just for the heck of it," Rachel repeated dully.

"It really paid off for her, though, didn't it? I can't believe she actually won! Hey, do you think she's the type to share?"

"This whole thing is utterly outrageous." This time Rachel was speaking to herself.

"What's outrageous?" Molly challenged. She sounded hurt. "We're just having a little bit of good luck lately, that's all. Me finding Jack Richter among the eight million souls wandering around New York City, not even realizing until I found him that I was looking for someone . . . Sis winning the lottery . . . It's great, Rachel! The Swanns have hit a real hot streak!"

"You think that's really all it is? Just coincidence?" Rachel asked doubtfully.

"What do you mean? What else could it possibly be?"

"You're right." Rachel laughed, more with relief than anything else. "I don't know what I could be thinking. What else *could* it possibly be?"

"Oh, listen, speaking of getting lucky, there's one more thing I've been wanting to tell you."

"Ummm?"

"You're going to think this is really crazy, I know. . . ."

"Oh, go on. Try me."

Rachel assumed that what was to follow was some imbecilic observation about Jack Richter, something along the lines of their zodiac signs being the most compatible combination in the entire universe.

So she was caught totally off guard when Molly said, "You're not going to believe this, Rachel, but without even trying, I've started losing weight!"

Rachel sat on the couch for a long time, wrapped in a blanket, shivering even though it was the middle of summer. She didn't even notice that day was giving way to night.

It *can't* be true, she thought. And yet . . . and yet every single wish I made at the art exhibition has come true.

Once again she replayed the scene inside the ridiculous toolshed that billed itself as a temple, reviewing the wishes she had made. Those she had made on her own behalf, that she get a boost to her writing career and a similar boost to her love life, were certainly becoming a reality. Sis, meanwhile, was rich. Molly had herself a new man, and—just in case the writing on the wall wasn't quite clear enough—was losing weight without even trying.

That last one was what really forced Rachel to confront what was happening. She had stood frozen as she listened to Molly giggling over the joyous if inexplicable phenomenon she had been observing over the past week. Her sister explained that she had been eating as she always ate. Translated, Rachel knew, that meant living for the moment, indulging in whatever goodies came her way, feeling secure that she was okay just the way she was . . . with Mike standing by, ready and eager to second that motion.

Yet even with no change in her habits, Molly reported, certain skirts were suddenly getting loose around the waist.

Belts easily hooked in a notch tighter. Jeans that had at one time been comparable to girdles were now comfortable. She had even overcome her usual resistance to stepping on the scale; instead of being fearful, she was actually excited as she peered at the minuscule numbers, the same size as those on the bottom line of the eye chart.

And there it was, in black and white: She had dropped six pounds.

That was the point in Molly's discourse at which Rachel had begged off, suddenly too dizzy to talk. She'd grabbed a blanket and created a cocoon, hugging herself and owning up to the fact that it was time to confront the truth.

She reexamined the past few days. The bizarre experience inside the Mocambian temple, the evening with Lance Firestone, the follow-up visit from Agnes the Avon lady, the note that had nearly singed the flesh on her fingers. The facts all pointed to one conclusion. It was no longer possible to plead an overly active imagination. Or coincidence, or bad luck, or anything else.

It was real. As crazy as it sounded, she really had struck a deal with the greatest dealmaker of all time.

Rachel knew then that she had to tell them. Molly and Sis had to know the truth. Her heart was as heavy as a marble paperweight, her stomach a cage for frenzied butterflies, but at least she knew what she was going to do. She would lay her cards out on the table, no matter how terrible the hand.

And then, hopefully, the three of them would put their heads together and find a way out.

Chapter
Fourteen

"*Sorry I'm late,*" Rachel said with a wan smile, plopping down onto an empty chair.

Molly and Sis were already sitting at a corner table in the restaurant she had picked for their lunchtime meeting, a nondescript place that was only a few steps up from a coffee shop on the evolutionary scale.

Now that they were facing her, Rachel wasn't sure if she was relieved or distressed. She'd been up most of the night, agonizing over how she was going to announce to her blood relatives that she had been negotiating with an individual even sleazier than a used car dealer—on their behalf as well as her own. Finally, at around four A.M., she'd concluded that she would have to come right out and tell them, then brace herself for the fallout.

"It's good to see you both," she offered feebly. She actually felt perkier than she sounded. In fact, her adrenaline was pumping so hard, she could have run the New York Marathon with one Nike tied behind her back.

Neither Sis nor Molly noticed.

"Oh, Rachel, what a great idea it was to meet for lunch," Sis gushed. "You know how lazy I am about coming into the city. But I took an early train so I'd have time to check out Bloomingdale's."

"How nice," Rachel said distractedly. "I bet they already have their fall clothes in."

"They certainly do. In fact, after this morning, I'm all set for winter."

There was an odd look on Sis's face. Even Rachel couldn't miss it. "What did you buy, Sis?"

"Well, they had these really terrific coats. . . ."

"You've got to go with one hundred percent wool if you want warmth," Molly interjected. "Those synthetics just don't make it. You did buy wool, didn't you, Sis?"

"Actually, I, uh, found something even warmer than wool."

"Warmer than wool!" Molly protested. "That's ridiculous. Nothing is warmer than wool! It sounds to me like some salesperson is pulling the wool over your eyes—if you'll excuse the pun. When you're buying a winter coat, you simply have to—"

"Uh, Mol?" Rachel interrupted.

"Hmmm?"

"What about fur?"

Comprehension began to register on Molly's face. "Oh, Sis, you didn't!"

Sis nodded up and down enthusiastically. "I did," she said, her eyes brighter than halogen light bulbs. "Full-length mink."

"Full-length mink!" Molly repeated.

"And, uh, this cute little sable number . . ."

"Sable!"

"And, uh, they had these darling little fox jobbies that I knew Shelley would love. . . ."

"What's gotten into you?" Molly demanded, suddenly furious. "What happened to your social consciousness? Where are your morals?"

But Sis just shrugged. She reached across the table, grabbed a roll from the basket, and began slathering butter onto it. "Those are your morals, Molly, not mine. Besides, Jerry has always said I'd look great in mink. One of his great regrets in life has been that he couldn't afford to buy me a terrific fur coat. So, now I can buy my own."

"Jerry," Molly groaned. "It figures he'd be behind this."

Sis looked at her blankly. "It was my decision, not his."

"Well, there you have it. They say power corrupts, and

here's living proof. You get a few bucks in your savings account, two million of them, in fact, and the next thing you know you're out slaughtering sweet little defenseless animals."

"I didn't slaughter anybody! All I did was whip out my charge card!" Her expression suddenly changed. "By the way, that's not all I bought today."

"Oh, really?" Molly countered. "What, did you buy a gorilla, stuffed and mounted?"

"Actually, I bought a computer." Sis paused for dramatic effect. "It's this really fancy Macintosh. The salesman assured me it was top of the line. Four-color screen, graphics, laser printer, the whole bit."

"That sounds useful," Molly said dryly. "Is that supposed to be a toy for Vincent?"

"No. As a matter of fact, I bought it for you, Molly. It should be delivered in a couple of weeks." Apologetically, Sis added, "They were out of stock on the fax machine attachment, so it's slowing delivery down."

Molly just stared at her.

"Close your mouth, Molly," Rachel muttered. "People are looking."

"You bought me a computer?"

"It's okay, isn't it?" Sis suddenly looked the way she did when she was a little girl, trying hard to win the approval of her two older sisters. "I mean, I know you've been using the one the school gave you. But you told me yourself that it's some ancient jobbie that belongs in a computer museum. And it seemed to make sense that having one right at home would be a convenience for you, what with all the writing you're always doing—"

"Why, Sis! That is the sweetest, most thoughtful thing. . . ." Molly reached over and gave her a big hug.

Rachel couldn't resist. "So I guess maybe it's okay for Sis to use her two million to buy whatever she sees fit, huh?"

"Well, if it's something useful. . . ." Molly stopped herself, quickly grasping the fact that she had just been backed into a corner.

Sis, however, had already turned her attention to Rachel. "I want to get you something, too, but so far I haven't decided what. I was thinking maybe something like a Club Med vacation. It wouldn't hurt for you to meet some new men. . . ."

Rachel cleared her throat. "Actually, I, uh, met someone new recently."

Sis was surprised. "You're kidding! You mean Howard is kaput?"

"Praise the Lord," muttered Molly, her eyes rising toward the ceiling.

"Yes. As a matter of fact, Ryder and I went away together this past weekend." Shyly she added, "I met him in the Ralph Lauren department at Bloomingdale's, just last week."

"Bloomingdale's!" Sis laughed. "I guess you can find just about anything you'd want there, can't you?"

"I found what I want at Rachel's office," Molly said provocatively. "She's not the only one who's had an upswing in her social life."

Sis looked at her with confusion. "Who are you talking about?"

"Oh, simply the most wonderful man in the world. His name is Jack Richter. He's an editor at *New York Life*. That's how Rachel came to know him—and that's how I met him."

"What about Mike?" Sis demanded.

Molly cast her a dirty look. "That's not fair. When Rachel told you about her new guy, you didn't say, 'What about Howard?' "

"That's different. Howard is . . . well, you know. He's . . . he's *Howard*. But Mike is sweet. Besides, you two live together."

"For now, anyway," Molly said.

"So you're basically two-timing sweet old Mike, huh?"

said Rachel. "Where's your social consciousness? Where are your morals?"

"My goodness, the three of us are certainly having a lot of changes in our lives, aren't we?" Sis observed brightly. They paused to order, then she reached for another roll, meanwhile offering the basket to Molly.

"No, thanks," she said. "Rolls and butter are a thing of the past for me. This is a new Molly Swann you're looking at. I've started losing weight without even trying, and now I want to help the process along as much as I can. . . ."

"Speaking of which," Rachel said firmly, clearing her throat once again, more out of nervousness than any desire to be more dramatic than she was already bound to be, "there's a special reason I wanted to talk to you both today."

Molly and Sis looked at her with interest. For the moment Rachel was the big sister again, about to bestow words of great wisdom upon their younger, less experienced minds.

"Now, what I'm about to tell you is going to strike both of you as something that's rather difficult to believe. Maybe even impossible."

"It's about this guy you met, isn't it?" Sis leaned forward, excited. "I can already tell he's special, just by the way you talk about him."

"He is special, but he's not what I want to talk to you about. Well, he is, in a way, because he's part of the whole problem. . . ."

"Problem? What problem?" Molly perked up instantly.

"Look." Rachel took a deep breath. This was going to sound crazy; in fact, she suspected that *she* was going to sound certifiable. Even so, she had to plunge right in, no holds barred.

"The reason all this stuff is happening—you winning the lottery, Sis, and you meeting Jack and losing weight without even trying—is that I, um . . . I made a deal with the devil."

As she might have expected, her words were greeted

with a long pause. But she was startled when that was followed by a hearty burst of laughter.

"Oh, Rachel, you're such a card," Molly cried. "Now,
quit stalling. Tell us about this new man of yours. What's
his name? Is he cute? More to the point, is he good in
bed?"

"You're not listening to me! I'm really serious about
this."

"Sure," said Molly. "And I'm going to be the next Roller
Derby queen."

"I could buy you a team if you wanted," Sis offered.

"All right, all right." Rachel held up both hands. "I knew
you were going to respond like this. And I can hardly
blame you. So please just do me a favor and listen to me
for five minutes. Don't talk, just listen."

She started at the very beginning. She told Sis and Molly
about going to the opening of the Mocambian exhibition at
the Metropolitan Museum of Art. She related her odd experience in the small temple built to honor the devil. She went
on to tell them about Gayle's offer of a blind date, her
strange evening with Lance Firestone, the visit from Agnes
the questionable Avon lady, the anonymous note that
burned her fingertips.

And then, slowly and carefully, she told them the specifics of the three wishes she had made, wishes for herself,
wishes for her two sisters. Molly and Sis listened, their
faces blank.

"There," she finally said, her shoulders slumping to indi-
cate just how draining her recitation had been. "Those are
the facts. What I can't explain are the feelings that go with
them. The feeling I got when I was in the temple at the museum, what I experienced while I was reading that note . . .
and then there's the fact that I can see so clearly how all
this fits together."

Nervously she looked at them, first at one and then the
other. "So? What do you think?"

"Hysteria," was all Molly said.

Rachel blinked. "Excuse me?"

"Well, it's all so easily explainable. The fact is that people see what they want to see. Look, Rachel, for whatever reason, you've simply hypnotized yourself into believing something that is totally outrageous but nevertheless still important for you to believe."

"And why on earth would I be doing that?" Rachel was indignant.

"I think what Molly is trying to say," Sis said in an overly gentle voice, "is that you're probably just overworked. And I'm afraid I have to agree with her. It does sound like you're . . . well, you know, imagining things. It's probably the result of taking on too much, don't you think?"

"Or maybe the result of low self-esteem," Molly countered. "Yes, that would explain it. Rachel, you're starting to get what you've always wanted for the first time in your life. And rather than simply accepting the fact that you've gone out there and gotten it for yourself, that you *deserve* a good man and a successful career, instead you've managed to convince yourself that it has to have been handed to you by someone else. Some force, something out of your control."

Sis, meanwhile, was nodding away.

"You've even gone so far as to pin a label on it," Molly went on calmly. "Not a very original one, I must admit, but one that, for whatever reason, works for you."

Suddenly a faraway look came into Molly's eyes. "You know, I think there may be a book idea in this. A sociological study of a brand-new phenomenon. For all I know, this could turn out to be a syndrome that's springing up all over America. Successful women—smart, ambitious achievers who are finally managing to balance career and family—are refusing to take any credit for it at all. Yes, I like it." She was growing more and more animated. "Rather than saying 'Look! I did this! I *earned* this!' they're saying 'I didn't do anything to make this happen. It was given to me by . . . by . . .' "

Already she was scrounging around in her purse, desperately looking for paper and pen. "I've got to jot this down while it's still fresh in my mind. I'll call it the Christmas-present complex. No, no, that doesn't work. The stocking-stuffer syndrome? No, not that, either. I need something catchy, something that really sums it up. . . . Oh, boy. I wonder if I could get on *Oprah* this time."

"Look," Rachel said patiently. "If you're right, Molly, if this really isn't the work of an outside force, how else could you possibly explain all the incredible things that have happened to us over the past two weeks or so?"

When her question was met with the same crazed expression that Molly had been wearing for the last two minutes, she turned toward Sis. "Well?"

Sis shrugged. "Coincidence."

"Luck," Molly offered.

"Maybe it's just time," said Sis. "Time for us all to start living better lives."

"Or perhaps the Swann sisters' moon just moved into the seventh house," suggested Molly.

"Oh, that's great," Rachel said dryly. "Those explanations are all so much better than mine."

"Now, wait a minute." Molly held up her hand. "Let's give Rachel the benefit of the doubt here—at least for a moment, okay? I mean, let's just assume that our dear sister really did make a pact with the devil."

"Molly," Sis protested, her voice filled with impatience, "I am not amused. In fact, I have to say that I'm finding this whole thing utterly—"

"No, wait. Let's give this idea a chance." She was in her authoritative-instructor mode now, in which she just assumed that people would listen to her. "If Rachel really *did* make this deal, what's so terrible about it? After all, we're getting what we want, aren't we?"

"I never asked for two million dollars," Sis insisted.

"You were playing the lottery, weren't you?"

Sis opened her mouth, then snapped it shut. She thought for a few moments, then said with much less fire, "But if anybody ever invited me to make a wish, I would wish for something like . . . oh, I don't know, world peace or an end to hunger or something really important like that."

Molly cast her a skeptical look. "Give me a break, dear. You really expect me and Rachel to believe that if you were offered anything in the entire universe—*anything*—you would be that giving? That there wouldn't be a shred of temptation to be just a little bit self-serving?" References to her recent spree in the pelts department were left unsaid.

"No matter what you might think, Molly, I'm not totally indifferent to the rest of the world, and neither is my husband. I belong to Amnesty International. Jerry and I give to the United Way. We *care*."

"Nobody is questioning that," Rachel said gently. "But Molly does have a point. Besides, think of the size of the contributions you can make to those organizations now that you've got all those zeroes in your bankbook. Don't you think you could really make a difference with two million dollars?"

Sis frowned. "I hadn't thought of that. Actually, Jerry and I have been so busy thinking about all the things we're going to buy for ourselves with our money—what's left now that the IRS has paid us a visit, that is—it never even occurred to us that we could give a lot of it away to charity."

"I rest my case," Molly announced. "Anyway, all I'm saying here is that maybe this deal isn't such a bad one. Sis has her fortune, Rachel has her career and her man, and I have Jack Richter and a lovelier, shapelier me."

With a grin she added, "Did I tell you I lost another three pounds? That's nine in all. Last night I bought my very first garment made of Lycra. It's a black miniskirt that can double as a headband. God, what a rush!"

"If this really is true—the way we're assuming for the moment—would that mean we were going to be sentenced to eternal damnation?" Sis asked nervously. "I mean, that's a pretty high price to pay for Lycra."

Molly looked at Rachel. "I'll let Rachel here field that one. After all, she's the Monty Hall of fates, not me."

Rachel swallowed hard. "I, uh, I'm not sure. The terms of the deal were, uh, never made that clear."

"Look, Rachel, I know all this pie-in-the-sky stuff is fun, in some bizarre, childish way. But it's getting boring. Why don't we step back for a minute and take a look at some of the facts?"

"Facts?" Rachel blinked a few times, looking as if she had never heard the word before.

Molly folded her arms in front of her. "It's not as if all this good stuff just happened to us in the past two weeks. Take you, for example. You've been plugging away at your career for years."

"More years than I care to think about," Rachel muttered.

"Right. So, okay, it's time. It's time for your career to take off. You've done the groundwork, paid your dues. . . . And so you've finally started getting the kind of assignments you've longed for practically your whole life. Okay, so the next thing you know you start feeling really good about yourself. You're a success. Your self-esteem is high, you're giving off these positive vibrations, you're practically glowing. . . .

"And then, wham! You run into this terrific guy at Bloomingdale's. By the way, you're hardly the first woman in New York to pick up a hunk in Bloomingdale's, courtesy of Ralph Lauren. Anyway, this man—Ryder, you said?— Ryder senses your energy, he's attracted to it, and the next thing you know, the two of you are off for a weekend of wild sex."

Rachel cast her sister the obligatory glare. But before she had a chance to speak, Sis jumped in.

"Molly is right, you know. It always happens like that. You know they say bad things always happen in threes? Well, good things tend to come clumped together, too. When you feel good about yourself, you also look good. You end up giving off a kind of glow. And people recognize that. They're attracted to it—just the way this Ryder guy was."

"Thank you, *Psychology Today*, for your deep, insightful interpretation of my life."

"Come on, Rachel. You know that what we're saying makes sense," said Molly. "As for me and my good luck, what happened between me and Jack was pure chemistry. It has nothing to do with wheeling and dealing. It was simply meant to be, that's all. And I've probably been losing weight because I've been so euphoric, walking around on cloud nine, sowing some wild oats, living the good life. . . ."

"Talking in clichés," Rachel mumbled.

"Losing nine pounds in two weeks isn't that unusual," Sis said. "Besides, most of it's probably water. You know, every time I eat pizza I gain four pounds overnight. All it is is water retention."

"See that?" said Molly, looking smug. "There's a perfectly good explanation for everything that's gone on with all of us in the past few weeks."

"But it's true!" Rachel cried. "The things I told you about really happened!"

"Okay, then. Let's see the note," said Molly. "You know, the one that melted your nail polish."

Sis leaned forward, her eyes glowing with excitement. "Maybe we could have the police look at it. Or the FBI."

"Sure, that makes sense," Molly agreed, her voice thick with sarcasm. "I guess dealing with Beelzebub does involve crossing state lines. So, Rachel, where's this note? Did you bring it with you?"

"I, uh, threw it out."

"You threw it out," Molly repeated. She and Sis exchanged knowing glances. "Well, then, how about introducing us to this guy Lance Firestone? The infamous blind date from hell?"

Sis giggled. "That's a terrific idea. And, you know, maybe I could come up with somebody who'd like to meet a nice Wall Street type."

"I guess I could call Gayle . . . except I'm not sure she even has his number."

"Um-hmmm." More knowing looks from both members of her audience, the looks this time tinged with concern.

"I guess that goes for the Avon lady, too, right?" said Molly.

Rachel nodded. "Look, you guys have got to believe me. I wouldn't make something like this up, would I? I mean, what would be the point?"

"Hey, come on," Sis said in a disturbingly calm voice. "I'm sure this kind of thing happens all the time."

"Sure. Stress-related symptoms are really common these days," said Molly. "Speaking of which, have you by any chance seen a doctor lately?"

"As a matter of fact, I have," Rachel replied. She sat up straighter, feeling for some reason that in beating Molly to the punch, she had scored a point for her team.

"And what did the doctor say?"

Instant letdown. "He said I, uh, was probably working too hard."

Sis reached over and took her hand, giving it a squeeze. "What do you say we order now? How about a nice bottle of wine? It'll relax all of us. They do have wine here, don't they? It's my treat."

Rachel opened her mouth to protest. She was about to argue that getting soused over lunch was not going to change the situation. She was determined to convince these two sisters of hers that what she was saying may have sounded totally ridiculous and utterly impossible, but was in fact actually true.

Suddenly she understood that she was wasting her breath. The bottom line was that Molly and Sis were simply not going to believe her.

And then another thought drifted into her mind, one that was the most comforting one she'd had in days.

Maybe they're right.

That one she liked.

Please, *please*, let them be right. Maybe I really am overworked, maybe I'm in some crazy state of self-hypnosis . . . maybe I'm even a little bit crazy.

As she picked up a fork to attack the limp salad that had just arrived, she had to admit that at this point even that last possibility sounded pretty good.

Chapter
Fifteen

As *Rachel let herself* into her apartment later that afternoon, the telephone was ringing.

"Let it be Ryder. Let it be Ryder," she muttered before answering. It was Ryder.

"I miss you," he confided.

"It's been only forty-eight hours," she protested. Then, "I miss you, too."

"So how about dinner?"

"I have Becky tonight."

"Does she eat pizza?"

He lived in TriBeCa, an area of lower Manhattan that had in just a few short years evolved from a high crime district to a high rent district. She and Becky brought flowers, figuring that a downtown "bachelor pad" was bound to be in need of cheering up. Rachel was expecting someplace two notches up from flophouse on the squalor scale. So she got the shock of a lifetime when, gay blossoms in hand, she stepped inside and found herself in one of the most wonderful living spaces she had ever encountered.

Ryder's apartment, the fourth floor in a warehouse building, had begun life as a coat factory. Now, instead of being divided up into smaller rooms, it remained one large open space. True, certain life functions had been delegated to special areas. There was a well-defined kitchen area, for example, as well as a home office. Rachel suspected there was also a bathroom or two tucked away behind closed doors.

The rest of the space was decorated like a furniture

showroom. There were several "living rooms," chairs and couches clustered around colorful area rugs or low tables. One near the kitchen, another by the largest window. One of these areas had a television nestled in its midst. A double bed was nearby, conveniently making the TV accessible to both the upright and the supine.

But the odd arrangement of the furniture was only the beginning. The walls were painted wonderful colors. A huge chunk of turquoise was cut off by yellow, followed by a splash of fuchsia. The different colors helped to define the various living areas: the blue and purple implied quiet time, the orange and yellow invited livelier interactions. Rachel guessed it was no accident that on the wall nearest the bed, hot pink collided with tangerine.

Then there were the toys.

There were dozens, even hundreds. They were piled up on the floor, on tables, on shelves that climbed up to the ceiling. In many cases they were large enough to be free-standing pieces of furniture themselves. A wooden hobby horse, for example, and a lavish Victorian dollhouse, completely furnished with everything from a grand piano in the front parlor to a dressmaker's mannequin in the attic to minuscule forks and spoons and salt shakers in the kitchen.

"Wow!" breathed Becky. "Mommy, what *is* this?"

"I think this is heaven. Why don't you go have a closer look?"

"Sure, Becky," Ryder said earnestly. "Feel free to check it all out. You, too, Rachel. Be my guest."

Wordlessly, Rachel wandered around. While her daughter was less restrained in her explorations, both had the same look: mouth open, eyes round, awed. Rachel observed that few of the toys were ordinary. Most were old, finely made, and well-maintained. A row of dolls sat sedately on one shelf, most of them porcelain, one of them a kewpie doll. Raggedy Ann and Andy were there, with their vacant stares and unwavering smiles.

Next she inventoried the stacks of old games. Their faded boxes suggested they were the original versions:

Candyland, Clue, Scrabble, Monopoly. A lot of them she didn't recognize, hardly surprising, since the games were stacked five and six feet high.

There were newer toys, too. On top of Trivial Pursuit and some of its variations were bins of hand-held computer games, everything from high-tech versions of ticktacktoe to war games. Baskets were filled with action figures: He-Man, Teenage Mutant Ninja Turtles, and some so new that Rachel had never even heard of them. Barbie and Ken were there with their complete wardrobes. The icing on the cake was an old-fashioned gumball machine, standing in a corner, patiently waiting to be fed pennies.

"Look at this place!" Rachel exclaimed. "You do love toys, don't you?"

Ryder laughed. "I guess you could say it borders on an obsession."

"Is this a toy store?" Becky asked.

"Not exactly." Ryder knelt down on one knee. "But if you see anything here that you'd like, maybe we could work something out." He looked up at Rachel and winked. "The same goes for you."

"Mommy," Becky asked, "can you go off and do grown-up things so I can play?"

"I like the way you think, Becky," said Ryder. "Hey, Rachel, know any good grown-up games?"

She laughed. "Come on. Let's go call up for that pizza."

They sat cross-legged on the floor, the pizza box between them, watching Becky balance a half-eaten slice on her knee as she dressed Barbie in her classic disco outfit.

"I can't help wondering," Rachel said, "how all this got started."

"I guess it began back when I was a kid—just like everybody else."

"Except that everybody else outgrew it."

"Hey, you don't think I'm strange or anything, do you?"

"Strange?"

"You know what I mean. Immature. Childish. Lacking in development."

"I've seen you in action, remember? I can testify to the fact that you're anything but lacking in development."

"Well, it certainly wasn't supposed to turn out like this. This wasn't what I was programmed for. By Mom and Dad, I mean."

"You mean there was a price tag on that idyllic childhood of yours?"

"That's an understatement. My parents, especially my father, had very definite ideas about how their son was supposed to turn out."

"Don't tell me. Doctor?"

"No."

"Lawyer?"

Ryder shook his head.

"Well, I'm not going to say the obvious. Besides, you don't have the genes for it.

"Although," she added, glancing around the room, "I'd be willing to bet the rest of this pizza that you have a headdress made out of feathers in here somewhere."

"In the cabinet over the fridge," Ryder replied matter-of-factly. "Right behind the toy tomahawks."

His expression grew serious. "What I was supposed to do was follow in my father's footsteps. He wanted me to be a banker, just like him."

"Is your dad one of those guys who sits behind a big desk and insists upon fingerprinting you before he'll cash your check?"

"Not exactly. He is—or was, before he retired—the president of Henries Vandergrift Thorn. You know, the investment bank."

"Oh. *That* kind of banker."

The president of one of the most prestigious investment banks in the city—if not the world. That certainly went a long way in explaining the Ralph Lauren sweater that needed exchanging. And the summer cottage that looked like Camp David. Not to mention the aura of confidence that Ryder gave off. That easy laugh, the comfortable way in which he approached every new situation, it was all rooted in a lifetime of the finest schools, the unending security, the abundance of opportunities, there for the taking.

"I suppose I should mention that my father was very disappointed in me."

"I'm afraid I don't quite get it." Rachel was already helping herself to a second slice of pizza. "I mean, unless I'm missing something, you seem to be doing fine."

"Maybe it looks that way to you, and ninety-nine percent of the world, but ... you see, in my family, I was always the rebellious one. Take my older sister, Prudence."

"Prudence?"

"Bitty for short."

Rachel nodded. "I'm beginning to understand where all those cutesy nicknames come from."

"Anyway, Bitty was the ideal daughter. She was always into the whole socialite thing—you know, parties, dating, the right clothes, the right *friends.* . . ."

"I know the type. I see their pictures in the *Times*'s wedding announcement pages."

"That's Bitty. Then there's my young brother."

"Don't tell me. Thurgood? Osborne? Witherspoon?"

"Thomas."

"Thomas! My, he got lucky, didn't he?"

"Hah. He probably would have preferred being named Witherspoon."

"A banker, right?"

"Just like Dad."

"So here's Ryder, the middle child. Let's see, thrown out of Andover, right?"

"Uh, Exeter."

"Barely made it through Harvard?"

"Brown."

"Goodness, you really are a degenerate, aren't you?"

But Ryder wasn't laughing. "It wasn't easy, you know. Trying to be forced into somebody else's mold. I *wanted* them to approve of me, but somehow . . ."

"So what happened after your near fall from grace at Brown?"

"Oh, boy. That was when things really came to a head." Ryder's distraught expression made it clear that even now, some twenty years later, thinking about it still hurt. "Dad just assumed I'd be coming to work at Henries right after graduation. I even went so far as to give it a shot. I got my hair cut, bought three suits at Brooks Brothers, the whole bit. Everything he wanted, just to show him I was willing to give it a try."

Playfully, Rachel nudged his side with her bare foot. "I bet you really shook the place up."

"I would have, probably—if Dad hadn't fired me after three days."

"Three *days*?"

Ryder let out a long sigh. "He said he'd always known I'd never amount to anything, that I just didn't have the stuff. You know, born to fail, no initiative, no respect for authority, blah, blah, blah. . . ."

Rachel looked at him with wide eyes. "What did you *do*, exactly?"

"I wore the wrong shoes."

"You what?"

With a chuckle, Ryder explained. "It was a bit more dramatic than that. And a lot more calculated. You see, on my third day at Henries, Dad decided to allow me the privilege of sitting in on a meeting with one of his most important clients. It was a super-big deal. He spent the entire day before prepping me. What to say, what not to say . . ."

"Everything but which shoes to wear, right?"

"Well, like I said, it wasn't quite that innocent." By way of explanation, he added, "This was 1969, don't forget."

"Uh-oh. What exactly was on your feet that day, Ryder?"

"Sandals."

Rachel burst out laughing. "Oh, *no*! I wish I'd seen that!"

"I was wearing my best suit, too." He smiled at the memory. "I tried, I really did. But I just couldn't go through with it.

"Besides, I thought it was kind of funny. Needless to say, Dad didn't quite share my sense of humor. He never has."

"Poor Ryder! So where did you go from there, in your Brooks Brothers suit and your sandals?"

"Out on my ear. Or some other part of my anatomy; I can't quite remember. I do remember that it was as if World War Three had struck. My mother was outraged, my sister wouldn't talk to me for months. . . ."

"Someone nicknamed Bitty would react like that, wouldn't she?"

Ryder was thoughtful as he continued. "Actually, I don't think any of them were particularly surprised. Maybe they were even relieved, I don't know. It was as if all their suspicions about me were finally proven correct. It turned out that they had been right all along."

Looking at her earnestly, he added, "Being right, in my family, is *very* important."

Rachel just nodded.

"Anyway, to make a long story short, I followed my instincts and started getting into my own thing. At that time, educational toys were starting to get really hot."

"Those were the *Sesame Street* days, right?"

"Right. That's when the whole concept of making learning fun was just getting started. Anyway, I had a couple of ideas, I tried them out, and bingo! Kidstuff was born."

"Without a penny from Daddy, I take it."

"No money. No support. Not even an encouraging word. He expected that I'd screw that up, too, just like everything else."

A hard look had come over his face. There was a cold glint that seemed very out of place in such blue eyes. "But I guess I showed him. Thirty million dollars in annual sales, distribution in seven countries . . . Kidstuff is doing great. *I'm* doing great."

"I guess you showed him, didn't you?" Rachel said softly.

The glint faded. The old Ryder was back.

"Maybe it's dumb for somebody to want to prove something to his father. But it was really important for me to show mine I wasn't the screwup he always thought I was."

He shrugged. "Maybe that's one of the reasons Kidstuff has done so well. I had something to prove. There was no way I was going to fall on my face with it. So I threw myself into it a zillion percent."

He smiled, remembering. "During the first two years I mastered the art of getting by on five hours' sleep a night. I was pretty crazed most of the time. But boy, was it worth it."

Rachel couldn't resist asking, "What's your relationship with your father like now?"

With a grin, Ryder replied, "I'm back to being invited to the Thorn residence for Thanksgiving and Christmas. And Bitty made me her daughter's godfather.

"Even so," he went on, "I always get the feeling that my dad is still waiting for me to fail. Sitting on the sidelines, watching me, not quite believing how well I'm doing, not quite feeling comfortable with it. . . ."

"It must be fun proving him wrong."

"I'll say. Almost as much fun as showing up at that meeting in pinstripes and a pair of water buffalos."

Suddenly Ryder let out a whoop. "Hey, let's clear this stuff away and dance."

"Dance?"

"Why not? I feel like dancing." He had already stood up, kicking aside the grease-stained pizza box.

Becky glanced up. "Can I dance with Barbie? She's wearing her disco clothes."

"Sure. Ask Ken if he wants to join in." Ryder snapped on the radio, and a pair of four-foot speakers filled the loft with a familiar rock and roll classic straight out of the fifties.

"Remember when this was big?" cried Ryder.

"Not really."

"Me, neither. Come on, let's jitterbug."

Becky and Barbie watched gleefully as Rachel and Ryder

launched into their best attempt. "Go, Mommy, go!" she cried, clapping her hands.

"I feel like I'm on *American Bandstand*." Rachel was already out of breath. "Got any poodle skirts?"

"Come dance with us, Becky!" Ryder called, holding out his hand.

On the spot the three of them invented a new variation on the jitterbug. Maybe it wasn't *American Bandstand* caliber, but it made them laugh so much, they could hardly hear the music. Finally they collapsed onto one of the couches.

"That was great," Ryder exclaimed. "Nothing like a little exercise to get the old blood pumping."

"Mommy, is that how you used to dance when you were still young?" Becky asked, resting her head against Rachel's stomach.

"Not quite."

"Becky, that's the way people used to dance in medieval times," Ryder answered seriously. "Ages before your mom was born."

She poked him. He responded by leaning his head against her shoulder. For a few minutes the three of them lay there, draped across each other, trying to catch their breath. Through it all, Rachel felt a kind of astonishment.

Slowly it dawned on her that there was a name for this unfamiliar feeling: contentment. It all felt so right, so easy.

Who cares what's responsible for me finding Ryder? she thought, glancing over at the man nestled beside her. What's wrong with finally getting what I've always wanted?

What's wrong with everything being perfect?

With one hand she reached down and stroked Becky's hair. With the other she took hold of Ryder's. And then she closed her eyes and smiled a smile of absolute bliss.

The next morning, after Becky's camp bus had whisked her off to the world of plastic lanyards and ice-cream-stick pencil holders, Rachel returned to her apartment, deter-

mined to dedicate the entire day to working. As she stepped
into the bathroom for a quick shower, she was already map-
ping out an hour-by-hour schedule. But just as she finished
smearing her wet head with a product promising to perform
an actual hair miracle in three short minutes, she heard the
telephone ring.

"Damn!" she muttered. She needed to make a choice—
and fast. Either let it go or wrap every moist surface in
towels and make a mad, damp dash for it.

The ringing continued. Letting out one more "Damn!"
for good measure, she grabbed a handful of towels and ran.

"Hello?" Her voice said, Whoever you are, this had better be good.

"Hey. It's Johnny."

Johnny, Mr. Timing himself. Even so, standing in the
middle of the living room and dripping all over the floor
was suddenly much more than a mere annoyance. It was a
thrill, part of the game. Who cared about the water stains
on her beloved dhurrie? What did it matter how quickly her
skin was growing clammy? Rachel Swann, Girl Reporter,
was on the job.

"I, uh, wanna get together again."

"Sure. Just name the time and place. Hang on a sec."

Rachel scrambled for a pen and a pad of paper, glancing
around the apartment in a near-panicked search. To say that
the place was in shambles would have been overly polite.
Two days worth of used coffee cups and empty bags of
Pepperidge Farm cookies littered the scene, unopened junk
mail covered the dining room table, laundry was strewn
decoratively throughout.

My Lord, just *look* at this mess! I'm turning into Jack
Richter!

That thought made her smile as she hurried back to the
phone.

"I'm ready. Shoot."

" 'Kay. There's a coffee shop right around the corner
from the Museum of Natural History." After filling her in
on the specifics—nothing quite as specific as an actual ad-

dress; Johnny was apparently big on landmarks—he added, "Can you meet me there in, say, half an hour?"

"Half an hour?"

Johnny lowered his voice seductively. "Listen," he said, "I got more names."

His words had their intended effect.

"A half hour. I'll be there."

As she was zipped across town by a taxi driver whose only English seemed to be "Where'd you learn to drive, New Jersey?" Rachel found that she was actually looking forward to her second meeting with Johnny. They were practically old friends by then, having shared both inside information about corporate corruption and the French fries on her plate.

Johnny, predictably, was already there. This time, though, instead of a well-worn T-shirt, he was wearing a crisp blue and white striped cotton shirt and a tie. *A tie.*

Rachel suppressed a grin as she took her place in the booth opposite him.

"You made it," he observed, smiling shyly.

"Of course."

Another greasy spoon, another ripped Leatherette seat, another red plastic menu. And another unwanted meal. This journalism business was getting fattening.

In response to her order, the waiter merely grunted. Rachel was beginning to wonder what it would feel like to live in a place where she actually spoke the language.

The business of summoning food concluded, she turned her full attention to Johnny.

"So, what have you got?"

"Like I said on the phone, I got names. Lots of 'em this time." He was clasping a manila folder protectively to his chest, acting as if he weren't yet ready to share the little tidbits of information he had in his possession. "See, most of the companies that have been involved so far, I already had a suspicion of who they were. I coulda told you their names last time. But I figured that before I could do that,

I had to have proof. I mean, we have to have hard evidence, right? Before we can go around incriminatin' 'em and everything?"

Rachel nodded. "You're absolutely right, Johnny. We have to be able to back up any claims we make."

"Yeah, well, it was your boss who told me about that."

"Grayson?"

"Mr. Winters."

"I see." With a frown she said, "So he already knows the names of the companies involved?"

"Some of 'em. I mentioned a few the first time I talked to him."

Rachel was picturing Grayson Winters sitting behind his desk, as always looking as smug as if he'd woken up that morning knowing things that nobody else knew. She found that her dislike for the man, a feeling laced generously with distrust, was growing stronger by the minute. Perhaps it just slipped his mind, she thought, trying to rationalize. It could have been an oversight.

Somehow, she found that a little hard to believe.

"Anyway, what have you got?" she asked.

Johnny looked around nervously. "Look, uh, if you don't mind, I'd rather just slip this to you and have you look it over later. You know, where we're not quite so conspicuous."

"Conspicuous. Right." Rachel glanced around. The Colossus of Rhodes coffee shop was practically empty, but it behooved her to play by Johnny's rules. With a nod she took the folder and tucked it underneath her purse.

"What I just gave you," said Johnny, gesturing toward the folder with his chin, "is Xerox copies of the letters some of the companies sent with their contributions. I also got a couple of copies of checks different companies made out to Grass Roots. No letters, just contributions."

"Great. This sounds like exactly what we need. Just as long as you're convinced these checks really are payoffs, and not something legitimate—"

"Believe me," Johnny said fiercely, "Grass Roots wasn't

selling nothin' that these companies would want to buy. The only thing they could buy with those checks was protection."

Stealing a glance at the contents of the folder, Rachel saw at least seven pieces of documentation. Her mind was already clicking away, running through the ways she would follow up his claims. Tracking down other Grass Roots people, checking out the employees of the companies allegedly involved, contacting the government's environmental agencies ... The mere thought caused buckets of adrenaline to start pumping through her veins.

"I'll read these as soon as I get home," she promised as their food arrived. She picked up her fork, wondering what on earth she and Johnny were going to talk about now that their business was concluded.

He, however, did not appear to share her concerns. He tugged on the knot of his necktie, cocked his head to one side, and in a pleasant, conversational tone said, "So, Rachel. You married or what?"

The copies inside Johnny's folders were as wonderfully incriminating as Rachel had hoped they would be. Everything was there, spelled out in black and white. Curled up on her couch back at her apartment, she pored over each one. And she grew more excited with each page.

Some of the firms slipping payoffs to the Grass Roots people were manufacturing concerns, some were service companies, but all dealt in some sort of material that was bound to be difficult—not to mention expensive—to dispose of properly. Four were companies hired by hospitals and clinics to dispose of medical waste, those bloodred Hefty bags filled with used hypodermic needles and surgical gloves and heaven only knew what else. Rachel could certainly guess the kind of deceit *they* were up to: red bags showing up in the most unlikely, and the most hazardous, places. She, along with everyone else who lived in New York and owned a television set, had come across that brand of scandal before.

The three manufacturing firms had similarly toxic by-products to deal with. Porter Industries of Ohio was a chemical firm. DayCo, down in Jersey, made paint. The third, Kepter Brothers, based in Southern California, produced office supplies, a wide variety of products ranging from glues and inks to plastic pencil cups. That translated, in part, to disposing of plastics. Not as sexy as toxic chemicals or medical waste, but problematic nevertheless.

There was quite a diversity here, Rachel observed. But all the companies had one thing in common: During the past year they'd made very generous payments to Grass Roots. Payment that, as Johnny had put it, could buy them only one thing: protection.

Now that she had names, it was time to do some digging. Already a To Do list was forming in her mind. She would start by learning everything she could about these companies, calling upon Dun & Bradstreet and annual reports and whatever other resources the New York University business school library could provide. Checking with the government's environmental agencies was a natural next step. After that she would seek out employees of the firms in question—or, better yet, disgruntled *ex*-employees. Perhaps one or two of their clients would have something to say. And as helpful as Johnny was, she also had to find other people intimate with Grass Roots willing to pour their hearts out in exchange for a cup of coffee.

Yes, it would take a lot of effort: phone work, footwork, brain work. But Rachel was energized by the very prospect. What to some might have been drudgery was to her as much fun as working on a jigsaw puzzle.

Chapter Sixteen

Molly *and* Sis *had begun* to complain that Rachel was keeping her "new man" from them, speculating pointedly over the phone that perhaps their older sister was ashamed of them. So Rachel had no choice but to accept Sis's invitation to another family barbecue chez Casamano.

That morning, as she packed up sun block, Allerest, and insect repellent, all the niceties crucial to a pleasant day in the country, she realized she was looking forward to the outing. The truth was, she was eager to show Ryder off—not only the man himself, but also how happy the two of them were together. She knew her sisters would be pleased for her. She, in turn, would enjoy basking in their admiration.

Becky was also excited. She dressed herself totally in lime green, everything from socks to hair ribbon. Barbie was considerably more tasteful in tennis whites.

It wasn't until Rachel, Becky, and Ryder were crawling uptown toward Molly's apartment that it occurred to her to worry about what he was going to think of her sisters.

"I think I'd better give you the lowdown on Molly and Sis," she said, suddenly uneasy.

"If they're related to you, I have nothing to worry about." He flashed her that smile that made her feel as if she were melting into the vinyl upholstery.

"It's not that there's anything really *wrong* with them," she tried again. "It's more that they're ... idiosyncratic."

"You mean weird?"

"I don't want to sound harsh or anything, but I suppose

you could use the word *weird* without being too far off base."

She tried to come up with a way of characterizing the Molly and Mike Show. Or the Sis and Jerry Hour. In the end she decided that any attempts to sum them up would prove lame.

"Look, you can make your own judgments," she finally said. "Just don't say I didn't warn you."

When Molly and Mike scrambled into Ryder's double-parked car a few minutes after Rachel buzzed their intercom, they were already embroiled in an argument.

"It's crazy," Molly was insisting as she went through the contortions necessary for climbing into the backseat of a two-door hatchback. "It's like ... like carrying coals to Newcastle."

"It's the thought that counts," Mike countered, looking like a marionette made of Popsicle sticks as he folded himself into the backseat next to Molly.

"Hello, Mike. Hello, Molly," Rachel said cheerfully. "Glad you could make it. This is Ryder—"

"We have to make a stop," Mike insisted. "There's a florist over on Broadway—"

"Watch out, Aunt Molly!" cried Becky. "You're sitting on Barbie's tennis racquet!"

"Sorry. Mike, this is ridiculous. Sis has a garden. You don't bring people who live in the suburbs *flowers* when you go to visit them. You bring them something they can't get out there, something like ..."

"How about some air pollution?" Rachel suggested. "Or maybe we could go all out and dump garbage on their front steps."

"Look, we'll let the two of you decide," said Molly. "Do you think we should stop and buy Sis flowers? Yes or no?"

"Oh, no, you don't, Mol. You're not getting me involved in sorting out your dirty laundry. Besides, aren't you even going to say hello to Ryder?"

Finally the flowers were forgotten. The conversation drifted on to predictions of the amount of traffic leaving the city early on a Saturday morning in August, and the mood became less toxic. It was almost fun, Rachel reflected as Ryder and Mike launched into a spirited discussion of decent restaurants in their respective neighborhoods.

"He's cute," Molly whispered once they had reached Sis's driveway.

"Cute?" Rachel repeated. "Your priorities are certainly changing."

"Oh, you know what I mean." When everyone had climbed out of the hatchback, Molly twirled around for Rachel, showing off the short skirt she was wearing with a skin-tight tank top. "What do you think?"

"You look great. Um, exactly how much weight have you lost?"

"Twelve pounds. By the way, the next time you make a deal with someone who wields major power, put in a bid for blond hair for me, will you? Jack thinks I'd look great as a blonde."

"That you can buy at a drugstore," Rachel snapped. "You don't need supernatural intervention."

"Just thought I'd mention it."

"How are things with Jack, anyway?"

"Wonderful. Simply wonderful."

"Then how come you're with Mike today?"

"Oh. Well." Molly frowned. "I haven't had the heart to tell him yet."

"What are you waiting for?"

"The right moment."

Rachel eyed her warily. "I just hope that 'right moment' doesn't come when Mike walks in on the two of you doing X-rated things on the kitchen floor."

Molly's eyes widened. "Oooh, what a great idea! Is that what you and Ryder do?"

It was just as well that Rachel never got a chance to answer. Sis had come bursting out of the house, dressed in rhinestone-studded pink sweats.

"Check this out," Molly muttered. "She looks like Imelda Marcos in search of an aerobics class."

"It's her money," Rachel reminded her. "She's welcome to use it however she pleases."

"Hey-y-y!" Sis cried, dashing across the lawn toward them. "It's so great to see you! Come around back. We're setting up outside, at least for now. They're forecasting rain." Giving Becky a hug, she added, "Great color."

Jerry was already in back with Shelley. All around were subtle signs of change, little things that only those who knew the Casamano family well were likely to notice. Even though the temperature was in the eighties, Shelley was flaunting her teenage curves in a pair of black leather pants. Jerry kept casting pleased looks at the pair of electric bug zappers that now stood at either edge of the patio. The lawn furniture was right off the showroom floor, white molded plastic stuff with pastel-colored webbing.

The changes in Vincent were less subtle. As he came shuffling around the corner of the house, it was obvious he'd been ordered to put in an appearance. He looked different. Not only were his glasses gone—contact lenses? Rachel wondered—he was wearing tight jeans and a black T-shirt printed with the insignia of a heavy-metal group. But the biggest change by far was that he was wheeling a pint-size motorcycle.

"What is *that*?" Rachel demanded.

"Dirt bike." Vincent was trying to act casual about his latest acquisition, but the glint in his eye gave him away. "Pretty cool, huh?"

"I'll say it's cool," his father said. "Best damn dirt bike money can buy. Jeez, I would've killed for something like that when I was his age."

Mike raised his eyebrows. "Some toy."

"Are you old enough for one of those?" Molly asked.

"It's not a toy. And sure I'm old enough." Thrusting his chin into the air, Vincent added, "I'm old enough for a lot of stuff I didn't used to be old enough for."

Leaning toward Rachel, Molly observed, "Apparently using smooth sentence structure isn't one of them."

"Vincent just loves this thing." Sis was beaming, looking

as if her thirteen-year-old son had just won the science fair, not joined the Evel Knievel fan club.

"So," Rachel said conversationally, "I guess a lot of other things around here have changed, too. Vincent, you're starting at a new school in a few weeks, right? How does it feel?"

Vincent shrugged. "I don't know. Okay, I guess."

"Well, I can't wait." Shelley, looking remarkably cool for someone swathed in animal skins from ankle to waist, finally deigned to speak. "Mom said I can get my hair cut in the city before school starts. Anyplace I want. And I can get as many new clothes as I want."

Molly sighed. "And to think, when I was in high school, I spent my summers getting a head start on the reading list."

"It'll probably be a big change, going to a fancy private school," said Rachel. "No doubt it'll take you and Vincent a while to settle in. . . ."

"Hey, Aunt Rachel, it's not Vincent anymore. It's Vince."

"Vince," Rachel repeated dutifully.

Molly was not as cooperative. "Aw, gee. And here I was all set to call you Easy Rider."

"That used to be my nickname," Ryder interjected, chuckling. "Get it?"

Up until now, Ryder had been a mere spectator. Rachel could only imagine what he was thinking. Much to her surprise, however, he actually looked as if he were enjoying himself. He was sitting comfortably on his molded plastic chair, sipping Bud from a can. A pile of barbecue-flavored potato chips was balanced on the flowered paper napkin spread out in his lap.

They were all settled in, in fact. Which was why it was such a shame that all of a sudden the storm that had been threatening to materialize made good on its threat. Dollops of rain began falling, the fat, noisy kind that promised it was only going to get worse.

"Shoot. I knew this would happen." Sis was dashing around, grabbing bowls of chips and piles of paper napkins.

Soon everyone was pitching in, and the transition from backyard to house took under two minutes.

The crowd reconvened in the living room, everyone taking more or less the same place as outdoors. Even the bowls of snacks followed; the dishes of chips and dips were arranged on the coffee table in the same configuration as on the picnic table.

"Too bad about the rain," Sis commented to no one in particular. "Well, might as well get lunch started."

"I'll help," Ryder offered. He followed her into the kitchen.

Rachel suspected he wanted to talk to her sister without distraction. She eased over to the kitchen door to do some spying, settling on a brand-new ottoman that just shouted Sears.

"I think I'll set up for lunch here in the kitchen," Sis was saying. It was as if in Ryder she felt she had found a co-conspirator in the ways of the successful hostess.

"Why not the dining room?" he asked. "There's probably more room."

Sis considered the possibility. "I don't know, I always like eating in the kitchen better. It's much more comfortable. More homey, don't you think?"

"It does seem to fit."

"Fit? Fit what?"

"This family," Ryder explained. "This family feels comfortable."

"Oh, you should hear us," Sis protested. "Everybody's on their best behavior today. That's partly because you're here—you know, an outsider, Rachel's new boyfriend—and partly because it's just easier if everybody's civil when we're all together like this."

"Tell me about some of those other times," Ryder urged. "I want to hear some really juicy gossip."

Sis laughed. "Well, I suppose I could tell you about back when I first got married to Jerry. Oh, boy. Things got pretty heated up then."

"Why?" Ryder sounded confused.

"Because my sisters didn't approve of him, that's why. Neither Molly nor Rachel thought Jerry was ... you know, good enough for me. Molly, especially. At least Rachel had the brains to keep her mouth shut. But Molly ... boy, you should have heard her."

She turned the faucet on full force. Rachel leaned forward, afraid of missing something. Through the doorway she could see Sis lowering the five-gallon pasta pot into the sink.

"I remember the day Jerry and I got married. Molly and Rachel were my bridesmaids. There were two others besides, Jerry's sister Marie and his sister-in-law, Angela. Anyway, there we all were, wearing these long, fancy dresses—I wanted coral for the bridesmaids, with full skirts and ruffles all around the hem and this really pretty scoop neckline. But instead of acting like princesses, the way I wanted, we were all fighting like cats and dogs."

She chuckled. "I can laugh about it now, but at the time I half expected Molly to lock me in my room and handcuff me to the dresser so I couldn't get to the church. It went on, too. After the wedding we didn't talk to each other for months."

"That's terrible!" Ryder exclaimed. "What finally happened?"

Sis paused, frowning as she opened a Tupperware container of homemade tomato sauce, trying not to spill it on her rhinestone-studded sweatshirt. She was quiet for so long that Rachel began to wonder if she was going to answer.

"We got over it," she finally said. Then she shrugged. "Of course we did. We had to. We're sisters."

"You're lucky." Ryder's voice was low, almost reverent. "Don't you have brothers and sisters?"

"One of each. But they don't do me much good."

In response to Sis's look of bewilderment, he added, "It's a long story. I'll tell you someday."

"You know, Ryder," Sis said, putting down her Tupperware, "I think you're okay."

"You're okay, too, Sis. Uh, it's all right if I call you Sis, isn't it?"

"Oh, sure. Everybody does." She looked at him earnestly. "I have this gut feeling about you. That you're good for Rachel."

"What does that mean?" he joked. "That I don't gamble, do drugs, or chase floozies?"

"No. Hell, how do I know if you do any of those things? What it means is that I can tell you really care about her."

"I just thought of something," interrupted Molly, barging into the kitchen after nearly tripping over Rachel and her ottoman. "Shouldn't somebody as rich as you have a maid?"

"I did. For a week, anyway."

"She quit, huh? Couldn't stand the heat?"

"Actually, I fired her."

"Didn't work out, huh? Then try someone else."

"Oh, she was fine. It was just . . ." Sis shrugged, waving her hand in the air. "It didn't work out. I guess the problem was that she just didn't do things the way I would have."

"You could have shown her," Molly insisted. "These things take time."

"It just didn't seem right, having somebody else clean up after me."

Molly stared at her, her mouth open. "You clean up after your kids! You clean up after Jerry!"

"That's different."

"Why? Why is that different?"

"It just is, that's all."

"Sounds reasonable to me," Ryder commented in a soothing voice.

Molly, however, was not in a pacifistic frame of mind. "Tell me why it's different."

"Because . . . because it makes me feel important, that's why. It makes me feel like I matter."

"Oh, Sis, you can matter to your family without being their slave!"

Sis cast Molly a weary look. "To me it feels like I'm taking care of the people I love. Maybe I'm nuts; I don't know. But that's the way I feel. So let's just drop it, okay?"

"Lunch almost ready?" Rachel chose that moment to make her entrance. "Don't tell me. Some delicious catered thing? Filet mignon? Lobster salad? Something with sun-dried tomatoes?"

"I'm making spaghetti." As if to demonstrate just how dedicated she was to that end, Sis pulled an apron out of a drawer and tied it around her middle.

"Spaghetti?" Molly chorused.

"Yes," Sis said simply, her mouth drawn into a thin line. "I *like* spaghetti."

"Hey-ey-ey. Can this lady cook or what?"

Jerry was sitting at the head of the kitchen table, an enviable position since it made him the only person in the room able to move his elbows more than three inches away from his sides. "Am I or am I not the luckiest guy in the world?"

Sis was blushing. "Oh, you," she said, waving her hands in the air dismissively. "You'd eat anything that was put in front of you."

But she was clearly pleased—so much so that for a moment it looked as if the two of them were going to excuse themselves from the table and head upstairs. Instead, much to their guests' relief, they dug into the spaghetti topped with Sis's special homemade tomato sauce—Jerry's mother's family recipe.

"This is wonderful," Ryder commented. He wasn't just being polite, either. He had already made impressive inroads into his first helping. "In fact, it's probably the best spaghetti I've ever had."

"Oh, go on," said Sis. "You mean to tell me my cooking is better than what you can get in those chi-chi restaurants in the city?"

"Now that you're Miss Moneybags," Molly ventured, "why don't you try some of those chi-chi restaurants and find out for yourself?"

"Nah. I wouldn't feel comfortable in a restaurant like that."

At first Molly looked as if she were going to try tackling that one. But after giving it more thought, she abandoned her line of questioning.

"Okay, then," she said. "So what *are* you going to do with all this money you now have?"

"I bet the IRS took a big chunk out of it," Mike said, his mouth full of pasta. "Probably enough to make a whole month's supply of bombs."

"Yeah, those tax guys came around the day Sis found out she won," Jerry said. "They sure don't let any Astroturf grow under their feet."

He was still guffawing to himself as Rachel said, "I can see you've made a few changes already. Private school for the kids, the new refrigerator . . . and wasn't that a new Mercedes I saw out front?"

"Oh, we just leased that," Sis explained. "I wanted to see how it felt, driving a car like that."

"And how does it feel?" asked Ryder.

"Well . . . actually, I don't use it very much. I mean, where am I gonna take it, the supermarket?"

"You should do something wonderful for yourself," Molly insisted. "Buy something you've always wanted. Travel around the world. Or . . . or just go crazy and do something wild."

"Actually," Sis said, sounding more serious than she had all day, "there is something I've been thinking about buying."

She put her fork down, as if talking about this were too important to mix with something as insignificant as eating. She looked around the table, testing the waters before going on. In the end, it was upon her husband's face that her eyes rested.

"I been talking to some people about the best thing to do with the money. You know, people who are experts in investing and all that. And, well, everybody pretty much says the same thing." Still looking at Jerry, she said, "I think we should sell this house and buy a bigger, more expensive one."

"What?"

Jerry's tone of voice caused all motion to cease. In a split second every person at the table became an eight-year-old kid, intimidated by the force of a parent's anger.

"What did you say?" he demanded once again. His face was red and his eyes showed a wildness that none of them had ever seen before.

"I said, everyone seems to agree that investing in real estate is the smartest thing for somebody in my position." Sis was trying to sound matter-of-fact, but she was unable to keep a slight waver out of her voice. "And you gotta admit, Jerry, this house is kind of small. Besides, the neighborhood isn't all that great, not if you're thinking about resale value down the line. And so investing in something that's going to—"

"I made this house what it is." Jerry's low, controlled voice was even more frightening than his bark. "You know that as well as I do, Sis. I put myself into every single room of this place. And I did it for you. You and me and the kids. This is *our* house."

Sis was keeping her eyes down. Distractedly, she picked at the crumbs of Italian bread sprinkled around her plate. "Maybe this isn't the best time to be talking about this."

"Hey, you're the one who brought it up," Jerry reminded her.

There was a long, painful pause. The spaghetti was getting colder by the second. Finally Molly piped up.

"I think Sis is right. This is between the man and the woman of the house, not a topic for general discussion. Mike, would you be a dear and pass me the salad?" Cheerfully, she added, "I'm really getting into salad these days."

"I noticed you lost a bunch of weight," Shelley said enthusiastically. "You look really great. How did you do it? Did you join a health club or something?"

Exhibiting a deftness that would have impressed a troupe of Chinese acrobats, the group moved on. For the time being the unpleasantness seemed to have been forgotten, or at least pushed aside for the host and hostess to deal with after the others had departed.

In fact, it wasn't until everyone was leaving that it was brought up again. Mike and Ryder were already in the car, and Molly and Rachel were saying their good-byes to Sis.

"Ryder and I had a great time," Rachel said. "Thanks for having us out."

"Yeah, it was fun," Sis agreed. "He's terrific, Rachel. I've never seen you looking so happy. Hang on to this one, okay? He's a real find."

Rachel laughed. "I'll do my best."

"And, uh, I'm sorry about that little scene at dinner. Between me and Jerry, I mean. I guess my timing was pretty lousy."

"So what are you going to do about the house thing?" demanded Molly. "It doesn't sound like upward mobility is your husband's thing."

"Don't worry," Sis assured her. "Jerry and I will work it out."

"I'm so sorry about all this," Rachel found herself saying without thinking. "I meant for the money to help, not screw things up."

Her sisters looked at her as if she'd lost her mind.

"Rachel, are you still harping on that ridiculous idea of yours that—"

Sis interrupted Molly, holding up her hand for silence.

"I'm telling you, my husband and I will work it out," she repeated. And then, sounding completely sure of herself, she added, "We always do."

Chapter
Seventeen

Rachel *awoke the next morning* to one of those Sundays a person could call "perfect" without exaggerating. With Becky spending the better part of the day at a birthday party, Rachel put on a pair of sneakers and headed downtown to Greenwich Village.

She was looking for more than a pleasant stroll. She needed a break from the *New York Life* article. For weeks she'd been eating, sleeping, and breathing Grass Roots. While she loved every minute, making probing telephone calls and doing face-to-face interviews and delving into every document she could get her hands on, she needed some time to clear her head. And trekking around Manhattan, where one street after another looked more like a movie set than reality, was the best way she knew.

As she emerged from the subway station, she found herself in the midst of Washington Square, today exhibiting street theater at its finest. She was hardly the only one taking advantage of the great outdoors. There was the usual sprinkling of mimes, their magic lying mainly in an ability to amuse at least as many as they irritated. The cardsharks were there, too, milking tourists with promises of easy money. Others—more enterprising, or, at least, less creative—hawked an impressive variety of wares: used books, used records, trinkets from Guatemala and India. The musicians made the whole scene festive, converting what could have been tawdry into something along the lines of a medieval festival.

As she paused to buy a cherry Italian ice from a street

255

vendor, Rachel thought how much more fun all of it would be with Ryder at her side. The trip to Long Island the day before had gone a long way in cementing their relationship. How cozy they had been riding back to the city, Molly, Mike, and Becky dozing in back. The radio played softly while the windshield wipers provided their own kind of music. She and Ryder were as comfortable as an old married couple.

But having played hooky all day, Ryder now had to do penance. Today he was slaving away at the office. Although it was only the beginning of August, Christmas orders were already pouring in. That was good news, of course, but it meant stacks of paperwork.

Still, it was fun, just being on her own. Rachel was enjoying the chance to sit back and relish the way things were going for her. Working on her article had been nourishing her mind. Ryder nourished her body and soul. Becky, too, was having a good summer. She loved spending her days toasting marshmallows and singing "Kum-by-ah." She had been spending some real quality time with her dad, too; according to her off-the-cuff reports, things between Boyd and Ariana were strained.

What else did she need? she wondered, giving a deep, satisfied sigh as her tongue made contact with the cold, sweet ice.

And then she stopped. It took only a fraction of a second for the face to register: that man, standing by a park bench, dressed in a T-shirt and jeans that looked as if they'd just come back from the dry cleaner, talking to a man who could have been his clone.

"Boyd?" Rachel muttered. "What's he doing here?"

Before she had a chance to slip away, he spotted her. His face first registered surprise, then gave way to a sardonic smile.

"Well, well, well," he said, watching her expectantly.

His friend glanced up, interested, as she sauntered over. "Hello, Boyd. I didn't know you ever went south of Fourteenth Street."

"I'm playing tour guide today. Rachel, this is George Drummond. He just joined the company last week."

"An out-of-towner?" Rachel asked politely, extending her hand.

"Yes, ma'am," he replied, grinning. "From Louisville."

"Kentucky?" Rachel's eyebrows shot up. "Then you'll definitely need an escort. Until you learn your way around, that is."

"Yes, ma'am."

"How's the writing business?" Body's smile had evolved into a smirk.

"Great, actually. I—"

"You're a writer?" George looked impressed. "What do you write?"

"Yes, tell us, Rachel," said Boyd. "I'm sure George would find it fascinating."

"Actually, at the moment I'm doing a piece for *New York Life* magazine." Daintily she nibbled at her Italian ice.

George let out a whistle. "Wow! *New York Life?* That's big-time, isn't it?"

"I can't wait to hear the topic," Boyd breathed.

"I'm not free to talk about the details, but it's an exposé of a major scandal."

Boyd looked unsettled for a moment. Then, "Oh, I get it. You mean like the latest on Liz or Ivana."

"To tell you the truth," Rachel said, leaning forward and lowering her voice, "I'm uncovering some pretty heavy-duty corruption within a nationally known organization. A humanistic one that prides itself on being squeaky clean. It turns out it's involved in payoffs, protection, all kinds of ugly things."

"Incredible!" George cried. "Sounds like you're right in the thick of things. I can't wait to read it."

"Me, neither," Boyd said dryly.

Rachel cast him her most dazzling smile. "Yes, the old writing career is definitely on the upswing. Did I mention that this will probably be a cover story? I predict that once this story breaks, I'll be able to write my own ticket."

"You'll be a household word," George exclaimed. "Like Woodward and Bernstein."

"Like Listerine." Boyd looked deflated.

Rachel just laughed. "And how are you, Boyd? Things going well with Ariana?"

"Fine. Couldn't be better."

George frowned. "Boyd, didn't you mention just the other day that you and Ariana were no longer—"

"We're going through a rough period, that's all."

"Poor Boyd," Rachel cooed. "Affairs of the heart can be so complicated. Well, I'd love to chat, but I'm on a tight schedule." She glanced at her watch.

George lowered his voice. "It's your article, right? Something too high-level to tell us about?"

"Picking up my daughter."

"*Our* daughter," Boyd grumbled. But Rachel had already turned away.

"Nervous, Rachel?"

"Oh, no. I always shake like this after drinking half a cup of decaf."

"Well," Ryder said with a sigh, "I wish I could say, 'Relax, honey. My parents are going to love you and they're going to do everything in their power to make you feel comfortable.' But I can't."

"Couldn't you lie a little, just this once?"

Ryder peeked into the rearview mirror to make sure no road terrorists were getting ready to pounce. Then he reached across the front seat and took Rachel's hand.

"It'll be fine. The one thing I can promise is that Eloise and Richmond are not going to cause you any physical harm."

"Maybe, but can you say the same for Bitty?"

Ryder and Rachel had sneaked away from the city early, wanting to beat some of the Friday afternoon let's-blow-this-joint traffic that was a part of summer in New York. So far they were lucky. It had been smooth sailing all the way. They were making such good progress, in fact, that they expected to reach the Thorns' Connecticut home by cocktail hour.

Ryder had assured Rachel that in the Thorns' Connecticut home there was indeed such a thing as a cocktail hour.

"Maybe meeting your folks would have been easier at their weekend place," Rachel offered. Her gaze left the monotonous green of the Connecticut Turnpike, lighting instead on the outfit she had chosen for this occasion: billowing off-white rayon pants and a turquoise silk T-shirt. It was wrong, she decided, all wrong. She looked like a Flying Walenda. "They wouldn't be able to scrutinize me as carefully up there, what with all the fuss about wet bathing suits and all."

"I don't think that would have helped much," Ryder said grimly. "Hey, look at it this way. Pretend you're on *Masterpiece Theater.* You know, acting in one of those dry drawing room comedies where on the surface everyone is completely civilized."

"Why, *Ry*-dah," she countered. "How veddy, veddy *clev*-ah of you!"

The Thorns' home was as imposing as Rachel had feared. The house was huge, the gardens impeccably manicured, the grounds appearing to stretch on forever.

"Oh, dear," she breathed as she climbed out of Ryder's Honda. He'd parked it in the semicircular driveway between his father's black Mercedes and his sister's bloodred BMW.

"You mean, 'Oh, de-ah,' don't you?" Ryder reminded her.

His expression dead serious, he reached over and gave her fanny a quick pinch.

"Ryder, darling, you made it!" A being who simply had to be Eloise Thorn floated down the front steps, one arm outstretched in a dramatic gesture. Her red nails were perfect talons, and the arm in question was covered from wrist to mid-forearm with gold cuff bracelets.

"And you must be Rachel."

Rachel smiled, not sure whether the words constituted an accusation or a simple statement of fact.

"Well, come inside, you two. I'm certain you must be *exhausted*. But there's good news: You're just in time for cocktail hour."

Ryder caught Rachel's eye and winked.

"Thomas should be here soon," Eloise told them as she drifted into the front room. She headed straight for the wet bar situated discreetly between a stone fireplace and a built-in bookshelf containing leatherbound volumes of all those classics that are no longer read by anyone besides junior high school students. "And Bitty's just arrived with Henry and the girls."

"The girls," Ryder explained, depositing their suitcases in the hall, "are Bitty's daughters. Emily is eleven and Gwen's thirteen."

"Oh, goody," said Rachel. "I've got a real way with teenage girls."

"Ah. Here's Dad," Eloise announced, dropping ice cubes into her glass.

Rachel expected to see Ryder's grandfather, a distinguished elderly Henry Fonda or Gregory Peck. Instead, a sprightly man, a peer of Eloise's, strode in, resplendent in black and white plaid pants and kelly-green golf shirt. "Dad," Rachel surmised, was Eloise's pet name for her husband.

"Hello, Dad," said Ryder with a curt nod.

Goodness, this is going to be confusing, Rachel thought, heading over to the bar herself.

Dad—Richmond—shook his son's hand, chairman-of-the-board style, then leaned against the mantelpiece. "So, old boy, you made it up here. We haven't seen you since—what is it, Christmas?"

"My business keeps me busy," Ryder said with a shrug.

"Ah, yes. The toy business."

Something that looked very much like a smirk played around Richmond's lips. Rachel, feeling protective, glanced over at Ryder. His mouth was smiling, but his eyes had that same hard look she'd seen once before, when he was telling her about his father. It was a look that frightened her.

"How are things going with your *toy* business?" Richmond's emphasis made it sound as if Ryder's enterprise were nothing but a folly. She couldn't resist rushing to the defense of her prince.

"This is an exceptionally busy time for Ryder's company," she said, sounding proud. "He's already caught up in the Christmas rush."

"Lots of demand for Hula Hoops these days, is there?" Richmond laughed loudly at his own joke, then came over to Ryder and slapped him on the back.

"Only kidding, son. You're man enough to take a joke, aren't you? You know I'm pleased that your . . . your business is doing well."

Ryder just grunted. It was actually a relief when Bitty appeared in the doorway, her two daughters in tow. She was everything Rachel had imagined, from her perky blond pageboy to her red plaid Bermuda shorts.

"Oh, *there* you are, Ryder, you naughty thing!" She dashed across the room to give her brother a big hug and then the obligatory peck on the cheek. "For months now the girls have been asking where their uncle Ryder has been keeping himself!"

"We have not," Emily insisted, plopping down on the couch. She began kicking it rhythmically. "Grandma, I can't believe you don't have Nintendo."

Ryder's eyes lit up. "Here, try this on for size."

He reached into his pocket and pulled out what looked like an oversize piece of pink bubble gum. He tossed it to his niece.

"What's this supposed to be?" Emily sounded more irritated than pleased.

"Yeah, what is that stupid thing?" Gwen came over to see what Uncle Ryder had brought along this time.

"You tell me," he said.

Emily pulled on it—and found that it stretched like real

bubble gum, bubble gum that had been chewed for a long time.

"Oooh, it feels so weird!" she cried, giggling. "Hey, look, you can change the shape. . . ."

"Hey, let me try." Gwen grabbed it, ignoring her younger sister's protests. "Wow, this is neat. It does feel funny. Like, like ooze or something. And it's—hey, look! It's changing color! It's turning purple! Gosh, how does it do that?"

"Actually, it's the heat from your hand that makes it change color." Ryder was pleased. "I call it the Rubber Rainbow. Pretty cool, huh?"

Turning to the grown-ups, who were looking on politely, he added, "And it's completely biodegradable. It's a brand-new item from our novelty line, Earth-lovers. We're launching the whole line this Christmas."

"How . . . how *nice*," said Bitty. Eloise and Richmond, meanwhile, simply looked confused.

"This is so cool," cried Gwen. "Look at this thing!"

"Hey, give it back," Emily whined.

"I want it. It's mine."

"I had it first!"

Rachel watched the two girls for a few seconds, then slipped her arm around Ryder's waist. "Ryder," she said softly, "I think you've got a winner on your hands."

By the time dinner was served, Rachel's mouth hurt from forcing a smile, a particularly difficult task since there was so little to smile about.

She did feel a new sense of closeness to Ryder, however, one that was rooted in having a better understanding of the kinds of pressures he was under. The two of them stayed close to each other, kindred spirits in an alien household. When Eloise announced that dinner was about to be served in the dining room, Rachel and Ryder grabbed two seats side by side.

Across from Rachel sat Henry, Bitty's husband. It was almost like sitting opposite an empty chair. How perfectly he played the dutiful husband, silent and meek beside his effervescent wife. He kept slipping Rachel secretive smiles, whether to show his support or to elicit sympathy, she couldn't quite tell.

Thomas, the latecomer to this impromptu little reunion of Thorns, sat opposite Ryder. Rachel sensed that this was an unfortunate arrangement. She hoped that dinner would be like a high-tech root canal: so fast and so painless it was over before you knew it.

"So, Ryder," said Thomas, leaning forward in an aggressive manner, "Dad tells me your little business is positively flourishing."

"It's doing well," Ryder said.

Already he was pretending to be more interested in the food on the table than in the company seated around it. Given the fact that everything on the table was a similar shade of beige, his performance was unconvincing.

"Ah, you're too modest," Thomas insisted. "Dad reports that you positively charmed the nieces with your latest invention. Some piece of plastic that stretches and changes color?"

Ryder nodded. "The Rubber Rainbow. Yeah, I think it'll catch on."

"I'm convinced it's going to be the next Koosh," Rachel burst out. Her only response was blank stares. Even the girls were looking at her oddly.

"I don't think these people are familiar with the Koosh ball," Ryder told her, sounding as if he were explaining the bizarre habits of some little-understood tribe. "In this household, people give Christmas presents like Burberry raincoats and shares of stock in conglomerates, not fun items like Koosh balls."

"I know what a Koosh ball is," Emily piped up. It was clear, however, that the Connecticut Thorns did not appreciate comments from children.

"You know, Ryder," Thomas said in a kind of singsong voice, "it's not too late for you to get a real job. I'm sure Dad and I could find a place for you somewhere at our firm.

"That is," he added, wearing what was clearly the family smirk, "assuming you've learned your lesson about how grown-ups behave."

"Thanks, but no thanks," Ryder said firmly. The skin on his neck, right under his jaw, was growing splotchy.

"Well, just file my offer away somewhere in the back of your mind," Thomas said. "You never know where life is going to take you, do you?"

"Meaning what, exactly?" Ryder countered.

Thomas laughed. "Meaning who knows how long you'll be able to make a living—assuming that you do, of course—based on the whims of teenagers with a few extra dollars to spend?"

"My goodness, can't we all talk about something more cheerful?" Eloise said brightly. "Which one of you big strong men is going to carve this turkey that Carmella spent the whole day preparing?"

As Ryder and Rachel lay together in bed that night, listening to the silence of the house, Rachel could feel the gloom hanging over them. She stroked his shoulder in a way that was meant to be comforting, getting about as much response as if she'd been fondling the pillow.

"Ryder, I feel like I'm lying in bed with an inflatable doll," she complained cheerfully. After a long silence she added, "That was supposed to be funny."

Ryder glanced over at her, a sad smile on his lips. "Sorry. Laughing and being in this house don't exactly go hand in hand."

"I know what you mean." She sighed. "Somehow, I'm having trouble remembering why we came here in the first place."

"Ritual, that's all. I met your family, so it was time for you to meet my family. I guess I feel it's only fair for you to get a look at the whole package. All the baggage I come with, I mean."

Rachel lay with her head propped up on her arm. With her free hand she traced the outline of the white eyelet that edged the crisp white sheets. "I've been trying to be open-minded. I hardly know your family. But, well, I can't help feeling like I'm spending the weekend in a wax museum."

"Hah! The dummies would probably be less antagonistic." Ryder's voice took on an odd, distant quality. "Can't you feel it? Isn't it almost like something in the air?" He appeared to be talking to the wallpaper. "It's like a . . . a curse or something. All of them, sitting back, watching me, waiting for me to fail. They actually *want* me to fail. They want my company to fall apart so they can wag their fingers at me and say, 'See, Ryder? You really are a failure! We told you so!' It's more important for them to be right than for me to be happy."

Rachel nodded. "Well, you know what they say," she said softly. " 'Living well is the best revenge.' You just have to do what's right for you, and forget them. If they're not on your side, then who needs them?"

As he looked over at her, she saw warmth in his eyes practically for the first time since they'd crossed into Connecticut.

"Ah, good. You're back," she muttered.

"I'm sorry they make me so crazy."

"That's okay. Families are supposed to make you crazy. It's their job."

"Your family doesn't make you crazy."

"I think you just happened to hit them on a good day." She smiled. "Besides, Sis thought you were the best thing since . . . well, since Jerry. If you don't mind the comparison, that is."

"I don't mind at all. I like Jerry. I like everyone in your family. What I like most of all is the way you and your sisters get along." Talking to the wallpaper once again, he added, "I hope our kids get along that well."

Rather than being surprised, Rachel just nodded. With the same matter-of-factness, she said, "I hope so, too."

Chapter
Eighteen

When Rachel answered the door the following Tuesday evening, she was expecting a low-key Ryder ready for a casual dinner at some neighborhood pub. Instead, she found a jubilant warrior, his face lit up like the Rockefeller Center tree on Christmas Eve. In one hand he clasped a bottle of champagne, in the other a huge stuffed tiger.

"Tonight, my dear Rachel," he announced, "you and I are celebrating."

"Terrific," she replied, blinking. "Uh, what exactly are we celebrating?"

He strode into the apartment, presented Becky with the tiger, kissed the baby-sitter on the cheek, and handed Rachel the Moët et Chandon.

"This afternoon I had a meeting with one of the buyers for Toys 'Я' Us."

"The big toy store chain?"

"None other. And to make a long story short, the buyer not only loved the Rubber Rainbow, he placed a big, fat order!"

Rachel threw her arms around his neck. "Wow! That's great news!"

He lifted her up into the air, Hollywood-style. Becky squealed and the baby-sitter sighed. "I feel like I've arrived, Rachel. Like I've finally hit the big time."

"I've always thought you were the big time."

"Come on, Becky," the baby-sitter said, reaching for her hand. "I think this is a good time for your bath."

Once the champagne had been poured, Rachel asked, "Have you told your father yet?"

Ryder shook his head. "Believe it or not, I'm not that interested in telling him. It's how I feel about it that matters."

Grinning, Rachel asked, "And how do you feel?"

"Fantastic. This Rubber Rainbow thing is something I've always wanted to do. Launching a new product, something the world's never seen before. Not to mention showing America there's such a thing as fun, creative toys that are good for kids *and* the environment." He shook his head. "I keep wondering if I died and went to heaven."

Glass in hand, he wandered around the apartment, too restless to sit. "Tonight let's eat at a really special restaurant. Anywhere you want. We can even . . . hey, is this the article you've been working on? The one that's practically taken over your life?"

"It's only a rough draft, not yet ready for human consumption." She grabbed it before he got a good look. "You'll just have to wait, like every other *New York Life* reader."

"You've been so secretive about it. Don't I get even a peek?"

"I'd rather not talk about it."

"Not even to me?"

"Not even to you."

She held her breath, expecting him to be offended. Instead, he shrugged and said, "I understand completely. I was the same way when the Rubber Rainbow was still in its planning stages. I didn't tell a soul. I was afraid I'd jinx it."

"That's how I feel."

"It's funny. You and I feel the same way about a lot of things."

"Very funny. Uncanny, even. In fact, you might even say it's too good to be true." Rachel was becoming uncomfortable, as she always did when the conversation veered this way. "So, uh, how about choosing a restaurant? Good news makes me hungry."

The same upbeat mood carried them through dinner. Rather than someplace fancy, they picked a small, raucous down-home restaurant with sawdust on the floor, the Gatlin Brothers on the jukebox, and the spiciest Tex-Mex food this side of New Jersey.

As they sat nose to nose, Rachel reflected once again on how perfect everything was. In fact, she couldn't imagine how things could get any better. And thanks to the two Mexican beers she downed, she barely gave a thought to how it had all come to pass. Instead, she concentrated on how it was about time.

She was still floating a few inches above the ground when she and Ryder reached her building. In the elevator Ryder commented, "That was pretty good grub, pardner. Too bad we were too full for dessert."

"I've got something in mind that's a lot better than after-dinner mints." Rachel slipped her arm around him, tucking her fingers inside his waistband. "Watch how fast I can get rid of the sitter."

But when she unlocked the door and let herself into her apartment, she found parked on the couch a disheveled heap of denim, leather, and fringe that was her niece.

"Shelley?"

The girl blinked. There was an incongruity between the pathetic little-girl expression on her young face and the makeup she'd smeared over it.

"Hi, Aunt Rachel."

The baby-sitter rushed in from the kitchen. "She said she was your niece, Ms. Swann. She even had a picture of Becky in her wallet, so I figured . . ."

"It's all right." Rachel turned back to Shelley. "What are you doing here?"

"Moving in with you, I hope."

Rachel cast Ryder a sidelong glance. "Oh, boy."

After hustling the sitter out the door, Rachel studied Shelley more carefully. She discovered she looked even worse than at first glance. Her leather pants had a tear in the thigh, her boots were scuffed, and the fringe on her denim jacket looked even more tattered than it was meant to.

As she sat down in the living room with her niece, Rachel knew instinctively that she had to handle this carefully. "Tell me, how long has it been since you've eaten?"

"Not that long." Shelley's defensiveness was automatic. Then, looking longingly toward the kitchen, she added, "I had an Egg McMuffin at eight this morning."

"Doesn't your mother feed you?" Ryder asked with forced joviality.

Haughtily, Shelley thrust her chin into the air. "I no longer live with my mother."

Rachel inhaled sharply. "I'd better make coffee."

As the three of them sat at Rachel's small table, it felt very late. Yet, outside the window the bustle of the city could still be heard. Shelley seemed oblivious of all but what was on her plate. In record time she wolfed down two cheese sandwiches, an overripe banana, a can of Diet 7-Up, and nine Mrs. Field's chocolate chip cookies, still half frozen. Rachel and Ryder looked on, sipping coffee, not sure whether to be amused or horrified.

"So what happened?" Rachel finally asked. "Did you and your mother have a fight?"

Shelley's face tightened defiantly. Her dark eyes were wild. For a moment it looked as if all the fury of the gods was about to be unleashed. Then, suddenly, her face crumpled and she burst into tears.

"I hate it! I just hate it!"

"What do you hate, honey?" Rachel asked in a gentle voice.

"All of it! I hate all of it!" Shelley let out a strangled snorting sound. "I especially hate my mother."

Rachel was tempted to throw her arms around her niece, but something warned her to treat Shelley like an adult, an equal.

"I see," she murmured.

Ryder caught her eye, giving her a look that said he clearly felt out of place given the situation. "Look, uh, I can see you two have a lot to talk about," he said awkwardly. "I think I'll just, uh. . . ." And faster than a speeding bullet, he was out the door.

So much for our celebratory roll in the hay, Rachel thought. She paused to dedicate a moment to her lost evening with Ryder. Then she turned her attention back to the matter at hand.

"I guess things have been pretty different around your house lately. Since your mom won all that money in the lottery and all."

"Yeah, you could say that," Shelley returned bitterly. "Like, how about she totally ruined my life?"

"How?" Rachel asked, startled.

"First of all, she redid my room. I loved that room! But Mom hired some ridiculous designer who talked, like, really affected to come in and redo the whole thing. First she threw out all my posters. Then she put in this ridiculous flowered wallpaper and these frilly curtains that look like something out of *Pollyanna*."

Rachel nodded understandingly.

"That's just the beginning," Shelley pouted. "Mom and Dad are fighting all the time."

"Sis and Jerry? *Fighting?*" Not the couple who wrote their sexual fantasies on Post-its and slipped them in between the salami slices in the meat storage drawer. . . .

"Mom keeps talking about moving. You know, selling the house."

"Oh. That again. Yes, I can see how that would cause friction."

"Friction! They're fighting like cats and dogs! My dad loves that house! He practically built the whole thing by hand! He made the baseboards, that entertainment unit thing. . . . He even made the hamper door himself!"

"Maybe moving wouldn't be so bad," Rachel said soothingly. "Maybe you'd get a house with a pool . . . a Jacuzzi. . . ." She shrugged. "I know your dad's attached to that place, but frankly, Shel, it just doesn't sound that bad to me."

"Well, that's not all. She also keeps buying me these clothes like you wouldn't believe. These weird designer things from Bloomingdale's. They're not what I want to wear."

"Honey, I know firsthand that your mom always felt bad that she couldn't buy her daughter wonderful clothes," Rachel told her sincerely. "I remember when you were born. I took her shopping for baby clothes on the Lower East Side. She kept saying that her new baby daughter was so wonderful, so special, that she wished she could buy her hand-made clothes from Saks."

"But don't you see?" Shelley pleaded, growing increasingly exasperated. "It's all what *she* wants, not what I want!"

Rachel was still pondering that when her niece said, "But the very worst thing is that she's going to send me to that yucky private school."

"But I thought you were excited about going there!"

"I was ... until I went to their geeky orientation tea. That was when I found out."

"Found out what?"

"That this place is like a detention home."

"Come on, Shel. You've been watching too many old movies."

"Oh, really? Did you know that the girls have to wear uniforms? Uniforms! Like ... like Nazi Germany or something. And they have rules you wouldn't believe."

"I'm sure you'll get used to all that in time. . . ."

"But I'm going to have to leave all my friends! And the girls at this new place are such snobs." She sucked in a sob. "They already hate me."

"Hate is such a strong word, honey." Rachel tried hard to sound cheerful. "I'm sure the girls at your new school won't hate you once they've had a chance to—"

"Aunt Rachel, they went into my purse and Crazy Glued everything in it into one big lump!"

"Ah." Rachel nodded soberly. "It does sound as if they're having some trouble accepting a new girl."

"Being new is only part of it. Most of those girls are so rich, you wouldn't believe it. They have their own cars, their own charge cards, their own horses . . . their own trust funds, for God's sake! A month ago I didn't even know what a trust fund was!"

"Well, your family's not exactly hurting, Shelley."

"Yes, but their fathers are brain surgeons and bankers and tax lawyers," she sputtered, wiping her raccoon eyes with the backs of her hands. "My father builds people's bathrooms."

"You never minded that before."

"It never seemed to matter before."

"How about Vincent?" asked Rachel. "How is he handling all this?"

Shelley rolled her eyes. "Oh, God, don't even ask."

"I'm asking, Shelley. Tell me—please."

Shelley looked at her earnestly. "I think he's getting into drugs."

"What?"

"You heard me."

"But . . . but just a few weeks ago he was showing off all his Boy Scout badges!"

"I know. Don't you see, Aunt Rachel?" Shelley wailed. "*Nothing* is the way it used to be!"

Rachel swallowed hard. "So what's the deal with him?"

"He's starting hanging out with this new crowd. They're kind of wild, you know? They all have those stupid dirt bikes. And, well, you know Vincent. He really wants to be accepted."

She shrugged, as if in defeat. "He's trying to prove how cool he is. That's where the drugs come in."

"My God! Can't he just act cool? Does he have to—"

"It's not the same thing, Aunt Rachel." Shelley cast her a cynical look. "And to tell you the truth, I can almost understand it. I feel like . . . oh, I don't know, going out and getting pregnant, just to show them all."

"Ah. Now, that would be constructive." Hastily Rachel added, "I'm just kidding, Shel. Really. It was a joke."

Shelley looked at her mournfully. "Can I stay here?"

"Of course you can. Tonight. And in the morning we'll—"

"I don't mean just tonight. I mean forever. I wouldn't be any trouble, I promise. I'd ... I'd help clean up and baby-sit Becky ... I could even help you with your work."

Rachel reached over and placed her hand lightly over her niece's. "Shelley, you can't simply run away from your problems. Besides, you have to go to school. You're only fourteen."

"I'm not going to that school!"

"All right, all right. Listen, here's my best offer. First, I have to call your parents and let them know you're here. They must be worried sick. But how about if I tell them you're going to stay here for a few days? You and I can talk, maybe go to some movies or museums, just relax a little. And when you're feeling up to it, we'll sit down together and have a long heart-to-heart talk with your mother, okay?"

Shelley nodded meekly. She seemed to believe that her aunt was going to make everything all better. Rachel only wished she felt that certain herself.

"So what'll it be?" Rachel asked cheerfully over breakfast the next morning. "The Museum of Modern Art or the Museum of Holography?" With Becky off to camp for the day, she was able to concentrate fully on her niece.

She studied Shelley, who pondered the possibilities as she worked on her second English muffin. Rachel had to admit that she looked a thousand percent better in the early morning light. All the makeup had been washed away, and her long, dark hair was neatly brushed and pulled back into a ponytail. In her aunt's pink chenille bathrobe she looked positively sweet. Rachel was surprised to find herself actually eager to spend the day with her niece.

"What are the choices again?" Shelley asked, blinking.

"Look, I have an idea. How about if I take it upon myself to—"

The telephone rang, a harsh reminder of life in the outside world. Rachel expected it was Sis, anxious about her baby bird's first solo flight. Or perhaps Ryder, seeking an update on last night's family crisis.

She was totally shocked when she heard Johnny's voice.

"I got more information to pass on to ya," he told her. "You know, letters, checks, the whole bit. Same deal as before."

"I see. So I guess you want to get together, right? Like today?"

"Yeah. Like now. This is the end of it. After I drop this stuff with you, I'm heading back out to the West Coast again."

"I see." Rachel glanced over at Shelley, who was heading toward the toaster oven with yet one more English muffin in hand. Surely the girl could occupy herself for a couple of hours. Maybe tidy up the place, as she'd offered the night before, to earn her keep.

"Okay, Johnny. We're on. Just tell me where and when."

Family matters put aside for the moment, Rachel was all business. Already she was worrying about whether or not it would be difficult to get a cab at that hour of the morning.

"So you're heading out west," Rachel said conversationally, taking one more sip of one more cup of coffee she didn't really want. She was developing her own medical theory about the correlation between high-stress careers and heart disease: It wasn't the stress that was the problem; it was all the coffee consumed in the name of being sociable.

Johnny nodded. "Yeah. I heard there's another movement starting up out there. Up in northern California, outside San Francisco. I'm gonna go there and check this SOP thing out."

"Sop?"

"Save Our Planet."

She smiled. "I'm really glad people like you are out there fighting for people like us."

"You could join me, y'know," Johnny said matter-of-factly. "I bet SOP could use a good writer."

"Maybe one day. But for now I've got my work cut out for me right here. You said you've got one more batch of incriminating evidence for me?"

Johnny was already reaching for his manila envelope. "Three more. Same deal as before. These companies were making generous contributions to Grass Roots, pretending they were supporting their efforts but in reality sending the message that if the Grass Roots folks were smart enough to know which side their bread was buttered on, they'd steer clear of 'em."

Rachel nodded. "More letters?"

"Yup. Mostly from folks at the middle levels. And all of it totally off the record, of course. These documents were meant only for the eyes of some of the higher-ups at Grass Roots."

"I'm going to read them the moment I get home," Rachel promised.

Johnny stood up, tucking a few bills beneath the rim of his saucer.

"You're taking off?" Rachel asked, surprised. She had just assumed that Johnny would stay until both their coffee cups were empty.

He nodded. "Yeah. My work is done here." He held out his hand. "Listen, it's been great workin' witcha. I'm really looking forward to reading your article."

Then, his eyes narrowing, he added, "And I really hope you nail the bastards to the wall."

That same melancholic feeling that Rachel had experienced upon saying good-bye to Johnny accompanied her as she opened the folder to look over the last bit of evidence he had unearthed. She was sitting in the backseat of a taxi, hurrying home to her niece; by comparison, the problems of her working life seemed like a breath of fresh air.

Even so, the awareness that this marked the beginning of the end of her first really important assignment made her sad. After almost four weeks of intense involvement, it was time to tie up the loose ends, insert the last of the information, tighten up the first draft, and deliver the manuscript to Grayson Winters. True, she was eager to hear his reaction or, to be more accurate, to hear him lavish praise upon her and her article. But for now it was the imminent termination of an all-absorbing project that was orchestrating her emotions.

She glanced through the papers in Johnny's folder, the hazy photocopies edged with fine gray lines. The first was a letter from a company in Texas that she had never heard of, the second a letter from a firm in Minnesota. . . .

And then her heart stopped. Everything stopped. It took only a moment for what she was seeing to register, a mere fraction of a second for its meaning to snap into place.

But that moment changed everything. Suddenly all of it—the sense of sadness, of finality, of relative peace—was completely shattered.

There it was, in black and white, staring her in the face. The letter was from Leonard Klein, an employee of Kidstuff, Incorporated. And stapled to the back was a copy of a check, made out to Grass Roots, for twenty-five thousand dollars.

Chapter
Nineteen

Rachel *had been trying hard* to compose herself, to keep from looking like someone whose entire world had just exploded. But as she let herself into her apartment, Shelley's first question was "Aunt Rachel, are you okay?"

She plopped down on the couch. "I'm fine, Shelley." Glancing up at her niece hovering in the kitchen doorway with a sponge in one hand and the latest issue of *Rolling Stone* in the other, she added, "Why shouldn't I be?"

"I don't know." Shelley deposited her playthings on the counter and sat next to her. "You look like you just saw a ghost."

What caused Rachel to turn around at that particular moment, to twist her shoulders one hundred eighty degrees so she could look behind her, she couldn't say. Never would she ever be able to understand what led her eyes to seek out the space directly under her word processor.

There, tucked beneath the straw basket that served as a trash can, was a piece of paper. She jumped up, dashed over, and grabbed it.

"What's that?" Shelley asked.

Rachel didn't answer. She was too busy unfolding the piece of paper, knowing all along there was no need to bother. She'd recognized it immediately.

"How am I doing?" it asked.

This time there was no heat. No sound of deep laughter. Only a gripping iciness that swept over her like the draft from a freezer with the door open.

"Aunt Rachel?"

Shelley sounded frightened. She was burrowing into the corner of the couch when her aunt whirled toward her, eyes blazing.

"Where did this come from?" she demanded. "Did you pull it out of the garbage?"

"No! Why would I go through your garbage?"

"Then where did this come from?"

"I didn't do anything!" the girl whimpered. "I promise, I didn't touch a thing!"

"You mean to tell me you didn't find this? On the kitchen floor, maybe, or under the sink?"

"No! I swear!"

Rachel got hold of herself. "Oh, my God, Shelley. I'm so sorry." She threw her arms around her niece. Rather than hugging her, she was clinging to her. "I didn't mean to accuse you, honey. None of this has anything to do with you."

When she pulled away, she saw that her words and actions—designed to be reassuring—had actually further alarmed her niece.

"What's going on?" Shelley's voice wavered. "Aunt Rachel, are you in some kind of trouble?"

"No, no, nothing like that. It's just . . . I'm sorry. You must think I've gone nuts. It's just that while I was out just now, I got some bad news."

Shelley hung her head, still not convinced she wasn't in some way to blame. Finally she ventured, "Is there anything I can do?"

"No, sweetie. I just need some time. I have to think. . . ."

"Uh, Aunt Rachel, while you were out, my mom called. She asked if you and I could meet her at the Metropolitan Museum of Art later. She said she couldn't sleep all night, and that she really wanted to talk."

"Fine. What time did she say?"

"Two o'clock."

"Good. That should give me just enough time. . . ." Rachel was studying her watch. "Shelley, I'm going to ask you to do me a favor."

"Anything."

"I want you to go to the museum by yourself. I'll meet you and your mom there at two, okay?"

"But I thought we were going to—okay."

"I'm sorry our plans got spoiled. It's just that this . . . this thing has come up. Here, let me give you some money for a cab."

"Don't forget, two o'clock," Shelley reminded her a few minutes later as she was heading out the door. "My mom said we should meet her at the entrance to the Mocambian exhibition."

Rachel swallowed hard. "Where else?"

When she was a little girl, Rachel was a straight-A student. That was hardly surprising, since she put all her energy into being the perfect, obedient child who took care never to make waves.

There was one time, however, when she was eight or nine years old, that she decided to step off the straight and narrow. She wanted to find out—just once—how it felt. The opportunity arose when her best friend at school came up with a plan for sneaking out of the lunchroom to take a peek into the teachers' lounge.

There, Debbie promised, the two of them would be able to see their teachers the way they *really* were. Inside that mysterious sanctuary, she had heard, they sat on comfortable chairs and crossed their legs. They laughed with each other conspiratorially. They drank coffee. They smoked cigarettes.

It was a daring undertaking, Rachel knew. But how delicious the rewards would be! She and Debbie made a point of sitting at separate tables during lunch period that day, not wanting to call attention to their absence when the two of them disappeared at precisely twenty-five minutes to twelve. The girls agreed to meet in the corridor, away from prying eyes.

It never even occurred to Rachel that her best friend might fail to follow through on her part of the plan. After all, she was not only the instigator, she was also the one who knew the secret route to the teachers' lounge, down the back corridor where hardly anyone ever went.

Rachel, standing outside the cafeteria for what seemed an eternity, began to wonder if she'd gotten confused about the plan. She tried to sort out the best thing to do, and in the end she went off on her own in search of the treasure at the end of the rainbow.

Taking that risk, it turned out, proved to be a fatal mistake. Wandering around school, lost and bewildered, she got caught. She was sent to be reprimanded by Mr. Snell, the principal. And sitting outside his office, waiting for the ax to fall with a knot in her stomach the size of a fist, she came to her own conclusion about the day's events: Perhaps going off in search of something you really wanted—something you weren't sure you were really supposed to have—invariably ended in punishment.

Sitting outside Grayson Winters's office now, waiting and watching Mary Louise typing away at her word processor, Rachel felt as she'd felt that day, waiting her turn at the principal's office. She was actually surprised when Grayson appeared in the doorway instead of Mr. Snell. And then her confusion passed even as the dread lingered on.

"So," Grayson said coolly, leading her into his office and then taking his usual place of authority behind the big desk. "You wanted to see me, Rachel?"

"Yes. Thanks for fitting me in on such short notice. Uh, something has come up."

Grayson frowned; this wasn't the kind of thing he liked to hear. "We're talking about the Grass Roots article, I take it?"

With a nod Rachel said, "Yes. I—"

"Don't tell me your informant hasn't come across with everything he promised?"

"Oh, no. Johnny's been great. I have all the evidence I need. I've even put together a rough draft of the article."

"Well, that's good news. After all, your deadline is next week, isn't it?"

"It's not writing the article that's the problem. It's . . . it's the effect that publishing it in *New York Life* is going to have."

Grayson's look of concern was quickly giving way to one of irritation. "We've known all along what the effect was going to be."

"Yes, of course. It's just that . . ."

Rachel could see that she had no choice but to lay all her cards on the table. She spread her fingers across her knees, staring at them instead of looking the editor in the eye.

"Grayson," she said in a soft, controlled voice, "I just found out that one of the companies involved in paying off Grass Roots belongs to a friend of mine."

Grayson's reaction was no reaction. "What's your point?"

Rachel was unable to contain her shock. "Good Lord, isn't it evident? The point is that writing this article and including all the information that Johnny has given me means destroying him. It means destroying someone I know. Someone I—" Her voice broke. "Someone I care about very much."

She was silent then, looking to Grayson for answers. Or perhaps a different perspective. Or, at the very least, a little sympathy.

She realized in that split second that she'd made a terrible mistake.

"Rachel," Grayson said simply, "I'm disappointed in you."

"What . . . I . . . but . . ."

"And here I thought you were a journalist. That you wanted to be working on tough, meaty assignments."

She had a vague recollection of words like that. The trouble was, it all seemed very, very long ago.

"Of course I do. But—"

"There *are* no 'buts,' Rachel. You should know that."

Grayson leaned back in his chair. There was a strange look in his eyes, something she couldn't quite define.

And then, suddenly, she understood. He was *enjoying*

this. He had, in fact, been waiting for a moment like this for a long time now, ever since the two of them had found themselves sitting together on the couch, right in this office. . . .

"Rachel," he said slowly, "the writing is on the wall. Either you do your job, or I find someone else to do it."

For a small eternity they sat opposite each other, their eyes locked.

"It's that cut and dried, is it?" Rachel finally asked, her voice cold.

But Grayson was matter-of-fact. With a small shrug he said, "Of course it is."

His response only made her more agitated. "But all I ever wanted was to go after the bad guys," she cried. "I never wanted to hurt any of the good guys."

Grayson shook his head, though whether in sympathy or disbelief, she couldn't say. "Haven't you learned yet that there's no such thing as good guys and bad guys? It's never a clear-cut case of us against them. If only life could really be that simple." He let out a long sigh. "The truth is, they *are* us, and we're them."

Rachel thought for a few seconds. "So the bottom line here is that if I don't go ahead and write this article, you'll find somebody else to do it."

He was actually smiling. "My dear Rachel, what else could you possibly expect? We have a story here, and we have to go ahead with it."

For a fleeting moment Rachel indulged in a delicious fantasy: taking all the evidence that Johnny had given her and burning it. He was gone, after all, vanished, off to the West Coast to do his part to save the world.

But that was only a fantasy. No doubt there were other copies of the letters and hundreds of other journalists around town who would kill for the opportunity to step in and take her place. *That* was reality. Besides, she knew, all of that was hardly the point.

The real point, of course, was that Grayson was right.

"All right," she said, standing up.

Grayson's eyes were following her, asking a question. "All right, meaning what? All right, you'll do it, or all right, I should find someone else?"

"It means, all right, I get what you're saying." In a softer voice she went on. "Can I take a day or two to think about this? It's important to me."

He shrugged. "Look, Rachel, aside from whatever personal agendas you and I may have in terms of working together, the fact remains that I've got a magazine to put out. I can't allow my writers to work out their personal problems on my time. The bottom line here is that either you're in or you're out."

He glanced at his watch, making no attempt to hide his annoyance. Rachel barely noticed; her mind was filled with the image of Boyd, the look on his face that day at the restaurant. The day a new side of him had emerged, a side that even she had never suspected. He remained a threat, with or without Ariana. He wanted blood. And she needed every bit of ammunition she could get.

She cleared her throat. "All right, Grayson," she said, her voice strained. "You can count me in."

"There she is! My best girl." Jack cocked his head to one side. Two pink splotches immediately decorated his cheeks. "Well, my second best girl, anyway."

"Hello, Jack," Rachel said distractedly.

"So what brings you to Dominion Publishing today?" He gestured toward the glass tank of water from which he was filling a tiny paper cup. "Looking for a little gossip around the water cooler?"

"Thanks, but I've heard about all the gossip I can handle for now."

"Too bad. I have a terrific little tidbit I was hoping to drop into your lap."

"Don't tell me," said Rachel. "You and my sister are running away to the South of France together."

He looked surprised. "Who told you?"

"Look, Jack, I'm not really in the mood for playing guessing games right now—"

"Of course, it's not the South of *France*, exactly; it's Texas."

"*What's* Texas?"

"The place I'm hoping she'll run off to with me."

Rachel took a moment to glance longingly at the elevator. Then, sighing, she let it close without her. "Okay, Jack. I've got five minutes and no more."

Once the door to his office had been closed, Jack let out an odd laugh, something between a chortle and a giggle. "I'm so thrilled about this, Rachel. I can't begin to tell you!"

"Try," she urged. "What's going on in Texas?"

"A job. Editor-in-chief of a brand-new regional magazine. It's called *The Great Southwest*."

"Never heard of it."

"Of course you haven't. No one has. It doesn't even exist yet. But it will soon. It's the brainchild of a Texas zillionaire who's distraught over the fact that local pride seems to be on the wane."

"And he wants *you* to run the show? You, a man whose idea of the wilds is Queens?"

Jack looked hurt. "There's more to me than you think," he offered in his own defense. "I love Tex-Mex food. I eat beef at least three times a day. When I was a kid I would drink my chocolate milk only out of my Roy Rogers mug."

"Right. And I had three Barbie dolls, but that didn't make me prom queen." She looked at him oddly. "You're really serious about this, aren't you?"

"Sho' am, pardner." Earnestly he added, "Hey, look. This is my chance to run the whole show."

"And it doesn't bother you that the show happens to be a rodeo?"

"Boy, Rachel. And here I thought you'd be happy for me."

"Oh, I am, Jack. Of course I am. It sounds too good to

be true. I'm just surprised, that's all. How did this guy find you?"

Jack shrugged. "Apparently he's been following my work for some time. He owns other magazines—trade publications, stuff like that—and he's been thinking about doing something on a larger scale for quite a while. He's decided that now is the time. And that I'm his man."

"Wow. Does Grayson know?"

"Not yet. I still need a couple more weeks to sort out some of the details."

"Right," Rachel said dryly. "Like finding out which states border Texas."

"Oklahoma is above it," Jack said. "And New Mexico is to the west. Or is it Arizona?"

Rachel laughed. "Sounds like you'd better hire yourself a research staff, fast."

Something had been nagging at her during their conversation, something she couldn't put her finger on. All of a sudden it kicked in.

"Jack, you're not smoking!"

"Nope." He smiled proudly. "I quit. It's been two weeks, three days, and—" He glanced at his watch.

"That's okay. What great news! What prompted you to do it?"

"The love of a good woman. What else?"

"Speaking of whom, how exactly does this good woman fit in to the Texas migration plan?"

"Actually, I was kind of hoping you'd be able to give me some advice on how to break the news to her."

"You mean you haven't told her yet?"

"Well, it's only been semidefinite, up until this morning. I just got off the phone, and . . . what do you think?"

"About what?"

"About whether or not she'll come with me?"

Rachel's mouth dropped open. "Wait a minute. Are you sure we're talking about the same person here?"

"Molly, right?"

"Right. Molly Swann. The Columbia University professor, the sweetheart of the talk show circuit, the ambitious career woman with the ego the size of . . . of Texas."

Jack was looking worried. "Yeah, that's what I've been thinking. She might not want to give all that up for me."

"Does this Texas zillionaire friend of yours have a private plane or two? You and Molly could try a commuter thing."

"Nah. That wouldn't work. Not for me, anyway."

"I know what you mean." Rachel was nodding. "It could get pretty lonely, sleeping alone Monday through Thursday."

"I'll just have to talk to her, that's all. There are universities down in Texas. There are even television stations."

"Right. The beef reports."

"Let's not jump to conclusions," Jack said brightly. "Molly and I will simply have to find a way to work all this out.

"Now, enough about me and my zany, madcap life. How's by you?"

Forcing a smile, Rachel prepared herself to offer Jack some witty reply. Suddenly her face crumpled and she burst into tears.

"What's the matter?" Jack rushed over and put a brotherly arm around her. "What happened? Are you all right?"

"Oh, I'm fine," she choked through her sobs. "It's just that my life is on the verge of being totally destroyed, that's all."

"Now, now. Tell Uncle Jack all about it."

In a few short sentences punctuated with hiccups and sniffles, she told him all about the man she had met in Bloomingdale's, about his toy company and his determination to prove to his family that he could make it just fine without their help. Then she filled him in on Johnny, their coffee-shop meetings, his manila folders full of evidence, and the discovery she had made while going over the last batch. Jack's first question caught her totally off guard.

"What did Ryder say when you told him?"

"W-what?"

"How did he react when you told him all the stuff you just told me?"

"I—I haven't told him yet."

"Well, doesn't that seem like the first thing you need to do? The man has a right to know about the dirt you've uncovered about his company. Besides, if he really loves you, the two of you should be going through this crisis together."

Rachel realized then she *had* known that telling Ryder was the right thing to do. She also understood that the prospect filled her with such dread that she'd filed it away in the dark, safe recesses of her mind.

"Yeah, you're right," she mumbled. "And you know what?"

"What?" Jack asked.

She grimaced. "Having to confront Ryder is the worst part of this whole thing."

In a weird way, Rachel was actually thankful for the distraction that her family was temporarily providing. As she skipped up the stairs to the front entrance of the Metropolitan Museum of Art at five minutes after two, she was driven by an energizing optimism, a sense that she was about to attack something both immediate and manageable. For now, at least, Ryder and Grayson and all the rest could be put on hold.

Even her apprehension over returning to the Mocambian exhibition was quickly dispelled. True, she moved hesitantly, waiting to feel a chill or perhaps the beginnings of a headache. Nothing. But her vigilance was completely forgotten as soon as she spotted Shelley and Sis.

They were waiting outside the exhibition's entrance, just as planned. However, they were sitting on opposite sides of a bench. The way they were both scowling made them look like a pair of gargoyle-shaped bookends propping up the three exhausted museumgoers wedged in between.

"Hi," Rachel called, beaming and waving as she hurried toward them. "Sorry I'm late."

"You're not late," said Sis, glancing up. She was wearing silk pants and a flashy loose-fitting jacket, an outfit much better suited to the PTA dinner than an art museum. Beside the jacket's gaudy pattern, her grim expression looked particularly out of place.

"I'm dying for a cup of tea," announced Rachel. "Why don't we go to the museum's restaurant?" Especially since it's about as far away from this exhibition as you can get without crossing Fifth Avenue, she added silently.

As she led her sister and her niece toward the cafeteria, she felt like a schoolteacher dragging a reluctant class on a tour of one of the most magnificent museums in the world. She kept up a nonstop monologue, so cheerful and energetic that even she found it irritating.

It was a relief when the three of them finally sat down at a table in the cavernous room, once a home for art but now a sort of fast-food pit stop for the culture monger.

"Now," she said firmly. "Sis, first of all, I think you should give Shelley a chance to air her complaints. And your job is to listen. Don't interrupt, just listen. And then it'll be your turn to talk. Okay, Shelley? Shoot."

She was afraid her niece would simply burst into tears. She had her paper napkin ready. Fortunately it appeared that a little time away from home had helped the girl put things into perspective.

"Here are the things that need to change before I'll agree to move back home," Shelley began with a haughtiness that would have been amusing if the words hadn't been so harsh. "First of all, I feel very uncomfortable with the idea of going to that new school you and Daddy are insisting I go to. The girls are snobs and . . . and I just don't belong there.

"Second, I want my room back the way it used to be. Third, I want your word that you're not going to sell that house, which poor Daddy practically built with his own bare hands. Fourth, I want that stupid motorcycle of Vincent's turned into scrap metal before he kills himself—or somebody else."

Shelley paused to take a deep breath. But Sis apparently interpreted it as a sign that she'd finished.

"It just so happens that I've got my own list, Shelley," she said, barely able to contain her anger. "And it starts with the fact that you, my dear girl, are a fourteen-year-old girl. You are, for all intents and purposes, a child. It is not your place to make decisions about where your father and I choose to live, or how we decorate our home, or what we buy or don't buy for our son. You are also too young to be able to understand clearly the importance of receiving a good education. . . ."

"Oh, fine. Great," Shelley burst out. "In other words, you don't care at all what I think. *I* don't count. *I* have absolutely no rights in that house."

"Um, this approach doesn't seem to be getting us anywhere," Rachel interjected gaily. "I was hoping for more of a . . . dialogue." Still in her perky mode, she added, "Sis, I think Shelley has brought up some valid points. I think—"

Sis turned on her with wild eyes. "Oh, yeah?" she countered, sounding exactly the way she had when she was six years old. "So what! It's *my* money!"

Rachel was stunned into silence. Shelley was, too, at least for the moment. When Rachel finally did think of something to say, she no longer had the patience to play the impartial mediator.

"Now, wait a minute," she said. "It's your money, yes. But I never intended for it to make the lives of every—"

"You never intended? *You? Hah!*" Sis let out a yelp, a cold, mean sound that Rachel had never heard from her before. "So *you're* responsible, *you*, with your stupid delusions . . ."

"What's going on here?" Shelley asked meekly.

"Nothing," her mother replied. "Your aunt just thinks she graduated to sainthood, that's all."

"That's hardly what I've been saying," Rachel protested. "Believe me, sainthood is as far as you can get from—"

"Look, Rachel." Sis was breathing heavily. "Why don't

you just butt out? Try minding your own business for a change.

"And *you*, young lady," she went on, turning to her daughter, "get your things together. We're going home. I've had about enough of this."

"Now, wasn't that productive?" Rachel said a few minutes later, talking to the empty table.

She took a sip of her tea, now cold, and looked around at the remains of the tea party. Even the ones she used to give when she was a little girl—for her teddy bear, her Betsy Wetsy doll, and all her imaginary friends—even those, with their invisible guests, had never seemed quite as lonely as this.

"Dr. Ashcrofton? I hope you don't mind my coming by without an appointment, but I happened to be in the museum and . . ."

Rachel let her voice trail off, the words hanging in the air uncertainly. She'd been about to leave the museum when she remembered that it was here all the problems had begun in the first place. Perhaps Dr. Ashcrofton might be able to provide a solution, or at least some information, some insight, that would help her out of the maze she had wandered into.

It was the end of the day, and the section of the building that housed the offices was nearly deserted. Fortunately the good doctor was in. But just barely. She was standing at her desk, which was piled so high with cardboard cartons that Rachel wouldn't even have seen her if it hadn't been for the little puff of white hair hovering over the horizon like cloud. She was packing away her books and papers, reminding Rachel that her stay here had, after all, been merely temporary.

Cornelia Pellings Ashcrofton, glancing up at the sound of a human voice, looked more bewildered than annoyed. She removed her glasses, letting them fall onto her chest, where they were held safely against the crisp blue flowered fabric by their chunky gold-colored chain.

"Dr. Swann, isn't it?" she asked, still trying to put things into perspective.

"Uh, Rachel Swann."

"Ah, yes." Slowly, Dr. Ashcrofton seemed to be remembering that not everyone in the universe possessed a Ph.D. "From that magazine, right?"

"From *New York Life* magazine, that's right. I wrote the article on the Mocambians."

"Ah, yes." This time the pronouncement was accompanied by a tightening of her mouth. Obviously Rachel's article had failed to meet with her approval.

"Dr. Ashcrofton, I can see you're busy. . . ."

"Yes. Now that the exhibition is all settled, it's time for me to move on." She looked around in dismay. "Packing up is such a chore, don't you agree?"

"Yes, I do. Uh, Dr. Ashcrofton, I was wondering if I might have a word with you. Just five minutes, that's all."

"Well . . . all right." Dr. Ashcrofton gave one more tired glance at her cartons and her piles of books and papers, then motioned for Rachel to sit down.

"I feel almost foolish telling you about this," she began, "but it has something to do with the exhibition. It has to do with the whole culture of Mocambu, actually. Their, uh, religion."

"Go on." The older woman was perched primly on the edge of her desk chair.

"The night of the opening, I wandered inside the temple that was on display here."

Rachel told her about all the events that had transpired since that evening. At first she was self-conscious, striving to sound impartial, detached, taking refuge behind the scientific language she thought Dr. Ashcrofton would feel comfortable with. But as she went on, her emotions came bubbling up, and just as she had while pouring her heart out to Jack, she ended by bursting into tears.

"My, my," Dr. Ashcrofton said, awkwardly offering her a white linen handkerchief. "You do seem to be under a lot of pressure, my dear. Have a good cry, now. It will make you feel better."

Rachel looked at her in surprise. "But it's not sympathy I want from you."

"What exactly is it you want from me, then?" Dr Ashcrofton looked uneasy.

"I want to know about other times this has happened."

"Other times?"

"Yes. You're the expert. You must know all about how the Mocambians handle their interactions with the devil Basically, I want to know how I can undo all this. How can I make it all go away? Is there some, some ceremony have to perform? Or some herb I should eat, or some offering, some sacrifice I have to make—"

Dr. Ashcrofton was staring at her in amazement. "My dear, you really believe all this, don't you?"

Blinking, Rachel nodded. "Of course I believe it. It's true. It's all true." But something in her was sinking, some small bit of optimism, of hope, that she had been clinging to. "It is true, isn't it? I mean, you have heard of this before, right?"

"I think," Dr. Ashcrofton said slowly, "you need to be talking to someone else about all this. I'm an anthropologist, not an expert in matters of this sort."

"What sort?"

"Psychological, uh, problems."

Rachel took a slow, deep breath, willing herself to regain control of her emotions. "You don't believe me."

"Ms. Swann—Rachel—I don't mean to be unkind. I can see how distraught you are. But maybe I can shed some light on the confusion you seem to be experiencing.

"The Mocambians' religion is like that of any other culture. It works because the people believe in it. The ceremonies, the incantations, the herbs . . . their power comes from the people's eagerness to accept them as truth."

"So you think I've been imagining all this," Rachel said slowly. "You don't believe a word of it."

"What I believe is that human beings are capable of con

vincing themselves of just about anything. And I think that, in your case, you want to believe that you—or some other force, some outside force—have the power to control every aspect of your life and the lives of those you love. In short, you want to believe that anything is possible, that everything is there for the taking, just because you want it."

"So you don't think I'm crazy."

Dr. Ashcrofton came over and put a comforting hand on her shoulder. "I think what you are is human."

Rachel was overcome with relief. So Molly and Sis had been right: She *was* imagining it. It was merely a question of self-hypnosis, of self-delusion, of an overly active fantasy life brought on by an overly busy schedule. She sighed.

"Which still leaves me with the problem of how I'm going to deal with the mess my life is in right now."

Dr. Ashcrofton sighed. "I'm afraid that that, my dear, is also part of being human." With an indulgent, almost motherly smile, she added, "That's one lesson I would have expected you to have learned by now."

Rachel stood up, ready to leave now that her business here had been completed. "Thank you for your time, Dr. Ashcrofton."

"Not at all." The older woman had already turned back to her cardboard cartons. When she spoke one more time, her voice was so muffled that Rachel nearly missed her words.

"It's not fair, is it, that we women are so often put in the position of having to choose between love and success."

Rachel, already halfway out the door, glanced back at her in surprise. As she did, she saw that there were tears in Dr. Ashcrofton's eyes.

A*s she rode up* in the elevator of her apartment building
minutes before Becky was due back, Rachel wished that
going home could mean what it usually did: retreating from
the big bad world, closing the door on whatever it was she
didn't want to face, hiding underneath the covers or in a
warm bubble bath or within the pages of a juicy novel. But
as she turned the key in the door, it was without the feeling
of relief that generally accompanied the sound of the tumblers rearranging themselves.

It was true that her little talk with Dr. Ashcrofton had
taken a load off her shoulders—a rather substantial load, in
fact. But even if there was no such thing as the bogeyman,
she still had to deal with the fact that inside her apartment
there was a telephone, and somewhere out there, at the
other end of it, was Ryder.

Her head was filled with images of him, the way the picture on a movie screen fills the theater. And not just Ryder's; she also kept seeing his father and his brother.

Yet she had to confront him; there was no way around it.
Her only course was to deal with the problem head-on. And
without delay. So focused on her thoughts was she that she
jumped to high heaven when she shuffled into the kitchen
and discovered that she wasn't alone.

"Uh, excuse me," she said to the bulky figure who was
half inside the cabinet underneath the kitchen sink. All that
was exposed was a broad back, not quite covered by a
white T-shirt, and a pair of worn-out jeans dipping dangerously low. A large field of coarse black hairs was in full

view, prompting Rachel to avert her eyes. "Is there, uh, a problem with the sink?"

The man lowered his head and ducked out from inside the cabinet. When he turned around, she found herself looking at a rotund, red-faced man with black hair, black eyebrows, and a thick black mustache. At his side, within easy reach, was a wooden toolbox. The stubby fingers of his right hand, stained with black smudges, were curled around a wrench. His left hand, meanwhile, held a burning cigar. A handyman, apparently, although he didn't look like one of her building's usual maintenance staff members. Then again, neither did he look like a deranged killer.

"You da lady who lives here?"

Rachel nodded, meanwhile holding up her key as proof. For a moment she forgot that he was the intruder.

"Uh, what exactly seems to be the problem?"

"Aw, ya got some leakage. Ya got a problem in here that's causing trouble for some of the other people who live around ya." He stood up, no easy task for someone with the physique of Alfred Hitchcock. "But I think we got it all under control."

"Good. I certainly hope so." Please, just get out, she was thinking, desperately wanting her own space back.

Unfortunately, he showed no signs of going anywhere. Putting down his wrench, he began to wander around the apartment at a leisurely pace. Nosily he poked at this and that, acting more like someone shopping for real estate than a plumber.

"So, you a writer?" he asked pleasantly.

Rachel bit her lip. "Yes, I am. Listen, if you don't mind. . . ."

"What, you write for magazines?"

"Yes. Yes, I do. Now, if you're finished here, I'd really appreciate it if . . ."

He had picked up the draft of her article sitting immediately to the right of her computer. He peeked over at her coyly. "Dis your article for *New York Life*?"

And then she knew.

That awful feeling, the feeling that someone was slowly running an ice cube down her spine, came over her.

"You're not really a handyman, are you?"

"I been called that," he said cheerfully. " 'Course, I been called a lot of things."

Still holding the article, he sashayed over to her couch and prepared to lower himself, grease stains and all.

"Wait! Don't—"

"Hmmm? Oh, it's okay. I won't get your couch dirty." Sitting down, grinning, he explained, "Makeup. Just for effect."

He settled back against the cushions. "So, Rachel, how's it going? I can't wait to read this article. I bet you're doin' a terrific job with it. Now, where exactly is the part about Kidstuff?"

"You knew, didn't you?" Rachel accused him. "You knew all along."

He shrugged. " 'Course I knew. It's my job to know."

Rachel stuck her chin in the air, attempting to inject a touch of arrogance. "You know, no one believes in you. Everybody I talk to tells me you're nothing more than a figment of my imagination."

"Oh, they do, do they?" He chose that moment to flick his cigar, causing a very large—and very real—clump of ash to plummet onto her carpet.

Rachel just stared. "That's right. Um, Molly and Sis and . . . and even Dr. Ashcrofton."

"Dr. Ashcrofton, huh?" He thought for a second, then, shaking his head slowly, said, "That's one broad I never cared for very much."

Indignantly, Rachel stood up as straight as she could. "What is it that you want, exactly?"

"Me? I already got what I want. And you got what you want, right? So everybody's happy, am I right?"

"Yeah, right."

With that, Rachel sank onto a chair, covering her face with her hands. "What am I going to do?" she sobbed. "Oh, God—"

"Don't call me that! I hate that."

"I'm in a no-win situation. No matter what I do, I lose."

The hulking figure chuckled. "Don't you love it?"

She looked up at him, her face streaked with tears. "Am I just a bad person? Is that what it is? Is that how I got here? Am I selfish and greedy and . . . and *bad*?"

"Aw, c'mon, Rachel," he said consolingly. "People are not 'bad.' There's no such thing as bad guys and good guys."

"That's what Grayson was saying."

"Now, *him*, I like. But he's right. And you know why? It's because people are not equal to the sum of their parts. The bad stuff, the negatives, do not cancel out the positives, like in a mathematical equation. Three good things do not combine with four bad things to make the person come out 'bad.'

"I'm tellin' ya, there's no such thing as a person who's totally 'good.' In fairy tales, maybe, but not real life. Ya got your jealousy, your greed, your sloth. . . . And the same goes for the other side of the coin. The worst criminal in the world will have people come visit him on death row. People who love him. People who see good in him, even if only a trace. There are always people who see him as good, people like his mother or his wife or his kids or his buddies."

He shrugged. "Believe me, I know. A bad man is hard to find."

"All right; so I'm not bad. Now what am I supposed to do?"

"What do you think you're supposed to do?"

"I think I'm supposed to talk to Ryder, tell him what Johnny found out, and try to work it out with him. I think I'm supposed to mind my own business where my sisters are concerned. And I think I'm supposed to try to find a way to live with the results of my actions, the good ones and the bad ones. That also includes the well-meaning ones that turn out to have bad results."

The handyman sighed. "You're handlin' all this so well. Do you have any idea how much that hurts me?"

"Well, what else can I do? Break down and cry?"

"Seems to me you been doin' a lot of that lately. It doesn't help things very much, does it?"

With great effort the large man pulled himself up off the couch. As he'd promised, there was not a stain on it. The carpet hadn't fared nearly as well.

"Oh, boy. This is no line of work for somebody my age," he wheezed. "Look, I gotta push on. I'll be back, of course, sooner or later. . . ."

"It's the 'later' part I'm worried about," Rachel returned.

"Oh, yeah. Before I forget, I'm supposed to give you dis."

"What now?"

She looked at the grease-smeared piece of paper he'd handed her. It appeared to be a bill for parts from a local plumbing supply store. There was some writing scribbled on back, hurried and barely legible, but Rachel barely glanced at it.

"Eighty-nine dollars for plumbing parts?"

"And fifty-three cents. What, ya think I do this for free?"

Rachel sighed. "Did you at least fix the sink?"

"Nah. Made it worse." He shrugged. "Whadda ya expect me to do, turn over a new leaf or somethin'?" With a loud guffaw, he added, "Get outa here!"

When he was gone, Rachel was, as usual, confused, dazed, not quite certain whether or not what appeared to have happened had, indeed, actually happened. For the moment, however, she had other realities to contend with. She hesitated for a moment, and then, knowing there was no point in putting it off any longer, reached for the telephone.

As she picked up the telephone, the doorbell buzzed loudly, causing her to jump.

"Who—or *what*—is it *now*?" she muttered in exasperation.

"Rachel, I have to talk to you," Molly sputtered, exploding into her sister's apartment. "I am ready to *burst!*"

Rachel almost would have preferred another visit from a diabolical being.

"Is it something I did?" she asked innocently.

"'Is it something I did?' she asks. Hah!" Molly let out a contemptuous snort.

Rachel braced herself for a tirade. Instead of letting loose, however, Molly sank onto the couch, her anger quickly giving way to despair. "Oh, Rachel, what am I going to *do?*"

Rachel sat down next to her and gently wrapped a protective arm around her sister's shoulders. "What is it?" she asked in a kind, grandmotherly voice.

"It's Mike. And Jack."

"A double whammy, huh? What happened?"

Molly looked at her accusingly. "The Jack part you already know about. He told me about the little talk the two of you had."

"Oh." Rachel, acting appropriately guilty, slumped her shoulders. "You mean the Texas thing."

"Yes, of course I mean the Texas thing!"

"Look, Molly. In the first place, I didn't say anything to you because none of this has anything at all to do with me. I was just trying to mind my own business, something I frequently find myself being encouraged to do, especially lately. In the second place, you've got to admit that being named editor-in-chief of this southwestern magazine is really a fantastic opportunity for Jack. . . ."

"But don't you see? I never had to deal with this kind of thing before. Mike's career was never a factor in our relationship. *I* was the one who counted. It was all *me*, me and what I needed."

She was close to tears. "All of a sudden there's this . . . this unsolvable problem of juggling two careers. And that's no easy task. I mean, what are my options? If I stay in New York and do what's best for my career, I lose Jack. If I go to Texas with him, I'm virtually flushing my career down the toilet. There's no way out!"

Molly made a fist with one hand and punched it angrily into the other. "Damn! If I hadn't met Jack in the first place, I never would have—"

"Ah. Now I get it. So that's the part that's my fault."

"Well, you *are* the one who introduced us."

"Hey, wait a minute! I didn't exactly sign you both up for the three-legged race at the company picnic, you know. You two just happened to spot each other—as you were coming back from the bathroom, as I recall."

However, Rachel could see that there was no place for logic in this discussion. "All right, all right. Don't panic. Look, if things were so simple back when you were with Mike, then drop Jack and go back to him."

"Yeah, right," Molly muttered grumpily. "As if that could ever happen."

"Molly, the man worships the linoleum you walk on."

"Until two days ago, you mean."

Rachel's heart sank. "Oh, dear. What happened?"

Molly avoided Rachel's eyes. "He . . . he walked in on us."

"Oh, Molly!" Rachel was genuinely chagrined. "What a way for poor Mike to find out!"

"It was an accident," Molly insisted. "He was supposed to be at work, computerizing somebody's . . . somebody's Christmas card list or something. Anyway, the next thing we know, the key turns in the door of the apartment, and there he is."

Something perverse in Rachel made her ask the question. "Uh, what exactly were you two doing?"

"I was smearing the crème fraîche Mike had bought specially for that night's raspberry *gâteau* all over Jack's, uh—"

"Oh, Molly! How *could* you?"

Molly hung her head penitently. "I know. And he'd made a special trip downtown to Balducci's to get it."

"My God, what's come over you?"

"I can't help it! Now that I've met Jack—and now that I've been losing weight and starting to feel, you know, really *sexual*—everything's different, somehow."

"So it seems."

"Anyway," Molly went on with a sigh, "Mike is moving out. Even as we speak, he's packing up his pastry blender and his wok." She looked particularly morose as she added, "Do you know what his parting words to me were?"

Rachel looked at her expectantly.

"He said, 'Molly, I hope I never make another crème brûlée for you again.'" She swallowed hard. "I think that was the part that hurt the most."

Nodding in sympathy, Rachel asked, "So what now? What are you going to do about this Texas thing?"

"Oh, why did this even have to come up in the first place?" Molly moaned. "Why did things have to get so *complicated*? Why couldn't everything have stayed the way it was? I was happy, Mike and I were in our routine, everything was simple."

Until I butted in, Rachel was thinking morosely. "I know what you mean," she said more to herself than to her sister. "All of the sudden nothing seems simple anymore, does it?"

Molly shook her head, then tightened her lips and stood up resolutely. "There's no point in beating this to death," she said. "What's done is done."

"Look, I have to go meet Becky at the bus," Rachel said, standing also. "What are you going to do?"

Molly cast her a wary look. "Oh, I'll probably just go home and have a good cry. What else is there to do?"

Rachel nodded. "Believe me," she said, "I know exactly how you feel."

"So, angel sweets, to what do I owe this welcome and unexpected invitation to spend the evening with my best girl?"

Rachel smiled wanly. "Angel sweets," "my best girl" . . . she and Ryder had adopted the lovey-dovey nicknames in perverse response to such typically ridiculous pet names as honey, sweetie, and darling—all the sickly sweet terms of endearment other loving couples were so fond of. The minute they'd found themselves joining the pack, they'd stopped, enjoyed a good chuckle, then decided there was only one way to deal with it: to overdo it.

Now, of course, the whole concept was nothing more than a tasteless joke. In the face of what she was about to say—the way in which she was about to test their relationship—the mere presence of such words made her squirm.

When he came over and put his arms around her, she stiffened immediately.

"Ryder, when I called you before and asked you to come over, it wasn't what you think."

"No?" His disappointment was sincere. "And here I thought we were going to celebrate Becky's first sleepover at somebody else's house."

"I asked you to come over because you and I need to talk."

As he picked up on her cues, his body grew similarly tense. "This doesn't sound good."

"No, it's not. Look, I don't know the best way to do this, so I'm going to just come right out and say it, okay?"

"Okay."

Rachel thought for a few seconds. Despite all the different ways she had rehearsed breaking the news to him, now that the moment had come, her mind was a blank. The only thing in there was the cold, blaring truth.

Her nervousness making her voice quiver, she began.

"Do you know a man named Leonard Klein?"

"Of course I do. He's our operations manager, in charge of the logistical stuff that goes along with making a company like mine run. Len's been with Kidstuff almost from the start. In fact, he's probably the one guy in the world who knows the company as well as I do."

Rachel swallowed hard. "So you two are, uh, close friends?"

Eyeing her oddly, Ryder said, "We're not exactly blood brothers. But we've had lunch together more than a few times over the years. Rachel, what's all this about?"

"Ryder, I think you'd better sit down."

There was a puzzled look on his face as he sat gingerly on the edge of the closest chair. "Is Len okay? Come to think of it, the last time I saw him, he did look a little flushed. I was even kidding him about it, telling him he looked like he'd suddenly aged ten years—"

"Ryder, let me do the talking. Please. It'll make it easier."

Rachel took a deep breath. She decided to avoid looking at him, to pretend she was making a speech to some faceless, anonymous crowd.

"Look, I'll start at the beginning. This article I've been researching for *New York Life*, the one I've been so secretive about, is an investigation of corruption inside the Grass Roots organization."

Shyly she glanced over at him to make sure he was following. His slow nod let her know that he was, indeed, familiar with Grass Roots.

"Okay. Apparently, what's been going on is that certain companies, companies who deal with toxins and plastics and medical waste and other substances whose disposal is rather, shall we say, controversial, have been giving 'contributions'—payoffs—to Grass Roots to keep themselves from coming under their scrutiny."

"That's outrageous!" Ryder cried, unable to contain himself. "Rachel, I'm proud of you. I know this probably sounds corny, but I'm really glad you're the one who's writing this article, the one's going after these guys who—"

Suddenly he stopped, his expression changing dramatically. "What does Len Klein have to do with this?"

Her silence gave him his answer.

"Oh, my God," he breathed.

"When I started going through the material that was given to me, I never in a million years expected that Kidstuff might be implicated." Rachel's voice was pleading—apologetic, even. "Most of the other companies were chemical manufacturers or drug companies or, or firms that disposed of medical waste for hospitals. . . ."

She could see what Ryder was going through as he sat before her, his hands clenched as he tried to digest the information. Surprise, disappointment, anger, fear, disbelief . . . one after another they all paraded by. It was all Rachel could do not to claim she was just joking, that she'd made it all up.

"So the bottom line here," Ryder said evenly, "is that Len Klein, my trusted employee, a representative of my company, has been slipping payoffs to Grass Roots, probably so that they wouldn't find out he was doing something illegal . . . something he was making a point of keeping from me."

She simply nodded. Somehow, his calm was even more terrifying to her than any explosion of fury.

In that same controlled voice he asked, "So what are you going to do?"

"What am I going to do?" she repeated.

"That's right. About the article, I mean."

"Uh, what about the article?"

"Are you going to write it? Are you going to take up your word processor and use it to destroy Kidstuff . . . to destroy me?"

"Oh, Ryder, I just don't know," she cried. "Believe me, I've been torn apart by this. I haven't known what to do, what to think. I even went to my editor to explain the situation. . . ."

"You told someone?" Ryder's entire body had grown rigid. "You mean somebody else knows about this?"

She looked at him in disbelief. "Well, of course. In the end, this isn't the kind of thing we'll be able to keep secret for very long. One way or another, it's bound to come out."

"Not if we're really careful!" Ryder seemed a million miles away. "There's got to be a way. . . . Boy, I can just imagine how my father is going to get off on this little tidbit. My brother, too. They'll be able to hear Thomas whooping with joy all the way on the other side of the Mississippi."

Turning back to her, he said, "Unless, of course, we can find a way to keep this quiet."

"That's just not realistic," she insisted. After a brief hesitation, she said, "I—I've been thinking that I have to go ahead and write the article, Ryder." She could hear the question in her voice and she hated herself for it.

"You would do that?"

"I have no choice. My ex-husband is threatening to sue me for custody of Becky. There's some woman he's involved with, but that's only part of it. He wants revenge. He wants to prove I can't take care of my own daughter.

"But beyond that, even if I decided not to write it, you know as well as I do that somebody else would." She shuddered at the thought of how gleeful Grayson would be. "Anyway, I was thinking that maybe when I write the article, I could sort of . . . downplay Kidstuff's involvement."

That thought was similarly chilling. Having admitted to her relationship with Ryder, she had virtually guaranteed that Grayson would highlight Kidstuff in the magazine. She could already picture it: an impossible-to-miss picture of Ryder striding out of one of the city's higher-priced restaurants, with the provocative caption, "The president and founder of one of the offending companies," or something along those lines. Perhaps he would even make the cover.

"Look, Ryder, I know this has turned out to be a total disaster," she said, close to tears. "But don't you see that I'm boxed in here?"

"What I see," he returned coldly, "is that you're about to screw me to the wall. And you actually seem to be enjoying it."

"That's not true!" she shot back. "Of course I'm not enjoying it! I feel just as terrible about this as you do!"

"Fine," he said, breathing hard. "Then don't write the article. Help me keep this quiet. Tell me—now—that you're not going to do this to me."

"Oh, Ryder." She sank onto the couch, suddenly having lost the strength to remain standing. "I can't."

He simply looked at her, wearing that familiar icy look. It was the same expression she'd seen at his parents' house, the one that came out in the face of apparent betrayal.

"Oh, Ryder," she said again, this time sobbing.

But he was already gone.

When later that same night the telephone rang, Rachel just knew it would be Ryder. Sure enough; in response to her tentative "Hello?" she heard a deep sigh that could only have come from him.

"Ryder?" she asked hopefully. "Ryder, is that you?"

"It's me." He sounded penitent—at least she thought he did. "I—I wanted to apologize for the way I acted before."

"Oh, it's all right, Ryder. I—"

"No, wait. Hear me out." The ensuing pause seemed to last forever. "I'm sorry that I tried to force you to make a choice between your career and me. That was really, really lousy of me."

He's apologizing. He's admitting he was wrong. Then why aren't I feeling any better?

"Of course you have to write that article. I never should have asked you not to. But the fact remains that ... that since you're the one who's going to be exposing what's been going on at Kidstuff, it's impossible for us to ... you know, be together."

"But, Ryder, I can help! I can give you a chance to tell your side of the story in my article! I can say that now that you know what's been going on in your company, you intend to fix it. And you really can. You can undo what's been done."

"Yes, at least I hope I can. I certainly intend to try. But the damage will still have been done. With my customers, my family—"

His voice broke. Rachel was tempted to indulge in a few tears of her own.

But she resisted. "Maybe you could use all the profits

from the sale of the Rubber Rainbow to clean up the environment. Something like that would put Kidstuff back in everyone's good graces."

"That's a nice idea, Rachel."

"You could get some good press out of it. You know, have it written up in local newspapers, maybe even go national. . . . You could take something bad and turn it around. Make it something positive."

"Maybe I will." Another pause, this one just long enough to break Rachel's heart. "Rachel, I'm sorry it turned out this way."

Yes, thought Rachel as she hung up the phone, moving in slow motion. I'm sorry, too.

Chapter
Twenty-one

The Beach Club Inn called heavily upon marine life as a decorating theme. The abundance of fishing nets went a long way toward setting the tone. But that was merely the beginning, since just about every available space in the restaurant was festooned with some lower form of life.

There were lobsters hanging on the walls and starfish on the ceiling. A menacing swordfish was stuck up near the rafters, glaring at all the patrons. Clam shells doubled as ashtrays. Predictably, the rest rooms were labeled MERMAIDS and MERMEN. All in all, it was a surprise that there wasn't a dish of Dramamine next to the cash register along with the after-dinner mints.

On this particular evening, all this yo-ho-ho-and-a-bottle-of-rum stuff was simply a backdrop for more important events. It was Thursday, amateur night at the south shore's most raucous beach club. Anybody with a song in her heart, rhythm in her bones, and enough guts to act on it was welcome to strut her stuff before an audience just sober enough to pass judgment.

"Too bad they don't allow minors in this place," Rachel observed, trying not to tip over the wooden barrel that doubled as her chair. "Becky's always wanted to see Disneyland."

"She's one of the lucky ones." Molly sipped her drink, meanwhile swatting at the fishing net that grazed her shoulder. "Boy, talk about ironic."

"To which particular aspect of my life are you referring?" Rachel returned. "There's so much irony in my life

these days that I've started cataloguing it all in a special
irony Filofax."

"I'm talking about you and me being here tonight
alone."

With a sigh she gestured toward the third Swann sister.
At the moment Sis was huddled behind the makeshift cur-
tain at the back of the club, giggling with her husband.
"We, the goody-goody, the ambitious, the successful, the
cautious, are here with each other. Sis, meanwhile, looks as
happy as a clam—if you'll excuse the pun."

Rachel craned her neck to see behind her. Sure enough;
her baby sister was radiating a kind of goofy joy, lit up by
the nervous energy that was precisely what she would need
to carry herself through her first performance as a country-
western singer with a New York metropolitan area flavor.

Still, despite the glowing, she did look rather ridiculous. There she was, in public, decked out in the same
outfit she had so proudly modeled for them a few weeks
earlier: the red vest with matching miniskirt, the red plastic boots, the fringe and the flash and that special glint
that could only mean "DuPont."

"How *dare* she look so happy?" Molly challenged. "It
just doesn't make any sense. I've never understood what
Sis saw in Jerry. He's so ... so. ..."

Rachel shrugged. "He adores her," she said simply.
"Surely that counts for something."

"Well, of course it does. But the really crazy part is that
she adores *him.*"

Rachel glanced back one more time. From what she
could tell, Jerry was giving his wife a pep talk. She could
imagine what he was telling her: that she was gonna knock
'em dead, that she was the greatest, that no matter how it
went, he still loved her. Her heart gave a little flutter, one
more of regret than anything else.

"So what exactly is going on with you and Jack?" she
asked lightly, turning her attention back to the sister at
hand.

Molly sighed. "I don't really know. I mean, he's all

psyched to buy a cowboy hat and move to Texas. Meanwhile, I'm completely rooted in New York. . . . Hey, we're talking two thousand miles here."

"You could go to Texas with him."

"Bite your tongue!" Molly snapped. "And give up everything I've worked for so long? Sacrifice my career, my connections, my ties to the university and the city?"

"It was just a thought," Rachel said, half apologizing.

"Yeah, well, I may not know for sure what's going to happen, but I can tell you one thing: I'm not about to start calling the Lone Star State home." Molly checked her watch impatiently. "When is this stupid floor show supposed to start, anyway? If I eat one more shrimp, I'm going to be seasick."

"Have another margarita," Rachel suggested. "You can pretend you're a Mexican sailor weathering a storm." Then, in a gentler voice, she asked, "Wouldn't you miss him, Moll?"

"Well, of *course* I'd miss him. But if I went to Texas, I'd miss my life here." She shook her head in dismay. "Boy, life has sure dealt me a complicated hand all of a sudden. I probably would have been better off hanging in there with Mike. At least with him everything was easy."

Rachel was about to voice the obligatory protests when Molly demanded, "And what about you? Do you miss Howard?"

"Howard?" Actually, Rachel hadn't thought about Howard in ages.

"And what about Mr. Wonderful? Speaking of which, where is Ryder tonight?"

"It's a long story," said Rachel. She popped a shrimp into her mouth and all but swallowed it whole. "Actually, it's a short story. I just don't feel like going into it right now."

"Saved by the dimming lights," said Molly. "Looks like it's showtime. Cross your fingers. It's our little sister's moment in the sun."

"Ladies and gentlemen—that is, assuming that you gals

eally are ladies and you guys might occasionally be mis-
aken for gentlemen, hah-hah . . ." The emcee had just
tepped onto the stage, clutching the microphone for dear
ife.

"Come on, come on," Molly muttered. "Let's get this
over with. Now *I'm* getting nervous."

Sis was scheduled to be the fourth performer. A magician
came on right before. He wasn't half bad, except for the
act that he spoke so softly that most of the audience
couldn't hear him. Not that Rachel and Molly were paying
much attention. It was their sister they'd come to see. Ev-
ryone else was superfluous.

"And now," said the emcee, "the Beach Club Inn is
pleased to present a little lady with more talent than Dolly
Parton—at least in *some* departments. . . ."

"Oh, God, this is painful," Molly moaned.

The man sitting at the table in front of her stopped guffawing long enough to turn around and shush her. He,
apparently, was into tasteless jokes.

". . . So let's bring her on with a warm round of applause. Let's all roll out the welcome mat for Maggie May
Casamano!"

"Maggie *May*?" Rachel whispered.

"Her stage name," Molly explained. "I kind of like it.
But we've really got to talk to her about the Casamano
part."

Even Rachel had to admit that as Sis walked woodenly
onto the stage, she looked pretty good. The fringe, the
cowboy hat, the nifty red boots: Somehow, it worked. At
least, by Memphis standards. Here on Long Island,
among the sea horses and fishing nets and clam-shell ashtrays, she looked . . . incongruous.

"Gee, that plastic comes across pretty nicely under the
lights, doesn't it?" Molly offered generously. "And check
out those sequins. The effect is quite striking."

Suddenly, from somewhere—a hidden sound system, no
doubt—came the notes of a twangy guitar. Sis's initial stiff-
ness faded, and she began to sway in time to her song's in-

troduction, her cheeks flushed as red as the rest of her outfit. Still, she looked like she was really getting into it. And the music was only part of it. Even more, it appeared that she loved being onstage.

"What is that song she's singing?" Molly frowned. "I don't think I recognize it. Of course, my cheap little radio doesn't pick up Nashville."

Rachel looked at her warily. "Actually, I understand it's something that she and Jerry wrote."

"*Oh*, boy."

" 'Ah *wait* . . . for *you* . . . at the shoestore. . . .' " Sis crooned. Her voice was high-pitched and twangy, her accent somewhere between that of an Oklahoma cowgirl and the checkout girl at the Kansas City 7-Eleven. " '*Over* . . . at . . . the mall. . . .' "

"She sounds . . . confident," Molly said uncertainly.

" 'We're headin' . . . over . . . to Jones Beach. . . . At least . . . if you show up at all.' "

"Oh, dear." Rachel was less kind. "Molly, is it just me, or are you also noticing that this is terrible? The song is terrible, Sis's singing is terrible. . . ."

"Yes, but check out all those rhinestones."

With that, Sis launched into the refrain.

" 'I'm *just* . . . a broken-hearted housewife . . . living . . . the split-level dreeeam. . . .' "

Rachel and Molly just watched, their eyes round, their mouths round, their frozen faces reflecting their disbelief. Sis had just launched into the second verse when they each felt a large hand clamp down on their shoulders.

"Is she terrific, or what?" Jerry's face, all smiles, was hovering above theirs. His eyes, meanwhile, remained glued to the stage. "What a talent that woman's been blessed with. Whoever knew?"

"Uh, that's quite a song," said Molly.

"Yeah, it's great, I know. I mean, sure, I mostly wrote it, but, hey, it was Sis's idea. The bleedin' heart of the Long Island housewife. What a concept, huh? Yeah, that might even be the good title for her first album."

"Album?" Rachel croaked.

Jerry, still wearing a dreamy smile, held his hand up, patting an imaginary puff of air. "In time, in time. We're just getting started."

"So who's her manager?" asked Molly. She winked at Rachel.

"Me, of course. As soon as I finish up a coupla projects I'm workin' on, I'll be free to do it full-time. Sis winnin' the money and everything is what's makin' it possible. She wants to ... oh, wait, wait, she's startin' her second song. She wrote this one all by herself."

" 'I met him in the frooozen food aisle. . . . He gave me a frooozen food smile. . . .' "

"I think I'm going to be sick," Molly mumbled.

"Too much shrimp!" Rachel said brightly. "Here, I'll go with you. Excuse us, Jerry, we're just going to the, uh, mermaids' room."

"Oh, God, Rachel, what are we going to *do*?" Molly wailed once they were inside the sanctuary of the rest room. "She's bound to ask us what we thought. What do we do, lie?"

"You've got it," Rachel shot back. "What else can we do?"

"How can we encourage this? Our little sister is out there making a total fool of herself."

"She is, isn't she?" Rachel was looking at her own reflection in the mirror. All around her, on three walls of the bathroom, was painted a mural depicting an underwater scene. It was all blue and green, dotted with Day-Glo fish. "But you've got to admit, she looks like she's having the time of her life."

"She does, doesn't she?" Molly agreed, similarly amazed.

"Maybe I'm even a little ... jealous," Rachel went on. "Sis really seems happy."

"Yeah, I would be, too, if I had all that money."

"But it's not the money!"

Even as she said the words, Rachel realized that it was

something she had known all along. Thinking that Sis's life was incomplete—*wrong*, somehow—had been entirely her own projection. There had never been the slightest hint from her sister that she actually felt that way. And wishing for all that money for her, when she was a woman who already had exactly what she needed, was simply proof that Rachel had no idea who her baby sister really was.

"I guess we'd better get back out there," she finally said. "You don't really feel sick, do you?"

"No. But I can guarantee that I'll never eat shrimp again, at least not in this lifetime."

"Come on, Molly. It's time to tell our little sister how great she was."

Sis's performance was just coming to an end, thanks to the three-song limit that the club's management had wisely set for amateur night. Smiling and waving, Sis strode confidently off the stage to the accompaniment of the audience's weak applause. She barely seemed to notice.

Her husband met her with a big bear hug.

"Honey, you were fantastic!" he cried. And then, reaching over into a dark corner, he produced, with all the smoothness of that night's performing magician, a bouquet of two dozen red roses. "Here, these are for my best girl."

"Oh, Jerry, they're beautiful."

"Hey," he said sternly. "*You're* beautiful."

Molly and Rachel stood by, watching, as Sis and Jerry went off to a quiet corner in the restaurant, their arms wrapped around each other so tightly it was a wonder no one was getting thorn wounds. When they were gone, the two sisters just looked at each other.

"So much for her asking our opinion," Molly grumbled.

"So much for her needing our support."

"Look at that. We've become irrelevant."

"Not really," said Rachel. She glanced toward the two lovebirds, nuzzling in the corner of the club, acting as if they were the only two people in the place. "All that's happened is that our baby sister has grown up and made herself a brand-new family."

* * *

Rachel was exhausted by the time she got back to her apartment that evening. Even so, she felt oddly at peace. Having seen Sis and Jerry together, having recognized at long last that they had created for themselves a life that worked just fine—certainly better than hers or Molly's—had encouraged her.

She also felt a little silly, realizing how unnecessary her supposedly charitable act had been. Jerry and Sis didn't need money; all they needed was each other. The only thing the money did was complicate things.

Not that any of that was helping her deal with her dilemma with Ryder. She glanced at the four tiny photographs of the two of them mugging together, still displayed prominently next to her word processor.

Another bit of irony, she thought. In writing the article for *New York Life* and establishing herself at last, she was in essence signing away any chance for a future with Ryder.

And part of her resented him for forcing her to make a choice.

"Why couldn't he have been a little more supportive?" she asked her reflection in the bathroom mirror. "Would it really have been so hard for him at least to *try* to see things from my perspective?"

She frowned at herself. This, my dear, is what happens to a sweet young thing like yourself who gets sucked into making a contract with the savviest dealmaker of all time.

The whole thing had been set up as a no-win situation all along, she mused, reaching for her Avon moisturizer. As she squeezed a dollop of the white goo into the palm of her hand, she noticed that it was almost gone.

Not that it did very much good, she thought, examining her skin in the mirror. Same old skin, same old fine, crinkly lines around the eyes.

As she lathered on that night's portion and put the tube back on the shelf, she happened to glance at it just a little more carefully than usual. Something printed on it had caught her eye.

Slowly she took it down from the shelf. On the back of the tube were printed words she had never bothered to read—typical advertising hype, she had supposed.

And indeed, words to that effect were printed on the back. But at the bottom also appeared the words *quadraginta quattuor dies.*

Quadraginta quattuor dies . . . familiar, but why?

She was growing more and more uncomfortable.

And then she remembered. The skin cream had not come from any usual source. Sure, it had the Avon name on it, but the Avon lady who had brought it had hardly been one of the company's usual staff members.

Besides, she could hear the phrase being spoken aloud. Her head spun as she tried to remember who had said it . . . and in what context. She was having such trouble focusing. It was as if her brain were so muddled, so clouded, she couldn't think properly. But she could hear it. Through the fog, through the haze, she could hear it.

Suddenly she snapped her fingers.

Of course! Lance Firestone! He had mumbled something like that. It was almost an afterthought, something he'd seemed compelled to bring up even though he'd tried to downplay the words. She hadn't paid attention at the time; she was too busy trying to hold on to her béarnaise sauce. But now, *now* . . .

Rachel's heart was pounding. She had just remembered something else: the bill the handyman had left for her. There had been handwriting scribbled on the back, she vaguely recalled, something she'd thought rather strange at the time but again had simply ignored. If she still had that bill . . .

Like a madwoman, she rifled through her drawers, checking under the furniture, shuffling through the messy stashes of paper that accumulated behind every corner of the apartment, junk mail and coupons and telephone numbers scrawled on bits of scrap paper. It had to be some-where.

She was at the point of giving up when she stumbled across it. Reading it, Rachel let out a little shriek. On the front was the bill for plumbing parts, an astounding eighty-nine dollars and fifty-three cents. And on the back was what appeared to be three sentences written in some kind of gibberish. Yet one phrase stood out from all the rest, under-lined twice with bold strokes: *quadraginta quattuor dies.*

What did it mean? Some evil incantation, some magical spell, some curse that had been put on her? Or perhaps something else altogether?

And what was the language? Something common like Dutch or Italian? Mocambian, maybe? Or something else, something too chilling even to contemplate? Rachel could only wonder.

But no matter what the language—of this world or beyond—one thing was certain: She had to find out.

Chapter
Twenty-two

First thing the next morning, after putting Becky on the camp bus and arranging an afternoon playdate with a friend's mother, Rachel called Madame Chrissie. She half expected to be screamed at, warned that darkening her doorway would result in immediate and forceful intervention by the law.

Instead, after some initial reluctance Madame Chrissie agreed to see her at the end of the day. Rachel was relieved; she was running out of energy and ideas and saw the psychic as her last resort.

"I must admit, I was a little surprised when you called," said Madame Chrissie, toying with the string of pearls fastened primly around her neck. "After our last meeting, I never expected to see you again."

Rachel, perched on the edge of the couch, sat up straighter. "That last session was kind of odd, wasn't it?"

"Odd?" Madame Chrissie shook her head. "How about catastrophic? How about disastrous? How about Twilight Zone-esque? Rachel, after the reading I was getting from you, I began to wonder if maybe my powers were going all kerplooie on me."

"I'm sure your powers are just fine," Rachel offered diplomatically. "I think the problem was that you were just dealing with—how can I put this?—a tougher case than most."

"Yeah, well, for the longest time I couldn't stop wondering what happened to you."

It occurred to Rachel that an effective psychic should not

have had to wonder. "If I told you," she said, sounding defeated, "you wouldn't believe me anyway." More to herself, she added, "After all, nobody else ever does."

"That may be true. But don't forget that I'm in the business of believing a *lot* of stuff that other people don't believe."

Madame Chrissie came over and sat next to Rachel on the couch. She took her hand and gave it a gentle, reassuring squeeze. "Tell me everything."

The warmth of the younger woman's hand, the concern in her voice, the feeling Rachel was getting—psychic or otherwise—that this was a place in which she could feel comfortable: Everything working together suddenly prompted her to spill out the entire story.

She went back to the beginning—her growing dissatisfaction, the sense that she was at an amusement park at which everyone else was having the time of their lives while she had yet to find the booth where they were selling the tickets ... her musings inside the Mocambian temple and the ensuing visits from beings who claimed to be out-of-towners on a very cosmic scale ... the wishes she made for herself and her sisters and the ways in which they'd all come true. Her voice broke several times as she detailed the complications that had followed: the discordance in Sis's once happy family, Molly's conflict between her career and the two men in her life, her own dilemma in the love vs. career debate.

Finally, somewhat sheepishly, she admitted that she'd learned there really was something to the saying Be careful what you wish for; you just might get it.

"And now?" Madame Chrissie asked as Rachel paused to draw breath.

"And now," Rachel replied in a feeble voice, "I want to get out of it. I want it undone."

Madame Chrissie just nodded. "And you want my advice, right?"

"Actually, I was hoping you'd be able to use your, you know, your powers to help me unscramble a phrase that has popped up a few times during this whole thing." Rachel be gan rifling through her purse. "Here, I'll show you. It printed on this free sample of face cream the Avon lad gave me. It's also handwritten on the back of this bill fo plumbing parts."

"Oooh, what is it? An incantation? Some magic words? Madame Chrissie was showing more animation than Rache had seen before. Obviously this was right up her alley.

"Here, I'll show you." Rachel handed over the evidence "Look, it's written here on this tube and over on the back of this piece of paper—"

"Eighty-nine fifty-three for plumbing parts?" Madame Chrissie cried. "Rachel, really. You don't have to be psychic to figure out that somebody's been taking you for a ride."

"That's not the important part," Rachel said impatiently. "Look, here on the back. See? Right here. It's even underlined."

Madame Chrissie frowned as she examined the words scrawled across the page.

"Quadraginta quattuor dies," she read aloud.

"That's it! You even pronounced it right!" Rachel cried. "At least, that's how it sounded when Lance Firestone said it. You know, the blind date. And that's how the Avon lady said it, too. What is it? A medieval chant? Some powerful phrase from a dead civilization? Do you know where we can find somebody who knows what it means?"

Madame Chrissie looked up at her. "I know what it means."

Rachel just stared.

"It means 'forty-four days.' "

"Forty-four days?" Rachel repeated. She didn't know whether to feel disappointed or exultant. "Uh, what is it, Madame Chrissie? Something from the tarot? Something you learned in your readings?"

"It's something I learned in eighth-grade Latin at Our Lady of Perpetual Agony."

"Latin?" Rachel blinked. "It's Latin?"

Madame Chrissie nodded. "Doesn't it stand to reason that the Prince of Darkness would speak Latin?"

"I knew I should have signed up for Latin instead of Spanish," Rachel muttered. She took a deep breath. "Okay, so it translates to forty-four days. But what do you think it *means?*"

"Well, I can't be sure," said Madame Chrissie, "but maybe—just maybe—it means that according to the deal you made, you get forty-four days to consider the offer. You know, before it finally goes into effect."

"I get it. You mean like the lemon laws that protect people who buy used cars."

Madame Chrissie looked at her in bewilderment. But Rachel was too busy muttering to herself to notice. "What's today's date? Let's see, it's August twenty-third. And the date of the Mocambian art exhibition opening was July tenth. . . ."

All of a sudden she turned white. "Oh, my God. Thirty days hath September. . . . Today is the forty-fourth day! Listen, I've got to get out of here."

Already she was on her feet, grabbing the tube of face cream and the plumbing bill and stuffing them back into her purse. "It's after five, right? Oh, no. How will I ever get uptown in time? The museum probably closes at six, and it's rush hour. . . ."

"You'll make it," Madame Chrissie said calmly. There was not a bit of tension in her expression as she watched her client heading out the door. "I just *feel* that you'll make it."

Rachel cast her a grateful look.

"I feel it in the same way I feel that when I send you a bill, you'll remit payment promptly."

So much for Madame Chrissie's psychic abilities, Rachel thought angrily. Tears of frustration stung her eyes as she pounded on the door of the Metropolitan Museum of Art, the door that had just been unceremoniously slammed not six inches in front of her nose.

"No, please!" she cried. "Open up! Let me in! You *have* to!"

But there was no sympathy in the muffled voice of the guard as he called back to her from the other side, "It's two minutes after six. Come back tomorrow."

"Tomorrow will be too late."

"We're *closed*."

Rachel stood frozen to the spot, leaning her face against the door. Its coolness was not the least bit soothing. She swore under her breath—at the heartless museum guard, at the congested rush hour traffic, at the taxi driver who was nauseatingly proud of the fact that he had lived in New York City his entire life yet turned out not to know that Fifth Avenue ran only one way.

Mostly she swore at herself. Why had it taken her so long to discover the clue that had been dangled in front of her ever since she'd first agreed to this deal? Some investigative reporter! Tom Brokaw, she wasn't. From inside the museum Rachel heard the sound of the tumblers being set firmly in place for the night. And then, right after, the deep evil laughter of the guard.

In defeat, she began the long climb down the stone steps. Down, down, down she went, her legs heavy, the force of gravity pulling them in the direction she was meant to go.

It's over, she was thinking morosely. I had an out, and I missed it. There's no turning back now.

And then, just as she was about to reach bottom, she noticed a pair of museum workers coming out the side door, the one meant for employees only.

Instantly the heaviness vanished, replaced by a burst of energy that carried her quickly to the door. Miracle of miracles, a polite young man actually held it open for her.

"Better hurry! They're closing up in there," he called after her cheerfully.

Rachel hurried inside, trying to keep her optimism in check. So far, so good, she told herself. At least she'd gained entrance to the museum.

But the ugly question "*Now* what?" loomed in front of
r. And there was no immediate answer.

"Oh, why didn't I study my Nancy Drew books more
refully?" Rachel moaned softly.

At that moment someone tapped her on the shoulder and
e jumped, barely managing to stay inside her skin as she
rned, terror-stricken, to see who it was.

"Excuse me, but aren't you Ms. Swann?" asked a young
oman.

Rachel studied the smiling face, puzzled. "Yes, that's
e."

The young woman snapped her gum. "I guess you don't
member me. My name is Patty Rogers. I'm the secretary
the special exhibitions department." In response to Ra-
el's hesitation, she added, "Remember? I helped you find
r. Ashcrofton's office a few weeks ago."

"Oh, yes!" Even if she didn't remember the face, Rachel
d remember the event. Grabbing the young woman's
nds, she cried, "It's so good to see you again! Listen, I
as wondering if you could do me a favor."

The friendliness in Patty's expression faded considerably.
Actually, I was just on my way out. It's six o'clock, you
now."

"Yes, but this is really important."

"Well. . . ."

"Look, all you've got to do is get me upstairs to the
locambian exhibit. I need two minutes in there. Two min-
es, that's it."

Patty glanced at her watch. "The museum is closed.
/e're not supposed to let anybody in after hours. They're
oing to turn on the alarm system in about fifteen minutes."

"Oh, come on," Rachel said with a wave of her hand.
Rules are meant to be broken. Especially by insiders like
ou."

"Well . . . since I know you and everything, I guess I
uld make an exception just this once."

Had there been more time, Rachel might have stopped to
rab her around the knees and kiss the hem of her mini-

skirt. As it was, she simply nodded curtly and then f
lowed her down the long corridor to some hidden stairc:
leading to the rest of the museum. Patty was chatting aw
going on and on about how spooky the museum alwa
seemed after hours. Rachel barely listened.

When the two women finally reached the Mocamb
exhibition, Rachel's sense of purpose suddenly gave way
total, all-consuming fear.

What if it doesn't work? she was thinking through l
panic. What if Madame Chrissie was wrong? What if it
ally is too late to undo what's already been done?

Yet she had to try.

"Thanks, Patty," she breathed. "You'll never know wl
you've done for me."

Without waiting for an answer, she sprinted across
huge exhibition hall, heading directly for the squat, u
temple in the middle. When she reached it, she took a qu
peek around, ducked down, and hobbled inside, all sens
on the alert.

Once she was tucked inside the small, dark space, s
felt nothing out of the ordinary. She was almost dis:
pointed. There was no odd smell, no eerie laughter,
sense of the preternatural.

But she knew she had to try.

"I want it undone," she whispered hoarsely. "Take
away. Make it stop. Take it all back. *Please!*"

She waited, wondering what more there was she cou
say. She was looking for a sign—the spontaneous lighti
of a candle, a gust of icy air, the barely perceptible sm
of incense. Nothing.

At last Rachel came out of the temple, her should
slumped. Her legs, once again, were so heavy that s
could barely force them to move.

It hadn't worked. Somehow she had miscalculated. It h
all been for nothing.

"All set?" Patty chirped. She was trying to sound che-
ful, but there was an impatient edge to her voice.

Rachel glanced up at her, her face slackened.

"Are you okay?" Patty's cheerful façade had vanished. You . . . you look like you don't feel too good."
Rachel just stared at her with empty eyes.

Rachel *lay still* for a long time the next morning, caug
in that fuzzy, confused state between sleep and wakeful
ness. The apartment was as silent as a tomb; when Beck
had telephoned the night before to beg for permission
spend the night at her friend's house, Rachel hadn't hes
tated to say yes.

She'd been completely worn out, no doubt from all th
emotional ups and downs of the day. Dinner had been to
much trouble. She hadn't even bothered to undress. Kickir
off her shoes, she'd fallen onto the couch and willingly su
cumbed to a dense, dreamless sleep.

Now, coming out of it, she felt rested. Her head wa
clear. She was amazed to find herself greeting this bran
new day with something that actually resembled optimisr
That she hadn't experienced for quite some time.

As she climbed off the couch, she felt oddly ligh
Weightless, almost. She went into the kitchen to make a p
of coffee, dazed by the peacefulness within.

With Mr. Coffee sputtering in the background, she sat
front of her word processor. Her nearly completed artic
was next to it, right where she'd left it. Just a bit more po
ishing and it would be ready to meet its deadline, two da
away. She glanced at the small pile of paper, expecting
experience an onslaught of emotions. Nothing.

Something was nagging at her, however. Something fe
different. Something *was* different. Rachel surveyed h
work area, straining to put her finger on what. At first sh

326

w nothing out of the ordinary. Papers, books, pens and
ncils, all strewn haphazardly across the table . . .

And then it clicked. The photographs of her and Ryder.
1ey were gone.

"Oh, God!" She sat very still, waiting for the chill to run
wn her spine, for the premonitory throb of a headache, for
e familiar odd feeling. Once again there was nothing.

"It's over."

She meant it as a question, a way of feeling things out,
f testing the waters. Instead, having said the words aloud,
1e realized it was true.

Rachel padded around her apartment, in a daze. Concen-
ating on her work was out of the question, so she tackled
1indless tasks: taking a shower, getting dressed, sipping a
1ug of coffee without tasting it. Through it all she mar-
eled over the fact that she was feeling so little. It was as
f her emotions were frozen.

When the telephone rang, she simply stared at it. She
vas afraid to answer it, frightened of who might be at the
ther end. But then she reminded herself that she had noth-
ng to fear. This, after all, was only life—*real* life, the one
1he had made for herself without any outside interference.
5he picked up the receiver.

"Hello?" she asked in an uncertain voice.

"Oh, *Rachel*! It's *over*!" wailed the tearful voice at the
ther end of the line.

"What's over?" Rachel demanded, caught entirely off
guard. "Molly, is that you? What are you talking about?"

"Jack. It's all over with Jack," Molly sobbed. "We—we
had a big fight last night, and he never wants to see me
again. He said I'm selfish and shortsighted and—and that
my priorities are all screwed up. He said that even if he
weren't going off to Texas to take that stupid job, he
wouldn't ever want to see me again!"

"Molly, I'm so sor—"

"And do you want to know the worst thing that . . . that
cretin said to me?"

Certainly not any threats concerning French desserts, R chel thought, bracing herself.

"He said that from now on the two of us should start ac ing as if we'd never even met!"

It took Rachel a few seconds to get her bearings. Whe she did speak, she was amazed by how matter-of-fact sl managed to sound. "Molly, what time did you have this a gument?"

Molly sniffed loudly. "It—it was about six-fifteen, guess. Six-ten, maybe. Why?"

Rachel let out a low moan.

"But believe it or not, there is kind of a happy ending. Molly went on.

"Don't tell me. Mike?"

"How did you know?" A few more sniffs for good mea sure. The storm was clearing. "He—he said we need to talk.

"Wait, let me guess. You two are moving in togethe again, right?"

"Rachel, are you becoming psychic or something?"

"Just seeing a pattern, that's all."

"What do you mean, a pattern?"

"Don't you see, Molly? Everything is going back to ex actly the way it was."

At the other end, Molly was silent for a few moments. " guess you're right. So what does that mean? That the way things were is simply the way they were meant to be?"

"Something like that." Trying to sound more cheerful Rachel asked, "So how do you feel about all this?"

"I'm not really sure. I mean, I'll miss Jack. At least, think I will. But I'm also glad Mike and I are getting back together."

She giggled. "Last night he made me a dinner like you wouldn't believe. Fettuccine alfredo, artichoke and hearts of palm salad, this really rich chocolate mousse cake . . ." She sounded almost gleeful as she added, "When I got on the scale this morning, I'd gained two pounds!"

"Oh, Molly," Rachel groaned. "I'm so sorry!"

"Sorry? What on earth for?"

Rachel wondered if she should bother to explain.

"Well . . . for a while it looked like you were heading in whole new direction." She didn't say a *better* direction, hich was what she really meant. "You know, trying out a ifferent kind of relationship with a brand-new man, losing eight, all that."

"Yes, but I feel so safe with Mike," Molly insisted. ounding almost timid, she added, "Doesn't that mean that 's what's best for me?"

Rachel swallowed hard. "It's true that you've al-ays seemed comfortable with Mike." It was the best she ould do.

"Well," Molly said brightly, "we'll have to have you ver for dinner soon. Maybe you could even bring some of at champagne you brought the last time you were here."

As Rachel hung up the phone, there was a thick, unpleas-nt coating in her mouth. Yes, she was watching it all hap-en with her own eyes. Or, rather, she was watching it all nhappen. She had to admit, it wasn't taking long for ings to go back to the way they'd been . . . before.

When the telephone rang again, she wasn't the least bit urprised.

"Hello, Sis," she said calmly, picking up on the first ring.

"How did you know it would be me?" Sis asked in mazement. Anxiously she added, "Rachel, the police idn't call you, did they?"

"The police? Why would they have called me? My God, is, what's happened?"

"Oh, Rachel. It's the most terrible thing. You'd better race yourself."

"Is it one of the kids? Are they all right?"

"Oh, they're fine. At least Shelley is. Vincent is, too— xcept for a few scrapes and bruises. At first we were fraid he had a concussion, but the doctor at the emergency oom said—"

"Emergency room! You'd better back up, Sis. What's go-ng on?"

Sis's voice was trembling. "Last night Vincent had an accident with that stupid dirt bike of his. He . . . it went ou of control." She paused to draw in a breath. "He was o something, Rachel. Drugs, I mean. Marijuana, the doctor told me."

"But he's okay, right?" Rachel interjected.

"Basically he wasn't hurt. I only wish I could say th same for the gas station he hit."

"Vincent's bike hit a *gas station*?"

"Well, one of the pumps. Right after he jumped off." Sh hesitated once again. "See, he was goofing around wit some of his new friends. They all have those dirt bikes, an four or five of the guys were riding around in a field oppo site this Hess station out in Islip. They were all stoned ou of their minds. Anyway, one of the guys apparently dare Vincent to take his bike out on the road, and, well . . ."

Sis sighed. It sounded as if she were getting tired of tell ing this story. "Of course, it wasn't the impact of the bik that caused all the destruction. It was the fire."

"The *fire*?"

"The gas pump exploded when the bike hit it. The bike' gas tank went, too."

"Oh, no! Sis, you're sure Vincent is okay?"

"He's fine, really." Another pause, this one somehov more ominous. "Unfortunately, the guy who worked ther wasn't so lucky. He got burned pretty badly."

"My God!" And then, a shift in mood. "Uh, Sis? Whe exactly did all this occur?"

"Yesterday. Last night, actually, It was just after—"

"Just after six o'clock?"

Sis gasped. "How did you know?"

"The guy who worked at the gas station—is he going t be all right?"

"He's going to live, if that's what you mean." Sis drev in another deep breath. "His family is suing us. We were u with a lawyer half the night."

"Oh, no. Don't tell me: They're suing for two millio dollars, right?"

"Five, actually. But our lawyer is pretty sure we can get them to settle out of court. For two, maybe one and a half."

"Two million dollars." Rachel swallowed hard, making a sound like a big gulp. "Exactly the amount you won in the lottery."

"Well, you know what they say." Sis laughed bitterly. "Easy come, easy go."

Rachel was shaking when the telephone rang a third time. She was tempted not to answer. But she had never been able to resist a ringing phone. This she found herself regretting immediately after she said "Hello."

"Rachel! It's so good to hear your voice!"

"Howard?" she squawked.

"None other than." A deep, hollow laugh. "So how the hell are you?"

"I—I'm fine. I was just. . . . Howard, this is such a surprise. You'll have to give me a minute to get myself together here."

"I've got a better idea. How about taking the whole morning . . . and then meeting me for lunch? I know it's Saturday, but I had some work to finish up this morning, so I had to come in to the city. The girls are with Sydney this weekend, so I'm free as a bird."

Rachel's head was reeling. "Howard, I, uh, don't know what to say."

"Then say yes. Better yet, say, 'Why, Howard dear, I can't think of anything I'd enjoy more.' "

Compared to that, saying yes was a piece of cake.

"You're looking lovelier than ever, Rachel. Working hard certainly seems to agree with you."

Rachel, sitting opposite Howard at an intimate midtown restaurant, smiled a mysterious little smile. It was true that she was looking her best. She'd made sure of it. After all, no way was she going to get together with Howard without gloating at least a little bit—and that meant pulling out all the stops in the looks department.

She'd spent the bulk of the morning tightening up her

New York Life article. But all the while she'd kept an eye on the clock, wanting to make sure she allowed enough time to put together a knock'em-dead look. And she'd been pleased with her efforts. Her hair was shiny and full, her makeup just right. She was wearing a billowy rayon pants outfit, a deep shade of mauve that had seemingly been created with her coloring in mind. The silver accessories she had chosen—large earrings, bangle bracelets, a dramatic oversize belt—added just the right amount of daytime glitter.

The Mona Lisa smile was the perfect finishing touch.

"My, my, Howard. You're certainly being complimentary. If I remember correctly, you used to say that kind of thing to me about as frequently as dear little Kimberly would say 'Please' and 'Thank you.' "

Howard threw back his head—even balder and shinier than she remembered—and let out a loud, fake-sounding laugh.

"You don't have to laugh *that* hard, Howard." Rachel glanced around the quiet restaurant in embarrassment. "I'm not Phyllis Diller opening at Caesar's Palace."

"Phyllis Diller, hah-hah! Caesar's Palace! That's a good one."

"A real knee-slapper," Rachel remarked dryly. "Howard, why am I getting the feeling you're about to ask something of me?"

Howard cocked his head to one side, puppylike. "What do you mean?"

"Oh, I don't know. I've got this sneaking suspicion that you're going to hit me up for a loan, or ask to borrow my apartment, or maybe suggest that I donate bone marrow . . . something along those lines."

Another ridiculous chuckle. "Rachel, Rachel, Rachel. God, I've missed you."

"Have you, Howard?" Borrowing a few moves from Bette Davis playing Queen Elizabeth, she reached for a roll, daintily broke off a tiny piece, and buttered it.

"Yes, as a matter of fact, I have. More than I can say." His expression had slackened into one that deserved a sign reading, "Caution! Tears Ahead!" "The girls miss you, too."

"The *girls*? Heather and Kimberly miss me?" And if you believe that one, perhaps you'd like to become part owner of the Brooklyn Bridge. . . .

"Well, sure. Just the other day Kimberly was reminiscing about the time we all went to the flea market."

"Ah, yes. One of my more memorable fiascos."

"And Heather has already worn those great sneakers you got her for her birthday so much that she's started hinting for a new pair."

"Now *that* I believe."

All of a sudden he reached across the table to grab Rachel's hand. Unfortunately, what was meant to be a spontaneous yet dramatic gesture nearly toppled her water glass.

"Uh, sorry about that," Howard mumbled as he set it right.

"You were saying?" Rachel asked sweetly. She was amazed at how much fun this was turning out to be.

"What I was saying, Rachel, was that lately I've uh, been thinking a lot about our decision to take some time off from each other."

"Um-hmmm."

Her hand may have been imprisoned in Howard's desperate grasp, but her attention had suddenly wandered. A party of three had just entered the restaurant: two men and a woman, so stiff and well-mannered that they were undoubtedly business associates rather than friends. At first she was attracted merely by the commotion created by their arrival. But at the sound of a familiar laugh, her heart began to tap-dance.

"Your usual table is free, Mr. Thorn," the obsequious headwaiter was saying, bowing his head ever so slightly. "Please, right this way."

Oh, God.

Rachel wrested free of Howard's grip and grabbed her water glass. Her eyes glued to Ryder, she gulped it all down. She watched him maneuver his way through the restaurant, taking care not to bump any tables or disturb any patrons. He looked very much at ease, orchestrating this luncheon with two important guests—buyers from an important toy store chain, she guessed, or perhaps inventors or designers or even potential investors. Her gaze never left his face as he sat down at the table next to hers, his chair directly opposite her.

And she was looking him straight in the eye as he glanced over at her, registered absolutely no sign of recognition, and turned his attention to the man sitting at his side.

All of a sudden she was on her feet, Howard and his Care Bears antics forgotten. She didn't even hear him as he called after her uncertainly, "Rachel? Is everything all right?"

She was a woman out of control as she strode over to Ryder's table, for once in her life not giving a moment's thought to how she appeared to others. She knew only that this was something she had to do.

And then there she was, standing at his side.

"Excuse me. . . ."

Ryder glanced up at her, the same blank expression on his face. "Yes?"

"I, uh, I'm sorry for disturbing you, but . . . don't I know you?"

The other man at the table let out a low, barely audible chuckle. The woman, meanwhile, glanced down at her salad fork. Ryder simply blinked.

"I'm sorry, but I don't believe so."

"My name is Rachel Swann," she said hoarsely.

He gave the name a few moments' thought. Then he shook his head. "I'm really sorry, but I think you must be confusing me with someone else."

Rachel just stared. The other man at Ryder's table had already introduced a new topic of conversation, looking for an easy way of ending an uneasy moment. Stunned, she went back to her table and sat down.

"What was all that about? You thought you knew that guy?" Howard asked, still bewildered.

Rachel kept her eyes down. "My mistake."

"Now, where were we? Oh, yes. I was just getting to the part where I tell you that I miss you. That I love you. And, well, that I want you back. There it is, Rachel. I'm laying all my cards on the table."

He was looking at her hopefully, like a cute little kitty begging to be let in out of the rain.

"I know it's sudden, but promise me you'll at least think it over."

The butterflies were back, Rachel reflected, the ones that for some mysterious reason seemed to thrive on the climatic conditions of Grayson Winters's office.

Having been invited in at all was a surprise. As she'd popped into the Dominion Building that Monday morning, completed Grass Roots article in hand, she'd expected simply to hand over the manila envelope to Mary Louise. So she'd been totally unprepared to hear that Grayson wanted to see her the minute she appeared.

What now? she was thinking nervously. Praise or condemnation? One never knew with Grayson.

Relax, she told herself. He probably just wants to give you a pep talk. You know, tell you what a great job you've been doing, maybe give you some spiel about how he's really looking forward to seeing what you've done with this challenging, career-making assignment, blah, blah, blah. . . .

As soon as he appeared in the doorway of his office, she knew. This time around, the butterflies had been right on target.

Without a word he strode in, leaned against the edge of his desk so that he was facing her, and folded his hands in front of him. It was clear that the ball was in her court—even though this was no game they were playing.

"I, uh, brought the Grass Roots article," she said, hoping this was the correct answer to an unasked question.

No reaction.

She cleared her throat. "I must say, I'm quite pleased with the way it turned out. Of course, I'm eager to see what your reaction is. . . ."

She was beginning to babble, she knew, but the silence was excruciating. She took the manila envelope that was balanced in her lap and held it out to Grayson. "It was really a fascinating assignment, and I was glad that I—"

She watched, astonished, as he politely accepted the envelope containing her article and then, without giving it so much as a glance, deposited it into the trash basket placed discreetly on one side of his desk. When he turned to face her, he was wearing a strange smile.

"Is—is something wrong?"

With a little shrug, he said, "We've been scooped."

"Scooped?"

"Surely you've heard the term."

"Of course. But . . . what . . . you're saying that somebody else is going to break this story?" Rachel's voice was little more than a whisper.

"Correction: Somebody else *broke* this story." He held up a copy of *Time* magazine. On the cover was Grass Roots' logo, the words "Good guys or bad guys?" written over it in red. "This week's issue, due out tomorrow. Sorry, Rachel. This baby's already old news."

He didn't sound sorry at all. Rachel just stared at him.

"In case you're wondering about the magazine's financial commitment," he went on, "you'll be getting a kill fee. Our standard rate. Don't worry; I've already taken care of it."

"But how did this happen?" she cried. Her hands were clenched into tight fists. "Who did this?"

"I must say, I'm not all that surprised. Disappointed, of course, perhaps even more than you, but not surprised. I knew this was hot. And, well, apparently somebody besides Johnny was willing to talk. In fact," he said, casually leafing through the magazine, "their main source was considerably higher up in the Grass Roots organization."

When he looked over at her, his mouth was twisted into a smirk. "Sorry, kid. Them's the breaks."

It's just like Sis said, Rachel thought less than three minutes later, in a daze as she rode down the elevator. Easy come, easy go.

Still, summing up that phenomenon with a neat little phrase was one thing. Actually living through it was something else entirely.

When Rachel came home and found a telephone message from Boyd, she wasn't the least bit surprised. With all the dominoes falling over one by one, why should the last remain standing?

He wanted to talk, he said on the tape, his voice sounding gruff. She could guess about what.

"I didn't really want to do this over the phone," he began hesitantly when she dialed his number.

"Consider the alternative," she shot back. "Look, Boyd, let's just get this over with."

"Then you know."

"Don't tell me. You and Ariana, right? She's back, and she wants to play house. And in order to do that, she needs a baby doll. Becky." She spat out the words, but inside she was crumbling.

"We can do this in a friendly way," he said smoothly, "or we can involve lawyers. Of course, that can get messy, not to mention expensive. I imagine you'll want to keep it simple." It sounded as if he were smirking as he added, "You never were one for a fight."

His words hit her like stones. He was right; she never had been one to fight. She'd always sat back, hoping, wishing . . . waiting. Suddenly, that wasn't good enough. Not when she was losing everything she'd once wished for. But the one thing she refused to lose was Becky. It didn't matter what it took; some things were worth fighting for.

It was then Rachel realized she was no longer the same person she had been back in July. In the past several weeks she had risen to heights greater than she'd ever imagined: getting the perfect writing assignment, finding the kind of man she had always dreamed of . . . in short, living the life that, up until then, had been a mere fantasy. As for her sisters, the two people she loved most in the world after Becky, she had seen them get the things she had always wanted them to have. She had had power. Success. Love. Happiness.

And through it all she had clung to the notion that it had come to her through some supernatural force. She'd ignored the fact that deep inside she knew that what she insisted upon believing was simply impossible. Had any of it really happened? She didn't know. She never would. But it no longer mattered. What she did know was what it felt like to have what she really wanted.

As she stood in her living room, still clutching the phone, she understood that it wasn't only her circumstances that had changed. *She* had changed. No longer was she willing to sit by, letting things happen, hoping that through some stroke of luck they would turn out to be what she wanted. She understood now that she had to *make* them happen. It was up to her. She had possessed the power all along. She had simply been afraid to use it.

When she finally spoke, she barely recognized her own voice.

"You want a fight? You've got it. And if our arena is the courts, so much the better. Because no matter what accusations you might make, the fact remains that no judge in the world is going to take Becky away from me. She's my daughter. And fortunately, even in this age of fax machines and synthetic cheese and . . . and rock stars prancing around in metal bras, there is still some recognition of the special bond that exists between a mother and her child. Whether you approve of my career or not, Boyd, I am a capable provider and a good mother. In the end, that's the truth that will prevail."

She took a deep breath, aware that the long silence at the other end of the line meant that, for once, Boyd had nothing to say. She felt different. It was that lightness again, the same way she had felt the morning after her second trip to the Mocambian temple. When she had banished the curse . . . or at least her belief in it.

All that was over. What stood in its place, she now understood, was belief in herself.

Chapter
Twenty-four

"No *one believes me* when I tell them it's just as well. . . ."

Sis's voice drifted through Rachel's semiconscious fog, as soothing as a lullaby. She lay on a lounge chair in the Casamanos' backyard, listening to many voices: Shelley's as she whined about the new clothes she needed for school; Jerry's, insisting he was the best barbecue chef in the free world; Mike's petulantly disputing his claim. Her arms and legs were so heavy, she seriously doubted she would ever move again.

Interestingly, she didn't care. It felt too good, just lying there, refusing to let in any thought more complicated than a vague curiosity about how high the temperature was on this last of summer holidays, Labor Day. In honor of the occasion, she was paying tribute to the concept of labor by leaving all the difficult stuff to the others, those demanding pastimes like making conversation, eating potato salad, and, of course, moving.

Besides, her brain would be back on call soon enough. Just the other day *Business Week* had called to ask if she was interested in doing another piece for them. Once she'd gasped yes into the phone, she was informed that they would be getting back to her right after the three-day weekend. Another assignment, another spurt of working like a maniac. All the more reason to squeeze in as much relaxation as possible.

"Hey, Mom?" Becky's voice rose over the din. For her, Rachel managed to raise one eyelid. She was towering

above her, grinning down. Her face was covered wi[th]
freckles, all that remained of her camp experience beside[s]
an entire shelf full of useless but beautiful objets d'art.

"What, sweetie?"

"I was thinking. You know Cheerleader Barbie?"

"Intimately."

"You know what she's doing when she's not cheerlead[-]
ing?"

The range of possibilities was endless. "What, Becky?[?]

The little girl's grin widened. "She's writing stories fo[r]
magazines, just like you."

"Oh, come on, Sis," Molly suddenly interrupted. "D[o]
you really expect me to believe that it didn't *kill* you t[o]
give up the whole two million? First a big chunk to th[e]
IRS, then whatever was left to some ... some grease mon-
key and his stable full of lawyers. . . ."

"It's a terrible thing that happened," Sis countered. "The
poor man is going to be scarred for life, and it's al[l]
because—"

"All because of a teenage boy's temporary lapse in judgment," Molly finished for her.

"No, because of his *parents'* lapse in judgment." Sis's
tone was firm. "We should have known better than to let all
that money get in the way. It came close to ruining everything that's important to us. My relationship with Jerry, my
relationship with Shelley ... And then there's this business
with Vincent. We allowed it to cloud up our original no-
tions about raising children, and so of course the whole
thing backfired."

"Well, it's a moot point now," Mike said cheerfully.
"But, boy, when I think of what I would have done with all
that money. Have you seen those Le Creuset pots and pans?
Man, what the French can do with cookware. . . ."

"Hey, Ma? You're never gonna believe this, but we got
more company." Vincent had just come skipping into the
backyard—or, more accurately, doing his own version of
skipping, one that required less coordination than the orig-

nal. "Some guy I don't recognize just drove up. He parked n the driveway, right behind Dad's truck."

For this I'll open my eyes, thought Rachel. But it'd bet-er be good.

Not only did she open her eyes; she also pulled herself o a sitting position. It turned out to be worth it.

Rounding the corner, his scrawny, pasty-white legs stick-ng out from a ridiculous pair of Hawaiian-print shorts, was Jack Richter.

"Jack?" she said aloud, wanting to make sure she was seeing more than just a mirage.

"Jack?" This came from Molly. It was more of a squeal than anything else—partly surprised, partly gleeful, partly appalled.

"Molly. I figured I'd find you here."

She put down the bag of potato chips she'd been hugging like a beloved pet. "But . . . but aren't you supposed to be shopping for a condominium in Dallas this weekend?"

"What the hell for?"

It wasn't until then that Jack noticed Mike, standing with his sticklike arms folded belligerently across his chest. Jack immediately copied his stance. The two of them looked like a pair of featherweight contenders mugging for the camera, promoting their next fight.

"Hello, Mike," he said with a brusque nod of his head.

"Jack." Same movement. "I almost didn't recognize you with your pants on." Mike glanced down at them. "Some pants."

"Yeah, well, you know the old saying. When in West Islip. . . ."

But Molly had no patience with polite small talk. "Jack, why are you here? What happened to Texas?"

Jack shrugged. "Texas will simply have to manage with-out me."

"But the magazine . . . ?"

"I told them no. My life is here in New York." He swal-lowed hard. "*You're* in New York."

"Hey, wait a minute here. . . ." Mike protested.

Vincent and Shelley, meanwhile, were loving every min ute.

"How romantic!" Shelley breathed.

Vincent peered at them both through his thick eyeglasse. "Wow, are these guys gonna fight a duel?"

"Whaddya talkin', a duel? *Marone!*" Jerry refused to ge excited. "Look, yer aunt Molly has two guys hot for her she picks the one that turns up her thermostat the highes What's the big deal?"

Indeed, Molly was at the moment looking from one to the other, acting as if she were trying to decide betweer two pastries in a glass case. In the end, it was Jack whc seemed to hold more interest for her.

"You really turned down that job?" she said, still no quite willing to believe it was possible. "It was your dream job. An opportunity that comes along only once in a life- time."

"Hey, Mol," he said gently, "somebody like you is an opportunity that comes along only once in a lifetime. If a guy's lucky, that is."

"Oh, Jack!"

"Well, if you think I'm gonna stand around and listen to this . . ." Mike sputtered.

"Good," said Jerry. "I need somebody to help me lug an- other bag of charcoal around from the side of the house. Gimme a hand, willya, Mike?"

Shyly, uncertainly, Jack and Molly took each other's hands. They were both blushing. And they both had glow- ing eyes.

"Nice shorts." Rachel couldn't resist. "Have you been shopping with Howard?"

"Hey, where is Howard? Isn't this the kind of thing he'd come to?"

Rachel shrugged. "Maybe. If we were still an item, that is."

"Didn't I hear through the grapevine that he'd come sniffing around, begging you to take him back?"

"Something like that." She made a face. "Hey, do you really think I'm that easy?"

"Poor Rachel," cooed Sis. "The last weekend of summer, and you don't have a date."

"You can take one of mine," Molly offered. She glanced over at Jack. "But not this one."

"That's okay. I think I've learned that you can't force these things. You just have to let it happen, you know?

"Besides," Rachel murmured, "I've got you guys. Two great sisters, the best daughter in the world, a wonderful niece and nephew, a brother-in-law who's a pretty good guy . . . all that's nothing to scoff at, you know."

She was even more surprised than Sis and Molly to realize how much she really, really meant it.

Corporate headquarters were in Astoria, Queens, not far from midtown Manhattan. It was the type of place Rachel would never have ventured without good reason. Writing an article for *Business Week* was a good reason.

It was turning out to be fun. Just getting to Astoria was an adventure: traveling out of Manhattan on a subway and emerging in a world entirely different from the one she'd left behind a mere subway token ago. Checking her map, she strode down streets lined with small shops and ethnic restaurants, crowded with people who all seemed to know each other.

Finally she turned down a side street, one that led to a block of monolithic warehouses.

"Two seventy-three, two seventy-seven . . . ah, there it is."

Feeling a mixture of relief and nervousness topped with a big fat dollop of excitement, Rachel took a couple of deep breaths and walked up the three flights of cement stairs to the main office. At the end of her climb she found herself in a tiny suite of tastefully decorated offices. Superimposed over the soft pastel colors were bright, colorful posters showing off the company's product line. She was pleased to see she recognized nearly every one.

A pretty receptionist smiled. "May I help you?"

"I'm Rachel Swann. From *Business Week.*"

"Oh, yes. We've been expecting you." The receptionist sat up a little straighter. "I'll take you right in."

"Thank you."

Rachel took a moment to straighten the skirt of her black T-shirt dress, today made suitable for the grown-up world of commerce with simple gold jewelry, a colorful scarf, and an oversize belt. Stylish without being overly trendy. She checked her shoulder bag to make sure it wouldn't be doing any of its famous sliding-off-the-shoulder tricks, then followed the receptionist down a short hall.

"The reporter from *Business Week* is here," the young woman announced, poking her head into the office at the end. Then, turning back to Rachel, she added, "There you go. Let me know if there's anything you need."

Rachel returned her smile. "Thanks, but I think from here on in, I'll be fine."

"Come on in," a male voice called from inside.

Rachel obliged, strolling into the large, cluttered office. "Hello," she said simply.

"Ms. Swann, isn't it?"

"Yes, that's right."

The man came around from behind his desk and extended his hand. "Pleased to meet you. I'm Ryder Thorn."